M000012184

Julie Anne Lindsey is an obsessive reader who was once torn between the love of her two favourite genres: toe-curling romance and chew-your-nails suspense. Now she gets to write both for Mills & Boon Heroes. When she's not creating new worlds, Julie can be found carpooling her three kids around northeastern Ohio and plotting with her shamelessly enabling friends. Winner of the Daphne du Maurier Award for Excellence in Mystery/Suspense, Julie is a member of International Thriller Writers, Romance Writers of America and Sisters in Crime. Learn more about Julie and her books at julieannelindsey.com

A *USA Today* bestselling author of over one hundred novels in twenty languages, **Tara Taylor Quinn** has sold more than seven million copies. Known for her intense emotional fiction, Ms Quinn's novels have received critical acclaim in the UK and most recently from Harvard. She is the recipient of the Readers' Choice Award and has appeared often on local and national TV, including *CBS Sunday Morning*. For TTQ offers, news and contests, visit tarataylorquinn.com

CLOSING IN ON CLUES

JULIE ANNE LINDSEY

LAST CHANCE INVESTIGATION

TARA TAYLOR QUINN

MILLS & BOON

First Published in Great Britain 2023
by Mills & Boon, an imprint of HarperCollins*Publishers* Ltd
1 London Bridge Street, London, SE1 9GF

www.harpercollins.co.uk

HarperCollins*Publishers*
Macken House, 39/40 Mayor Street Upper,
Dublin 1, D01 C9W8, Ireland

Closing In On Clues © 2023 Julie Anne Lindsey
Last Chance Investigation © 2023 TTQ Books LLC

ISBN: 978-0-263-30746-7

1023

CLOSING IN ON CLUES

JULIE ANNE LINDSEY

For my incredible friend Nicolé Homes.

Chapter One

Nicole Homes checked the clock for the tenth time in half as many minutes, a routine she'd perfected hours before, when her younger sister, Cari, went from being inconsiderably late to unfathomably so. There'd been a time in Cari's teen years when staying out all night without calling meant she'd fallen back into bad habits and unhealthy patterns, but she'd been clean for thirty-five months. And since the birth of her daughter, Blakely, in the spring, Cari tended to come home early more often than not.

So where was she now?

"Of course I've tried calling," Nicole explained to a painfully calm officer on the other end of the line. "I get voice mail every time."

She paced the living room carpet with impatient steps and a biting urge to scream. If it hadn't been for her sweet niece, playing happily in the nearby playpen, she might have.

"Something's happened to my sister," she repeated. "I know it."

And whatever it is, it's bad, she thought, and her breaths grew increasingly shallow.

"I understand your concern, ma'am," the officer replied. "I do. But without any evidence of foul play, your sister is just considered late at this point. You said she worked last night."

"Only until eleven."

"All right. Maybe she got caught up. Maybe the party where she worked went on longer than expected, or she went out with friends afterward and fell asleep."

"Okay," Nicole conceded. "Then where is she now? It's nearly lunchtime."

The officer inhaled audibly, then released the breath on a slow exhale. "It's barely ten a.m. She could still be sleeping if she had a late night. Maybe she had car trouble. Maybe her phone is dead, because she didn't take a charger to work with her. Any number of very common, non-perilous things could've happened, and nine times out of ten, that's all it is. Hang tight until this evening, and if she's still not home after twenty-four hours…"

The man's words faded as Nicole circled their small living room, peeking through the window toward Cari's designated parking spot on each pass. Empty. As it had been since last night. Nicole had received all the same advice and sentiments when she'd made her first call to the police department at two in the morning. The officer on duty then had encouraged her to get some sleep, claiming circumstances often looked different by light of day.

Currently, they did not.

Blakely squirmed in her playpen, probably sensing the tension rolling off her aunt in waves.

Nicole's eyes misted with fatigue and frustration as she paused to stroke her niece's round cheek.

She'd been eight years old when Cari was born. And remembered clearly how she'd looked the first time she set eyes on her, wrapped in a pink blanket, dark curls springing out in all directions. Wide brown eyes fixed on hers.

Cari had looked then exactly as her daughter did now.

"Thank you," Nicole said abruptly, interrupting the officer. "I'll call back in a few hours." The fierce protectiveness she'd felt every day as a big sister blazed to life once more. The police weren't ready to look for Cari, but Nicole was.

She set her phone aside and lifted her sweet niece into her arms. "It's okay," she cooed, stopping the infant's small fussy sounds. She cradled Blakely's warm little body against hers, and their dark brown locks mingled against her shoulder. Homes women looked a lot alike, but the similarities always stopped there. Cari was carefree and energetic, afraid of nothing and happy in a nearly contagious way. Nicole was pragmatic and steadfast, a troubleshooter by nature, and on occasion slightly harsher than necessary, which she didn't mind if it got the job done. Her mother had insisted their differences were what made them a formidable team.

It was time to find her teammate.

"How about a drive?" she asked Blakely. "Fresh air. Sunshine. Sound good?"

If she happened to discover her sister's car abandoned, or some other evidence to suggest Cari wasn't just being irresponsible, then the police would have to listen.

She buckled Blakely securely into her rear-facing car seat and thanked her stars she'd made the purchase. "Your mama wanted to save money by sharing a car seat," she told her, before pressing a kiss to the baby's forehead. "If I'd listened to her, she might've taken the seat with her last night. Then we'd be stuck at home instead of on our way to save her."

What she wouldn't give to have that argument with Cari again right now. She'd cheerfully fight about anything if it meant her sister was safe.

She climbed behind the wheel of her small gray SUV, and they were on their way.

Cari set her phone to Do Not Disturb while she worked, but always left the address where she could be found in case of an emergency. If her baby needed her, Nicole was to come straight to the source, etiquette be darned.

Not surprisingly, the GPS led them away from the valley, where single-family homes and apartment buildings peppered the landscape near a historic downtown. Warm southern sun heated her skin through open windows, while the balmy breeze did its best to ease her nerves. Coastal North Carolina was a sight to behold in every season, but their little inlet town was downright breathtaking in summertime. July was possibly the prettiest month of all.

They wound their way along the smooth black ribbon of road, past big white dairy barns and emerald fields, then upward, past miles of vibrant wildflowers and cookie-cutter neighborhoods into the mountains. Rugged, jutting rocks lined the road on one side, climbing into the sky, while a great precipice overlooked the sea on the other.

When houses appeared once more, they were massive and sprawling, nothing like the farmhouses and cottages of the working class, found closer to sea level. These properties were owned by folks who probably never got their hands dirty. If they did, there were luxurious in-ground and infinity pools waiting out back to wash away their cares.

Finally, the small voice on her phone announced their arrival, and Nicole slowed near a multilevel Frank Lloyd Wright knockoff on the corner of multiple entwining roads. It was a wonder residents ever learned their way around.

"This is it," she told Blakely, catching her eye in the baby mirror she'd attached to her car's back-seat headrest. Blakely chewed contentedly on one pudgy fist, her face reflected in the shiny silver plastic, then again in Nicole's rearview. "Your mommy was here last night. Working hard to buy you nice toys so you can chew on your fist instead."

Blakely hiccupped a laugh against her knuckles, and Nicole smiled.

None of the cars parked along the street were Cari's.

She circled the area once more with identical results.

Unease pooled and coiled in her core as she passed the house in question for a third time.

Cari had been fine before the fancy party. She'd come home and showered after her waitressing shift at a restaurant in town. She'd kissed Blakely good-night a hundred times and promised to be home as soon as possible. Extra shifts and gigs at private parties had become part of her routine since Blakely's birth. And she'd taken full advantage of the free babysitting opportunities afforded by a sister who had the summer off from teaching second grade.

Nicole never minded. She loved the extra time with her niece, and seeing her sister thriving was a joy all on its own. Life hadn't always been this way for Cari.

She thought again of the short video Cari sent for Blakely. Nicole had replayed it several times throughout the night, but there were only notes of happiness in her voice and smile. No signs anything was amiss.

Aside from the video, Cari had sent a single picture of a small bridge illuminated in fairy lights. Presumably a landscaping feature in the homeowner's backyard. Something Cari would insist they make for Blakely somewhere, someday.

Nicole exhaled a heavy breath and pulled onto the home's double-wide driveway.

The garage door opened and a man stilled when he saw her exit the SUV. "Can I help you?" he asked.

"Yes. Hi," she said, opening the back door to gather Blakely into her arms. "I hope so." She stepped around her car, moving in the man's direction. "My sister worked at a party here last night. She hasn't come home, and I'm starting to worry.

I thought you might remember her, or could put me in contact with the company you used for the catering. She was a member of the waitstaff."

His eyes widened slightly at the announcement Cari hadn't come home, then narrowed suspiciously when Nicole made her request. "I'm sorry. You must be mistaken. I haven't hired any catering company. Now, if you'll excuse me, I have to get to work." He dropped behind the wheel of his high-end sports car and drove away.

The garage door shut emphatically behind him.

She shook off the urge to retreat and marched to the home's front porch instead.

A phone rang somewhere inside while Nicole pressed the bell.

Long seconds passed before the clicking of heels carried to the door.

She stepped back as the great wooden barrier swept open, revealing a thin blonde in a fitted red dress, a pair of fawn-colored heels on her feet. "Can I help you?" she asked, fastening a golden hoop to one earlobe. Her skin was clear and tanned, her makeup flawless and her smile warm.

"Hello," Nicole said gently, putting on the voice and smile she used on parents and new students at the beginning of each school year. "I'm looking for my sister. She was part of the waitstaff at a party here last night, and I wondered if you could look at a photo of her and let me know if you remember seeing her?"

She freed her phone from one pocket and swiped quickly through saved images. "I understand if you didn't have time to meet every server, but it would mean a lot if you would just look. Or if you can tell me the name of the company you used to hire the servers."

She settled on an image of Cari with a wide-open smile and

Blakely in her arms. "This is her. Her name is Cari Homes. She's twenty-three and—"

"No," the woman said sharply, smile fading as she scanned the street over Nicole's shoulders, probably looking for nosy neighbors. "There wasn't any party. I can't help you, and I didn't see your sister." Her gaze swept briefly to Blakely. "I'm sorry. I have to go," she added more softly, then stepped back and closed the door.

Nicole stared at the brass knocker, fighting the urge to rap it a few times, or maybe try the bell again. Instead, she turned, stunned silent, toward her car.

Blakely squirmed, and Nicole adjusted her niece in her arms. Blakely's fair baby skin was turning pink beneath the beating southern sun, and sunscreen hadn't crossed her aunt's harried mind.

"Poor sweetie," Nicole said, hurrying to secure her inside the car and out of the dangerous UV light.

It was possible Cari had written the address incorrectly, accidentally flipping two digits on the house number or mis-understanding the street name, but that seemed even more unlikely than the possibility nothing was wrong.

Unwilling to give up just yet, Nicole drove aimlessly through the neighborhood in search of Cari's car. She tried to imagine a scenario where Cari would lie about where she was last night but came up empty-handed.

When she wondered why a wealthy couple would lie about having a party, nothing good came to mind. She supposed it was possible the wife didn't know the husband had a party. Or maybe the call Nicole heard ringing while she'd waited on the doorstep was the husband instructing his wife to lie if she was questioned. Maybe they both knew something went wrong and were covering their backsides by pretending it hadn't happened.

The potential reasons were increasingly grim.

Nicole's chest constricted as she imagined gruesome accidents of every variety, and she pulled over to catch her breath. A small park caught her attention. A handful of kids played at its center, one of whom wore a coat that looked a lot like the one Cari had left home in the night before.

Nicole was out of her car in a heartbeat, pulling Blakely from her five-point safety harness and moving across the street at a clip. "Excuse me," she called, forcing a smile and waving an arm. "Hey! Hello!" She broke into a jog when the group looked her way.

The children ranged in age from ten or so to a pair of girls in their teens. They all stared as she approached. One of the younger girls wore the cropped lavender coat over a tank top with cutoff shorts and flip-flops.

"I'm Ms. Homes," she said. "I'm a teacher at Marshal's Bluff Elementary School. I think my sister lost her jacket. She was in this area last night, and it looks a lot like that one." She smiled at the young lady in question. "How long have you had that?"

The coat could belong to the girl, she supposed, but given the current temperatures, and her weather-appropriate outfit, otherwise, she doubted the kid had left home in a coat. Especially one clearly not her correct size.

The child looked at the teen, who raised her eyebrows in turn. "Fine," the kid said, sloughing off the coat. "I found it under a park bench and put it on. Purple is my favorite color, and no one else was around. I thought it was finders keepers."

"Which bench?" Nicole asked, fear gripping her chest as she reached for the coat.

The child pointed, and an anvil pressed against Nicole's lungs.

"Told you it was lost, dummy," another child scolded.

One of the teens shoved him in response. "Don't call names."

Nicole turned the jacket around in her hand, careful to keep Blakely secure as she looked. A small nail polish stain near the zipper sent her back to the day Cari had selected the coat and they'd gotten manicures together at the mall. She worked to press words through her tightened throat. This was her sister's coat. Why was it under a park bench? "Thank you."

The benches were all empty now, and the group of children moved away.

She hugged Blakely and clutched the jacket against them both. "Where did you go?" she whispered into the day.

With a deep intake of air, she moved back toward her car, planting comfort kisses against her niece's head as they moved. Blakely smelled like love and hope. Nicole needed both, and Cari probably needed them more.

The sharp roar of an engine stopped her short of stepping onto the road. A sleek black sedan barreled past, engine growling. The vehicle turned the next corner with a piercing squeal of tires and disappeared.

Nicole shook away the rush of gooseflesh and foreboding that had appeared with the car, then ran to her SUV and secured Blakely in her car seat.

She pulled carefully away from the curb with a multitude of backward glances, praying her sister would appear. Somewhere on the fringe. Unharmed and oblivious to the lost time. Instead, she told her phone to direct her home.

Something dark flashed across her rearview mirror as she rolled forward, under command of her GPS.

The black car that had screamed past the park earlier was now behind her and quickly drawing near.

Nicole toed the gas pedal with increased purpose, stretching the space between them.

Blakely's eyes drooped in the reflection of her toy mirror,

lulled by the heat of the day and the gentle rock of the SUV in motion.

The black car snarled loudly, reclaiming the little space Nicole had gained. It quickly matched her speed on the narrow curving roads. Tint on the windows, combined with glare from the sun, made the driver invisible, but everything about the moment felt pointed and intentional.

Nicole's speed edged higher, nearing ten miles over the posted limit, and she wondered if she should pull into someone's driveway. Maybe make a run for their front door. Would the other driver give chase on foot as well?

Was she being chased?

The time it would take to get Blakely into her arms, and the possibility no one would answer the door at a randomly selected home, tore her rattled heart into pieces. How could she escape this car?

The sudden growl of the vehicle's engine snapped her eyes to the rearview mirror in time to see the sedan lurch closer, slowing only when its front bumper disappeared.

Nicole cussed.

Blakely burst into tears. The engine noise and her aunt's outburst had apparently tipped the scales against her prospects for sleep.

"Sorry," Nicole chanted, her fingers painfully tight around the steering wheel. "Shh. It's okay."

The incredibly steep road back to town came into view. Light glinted off the sun-bleached rock face on her right, and danced over the inlet waters on her left, hundreds of feet below.

She braced to hold her ground as a final, teeth-rattling groan shot the black sedan forward and into the oncoming lane.

The driver darted in front of Nicole, causing her to swerve and slam the brakes before it zoomed away.

She eased into the next available space along the road's shoulder and cried with Blakely as the car's taillights vanished into the distance.

Nicole didn't have proof her sister was in trouble, or that the black sedan had just delivered a warning, but she knew in her bones both were true.

And there was only one man on earth who would believe her.

Chapter Two

Dean Beaumont fastened the latch on his tackle box and set it with the rest of the gear collecting on his front porch. Long, lazy summer Sundays spent fishing with his brother and business partner, Austin, were a tradition he enjoyed with increasing appreciation. This week, he craved the respite more than ever.

Folks always assumed being a private investigator in a town as small as Marshal's Bluff would be a bore. But there were awful people everywhere. Even in nice little towns where nothing ever seemed to happen. Because people were just like the waters he liked to fish on. Calm and inviting on the surface with a whole lot going on underneath.

He exhaled a long breath and readjusted the ball cap on his head. With a little luck there'd be a breeze on the harbor today, because he'd been outside for all of three minutes and already felt the familiar prickle of sweat beading across the back of his neck. According to the thermostat on his porch post, it was nearing ninety. It'd be even hotter on the water with the sun's rays reflected back at him from every direction.

He peered down the long gravel drive toward the main road, willing Austin's red-and-white Ford to appear. An apparition of heat hovered over the distant ground.

Austin was notorious for running late, but that never

stopped Dean from worrying. Call it paranoia, or a protective instinct, but he doubted there'd ever be a day he didn't fear that the ugly things they investigated might come calling for his brother.

If Austin was on task, as he should've been, he'd delivered a pile of incriminating photos to an unfortunate client this morning. Definitive proof the client's spouse was cheating. It was one of their easier jobs. Because when a client suspected their significant other was stepping out on them, they were almost always right.

The downside was that jobs like these weren't exactly improving Austin's outlook on relationships or commitment. Which was something they could be talking about while fishing, if the knucklehead ever arrived.

The thought of failed commitments sent Dean's hand plunging into his pocket. A habit he'd developed a while back. His fingers found the penny with ease, and he relaxed by a small measure. He'd won the coin with a heart-shaped hole punched through it at a carnival and given it to his fiancée, Nicole, one balmy fall night. She'd kissed it and handed it back, telling him it was his, and he could carry her heart with him wherever he went. The coin had become a talisman. He never left home without it, though he hadn't spoken to her in more than a year.

He released the coin, unwilling to look too long or hard at why he couldn't leave the penny behind. Still, the memories of their demise poured back unbidden. He'd let his devastation over a child abduction case drive him half-mad when they were together, and he'd practically pushed her out the door when the missing boy's body was discovered. He'd shouldered that burden as if he were the cause, when he should've trusted her to help him process the pain.

He scrubbed a hand over his unshaven cheeks and headed

inside for a tall glass of water. He poured, then drained the glass, wincing at the way it burned his tightened throat.

Then, finally, the sound of tires on gravel turned him toward the door.

He set the glass aside and cast his gaze over the small log cabin, double checking things before they left. Windows were shut. Stove burners off. Lunch was in the cooler.

The truck door closed before Dean reached the porch. He felt his brow wrinkle when the door closed again.

"What the heck took you so long?" he asked, swinging onto the porch with a smile.

But it wasn't Austin's truck in the driveway. Or his brother climbing the steps.

It was Nicole.

And a baby.

Dean's gaze jerked from Nicole's anguished face to the tiny look-alike in her arms, and a string of unintelligible sounds escaped his mouth.

"Dean," she said, voice strangled and gaze pleading. "I need your help."

He was at her side in the next heartbeat, ushering her into his home. "Of course. Here. Sit. I'll get you some water." He crossed to his kitchen several feet away and returned quickly with her drink. The flush in her cheeks and red in her eyes told him whatever had happened wasn't good. His heart pounded at the thought of her pain.

She sat on the edge of his couch, limbs trembling slightly as she lay the child on the cushion at her side.

"What's going on?" he asked. "What can I do?"

She accepted the drink and gulped it, visibly straining against a breakdown.

His gaze strayed to the dark-haired baby with wide brown eyes and perfect curls. He'd cared for dozens of little ones, thanks to life on his parents' ranch, where troubled teens, often with children, stayed until their circumstances improved. Nicole's sister, Cari, had spent time on the ranch once, too. It was how he'd met Nicole.

The baby before him appeared to be four or five months old. Add nine months for a pregnancy, and the child must've been conceived while Dean and Nicole were together, though admittedly near their end.

"Nicole?" he pressed, panic welling in his chest. Not because he could be a father, but because Nicole was scared speechless, and suddenly it felt as if his entire world was at stake.

"My sister's missing," she said. "She's in trouble and no one will listen to me. I've been babysitting Blakely since yesterday, but Cari never came home. Her phone goes straight to voice mail. The police say more time has to pass before they open a case, but something is wrong." Her voice shook on the final word. "I can feel it. I didn't want to just show up here like this, but I don't know where else to turn. I'm trying to hold it together, so I won't scare her baby, but I know she can sense my stress." Her eyes turned cautiously toward her niece, and the child cried, as if on cue.

"Hey." Dean crouched before her and took the empty glass from her hands. "We can figure this out. It's going to be okay."

She swallowed audibly and pulled the baby back into her arms. "I'm so scared," she whispered. "It's been a long time since I've been this afraid."

"Well, you're with me now," he said gently. "I've got you. And… Blakely?"

She nodded.

Her niece. "I can't believe I didn't know Cari had a baby. You're an aunt."

Nicole's frail smile quivered. "Yeah."

Dean forced himself to refocus. He could regret all the things he'd missed in the past year later. Right now, Nicole needed his help. "Tell me what you know about the situation with Cari, and we'll think this through."

Nicole exhaled a shuddered breath, then began to tell her story.

Ten minutes later, Blakely was fast asleep in Dean's arms as he paced the small cabin's floor.

Nicole curled on the couch, clearly exhausted, her face in her hands.

"Finn's on the way," he said, tucking his cell phone back into his pocket. "He'll open an official case and help us get things started." Having a local detective for a brother came in handy from time to time.

"Thank you," she said, scanning him with wary eyes. "For all of this."

He followed her gaze to the baby. "Anytime."

"What do you think about the homeowners?" she asked. "They were being weird, right? Or am I overthinking? I am a stranger who approached them without warning, asking about a missing person."

"I wasn't there, but it sounds like they might be hiding something," he said. "You're usually a good judge of character, shaken or not. If you think they seemed on edge, you're probably right. The reason might not have had anything to do with Cari, but maybe it did. Either way, it doesn't sound as if this pair were seasoned criminals. That works in our favor. The nervous ones either come clean or get caught faster."

Nicole straightened and met his eye. "Faster sounds good."

"Can I see the video you mentioned?"

Dean adjusted Blakely in his arms and prepared himself for potential bad news. Users and addicts were master manipulators, and Cari had struggled with sobriety once. She might not have checked all the boxes as an addict, but he suspected she would always be one temptation away from a free fall. And like every loved one of someone with substance abuse problems, Nicole wouldn't want to accept that her sister was using again. Even if the evidence was clear.

He pressed a kiss to the top of Blakely's head while he waited for Nicole to find the video. As the child of an addict, Dean knew a little something about the lifelong turmoil Blakely had ahead of her, if Nicole was wrong about Cari's sobriety. Dean and his biological brother, Jake, had been luckier than most, fostered, then adopted, by the Beaumonts while they were still young. The Beaumonts had made every right move to protect them.

Nicole would do the same for Blakely, but it would never completely eliminate the mark a parent's addiction left on the kids.

"Here." She stood before him, arm extended, her phone turned in his direction.

A video centered the screen. Laughter and chatter mingled with music in the background. Cari held the camera close. Her hair and makeup were done. Her eyes were clear and focused.

"Good night, sweet angel baby girl," she cooed. "Mommy's sorry she isn't there to tuck you in tonight, but she's got to take advantage of your auntie Nicole while she can." She grinned widely in the teasing, practiced way of younger siblings. "Dream sweet dreams until I get home to snuggle you up. I'll be there soon." Cari blew a kiss and the video ended.

"They were outside somewhere," Nicole said. "There seemed to be a group of other women with her. All in black dresses. All hyped up and happy. I've watched the clip a dozen times, and nothing seems wrong. I tried freezing the frames and zooming in on the other faces, but it's too dark and blurry. And I don't know any of her friends anymore." She shook her head, as if casting the idea aside. "She basically doesn't have friends anymore. She has me and she has Blakely."

Dean wet his lips, preparing to tread gently. "You said they were catering a party?" The women had been dressed as if they were going out.

She nodded again. "Serving at a private party. Cari waitresses at the diner downtown, and she started taking one of these side jobs every week or so. She's paid in cash and asked to wear a simple black dress. No aprons or anything like that. She says the servers are told to blend. She's always home on time. And she always calls when she's on her way."

Nicole's composure cracked, and Dean pulled her against him with one arm, careful not to wake Blakely in the process.

His heart swelled at the feel of her, the scent of her, the warmth. He also felt her pain and would do anything to make it end.

His front door swung open, and Austin's voice filled the space. "Hey, whose SUV is—"

Nicole stepped away and wiped her eyes. "Hey, Austin."

His mouth opened, and for a single beat, he was silent. "Nicole?" His smile emerged, and he dived for her.

Dean backed up a few paces, shielding Blakely as his brother spun Nicole off her feet. "What are you doing here, gorgeous? Change your mind about this old man?" He thrust a thumb in Dean's direction, then stilled when he finally noticed the baby.

Austin's eyes widened as he looked from Blakely to Dean and back.

"She's not mine," Dean said, hit with an unexpected pang of regret. "This is Cari's baby. You remember Nicole's little sister."

His smile returned. "Of course I do. I love that girl. I can't believe she's a mama! How is she?"

"Missing." Nicole released the word on a sigh. "I'm here for help."

Dean shook off the hit of rejection that came with her words, reminding him she wasn't here for him. She just needed his help. Something he would never deny her. Then he delivered the quick facts on the matter to his brother.

"Did you call Finn?" Austin asked.

Before Dean could answer, Finn's truck pulled into the drive behind Austin's.

"Guess that answers that," he said, moving to open the door for their newest guest.

"Not my first rodeo," Dean said. In case Austin forgot this was exactly the sort of thing they did for a living.

Nicole greeted Finn with a hug. He'd worked this case once before, when Cari was a runaway in need of a detox and complete reboot on life. He'd found her with a small crowd of users and young people near the industrial section of town. Finn had recommended a facility for her rehabilitation and the Beaumont Ranch for some downtime once she was clean.

Dean's gut tightened with the realization that Nicole was reliving her worst nightmare.

"All right," Finn said, motioning Nicole to sit. "I know you probably don't feel like eating, but it sounds like you're running on no sleep, and I'm guessing you skipped your meals, too."

Austin ambled in Dean's direction, arms outstretched for the baby. "I'll take care of this little cowgirl, so you can make sandwiches."

Nicole smiled, and Dean frowned.

"Coming right up, I guess." He released Blakely into Austin's care, then gathered the ingredients for a few ham and cheese sandwiches and got to work.

"Did you get a look at the car?" Finn asked.

Nicole shook her head. "It was black. Ridiculously clean. Probably new. High end. Fast. It was behind me a while, but when it cut me off, it was out of sight in seconds."

Finn nodded. "We'll take a look at some images online."

Dean set a plate with stacked sandwich halves on the table, then poured a bag of chips into a bowl. "Let me grab my laptop."

He returned to the kitchen table and searched for fast cars in black to help her with recognition, then he narrowed the search to only include sedans in the newest models.

Nicole selected a sandwich half, then scrolled through the resulting images.

His brothers exchanged looks but didn't comment on whatever they were thinking.

"Cari sent a good-night video for Blakely," Dean said. "She looked good in the clip."

They nodded, picking up on the thing he didn't say. Cari had been sober, with no indication of intoxication or an otherwise diminished capacity. At least at the time of the video.

"Good," Finn said. "Consider the case officially opened. I'm heading back to the station to see what I can learn based on what you've told me." He grabbed another half sandwich from the pile and stood. "I'll keep you in the loop as things progress. You." He pointed to Nicole. "Rest. Then get a list together of anyone you think might know something you don't about your sister. Hangouts. Interests. New people in her life. Old acquaintances making reappearances." He held her gaze for a long beat.

No one wanted to think Cari would make terrible choices at this point in her life, or that she would risk everything when she had a daughter to care for, but everyone in the room knew things happened, and humans didn't always make the right choices. Even the best of them.

Finn released her from his stare and tipped his hat before seeing himself out.

Blakely whimpered, and Nicole stood to relieve Austin.

"She's having a rough day," she said. "I can take her."

Austin turned away, an expression of exaggerated offense on his face. "I've got her. You eat. Rest. Talk things out with your man." He winked, and Dean made a mental note to throttle him.

That plan changed when Nicole walked straight into his arms and held on tight.

He wrapped her up protectively and pressed a gentle kiss against her head. "We're going to find your sister."

Chapter Three

Nicole climbed into the passenger seat of her SUV while Dean secured Blakely in the back. Asking for his help had been easy. Cari needed it. Letting him step in and ease Nicole's burdens was something else. She'd learned years ago, when Cari was at her worst, and their parents were either fighting or sobbing, not to be one more person in need. But Dean and his family were wired to get involved, however they could, whenever needed. And she'd never been so thankful for those qualities. It was no wonder he'd once meant everything to her. He was the perfect hero.

If only he'd learned to be a partner, too. She appreciated his big, giving heart, but she couldn't settle for anyone who refused to be her teammate.

At least the Beaumont brothers were working together to find Cari. She could never thank any of them properly for that.

Nicole took a few slow, cleansing breaths to re-center herself. Giving in to her heightened emotions when so much was at stake felt unreasonably selfish. It was time to get her head together and think of ways to help the Beaumonts. But when she'd arrived on Dean's doorstep unannounced, asking for help, and he'd immediately accepted, she'd begun to feel herself unravel. He hadn't even waited to hear what she needed.

He'd just brought her and Blakely into his home, then started giving. And it was as if a dam had broken loose inside her.

"Ready?" Dean asked, shifting into Reverse.

"Yes." She met his eyes with gratitude when further words failed.

They rode in companionable silence for several long minutes, heading back to the neighborhood where Cari had worked the night before.

"You doing okay?" he asked, eyeing her carefully as they made the ascent along the water.

She nodded, but her stomach clenched. "Actually, no," she admitted. "All this fear is triggering old memories. Part of me is trying to be angry, doubting her word about the job and address. Which is nonsense. She isn't that person anymore. And I kind of hate myself for having such awful thoughts."

The SUV leveled out at the top of the hill, rolling slowly to a stop sign inside the high-class neighborhood.

"Don't beat yourself up. That's normal," he said. "You lived in fear of losing her for years, and on the surface, today looks a lot like all those times before. You're experiencing the same emotions. Your brain is being flooded with all the same signals. It's trying to make sense of things by connecting this to old patterns."

Nicole wet her lips and nodded. More than one counselor had told her similar things over the years. "Is it ridiculous that I'm also feeling guilty for being so upset? I keep thinking if I'm this scared, how terrified is Cari? I'm still safe. My world is stable. But I still can't stop shaking."

"Your world is upside down," he countered. "Her traumas have always been your traumas, too. They always will be. She's your sister."

Nicole wiped a renegade tear from her cheek and concentrated on steadying her breaths.

"Nicole?" Dean said softly.

Her name on his tongue was nearly enough to crack her newly rebuilt composure.

"Did I make it worse?" he asked, sneaking peeks at her as he drove.

"No." Dean always made everything better. "Thank you for the reminder," she said. "And for being here."

Emotion rolled over his handsome features. "Where else would I be?"

Soon they passed the home where Nicole had knocked earlier, but Dean didn't stop. He made several loops through the winding streets, examining this world through sharp, trained eyes.

Nicole looked pointlessly for Cari's car, still nowhere to be found. "I can't decide if I'm more afraid she never made it here, or that she just never made it home from here. Without her car in the area, it makes me wonder if the people I spoke to really never saw her."

What if there wasn't a party? She dragged anxious fingers through her hair, hating the thoughts of doubt. "I know she was here," she said, as much to herself as to Dean.

"I believe you," he said. "And we believe Cari. Can you point me to the park you mentioned?"

Two turns later they pulled against the curb where Nicole had parked earlier.

"Here," she said. "I thought this was someone's backyard at first, but there are benches. And a group of kids were here." She twisted on her seat to fish Cari's coat from the floor of the back seat. "This is the coat I told you about."

Dean settled the SUV's engine and gave the lavender jacket a thorough exam.

Nicole had already done the same. No obvious damage. No

hidden pockets or other places the destination of her where-abouts might be concealed.

She returned the item to the back seat when he finished.

"Okay. Next step." He opened his car door and smiled. "Let's see what else we can find in the park."

With Blakely in tow, they crossed the street and began a methodical search.

Dean peeked under every bench, carefully running his hand through the lush green grass.

Nicole turned in a slow circle, acclimating herself to the surroundings. "The party house is on top of that hill," she said. "If something frightened Cari and she left, moving downhill also makes sense. Town is downhill. So is the police station. Home. Safety."

Dean stretched onto his feet and rested both hands on his hips. "Agreed." He fixed his eyes on the horizon and whispered into the heated air. "Where did you go next, Cari Homes?"

Nicole had asked the universe same thing.

And still there wasn't an answer.

DEAN WATCHED NICOLE with her niece, hating that there wasn't more he could do for either of them. Missing persons cases took time. They'd started early, which was good, but they had little to go on. And from the looks of the ladies in front of him, they could both use some rest.

He rubbed his palms together, fingers outstretched. "What do you say about getting out of the sun? Maybe taking the little one home. Cooling off. Getting some rest. Waiting for input from Finn and Austin. Maybe having a look in Cari's room?"

Nicole's brows rose and relief softened the tension in her face and shoulders. "I think that sounds really good. Blakely's been on the go all day. She should be in her bed for naps. Someplace familiar and comforting."

"Well, then," he said, spinning the key ring on one finger. "Point me to your home."

The look of appreciation on Nicole's face each time he expressed the smallest kindness was enough to break his heart. Didn't she know she deserved so much more? Kindness wasn't even the tip of the iceberg.

He drove back through the quiet tree-lined streets, then began the descent into town with a heavy heart. Missing persons cases always took a toll on him, and leaving Cari's last known location empty-handed felt a lot like defeat.

Nicole kneaded her hands in her lap, probably feeling the same.

Dean set his fingers over hers on instinct, and she stilled. He stiffened slightly in response, having momentarily forgotten he had no right to touch her anymore. No claim to this access. Still, pulling away now could feel like rejection, and she hadn't immediately shaken him off.

He cleared his throat and gave her hand a gentle squeeze. "We'll figure this out." He'd said something similar before, and he would repeat the words as many times as she needed. He would find her sister.

"Thank you."

In cases like this one, things generally didn't get dicey until three days or more had passed. There was still room for hope. With some persistence and a little luck, Cari could be back safely long before then. "When we get to your place, we can reach out to Finn and Austin. See if they have anything."

"I still have Finn's number," Nicole said. "I can text him now."

Dean nodded. Contacting Finn would give her something to do, which would make her feel less powerless. And the reminder a local detective was actively working the case would be a bonus, even if he hadn't learned anything new.

Dean opened his mouth to say her suggestion sounded good, but a small sound escaped her. Prickles of foreboding climbed Dean's neck and arms. "What is it?"

She pointed to the windshield, indicating an oncoming vehicle still too distant to be more than a silhouette. "That's the car."

He frowned, straining to make out the details as it rumbled nearer.

"That sound," she said, rubbing gooseflesh from her skin. "I don't think I'll ever forget it."

The late-model Dodge Charger flew past them at double the speed limit. No plates, dark tint, just like she'd described earlier. And the signature engine growl was one enthusiasts worked long and hard under the hood to perfect. A glance in his side-view mirror revealed a hint of brake lights before the car zoomed away.

"What do we do?" she asked, voice thick with fear.

"Let Finn know we saw the car. It's a late-model Dodge Charger. He and local law enforcement can keep an eye out for it. See where it's spotted and who's driving. Meanwhile, we'll head to your place as planned."

She twisted in her seat, checking on Blakely before facing forward once more. She dug her phone from her purse. "It's not the same car I saw the guy at the house get into. Do you think that means anything?"

"Maybe," Dean said. Though at this point nothing was off the table for theories. "Did you get a look in the garage when the door went up?" There could easily have been two, possibly three other cars inside.

"No." She exhaled softly. "I was only thinking of Cari. Maybe even hoping she'd bounce into view apologizing for scaring me. As if she might've been working, then fallen asleep in a spare bedroom, and the family was just too nice to wake her."

Before he could turn an encouraging smile her way, the Charger reappeared. This time in his rearview mirror. "You should probably pass the information on to Finn."

Nicole's wide eyes were already on the mirror. "Okay."

The car roared closer, riding their bumper along the two-lane road above the water. The experience, given the infant in the back seat, Nicole at his side and a single lane separating them from a plummet into the sea, was genuinely terrifying.

The battered guardrail had never looked so flimsy. The barrier would be useless if the other driver chose to ram their SUV.

"We're on Highway 12," Nicole said into her phone, apparently having called Finn rather than texting. "Coming back from the address I gave you this morning."

Dean gauged the car's distance and considered his options as town drew near. "Tell him the engine's been souped up. Heavy tint. No other identifying features."

She repeated his words as the road angled away from the sea, cutting through fields and farmland instead of rock and mountain. "I'm putting you on speaker."

Finn repeated the description of the car for clarification while Dean began a series of turns and switchbacks when other roads became available. A procedure designed to lose their tail.

Nicole confirmed the description, and Dean took another wild turn.

"We're almost to the high school," he said, projecting his voice in the direction of the phone. "He's on us like a bumper sticker."

"Head toward the precinct," Finn advised. "I'll move your way. Don't let him rattle you. Mind your speed."

Dean fought the urge to remind his younger brother he'd learned to give advice like that from Dean. At thirty-four, he was hardly a novice prone to panic. "I've got this," he said instead. "Just get out here and do your lights and sirens thing."

Nicole raised the phone as she peered behind them. "I knew this guy was a threat, or at least a message the first time he followed me. There are plenty of other vehicles on the road to torment. He's chosen mine twice."

The car gave a louder, more menacing growl and launched into the oncoming lane, then in front of the SUV, barely avoiding a head-on collision with a pickup. A moment later the car was gone, vanished into the distance as quickly as it had appeared on their tail.

Nicole stifled a scream, and Blakely burst into tears.

"What happened?" Finn barked.

"We lost our tail," Dean said. "Too many witnesses, maybe."

"Or," Nicole panted, dropping her fingers from her chest to tap against her phone screen, "he saw me recording him."

Dean's lips quirked into a smile. "You got that on video?"

"Yep."

"Good thinking," Finn said. "I'm going to need that file."

She composed her features into a satisfied grin. "Already done."

DEAN SENT HER a look of unfiltered pride, then took a long, convoluted route to Nicole and Cari's apartment, assuring the Charger didn't manage to follow or find them.

Blakely calmed with some soothing comfort from her aunt.

Nicole had always been a troubleshooter and quick thinker. Those characteristics had likely paid off today in droves.

Video of the car would go a long way in helping Finn nail down the driver or owner. He couldn't imagine how she'd remained calm when it'd been her behind the wheel, especially considering she'd just realized her sister was missing and something strange was going on. A strong testament to her grit and character.

They parked outside a three-story apartment building and made their way to the front. A single camera pointed at the parking lot and street.

An older gentleman paused to hold the door open for them on his way out.

"Thanks," Nicole said, moving swiftly inside.

"Did you know him?" Dean asked, hating the ridiculous lack of security.

She stuck her key in a first-floor apartment door lock. "No. Why?"

"Do you think he recognized you, or knows you live in the building? Do you know your neighbors?"

She frowned. "Probably not, and maybe," she said. "Everyone keeps to themselves here. It's mostly working couples. A few older folks, but it's usually pretty desolate during the workday." She swung the door open and motioned him inside. "This is it."

He gave the long, quiet hallway a final look before stepping inside. The small space had an open floor plan, much like his cabin. An island bar separated the kitchen and living room. A hall led from the main hub, presumably to the bedrooms and a shared bath. The decor was inviting and overrun with charm.

"It's not usually this clean," she said. "I couldn't sleep last night, so I scrubbed everything while I waited for Cari to call or show up."

Dean snorted softly. "Most people tell folks to excuse the mess, when there's obviously nothing out of place."

She rolled her eyes. "Yeah, well, our place is usually a disaster. Especially during the school year. Cari works nights after I get home, so Blakely never has to go to day care. She can't afford it, and everything is covered in germs there. We basically run in circles just trying to care for the baby and get where we need to be on time. No one here has had a full night's sleep in six months."

"Is that Blakely's age?" he asked, reevaluating the little girl. Was she a couple of months older than he'd guessed?

Nicole deftly prepared a bottle in the kitchen, cradling Blakely in her opposite arm. "She'll be five months this week. But Cari was on bed rest for most of her last trimester. This kiddo was in a big hurry to meet me, I guess." She moved to the couch and rested her niece on her lap, then slid the bottle's nipple into Blakely's mouth with a smile. "We thought we were going to lose her for a while. Then, one day the time was finally up, and here she is."

"And she's perfect," Dean said, enjoying her story and the love evident in her voice.

"Absolutely."

"Sounds like the three of you have been through a lot together," Dean said.

Tears welled in Nicole's eyes as she dragged her gaze away from Blakely. "What if Cari doesn't… What if she's already…"

Dean moved to Nicole's side and crouched before her. "It's not time to think like that. If we get evidence to suggest you should prepare for the worst, I'll be straight with you. I promise. But we aren't there yet. Not even close. Your sister is a fighter and a survivor. Just like you."

Nicole's expression hardened, and she rose with the baby.

Her shoulders squared, and her spine straightened. "You're right. We need to keep going."

Dean stretched onto his feet beside her. "Where are we going?"

"To her room." Nicole moved into the hallway. "I'm not going to love doing this, but we should search Cari's things."

He followed her with a fresh jolt of purpose. This was what he did best. "Any chance she left her laptop?"

"On her desk." Nicole opened the device and stepped aside, giving Dean room to work.

"Perfect." He hunched over the lock screen, fingers resting on the keys. "Any guesses about the password?" If not, he doubted it would take long to crack. Most people weren't very creative.

"Try heart of hearts," she said. "Capital *H*s and a zero for the *o* in *of*. That was the password when she was still pregnant. I used her laptop at the hospital. If she was feeling really clever, she might've used threes in place of the *E*s."

Dean tried the suggested passwords, and Cari's desktop appeared. "Looks like she was feeling clever."

Nicole smiled and moved Blakely into position at her shoulder. She patted the baby's back and shifted foot to foot. "Now what?"

"Now we see what she's been up to online. Find out what she's researched. Who she talked to. What they said." Dean accessed the device's browsing history and opened a few web pages. "Looks like she's still logged into her email and social media accounts. That'll save us some time."

"Good," Nicole said. "So why are you frowning?"

He did his best to clear his expression, then angled the device in her direction. There were at least a dozen recent exchanges between Cari and a guy whose profile image involved a crude hand gesture and a lolling tongue. "Who's Mikey Likey?"

"Ugh. Her ex." Nicole peered over his shoulder at the screen. "She dated him before meeting Blakely's dad. She and Mikey stayed friends."

"And Blakely's dad?" Dean asked.

"Became vapor the minute two lines appeared on the pregnancy test."

Dean bit back his opinion on anyone who'd abandon their baby and her mother. Instead, he doubled down on the task at hand. "Then let's start with Mikey."

Chapter Four

Nicole curled on the couch after dinner, eyes fixed on the clock. Tension only slightly eased from a long cry in a steaming-hot shower. She'd fed and bathed Blakely, then helped her fall asleep for the night. Now the apartment was still, aside from the tick of the clock's second hand.

There were no new leads on Cari.

And she'd been chatting regularly with Mikey. A terrible influence from her past. Why? And what else was going on in Cari's life that Nicole didn't know?

"Hey," Dean said, taking the seat beside her and offering a mug of steaming tea. "You still like lavender and vanilla. The cupboard's full of it."

She smiled. "There was a sale."

Dean used to bring her a cup when she stayed up late grading art projects and worksheets from her classroom.

"Thanks." She held the tea beneath her nose to inhale the soothing scents. It was time to refocus. Think of something that could help the Beaumonts make headway in finding her sister.

But her tired, desperate mind had lost its clarity, and Blakely would be awake and hungry before dawn.

Dean sipped from his mug, the contents of which smelled distinctly like black coffee, and guilt tugged at her heart once more. She'd taken him away from Sunday fishing without any notice. He looked forward to the time with his brother, alone on the lake. He'd once told her those trips helped him re-center himself after a long week of turbulence. But this week, she'd barged in needing help. Then she'd monopolized the rest of his day, and the foreseeable future, with her problem. And guilty or not, she couldn't bring herself to tell him he could go home if he wanted. She prayed he didn't want to, because she was holding on to sanity by a thread, and his presence was making her whole impossible situation survivable.

Blakely deserved at least one adult who wasn't falling apart.

The thought of other adults sat Nicole upright. She'd been putting off the inevitable all day, and she couldn't wait any longer.

Dean lowered his mug and furrowed his brow.

"I have to call Mom." She set her tea aside and dropped her face into waiting palms. "I didn't want to have to make this call. Every time I've thought about it, I decided to wait a little longer, hoping I wouldn't have to do it at all." Cari had been gone for twenty hours. "She's going to be a mess, and there's no one to comfort her. Plus she's sure to be upset with me for waiting so long to tell her." Nicole lifted her head and turned tired eyes to meet Dean's. "Making this call means this is all real. And I really, really don't want it to be."

He rubbed a palm over her back, smoothing the soft cotton of her T-shirt, offering companionship instead of words. "Why doesn't she have anyone?" Dean asked. "What about your dad?"

Nicole's last bit of energy seemed to drain. Apparently a lot could happen in a year. "Mom moved to Charleston a few months ago to take care of her parents. Grandpa had a stroke and they needed to hire a caretaker but couldn't afford one. Mom was struggling financially after the divorce, so moving in with my grandparents has helped all three of them. She misses us, but she's glad to be able to do this for her folks. She calls most nights around ten."

According to the clock, that was in less than an hour.

Dean twisted on the couch for a better look at her. "Your folks got divorced? I'm sorry to hear that."

She sighed. "I want to say me too, but I don't know."

Cari's teenage issues had taken a toll on everyone and strained the family in a dozen ways. Their mom had internalized it, wondering where she'd gone wrong as a mother and how she'd failed Cari. Their father had grown distant, unwilling to show or deal with his pain.

Eventually, Cari put her life back together, but their parents' marriage had broken irrevocably. That was the thing most people didn't realize. Drugs crushed everyone in their reach. The waves and ripples of pain went out in long arcs, breaking up friendships, driving away peripheral people and annihilating support systems for everyone in the family.

"He remarried," Nicole added. "They have a baby a little older than Blakely."

Dean's brows rose. "How long have they been divorced?"

"Not long enough for them to have a baby Tony's age. Dad and Heidi eloped a few months after he moved out. We learned about her and the coming addition to our family in the same conversation."

"Wow."

"That's what we said, too." Nicole smiled. "There was also a little cussing."

Dean laughed. "I guess so."

"Once Tony was born, Dad sent photos and confessed to meeting his new wife while he was still with Mama. He blamed her for pulling away in their time of crisis. He thought she'd prioritized Cari's situation over his needs and their marriage, so he was forced to find comfort elsewhere."

Dean's mouth turned down and his eyes flashed hot.

Nicole sighed. "I should probably call Dad, too."

"Why don't you let me call him?" Dean suggested. "He knows me well enough, and I can relay anything he needs to know. Tell him you're with Blakely right now if he asks for you. You can concentrate on that call to your mama."

"Would you?" Her words caught in her throat, and she blew out a long shaky breath.

"I've got this. Text me his number."

Nicole did as Dean asked, grateful for a partner in this moment and glad to skip that particular call.

She dialed and waited. Dean did the same.

When her mom's voice mail picked up, Nicole was equally sorry and relieved. She left a message in her most casual tone possible and asked her to return the call.

Dean pursed his lips. "No answer. I didn't leave a message. I thought a voice mail from me might tip him off to the problem, and I heard you leaving a message for your mama. I'll try again in an hour."

She returned to her tea, taking several long sips as she unwound. "I can't believe Cari kept in touch with Mikey. I know that's the least of our problems right now, but I'm truly stunned. He played a big part in some of the worst days of her life. Why would she want to talk to him? And why would she keep it from me? I guess this is my answer. Look at how judgmental I'm being."

"You're upset," Dean said. "Give yourself a break. We'll know more after he responds to your message. If he doesn't respond by morning, we'll go find him."

"Okay." That seemed reasonable, and it gave her a new purpose. Tomorrow they would look for Mikey.

A few hours ago she'd typed three little words into the chat box on Cari's laptop.

Can we talk?

She hadn't let him know it was her. With a little luck he'd agree to meet her somewhere, then she and Dean could corner him for information. Instead of giving him the chance to simply stop responding.

"Your sister's going to be okay," Dean said softly, apparently seeing where her mind had gone. "She's tough, smart and resourceful. Finn and Austin are chasing leads. You and I will keep caring for her little girl and pulling any thread we find."

Nicole turned on the cushion, tucking her feet beneath her and leaning against his side. Greedy for a little of his strength and assurance. "I felt like I failed her as a big sister when I found out she was using. I blamed myself for not seeing the signs. And I kept that up right through her time at your family's ranch. I'm feeling exactly that way again now. I didn't think I ever would."

Dean's arm looped around her shoulders, pulling her in close. "I know." He held her silently while she worked her way through the tea. When she set the empty mug on the coffee table, he offered an encouraging smile. "Aside from becoming World's Best Aunt, what have you been up to this year?"

Nicole smiled, glad for the mental and emotional break. "I'm still teaching at the elementary school, and I still love it. Half my wardrobe has glitter in places it will never come out. I helped Cari through her last trimester. I was her birthing coach through a pretty traumatic labor and delivery. Saw things I'll never unsee." She slid her eyes to Dean.

He laughed.

"And now I've got this perfect little niece. My sister is a wonderful mom. She's become my best friend. It's the closest we've ever been, and I've been really happy."

The eight-year age difference between them had made a relationship on any kind of equal ground nearly impossible until Cari became a mom. She'd still been a kid when Nicole was in high school. She'd still been learning to drive when Nicole had graduated from college and started teaching. What they'd created this year was real, and it hurt all the more to lose her now.

"I'm glad y'all found your ways to each other," Dean said. "I've always liked Cari. Lots of people take wrong turns in life, but I knew the moment your folks brought her to the ranch she was going to be okay."

"Thanks." She smiled. "What about you?" Nicole asked, realizing for the first time that Dean could be married or engaged, or even have a baby of his own in the time they'd been apart. They'd barely spoken about anything other than Cari's disappearance, and suddenly she wanted to know everything. Especially the parts about a potential love interest or child. "What did I miss in your life this year?"

Dean stilled for a long beat, and Nicole found herself doing the same. "I've been working through some things," he said finally. "It took me a while to find my way back after you left, but for what it's worth, I know you were right for leaving. I let that case and that family's tragedy derail everything in my life. It wrecked me, and that hurt everyone who loved me. Not to mention all the cases I had to turn down while I got myself together. I wasn't helping anyone else who needed help. Thankfully, I've probably got the best support system on earth, and I figured things out eventually."

Nicole had been part of his system once. Maybe she'd failed

him by walking away when he was at his worst, but knowing the strides she'd made with Cari these last few months, it was hard to want to change anything about the way things had gone. And selfish as it felt, Nicole stood by her reason for leaving. She wanted a partner in all things, and Dean had stopped letting her in. He'd pulled away in his pain just like her dad, and look at how that had ended.

"I'm glad you're okay, Dean," she said. "And I'm really thankful you're here."

"Me, too."

Nicole groaned and shifted, sore from a restless night on her couch. Shafts of light through her living-room curtain stung her tired eyes.

Sounds of movement somewhere in the apartment set her heart and mind on alert.

For the briefest moment, she thought Cari and Blakely were sharing breakfast or playing together.

Then the previous day came crashing back.

Dean's muffled voice slowly reached her on the still morning air, and she pushed herself onto her feet.

She gripped and kneaded the aching muscles along her neck and shoulders where tension and a night on the couch bit and cramped them. Exhaustion had pulled her under, but she'd barely slept during the eight hours that had passed.

Blakely must've been awake for nearly three.

Nicole padded down the hallway to Cari's room, where Dean paced the carpet, a cell phone pressed to one ear. Blakely rocked in her front carrier, attached to his broad chest. A pink pacifier bobbing double time in her little rosebud mouth.

Cari's normally cluttered space was tidy. Her things organized and stacked in neat piles along the wall and on her bed.

Dean had inventoried her room.

He turned when she arrived in the open doorway. "Good morning."

"Hey." She forced a smile, taken aback by the wave of emotions. Seeing him in her apartment was strange. Seeing him with a baby in a front carrier was something else altogether. And seeing her little sister's room processed as if it was a crime scene was enough to make her stomach bottom out.

Dean wet his lips and turned slightly away. "Nicole's up. Keep me posted." He ended the call and tucked his phone into the pocket of his jeans.

Blakely cooed and babbled. Her wide brown eyes danced with pleasure, enjoying two of her most favorite things at once: her pacifier and being carried.

"She woke at dawn, so we've been hanging out," he explained. "Were you able to rest on the couch? I thought about carrying you to your bed, but that seemed—" He cringed. "And I didn't want to wake you, so…"

Memories of being carried to bed by Dean stunned her brain momentarily, fully eliminating any fog that had remained after a restless sleep. "I'm okay," she said. "Thank you for caring for Blakely. And doing all this." She motioned to the room. "How's that going?"

"I don't know her like you do, so nothing stood out to me as unusual. But I've organized as much as I can to make it easier for you to take a look and see what you think."

"That's good, I think," Nicole said. "I'll look as soon as I've had some coffee. I don't want to miss anything. Do you want some?"

Dean lifted a small stack of papers from Cari's desk. "Sounds good. I wanted to show you these. I found them hidden inside the album covers of her old vinyl record collection."

Nicole's heart stuttered, her outstretched hand frozen a

few inches from Blakely before she regained herself enough to carry the motion through. She stroked her niece's chubby cheek and planted a kiss on her head before stepping back. She met Dean's steady gaze with utter fear. "What is it?"

"Five college acceptance letters."

Nicole blinked. Of all the things he could've said, this was at the bottom of her expectations. "Colleges?"

He passed her the findings with a shy smile. "All sent in the last two months."

The papers were heavy in Nicole's grip. Cari hadn't told her about this, either. "I had no idea she was thinking about going to college. Or that she'd applied."

Her attention moved to the top line of each letter.

Congratulations Carolyn Homes! We're honored to announce your acceptance for enrollment in the fall semester.

"She got in," Nicole repeated, sifting through the pages. "Everywhere."

Dean's hands covered hers as they began to shake. "Cari was planning a better future. The extra catering jobs she took were probably meant to help with tuition. And maybe this was going to be a surprise."

Nicole's gaze snapped back to Dean's. Her sister wanted to go to college. She wasn't falling into trouble with old connections. She was rising above her challenges, like she always did. "We need to talk to Mikey."

Chapter Five

It was nearing lunchtime when Dean and Nicole finally left the apartment with Blakely. Nicole's sweet little niece had fallen asleep while the adults had breakfast, and neither of them wanted to wake her. Instead, they'd drifted into easy conversation that had reminded Dean how much he'd missed talking with her. Nicole was intuitive and kind in ways most people weren't, and her levelheaded approach to life was something he could use more of.

She strapped Blakely into the rear-facing car seat, then took the seat at Dean's side, allowing him to drive her SUV again. "Ready."

Dean waited while she buckled up, then reversed out of the parking lot and onto the residential streets of her neighborhood. The hot summer sun beat down on the pavement, creating an apparition of heat over the asphalt.

He needed to make a pit stop at his place. He hadn't expected to spend the night at Nicole's, and he needed some basic things, like a change of clothes and his own toiletries. "Care if we swing back by my house after this?"

Thankfully Nicole had provided an unopened toothbrush, but his deodorant was pushing the boundaries of its advertised twenty-four-hour protection.

"Of course." She looked nearly as exhausted as she had last night, despite the hours of rest on her couch.

Dean made a mental note to create an opportunity for her to sleep again soon.

Aside from the tension rolling off her in waves, Nicole looked as beautiful as ever. She'd hidden warm brown eyes behind mirrored sunglasses, and her thick dark hair fell over her shoulders in matching French braids. She wore a simple blue tank top that hugged her curves and jean shorts that would've been his undoing in any other situation.

She caught him staring, and he returned his attention to the road.

"Where are we going?" she asked. "The police station? The diner where Cari works?"

Dean adjusted his grip on the wheel, bracing for what he was about to say. "I thought we'd start down by the docks."

Nicole stilled, and her gaze flickered to the window.

Marshal's Bluff law enforcement had recovered Cari from the docks when she'd gone missing years ago. She'd been high and sleeping on the concrete beneath highway overpasses as if she were homeless, instead of breaking her entire family's hearts.

Dean helped locate missing people in similar situations every month, but he hadn't been to the docks in some time. Local police frequently set the homeless community on the move, attempting to get as many as possible into shelters and return the runaways to their families. Eventually, the group always reunited in a new location. Or in one of their previously vacated favorites.

For most folks, it was probably hard to believe Marshal's Bluff had a homeless population or any amount of addicts. The streets were clean, crime was low, and the town was inarguably charming. But anywhere there were people, there were problems.

They motored along residential roads toward the sea, eventually trading houses for small businesses and cafés in the picturesque downtown. Historic and postcard-perfect, the blocks from Main to Bayview were pristine, lined with trees and doused in an abundance of cheerful potted plants.

Several blocks and one turn later, large utilitarian buildings rose from the concrete, turning the quaint, colorful surroundings gray and sparse. Scorching sunlight glinted off harbor waters, and exhaust rose from ships and semitrucks delivering large-scale shipments.

The types of pedestrians changed with the scenery. No more couples holding hands and smiling singles walking dogs or families pushing strollers. In this area of town, individuals stood on corners looking defeated, lost or angry, often staring down commuters who dared drive past. Some were lookouts, watching for signs of the authorities while their counterparts engaged in unsavory or illegal activities. Others were just getting by, passing time without purpose or plan. By night, these blocks weren't safe for anyone without a connection to the various crimes or a weapon for protection.

Dean always traveled with both. "I've got a few contacts down here, but they don't spend a lot of time with the community we're going to talk to," he explained, scanning the area for a place to start asking questions. "We'll reach out to them next if this is a bust."

The highway overpasses came into view, and Dean slowed to a crawl. The bridges offered shade and acted as a hub for those folks with nowhere to go while the rest of the world was on the clock.

Nicole straightened as they reached the edge of the first bridge.

The sidewalks were lined in trash and makeshift shelters. A mass of young people meandered in the grassy space beyond the road.

"Do you think she could be here?"

"No." Dean covered her hand with his and offered a squeeze. "But I'm hoping Mikey is, or someone will know where we can find him."

He parked the SUV along the curb and climbed out.

Nicole followed suit, sliding Blakely into a sling on her hip.

Several people took notice immediately. Some standing taller, as if they might want trouble. Others appeared frightened, clearly unsure what to make of the newcomers. Dean reached for Nicole's hand and glanced at her to be sure he hadn't overstepped. "Okay?"

She nodded.

His gaze jumped back to the appraising groups. None of the wary or hostile faces looked like Mikey's profile photo.

Dean rolled his shoulders back and flattened his expression, then raised his cell phone, Cari's image already on-screen. "We're looking for a missing woman. She used to come down here a few years ago. Her name's Cari," he told the group.

Mentioning Cari's former affiliation with the area softened a few faces and gained the interest of others.

He extended the phone in their direction as he walked slowly past. "She's been gone more than a day now. Her family's worried. She stays in touch with Mikey, and we thought someone here might know where we can find him."

An older woman with a long gray ponytail and scar along one cheek stepped forward. "How do you know Mikey?"

"We don't," Nicole said. "But he's Cari's friend, and I'm hoping he can help me find her. She's my little sister, and I'm scared. I don't know what else to do."

The crowd shifted and murmured. Several people dropped back, interest lost.

A trio of men Dean guessed was the group's muscle lined up and moved in his direction.

The older woman outstretched an arm at her side, palm

up, stopping them in their places. "Cari with the stars on her wrist?" she asked. "Young. Short hair. Fancy life?"

Nicole exhaled a shuddered breath, and Dean squeezed her hand again. "Yes," she croaked. "She's twenty-three now. Her hair is long, and she's put on weight. This is her daughter. I was babysitting when she went missing."

The woman examined Blakely from several feet away. "Mikey said she got clean."

"She did." Nicole nodded and sniffled, voice wavering. "She's my best friend and a really, really good mother."

Dean gritted his teeth against the lump rising in his throat. Nicole and her family had been through so much already. He hated that fate had brought them back here again. And he couldn't do a darn thing about it.

"She catered a party on the night she went missing," Nicole pressed. "Do you know anything about that?"

The woman shook her head. "No, but Mikey delivers pizzas for the place on Main Street with a rocket on the logo. Sometimes he comes by and brings food."

"Thank you," Nicole said.

The light in her eyes dimmed as she looked at Dean, and he knew what she was thinking without having to ask.

He removed his wallet from his pocket, tucking the cell phone away. "There's a ranch outside town where Cari spent a few weeks when she needed time to get herself together," he said, projecting his voice through the sudden silence. "Anyone is welcome, as long as they stay busy and sober. The facilities are clean and safe. Food's hot and good. The folks there will stand by you until you're ready to leave. Long afterward, too, if you let them." He pulled a battered stack of business cards from his wallet and offered them around.

One of the tough guys took one, then tossed it on the ground. A couple of others laughed, but took a card, too.

A small brown-haired woman covertly slid a card under the tattered cuff of her shirtsleeve.

He hoped that meant he might see her again.

"Let's go," Nicole whispered, offering a small, hip-high wave to the older woman.

And they hurried back to the SUV.

NICOLE'S HANDS SHOOK and her knees trembled as she buckled into the passenger seat of the SUV. She hadn't been anywhere near the industrial section of town since a detective had pulled her unconscious little sister off the ground in the middle of winter, high and barefoot. Being there again, with Cari missing, stole her breath and broke her heart.

Dean pressed the speaker button on his phone and dialed, then dropped the device into her cup holder before pulling onto the road. The word *Mama* appeared on the screen.

"Hello, baby boy." His mother's voice rose through the car, and Nicole's heart ached anew. She'd missed Mrs. Beaumont and Dean's entire family when they'd parted. She hadn't fully realized how much until now.

"Hey, Mama," Dean said, a broad smile curving his lips. "I've got you on speaker. I'm here with Nicole and Cari's little girl, Blakely."

"Hello, Nicole!" Mary Beaumont sang. "I've heard all about what's going on with Cari, and I'll tell you what I told Finn and Austin. Whatever trouble Cari's in, it's not her doing. Your sister's a good girl, and she left here with her head on straight. My boys will figure this out."

"Thank you," Nicole said. "I've really missed you, Mrs. Beaumont."

"Well, don't be a stranger. Come over. Let me get my hands on that niece of yours."

Nicole smiled, stealing a glance at Dean.

He bobbed his head, never one to say no to his mama.

"I will," Nicole said.

"Mama," Dean interrupted, making the final turn back onto Main Street. "I don't mean to rush you, but we're almost at our next stop. I called to tell you we were just down at the overpasses, and there's quite a few folks staying there again. I thought you could make sure they had something to eat tonight. I handed out a few cards. So you should probably know that, too."

"Good job," Mrs. Beaumont said. "I'll make up some sandwiches and send your dad down that way in a bit. I'll tell Lincoln to ride along."

Dean's brows rose and Nicole grinned.

The youngest Beaumont brother, Lincoln, had excelled in the military until he was captured during a mission that took the life of the younger soldier who'd gone with him. He'd returned home physically, but it'd been a long, slow process for him mentally and emotionally. Last she'd heard, he was doing okay, working as a ranch hand on the farm and not a fan of anyone or anything. Except maybe the young stables manager, Josie, but she was a whole lot of sunshine and he was a bit of a storm cloud.

Hopefully none of the tough guys they'd seen beneath the bridge gave him any trouble. Or back talk. Or sideways looks. They would unequivocally regret it.

"Now," Mrs. Beaumont said. "Nicole. How's your mama taking this? Is there anything I can do for her?"

"No, ma'am." Nicole cringed. "Mom's living in Charleston with my grandparents, and I haven't been able to reach her." It was one more thing on her growing pile of tasks and concerns.

"Has her number changed?" Mrs. Beaumont asked.

"No."

"That's settled then. I'll get a hold of your mama and invite her here to stay with me while this is sorted. How's that?"

Nicole's chest expanded with relief and gratitude. "I know she'd appreciate that."

Their mothers had become friends during the time Cari spent on the ranch, and the Beaumonts' property was large with numerous outbuildings turned guest rooms for anyone in need.

"Say no more," Mrs. Beaumont said.

"Thank you," Nicole repeated, meaning it to her core.

"All right, Mama," Dean cut in. "We'll swing by when we can. Love you."

"Love you, too, darlin'. See you soon, Nicole."

"Bye, Mrs. Beaumont," she called, missing the other woman, and her mother, so badly it hurt.

The call disconnected, and Nicole blew out a shaky breath. "I love your mama."

Dean slid her SUV into one of the spots on the street outside Ricky Rocket's Pizzas. "She loves you."

He climbed out and freed Blakely from her car seat, then met Nicole on the sidewalk and passed the baby her way.

She settled her niece into the sling and followed Dean into the pizza parlor, sending up silent prayers that Mikey would be there. And willing to talk.

The warm, rich scents of rising dough, stringy cheese and zesty sauce enveloped her as she crossed the threshold onto black-and-white-checkered flooring. Her stomach gurgled in response. A counter stretched across half of the back wall, leaving room for a small hallway on one side. Sets of round tables with chairs were scattered across the space, each with a metal napkin dispenser and shakers for Parmesan and pepper flakes.

A young woman in a Ricky Rocket's T-shirt and ball cap

waited at the register. Her curly brown hair was thick and partially covered one eye. "Can I get something started for you?"

Dean made his way to her, full swagger activated.

Nicole followed, heart pounding.

"Hi," Dean said, resting a hip against the counter between them. "I'm Dean."

"Laney."

"Hi, Laney. I'm looking for Mikey. Any chance he's working today?"

Laney's gaze flickered to Nicole and Blakely.

Nicole tried to appear casual. "Mikey's a friend of my little sister."

The young woman's smile faltered, setting off alarm bells in Nicole's head. A quick look at Dean suggested he'd picked up on it as well.

"We were in the area and thought we'd stop by and see if we could catch him," Dean said, drawing her attention back to him.

"He's out right now. He's our only driver this shift, so he's just stopping in between deliveries to get the next bunch of orders."

Dean unleashed his full smile, and the girl's cheeks turned pink. "We'll wait," he said. "Can we get a couple of pepperoni strombolis in the meantime?"

"Sure."

Dean paid by credit card, then passed her some folded bills when he took his receipt. "Let me know when he gets back."

The young woman darted into the kitchen.

Nicole chose a table with full view of the front door and small hallway marked with signs for an office, restroom and exit. "I almost feel bad for her," she said, stroking Blakely's downy hair and clucking her tongue at Dean.

"Who?" He looked at the empty counter where the young woman had been. "Laney? Why?"

"You know why. You pull out that charming smile and lay on that sexy drawl and it confuses people. They probably never even know what's hit them."

"I was being polite, like my mama taught me," he countered. "I couldn't exactly come in here demanding to speak to Mikey. She wouldn't have wanted to help me."

"Oh." Nicole chuckled. "She definitely wants to help you."

Dean grinned and leaned his elbows on the table, crossing his arms before him. "Any chance you're speaking from experience?"

Nicole pursed her lips, fighting a silly smile. Her body and soul reacted to him the same way now as they had when they'd been together, even in the midst of a crisis. But she would never tell. "You drew me in with your quiet confidence at the ranch. My life and family were in chaos, and you had a profoundly peaceful vibe that I craved. The smile. The voice." The face and body… "The rest was just icing."

"And you think Laney liked the icing?" he asked, tipping his head to the register without breaking eye contact.

"Most folks do."

"What about you?" he asked.

"I've always been partial to the cake."

Dean barked a laugh, and Blakely jumped.

Nicole held her niece close, giggling softly into her curls.

It was just so easy to be comfortable with Dean. *Too easy*, she thought. And there was too much at stake for her to lose focus right now. She opened her mouth to change the subject, and the back door swung open.

A narrow figure strode inside and made an immediate turn away from view.

"Hey, Mikey," a deep male voice called in back. "Where ya been? You gotta move. We're backed up to Tuesday."

Dean was on his feet in a heartbeat, moving toward the counter.

Nicole stayed on his heels.

Workers were visible in the kitchen, preparing foods and hustling around the space.

Laney spoke to a guy with shaggy black hair, ripped jeans and a matching Ricky Rocket's T-shirt and hat. His Converse were tattered, and he had piercings in one eyebrow.

His face jerked in Nicole and Dean's direction, brow furrowing for one long beat before he broke into a run, scattering pizza boxes off the metal workstations in his wake.

"Hey!" the kitchen staff protested.

Mikey's shoes squeaked and slapped against the tiled floor a moment before the back door banged open, then shut.

Dean cussed under his breath, then looked at Nicole.

"Go!"

He bolted down the hallway and through the back door, seconds behind Mikey.

Nicole pulled her phone from her pocket and hurried outside, eager to see the apprehension and notify Finn of the situation.

By the time she reached the rear lot, both men were gone.

Chapter Six

Nicole scanned the crumbling asphalt parking lot, the over-flowing dumpster and handful of employee cars. The sedan with the delivery light on top was likely Mikey's, given that Laney said he was the only driver this shift. But if the car was still there, the two were clearly involved in a foot chase.

She stroked Blakely's hair and rocked gently back and forth, soothing her niece before she decided to fuss. It was nearing her next meal time, and Nicole had left her bag in the SUV, not expecting to be inside the pizzeria for more than a minute or two.

"Where did Uncle Dean go?" she whispered, straining her senses into the bright, sunny world.

Sounds of bleating tugboats and the rumbling of a distant train were all that could be heard, aside from the smooth crawl of tires over the street out front.

"I guess we'll wait inside," she told Blakely, tucking the cell phone away and turning back for the door. Dean would be back when he finished talking to Mikey, and if they were still running, she didn't want to interrupt. Mikey likely had the answers she needed. "First, we'll grab your bag and get your bottle ready. How does that sound?"

The strombolis Dean had ordered suddenly sounded like heaven. The toast and coffee she'd had at breakfast weren't nearly enough to get her through her day. And suddenly, she was famished.

She turned to tug the handle on the metal door behind them, but the door didn't budge. She braced her opposite arm around Blakely, careful not to jostle her, then tried again, harder this time. "Shoot."

Locked.

She blinked at a keypad above the knob. Employees probably had a code.

The sounds of footfalls turned her around once more. "Dean?"

The lot was empty.

Goose bumps raised the hairs along Nicole's arms and down the back of her neck. She moved to the edge of the building and wrapped her arms around Blakely on instinct, ready to make a run for the sidewalk out front.

A rough hand clamped over her mouth before she'd taken another step.

The man's large frame pressed against her back. His opposite arm curled over Blakely, crushing her against Nicole and causing her niece to scream in protest. The scent of something familiar and metallic, but unplaceable, sizzled in her rattled mind.

The sharp point of a blade pinched Nicole's side, and a whimper rattled up her windpipe. The cry was muffled against his unyielding palm. If she struggled, her attacker's weapon would win the battle. If either of them moved too much, or too suddenly, it would be Nicole who paid the price.

And if she fell, Blakely would fall with her.

A thousand horrifying thoughts raced through Nicole's mind. Was this what Cari had gone through? It couldn't be a coincidence that both sisters were in trouble only days apart.

Was she going to die without knowing her sister was okay?

The assailant's breath was hot against her cheek as he pressed his unshaven face against her temple. His mouth brushed her ear. "Stop looking for her," he whispered. His hold tightened, eliciting a primal scream from Blakely. "Understand?"

Nicole's eyes fell shut. She willed Dean to return to her. Or another employee to exit the rear door. For any kind of help at all. And above everything, someone to protect Blakely.

The knife pressed deeper, puncturing her shirt and tearing her skin.

She gasped as pain and panic flooded her system.

"Nod if you understand," he seethed.

She did as he asked, repeating the fervent, silent prayers for intervention.

"Good. Because the next time I come for you I'm taking your baby."

DEAN JOGGED BACK toward the pizzeria, eager to be with Nicole and Blakely again. A little embarrassed to say Mikey had gotten away. So much for being her superhero. Hopefully she wasn't worried when he didn't return immediately. He'd never dreamed a lanky man in worn-out Chucks could best him. Yet here he was.

He picked up his pace, surprised by the number of blocks he'd covered while lost in the chase. He could only hope, belatedly, that Nicole wouldn't see this as evidence of him choosing the job over her again.

He scrubbed a frustrated hand over his head, the hair hot from a beating sun. He hadn't caught Mikey, but the manager on duty might be willing to talk. Maybe he'd give up Mikey's contact information. Or perhaps the young woman from the register would. If not, Finn could get involved. Folks tended to comply when a badge showed up. His mind raced to piece together fresh backup plans for his backup plans so Nicole wouldn't feel more defeated than she already must.

The piercing scream of a baby broke his concentration and instinct jolted him into a run, his mind catching up a heartbeat later.

Blakely.

Sudden desperation moved him through the streets and alleys at fresh new speeds, warming his skin to combustion.

What was happening? Was it even Blakely who cried?

Every fiber of his being said yes. And he'd never heard her scream like that before.

He made the final cut through an alley and into Ricky Rocket's rear lot, then skidded to a stop.

A man had Nicole in his arms. His face pressed against her cheek from behind, dwarfing her narrow body. The assailant was at least half a foot taller than her and nearly doubly as broad. A dark hoodie pulled over his head hid his features, hair color and anything else Dean could attempt to use as identification.

Blakely's continuous screams wrenched Dean's gut.

"Freeze!" He shouted on instinct. His voice erupted in a deep, menacing growl. The words rumbled from his chest as he stalked forward, anger twisting in his veins. If this man so much as bruised either of them, Dean would make him live to regret it. "Let them go," he warned. "Now!"

Then Nicole was falling, shoved in a burst from the man's grip, and her attacker was bolting away.

Dean launched toward them, too far away to break their impact and terror-stricken by the possibility she wouldn't catch herself before hitting the ground.

"Nicole!"

Her knees collided with the pavement in a bone-jarring scrape. Her right palm slammed against the broken asphalt.

Blakely's scream was blood-chilling.

Dean slid across the ground to collect them, helping support Blakely's weight as Nicole lifted her torso, then collapsed onto her backside.

Tears streamed down her face as she stared at him and raised a palm for inspection, the skin covered in blood.

"I've got you," he cooed. "I'm right here. You're okay. It's okay. I'm so sorry I left you. I won't do that again."

Nicole raised stunned eyes to him, then collapsed.

"Nicole!" Dean pulled Blakely from the sling and cradled her to his chest, then dug the phone from his pocket. "Shh," he soothed. "Shh."

The baby arched and screeched as he held her tight, struggling to dial his phone with trembling hands. He curled her against him, hating that he hadn't been there to protect her. Hating Nicole's still frame, despite her niece's distress.

Then he saw the blood on Blakely's clothes and the sling, still hooked over Nicole's head.

TWENTY MINUTES LATER, Nicole was awake inside an ambulance, being cared for by an EMT, and Blakely had devoured a bottle before going straight to sleep in Dean's arms.

His heart rate had barely slowed at all. The man who'd threatened Nicole had cut her, leaving a gash in her side. The wound had bled tremendously, but the responding EMT claimed it wasn't deep enough to necessitate stitches. Which was doubly good news since Nicole had made it clear she wasn't going to the hospital, where sutures were administered.

Instead, the EMT had cleaned and treated the area with glue and butterfly bandages. She'd apparently collapsed from stress and exhaustion; the shock of her assailant's shove had been her body's final straw.

Seeing Blakely soaked in blood and watching Nicole pass

out was nearly Dean's unraveling. He wasn't sure he'd ever relax again.

Finn moved into view, stepping around a group of bystanders, being questioned about the man they'd witnessed running away from the scene of the attack. "How are you holding up?" he asked, stopping in front of Dean and Blakely.

Dean didn't have words for half of the things running circles in his head, so he stuck with the tried and true. "I'm okay. Did you get the jacket from the SUV?" He'd forgotten Cari's lavender jacket was in the back seat until he'd gone to retrieve Blakely's diaper bag. He should've delivered the evidence into Finn's hand the day before, but things had gotten out of control. Just as they had today.

"Already bagged and headed to forensics." Finn watched him closely, undoubtedly seeing more than Dean wanted to share. "This is a good look on you." He nodded to the sleeping baby in his brother's arms.

Dean glanced down as well. It wasn't a secret that he wanted a family of his own one day. Children he would keep and protect to his last breath. "Thanks. She's going through a lot. I can't imagine what her little mind is thinking. I hope she forgets as much of this as possible."

Finn shifted, offering a small smile. "If it helps, I don't know anyone who remembers anything from this age."

"It helps."

"How's Nicole doing?"

Dean's gaze moved to the open ambulance doors where Nicole spoke with the EMT. "He's forcing an IV of fluid on her, hopefully with something mild for pain. No stitches, as long as she takes it easy."

Finn snorted. "Good luck with that."

Dean swallowed a groan. "Yeah. Thanks."

Nicole's sister was missing, and the man who'd just knifed her admitted to knowing something about the situation.

Nicole would very likely need the stitches soon.

He ran a palm down his face, then tipped his head toward the remaining bystanders. "Were you able to get a good description?"

Finn's expression said the answer was no. "We've got a good start," he hedged. "More than a dozen people saw a man in a dark hoodie running from this direction. Only about three of them had details beyond that, but those all matched, so it's something."

"He was tall," Dean said, recalling the horrific scene with perfect detail. "At least my height. And broad. Her shoulders were completely concealed by him. I could only see her legs and hear Blakely's screams."

Finn dropped his gaze to the baby once more. "Did the EMT take a look at her?"

"Yeah. Nicole refused treatment until Blakely had been evaluated. Any new leads on Cari?"

"Aside from this guy?" Finn asked. "No. But Nicole says he didn't know Blakely was Cari's kid. He referred to her as Nicole's child. So he doesn't know Cari personally. That goes along with what we expected. Whatever she's gotten wrapped up in isn't about her. I'm not sure how much Mikey could've helped, even if you'd caught him."

Dean narrowed his eyes. "Thanks for reminding me of that."

Finn laughed. "Hey, what are little brothers for?"

"Finn?" Nicole's voice drew their attention to where she crouched at the edge of the ambulance bay, one hand pressed to her newly bandaged side. "A little help?"

Finn obliged.

Dean followed him, watching carefully as his brother helped her down.

Her body language and facial expression suggested significant pain and discomfort. Given the way things could've gone today, Dean chose to be thankful.

He also told himself she'd asked Finn, instead of him, for help because Blakely was asleep in his arms, and she didn't want to risk waking her. But he couldn't help wondering if Nicole was upset with him for leaving her unprotected.

"We can go," she said.

The EMT frowned as he peeled protective gloves from his hands. "If you don't want to go to the hospital for stitches, you're going to have to rest and be still so your body can do the work." He shot pointed looks at Dean and Finn, then fixed her with a hard stare. "I mean it. No overexertion. Change the bandage regularly and go to the ER if you have any of the symptoms we talked about."

She responded with a polite but dismissive smile. "Thank you."

She looked longingly at Blakely, but didn't ask to hold her. "All right. What did we learn?" she asked, bouncing her attention from one Beaumont to the other.

"We're working on it," Finn said. "Folks on the sidewalk reported a guy roughly our size—" he motioned from himself to Dean "—wearing a dark hoodie, sneakers and jeans. Possibly with shaggy brown hair."

Nicole visibly deflated. "After all this, we don't even have a thorough description?"

Finn looked a bit sheepish, though he'd done all he could do. "We're pulling security video from shops on the block. I'll keep you in the loop as new details come to light."

She hugged herself and nodded. "He was heavier than the two of you, less…fit. His breaths were rough instead of even, and I could feel his middle pressed against me. He was soft, not—" Her cheeks darkened.

Finn grinned. "Fit? Like me?"

Dean frowned.

"Yeah." Nicole laughed softly, then winced, presumably at a jolt of pain.

"Assailant with a dad bod," Finn said. "That helps. Anything else?"

"Maybe. He smelled like something vaguely familiar, but I haven't decided what yet. In the moment, I was too panicked. Right now, my mind feels a little warped. I'll let you know when it comes to me."

Finn nodded. "Sounds like a plan."

The pizzeria's back door opened, and a man in a white T-shirt and apron appeared with a piece of paper in hand. "Detective Beaumont?"

"Right here." Finn moved across the lot to accept the paper.

The man retreated inside.

"What's that?" Nicole asked, taking the words out of Dean's mouth.

Finn smiled. "Mike Litchfield's contact information and work schedule for the next two weeks."

Nicole's expression brightened. "That's good. Do you think he'll go home? Or hide out? Will he even come back here after Dean chased him?"

"We'll know soon enough," Finn said. "I'll get a man outside his home and the pizzeria. The manager knows to contact me if he hears from Mikey."

"Any word on the black sedan?" Dean asked.

"Not yet, but I'll be in touch if that changes." He stepped away with one hand raised in goodbye. "I've got to get back to it, but y'all take care and keep in touch. Rest, Nicole."

She sighed but didn't protest.

Instead, she slid an arm around Dean's back and let him curl her against him in a gentle embrace, while Blakely snored softly between them.

Chapter Seven

Nicole changed into yoga pants and an oversize T-shirt when they returned to her apartment. Excess adrenaline poured through her, trembling her limbs and rattling her thoughts. Was this day even real? It didn't seem possible, and yet she would surely have a scar to prove it.

She could only pray Cari wasn't faring any worse.

It only took a minute for Nicole to choose her bed over the couch for rest, even as Dean tucked Blakely into her crib, then went to make tea. She slid beneath the cool covers, then pulled the fabric up to meet her chin. She'd thought the night Cari didn't come home from work was the worst of her life. Then last night, when she still hadn't come home, and Nicole had been chased by a black sedan twice, she'd been sure that was as bad as it could get. This morning, when she'd had to face the awful reality of the industrial park and confront the internal demons from her past, she'd never guessed that would be the easiest part of her day. Never dreamed she'd be held at knifepoint. And stabbed. The idea was inconceivable. And terrifying. Blakely had been right there in her arms.

A tear slid over her cheek and onto the pillow where she'd rested her head, knees curled up to her chest. The sting in her bandaged side grew, and she longed for sleep. But guilt and worries crept in. Blakely would wake again soon, and Nicole couldn't keep asking Dean for help. It was Nicole's responsibility to care for her niece. And she was failing.

She had naively believed she could protect her sister, too.

She closed her eyes tight and willed an untapped sisterly instinct to manifest and reveal Cari's location. Instead, her attacker's unshaven face and sticky breath on her skin came back with a crash. Her eyes opened, and her gut coiled. That man knew where Cari was. He knew what was happening to her. The answers Nicole needed had been so close, and now they were gone.

A gentle rap against the doorjamb drew Nicole's attention.

Dean stood in the hallway with a tray. "Sorry. I knocked lightly to see if you were asleep."

"I'm not." She wiped her tears discreetly and scooted upward on the mattress, rearranging her pillows to support her back against the headboard. The scents of her favorite comfort foods made her stomach shout with glee. "Is that for me?"

"Chicken noodle soup and grilled cheese." He carried the tray into her room and lowered it onto the nightstand. "You only had toast at breakfast. I thought you might be hungry. I also brought water. And these." He opened his palm to reveal a pair of over-the-counter painkillers.

Nicole took the pills and opened the bottle of water. "Thank you. Are you eating?"

"I will. I wanted to check on you first. It's not exactly Ricky Rocket's stromboli, but…"

"It's better," she said, carefully moving the tray onto her lap. She swallowed the painkillers, then lifted one of the sandwich triangles in Dean's direction. "Sit. Share with me."

He accepted, reluctantly taking a seat at the edge of her bed. "When I chased Mikey, I wasn't choosing work over you and Blakely," he said, looking strangely pained.

She frowned. "I didn't think that." She reached for him on

instinct, curling her free hand over his. "Not for a second. And I don't blame you for what happened to me today, in case that's where this is going. I wanted you to chase Mikey. I think he could know something useful. I blame myself for following you outside. In my mind, I was going to find the two of you arguing in the lot. Even though we were followed twice yesterday, it never occurred to me that we might be followed again today."

"I looked for it," Dean said. "The black sedan. When we were in the SUV, I was watching. When we were talking to the folks at the underpasses, I was watching. Once we parked on Main Street, my focus changed, and I should know better. It's my job to be vigilant and cautious."

Nicole bit into her half of the sandwich, unsure anything they could've done differently would've mattered. Aside from giving up the search for Cari, and that wasn't happening. "This isn't the same as your other jobs," she said. "You usually work alone, or with your brothers who are trained to handle those situations. I'm sure they could've defended themselves."

"They all carry weapons, not babies," he said, remorse still etched across his face. "I'm not sure what anyone could've done in your shoes."

"Still," she said. The Beaumont men were tall and lean. They'd grown up working the land and helping with the ranch. She'd called them fit earlier, but that didn't begin to describe their sheer muscle and utter capability. They'd all spent time in the military, been trained to remain calm and handle any type of pressure. Not to mention their hand-to-hand combat skills were action film-worthy. Watching them spar for fun had always been Nicole's guilty pleasure when she and Dean were together. Frankly, she wouldn't say no to watching a match now, either. "I shouldn't have let myself get into that situation," she said. "It won't happen again."

Dean didn't push. He stroked his thumb along her fingers and took a bite of his sandwich.

It had always been moments like these that turned her to putty for Dean Beaumont. The cups of tea and grilled cheese sandwiches. The way he listened when she spoke and remembered the things she said. He treated everyone as if they were his top priority, and he treated her as if she mattered most in the world.

Nicole could be vulnerable with Dean. She could be anything with Dean.

He polished off his half of the sandwich and grinned. "Not bad."

She agreed. Something about the moment felt hopeful. "I wish I could tell Cari how hard we're working," she said. "If she knew we were all out here looking, that Blakely is okay, and your mama is inviting our mom to stay at the ranch until Cari's home... I think that would give her hope." Nicole pressed her lips tight. "I wish she knew we were coming."

"She knows," Dean said, his low, confident voice making it impossible not to believe.

"Yeah?"

"Nicole." His expression caught somewhere between sincerity and disbelief. "Everyone who's ever met you knows you would move mountains for your sister. She does, too. And she's going to keep fighting until you get there, because Homes women don't quit."

Nicole's throat tightened, and she wiped her face with a napkin from the tray. "Sorry. I can't seem to stick with one emotion for more than five minutes."

"Extreme exhaustion and a recent stabbing will do that," Dean deadpanned.

She laughed. "See? Ow." She pressed a palm to her burning wound. "Stop."

He raised his hand in innocence, but mischief twinkled in his eyes. "All right. I'll leave you to finish your soup. Drink the water. Later, we'll think of something we can do from the apartment to generate a new lead."

"Deal." She dipped a spoon into the soup, watching with regret as he moved back through her door. She gave silent gratitude for every bite of a meal she didn't have to make, and for each minute Blakely continued to rest.

When the bowl was empty and her half sandwich gone, she returned the tray to the nightstand and scooted under the blankets. Then she closed her eyes.

When Blakely's laughter roused her sometime later, Nicole was surprised to learn nearly two hours had passed. Her side was tender as she moved to sit up, but the pain she'd felt earlier was significantly dulled.

Dean's rumbling chuckle brought a smile to her lips, and she swung her legs over the edge of the bed.

A few moments later, her niece and her hero came into view on the living room floor. Blakely wore a black bodysuit and rainbow-colored tutu. The short hair at the top of her head was arranged into two tiny pigtails that looked a little like antennae.

Blakely erupted in giddy screeches as her pony-shaped teether galloped over her round tummy, powered by the handsome sitter at her side.

Dean made clip-clopping hoof sounds, then laughed again when Blakely couldn't seem to stop.

The scene gripped Nicole's heart. Want, regret and a whole host of other emotions she wasn't ready to unpack rose to the surface. But she pressed them all back down.

"Hey," Dean said, crunching effortlessly into a sit. "How'd you sleep? Better than last night?"

"Much." She moved in his direction, catching her niece's eye. "Thank you again."

Blakely made spit bubbles and kicked her chubby, dimpled legs, vocalizing her joy at her favorite aunt's appearance.

Dean scooped her off the floor and stood before Nicole could bend to lift her. "I've got her," he said. "No need to dead lift this chunk when I'm a perfectly good delivery option." He passed her yammering niece into her arms.

Nicole pulled her in close and nuzzled her warm soft skin. "I love you so much," she whispered, dotting Blakely's face and hair with kisses. "You have no idea."

"Maybe you should sit," Dean suggested.

"No time," Nicole said. "Right, Blakely?" She turned back toward the hallway with a fresh idea in her rested mind. "I think we should message Mikey again. This time we need to come clean. Let him know it was us at the pizzeria and why we were there. Otherwise, who knows what he thinks is happening. He might avoid his home and the pizza shop if he's in some kind of trouble and thinks you're after him."

Dean's soft footfalls moved down the hall behind her, never missing a beat. "It can't hurt. We've given him plenty of time to respond to our last message, and he hasn't."

"Exactly what I was thinking. And if he cares about Cari at all, and isn't part of the reason she's gone, he should want to help us." Nicole sat at the small computer desk in her sister's room and balanced Blakely on her legs.

She set one hand on the keys, but the words didn't come.

Dean moved to her side. He placed a palm on her shoulder, offering his silent strength.

"You're right," she said, grabbing on to the unspoken encouragement. "I just need to do it." She blew out a breath and began typing. "Hi Mikey," she spoke the words as she typed. "I'm Cari's sister, Nicole. Maybe you've heard of me."

The story unfolded as she pecked, one-handed, at the keyboard, cradling Blakely with her other arm. Within minutes, Nicole had outlined her last two days and added a plea for help. "Anything you might know about what she's been up to, or who she's been with, anything at all might make the difference between finding her in time or after it's too late. Please. Please help me."

Blakely slapped a drool-covered hand against her aunt's chest and squealed with delight.

Nicole stifled a desperate scream. How had all her hope landed in the hands of a pizza guy who ran when anyone asked for him? "I hope that enthusiasm means you think this message was perfect, Blakely."

Dean dropped into a squat beside her chair. "I think our little ninja ballerina is right."

"Is that what you've dressed her as?" Nicole asked, swinging her face toward his. She'd assumed the look was unintentional, a result of Dean pulling wardrobe pieces from Blakely's drawers at random.

He glanced her way, brow furrowed. "Well, yeah. But look."

She followed his gaze to the screen.

Three tiny dots bounced beneath her message. Mikey was typing.

Nicole reminded herself to breathe.

Then the dots stopped.

"What happened?" she asked, looking frantically from the screen to Dean and back. "Where'd the dots go? Why'd they stop?"

Before Dean could answer, Cari's laptop emitted the sudden peppy bing-bong sound announcing an incoming video call.

"He's calling," she whispered. "What do I do?"

Dean reached for the device and accepted the call.

Mikey wore a beanie over his shaggy dark hair, despite the heat. He chewed the skin along the sides of his fingernails, gaze darting as he moved along an empty sidewalk.

"Hi," Nicole said. "Thank you so much for calling. I didn't know who else to ask for help. You've known her for years, and I'm just hoping—"

"Stop," he said, eyes snapping back to the camera. "Stop. I don't know what's going on with your sister. I can't help you."

Nicole's hopeful heart crashed. "But—"

"Listen lady, I said I don't know. And I don't."

Dean turned the laptop in his direction by a half inch, bringing him into the frame. "I'm Dean Beaumont. I'm a private investigator and personal friend of Cari's and Nicole's. You should know a man held Nicole and Cari's baby at knifepoint today. He stabbed her when I got back from chasing after you, so this is serious, and you need to treat it that way."

Mikey stilled, and his gaze jumped to Nicole. "Seriously?"

She nodded, holding Blakely closer and fighting the surge of mixed emotion. "Please help us."

Mikey cursed. He rubbed his cheek, then scratched his head, fidgeting and shifting his weight as he paused outside a boarded-up garage. "I want to help, but look, I'm not the hero to your story. I'm not the hero in any story."

"Mikey," Dean cut in. "My brother is the detective assigned to Cari's disappearance," he said. "He's good at what he does, and so am I. So is my partner. Anything you can tell us has the potential to help save your friend's life."

Mikey debated a long moment, then caved. "Fine. I'm the one who helped Cari get the party gigs, but I didn't talk to her last night. And none of the servers have to do anything they don't want to do."

Nicole's gut twisted instantly, fear and nausea fought for position with her anger. "What does that mean?"

He crunched his features into a look of disbelief, as if she were the one saying ridiculous things. "It means the jobs pay well for a reason. Servers take the money and keep quiet about what they see or hear. If they ever want in on a chance to make more, those opportunities are there, too."

Nicole couldn't bring herself to ask the next, most obvious, question.

Dean's fingers curled into fists on the desktop, and he pulled them onto his lap. "Did Cari ever take on any of the extra opportunities?"

Mikey's expression turned instantly to offense. "Hell no. Man, I thought you said you knew her." He swung his attention back to Nicole, as she sank against the chair with relief. "Cari was always cautious, and she was saving money. She never said why. Baby stuff, I guess."

"She applied to colleges," Nicole said, pride thick in her voice. "She was trying to make a better life for her and Blakely."

Mikey bobbed his head. "Yeah, that sounds like her. It's why I told her about the special gigs. But I can't talk to you anymore. Either of you," he said, shooting pointed looks at Dean, then back. "So stop looking for me, and stop messaging me, because I don't have anything else to say. If something bad is going down, then you guys have already put a target on my back by coming to work and chasing me around. I've got enough problems. You know what I'm saying? Anyone who didn't know I had a connection to a missing girl, or these gigs, probably does now. And that's no good for anyone. So I'm out. Stop coming for me or I'll be next."

"Who's your contact for the parties?" Dean asked. "How can I get in touch with them?"

Mikey shook his head, flashed a peace sign and disconnected the call.

A moment later, the app showed he'd signed off.

Mikey was gone.

Chapter Eight

Dean returned to the living room, giving Nicole the space she requested after the call with Mikey. The video chat had only lasted a few minutes, but there had been plenty to process. Like the fact that Mikey was clearly scared, which didn't bode well for Cari. Mikey was mixed up in something dangerous and probably illegal. He hadn't been specific, but the implications he'd made were enough.

Dean dialed Finn to fill him in on the new information, but the call landed in voice mail. He sent a text instead of leaving a message, asking him to get in touch.

His next text went to Austin. As private investigators, Austin and Dean had a handful of informants and a whole lot of experience navigating the unsavory groups in town. If Cari's disappearance wasn't a random kidnapping or carjacking, the PIs' connections would go just as far as the long arm of the law.

The message was barely marked as delivered before Austin's response returned.

Austin: omw

On my way.
Dean blew out a breath of relief and poured a glass of

water. Sitting on the sidelines when something needed done wasn't his style, but someone had to be there for Nicole, and he couldn't think of anyone else he'd want to take his stead.

She appeared with Blakely a long while later. Her hair had been swept into a ponytail, and her smile was an obvious ruse, likely meant for her niece. The hope he'd seen in her eyes before speaking with Mikey was long gone. "My mom called."

"Yeah?" Dean asked, mildly glad to know she hadn't simply been avoiding him all this time. Still, his muscles bunched with tension. Every polite follow-up that came to mind was ridiculous. *How's she doing? How'd it go? Are you okay?* Those answers were so obvious, he couldn't bring himself to speak the words. Instead, he did his best to appear calm and casual, encouraging her to elaborate when she was ready.

"My grandpa had a medical scare yesterday. Mom spent the day at the hospital while they ran a gamut of tests and kept him for observation. She got my message, but I didn't tell her what was going on, so she waited to call until she got some sleep. Grandpa's home now, and Grandma made an appointment for him to see a specialist next week."

"He's okay?" Dean asked.

"Mom thinks so, but she'll know more after the next appointment. Meanwhile, she's on her way here. Your mama left a message for her, too. I told her to give Mrs. Beaumont a call when we hung up. She's going to take her up on the offer to stay at the ranch for a while. A neighbor is going to check in on my grandparents and make sure Grandpa gets to his next appointment if Mom's not back in time." Nicole bounced Blakely gently as she rocked foot to foot. "Mom's having a hard time."

"Being here will help," Dean said, wondering just how awful it must feel for Mrs. Homes to know her aging parents needed her, but so did her daughters, and she couldn't be in two different states at once.

He longed to reach for Nicole. He ached to comfort her. But he wasn't sure how to do that without overstepping. Caring for Blakely, making sure Nicole rested and was fed, that was easy. That didn't involve getting into her space. Suddenly, the shared history that'd made it so easy to drop everything and help her felt like an impossible divide.

They'd been in love once, and they'd hurt each other badly. He'd been a terrible boyfriend, retreated inward when he couldn't deal with the loss of Ben Smothers, the eight-year-old boy he didn't find in time to save. After seeing the way Nicole had stuck by her sister, he'd wrongly assumed she'd stay through his crisis, too. But she'd walked out on Dean at his lowest point. She'd drawn a line for him. And he hadn't fought to keep her. She'd done what she had to do to protect herself, but it'd felt like abandonment in the moment nonetheless.

He'd let her leave, but he'd never really let her go. He wanted her in his arms and in his life again, right now. Same as always. He wanted Nicole in a real and long-term way, but there was a mountain of old wounds between them. And right now, all that mattered was finding Cari.

Nicole made a bottle for Blakely, then carried both into the living room, sharp eyes fixed on him. "You okay?"

"Yeah, sorry." He forced his thoughts to the moment at hand.

Her head tilted slightly over one shoulder, and her eyes narrowed.

A knock at the door saved Dean from a conversation he wasn't ready to have.

He hurried in the direction of the sound. "That's probably

Austin," he said, pausing to check the peephole before letting his brother inside.

"Hey." Austin greeted Dean with a loose one-armed hug. "How y'all holding up?"

Dean nodded in answer to the inane question then locked the door while Austin greeted Nicole and Blakely.

"Has there been any news?" Nicole asked, a cautious thread of hope in her tone.

Austin's polite expression faltered. "I'm just here touching base."

"I thought we should fill one another in on what we know," Dean said.

Austin slowly extricated the baby from Nicole's arms. "Your auntie isn't supposed to exert herself, so I'm going to sneak in here and make you love me best."

He turned to Dean with a wink.

Nicole rolled her eyes but didn't argue. "I'll put on the coffee."

Within minutes, they'd settled around the small kitchen table, floral-patterned mugs in hand. Nicole reported on the details of her attack and the conversation with Mikey, answering Austin's questions as they came. Dean did his best to maintain his cool facade, though both stories made him want to run his fist through a virtual stranger.

"How about you?" he asked his brother, when the volleys between Austin and Nicole had gone silent.

Austin cleared his throat, the only sign so far that Nicole's awful day had affected him, too. "I spent a little time with Finn at the station," he said. "He's got a plan in motion, but he's shorthanded, so I'm helping with legwork. Small towns, small police departments," he explained to Nicole, though she'd spent enough time with his family to fully understand.

"Tell me more about the plan," she prompted.

Austin shifted, shaking a rattle at Blakely, safely strapped into the high chair at his side. "Tech support is pinging Cari's phone. It hasn't been on, so there's no signal, but they're looking. The next time it's powered up, they'll be able to track it."

Dean turned his mug between his palms, fighting the creeping feeling of failure. "I think we need to track down Mikey. He was scared, and I think he's in trouble. He was convinced Nicole and I had caused him real problems by showing up at the pizzeria. I don't want that to be true. I'm hoping our folks will intervene, give him refuge and a chance to change his trajectory in life, if you can find him."

"I'll see what I can do," Austin said. "Finn's got a cruiser watching the guy's house and Ricky Rocket's. I'll ask around downtown, see if anyone knows him. Maybe talk to the staff in some local shops, the record store, bookstore, skate shop. Someone's seen him, or seen him with someone they know. I'll follow the bread crumbs until I've got him."

"Let's hope you're faster than whoever he thinks is after him."

Nicole pulled her hair from its tie, finger-combing it as she listened, then put it up again. She dragged her gaze from one brother to the other. "What do you think Mikey meant when he said the waitstaff had opportunities to make more money if they wanted? Was he talking about…" She tensed, expression flat. "Prostitution? Drugs? Something else? Something worse?"

Dean's hand drifted in her direction, intending to cover and squeeze her trembling fingers, but their eyes met and he withdrew.

Austin's eyebrow ticked. Of course his brother had noticed.

That was the problem with belonging to a family of investigators. They saw everything. And if what they saw was even remotely related to romance, their mama would know inside the hour. Sometimes they didn't even have to report it to her. She just knew.

"We'll have answers when we catch up to Mikey," Austin said. "Speculation will only distract us and waste time. Better to get the facts from the source. What did you notice in the background during the call? Any idea where he was?"

"He kept the camera close, but he seemed to be on an empty sidewalk somewhere," Dean said. "No passing cars. No shoppers. Not downtown. I didn't hear the tugboats or see water either, so probably not near the docks."

"What about traffic sounds? Could he have been near the overpasses?"

"No." Dean imagined the area his brother mentioned, and another thought came to mind. "I asked Mama to get some food out that way tonight. Any chance you've talked to her? There were quite a few folks down there who looked like they could use a meal. She mentioned sending Dad and Lincoln."

Austin's lips twisted into a wry smile. "Lincoln told me all about it."

Nicole tensed. "Is everything okay?"

"Dad stood him up," Austin said. "Then the next thing Lincoln knew, Josie's on her way to the truck with Mama's sandwiches."

"No," Nicole whispered, delight lifting her features. She leaned over her mug, awaiting details.

Dean snorted. He'd forgotten how invested she'd always been in the unlikely pairing. It was no wonder Nicole and his mother got along so well.

Lincoln and Josie had some sort of connection that neither of them talked about and both refused to act on, as far as anyone knew. Dean suspected a big part of the reason was his brother. It'd taken three years for Lincoln to come back to himself after the things he'd endured as a soldier. He was darker now, more withdrawn and cautious. Except when it came to Josie.

Josie was several years younger than Lincoln. Their folks had taken her in when she was a teen struggling with a series of bad choices and no support system. Lincoln had been in the military at the time and only met Josie when he was home on leave, but the Beaumonts suspected part of Lincoln still thought of Josie as a kid, or worse, as kin. If they were right, it was easy to see why he'd struggle with the obvious attraction. Mama assumed Lincoln was letting Josie set the pace, and their dad said Lincoln was taming his own demons before letting anyone else get close enough to be hurt by them.

Whatever the reason, the slow burn had been killing the lot of them for years.

"Cops are still pulling security footage from shops near Ricky Rocket's," Austin said. "So far the images of the assailant are too distant and pixelated to make a solid identification. Finn's asked the tech lab to look for signs of the black sedan that followed you as well. If we can't get an ID on the man, maybe we can get a plate on the car he's driving."

"Assuming it's his car," Dean said.

Austin clasped his hands on the table, shooting Dean a bland expression. "No matter whose it is, the car's a lead." He turned back to Nicole. "Even if the car was stolen, it's a lead. We can look at who it was taken from and where, then scope out that person and their location. Things don't happen in a vacuum. There's always a witness or loose end. We just have to find it and pull. Any chance you got a screenshot of Mikey's face?"

"No," Nicole answered. "But I saw photos of him on Cari's computer. I can get those for you if you want."

"I'd appreciate it," he said. "Text them to me and Finn when you get time. Also, send any social media handles you have for him. Dean told me about the Mikey Likey account, so I'll do a deep dive on that later, see who his contacts are, where he frequents and who he's in photos with. I'll look into the friends' accounts, too. See if I can find any connection to a catering service or restaurant, other than Ricky Rocket's. Finn's already interviewed everyone there. I'll also look for a connection between Mikey's online acquaintances and the homeowners at the address where Cari last worked."

Dean rubbed the backs of his fingers along his unshaven cheeks. "Sounds like a plan."

Austin fought a smile, eyeballing Dean's unusually scruffy face. "It's something. You growing a beard or what?"

"I need to get home and pick up some things. My truck, too. I didn't expect to be gone for the night when I left yesterday."

"I've got a go bag in the truck, if you want it." His gaze flickered to Nicole, then Blakely. "It'll set you up for two or three days if you're not ready to make the run home."

Dean sighed in relief. He hadn't wanted to go back out today, but he was in need of a shower and fresh clothes. "Thanks. I'll take it."

Austin rose and carried his mug to the sink. "Thank you for the coffee and company, Nicole." He patted her shoulder playfully on his way to the high chair, where he blew raspberries against Blakely's neck.

She erupted into laughter that spread through the adults in the room.

"Hold on." Nicole rose and wrapped her arms around Austin's middle, flinching slightly with the movement. "I've missed you. And I really appreciate all you're doing for my family."

"Anything. Anytime." Austin pulled back and looked into her eyes. "We're going to find Cari and bring her home.

Now go sit yourself down and get your feet up. You were stabbed today."

Dean's gut twisted at the scene, the sweet familiarity between them, and longing for what might've been.

Nicole went to the couch and made a show of putting both feet up.

Austin grinned. "I'll be right back."

Dean lifted Blakely from her high chair and waited for his brother to return with the bag.

He reappeared a moment later. "Keep me posted if you hear anything new or have something else I can grab on to."

"Count on it."

Chapter Nine

Dean woke with the sun and an aching back the next morning. Nicole's living room was not suited for sleep. No wonder she hadn't felt rested the night before, stress and anxiety aside. He'd felt better after three hours on her recliner than following an entire night on the sofa.

He arched his back and rolled his shoulders, working out the knotted muscles as he paced her living room.

Nicole had fallen asleep shortly after Blakely, a testament to her pain and fatigue. She'd surprised him with her willingness to take more over-the-counter medication after changing her bandage and calling it a night.

If he had to hazard a guess, he'd say her reasons for taking such good care of herself had more to do with healing quickly for Blakely's sake than her own. But the reason didn't matter. He was just glad not to have to fight her on the pills and rest.

Dean toted Austin's blessed go bag to the bathroom and rushed through his usual morning routine. Showered, shaved and dressed in a navy blue T-shirt and jeans, he was ready for a whole lot of black coffee.

Blakely rose before he'd poured his second mug, and he nabbed her from her crib before she got too wound up.

He'd wisely moved the baby monitor's speaker from Nicole's room the night before so she wouldn't be disturbed this morning. He'd left the device in the kitchen while he brewed coffee.

He made a mental note to thank his mama for letting him and his brothers help out with babies and toddlers over the years. He'd been calling on that experience and training more every day since Nicole and her niece had arrived at his place. *Keep 'em fed, clean and dry* were his mama's words of wisdom when he'd struggled to make his foster brothers and sisters happy. Her follow-up advice had always been, *hold 'em and entertain them. If none of that works, call Mama.*

Thankfully a dry diaper and full bottle had pleased Blakely. From there, he'd taken her to the room she shared with Cari. "Time to get you out of these goofy pajamas," he suggested, peering into the closet of pint-sized clothes. Her black-and-white ensemble was hilarious but unfortunate. "You look like you just busted out of an old-timey jail," he said. "What is your auntie doing to you?"

Dean selected a red plaid sundress and socks that looked like cowgirl boots, then rested her on the changing table. "Did you know everyone I love is out there looking for your mama right now? No one's going to give up until she's back here with you. They're all very good at their jobs, even if one or two of them look too young or as if they aren't paying attention. Then again, there probably aren't a lot of people who look young to you."

He tugged the dress over her head and the socks onto her feet. "I'm hoping to stay here and help your auntie while she heals. She loves you and your mama very much, and this is a tough time for her. Don't tell her I told you this," he said, stretching a springy headband with a big fake flower over her wispy brown curls and arranging the flower near one ear. "But she's very important to me. Has been for a long while, and I can't imagine that ever changing. I can promise you I won't let anything bad happen to her again. She's stubborn, so she won't like knowing I'm looking out for her too closely. Which means I'm trusting you to keep this intel on the DL. That's the down-low. We'll learn more PI terms after breakfast."

Blakely cooed and babbled as he curled her against his chest and headed back down the hallway, past a closed bedroom door.

His footfalls slowed when Nicole came into view at the kitchen table, a mug of coffee poised at her lips. The baby monitor glowing merrily on the counter at her side.

He willed his expression to remain unmoved, told himself she somehow hadn't overheard his conversation through the speaker sitting three feet away and hoped he hadn't just added more stress to her life. "Morning."

"Morning," she said. The slight curve at the corner of her mouth suggested she'd heard every word and maybe wasn't mad about it. "Were you able to sleep?"

"A little. You?"

"Mmm-hmm. I just took a couple more pain pills with water and helped myself to coffee. Feel like joining me for a bagel?"

"Sure." He put Blakely into her playpen and started the mobile of tiny hedgehogs for her entertainment.

Nicole pushed two bagels into the toaster. "Great. After this, I thought we could go for a drive."

NICOLE STRETCHED HER arm through the open window on the passenger side of her SUV. Dean had graciously agreed to drive her and Blakely around again, which was good, because Nicole had never been good at staying inside for long periods of time. Walking or jogging in the fresh air was her go-to method for processing emotions. She'd experienced more turmoil in the last few days than in the past year, and she wasn't in any condition or position to go out alone.

The wound on her side was trying to heal, and the area was tender, sensitive to movement. Changing the bandage had revealed the glue and tape were working their magic. Still, going anywhere alone seemed unwise. And she'd likely feel the larger effects of her attack long after a permanent scar had formed. The follow-up appointment she truly needed was with a licensed trauma counselor, not an MD.

Nicole opened and closed her hand against the beating wind as Dean drove along the coast. Her favorite summertime playlist rose from the speakers on shuffle. She did her best to soak up the sun and find peace in the moment, but it proved an impossible task.

She was outside, but she wasn't walking or running or pushing away her cares. She was in a car with a man whose entire family was helping her find her missing sister. And no part of her could forget that for a millisecond.

"Maybe we should visit the people who helped us find Mikey before," she said. "They might know more now, or there could be someone new." She stared at Dean's freshly shaven cheek, aching to stroke it with her fingertips and turn him to face her. "Please?"

Dean cast a wary glance in her direction, then made the next available turn.

She smiled, and her shoulders sagged with relief. "Thank you."

"I thought about that group all night, wondering what kind of impression Lincoln made. I'm hoping the food and added interaction built some more trust. I know it's not too late for any of them to turn things around, and I know my folks can help."

Nicole watched intently as the scenery changed, anxiety

rapidly climbing over her. Just as it had the day before, and as it always would when visiting this particular part of town.

She straightened when the overpasses came into view, the space unchanged, the view drastically different. "What's going on?" she asked, pulling her sunglasses from her eyes. "Where'd they all go?"

Dean stopped in the middle of the desolate street, in the shadow of an overarching highway system. Twenty-four hours prior, there had been a dozen people lingering there, along with makeshift tents and other evidence at least a few had called this place their home. Now there was only scattered debris and silence.

"I don't know." He eased the SUV forward, eyes clinging to the emptiness.

"Were they here when Lincoln and Josie brought sandwiches?"

"I think Lincoln would've called if they weren't," Dean said, returning his eyes to the road. His tone and expression were the perfect picture of calm, but there was tension in his jaw and grip on her steering wheel.

Dean was clearly as startled as she was. He was just better at hiding it.

She'd always envied that. Her emotions were written in neon across her face and heart, hanging perpetually from her sleeve.

"Do you think something bad happened to them?" she asked.

Mikey had been afraid when they chatted last night. He thought she and Dean had put him in danger by looking for him. What did that mean for a group of people they'd actually had the chance to speak with?

"I don't know."

Nicole's mind raced with awful possibilities. "Can we drive by the house where Cari worked?"

He cast another cautious glance in her direction. "Why?"

"I don't know. I guess because it's the last place she was supposed to be. What if I missed something before?"

Dean nodded, apparently lost in thought.

Behind them, in her rear-facing car seat, Blakely made enthusiastic baby sounds, kicking her dimpled baby feet into view.

"She's happy," Dean noted, catching Nicole's eyes as she turned back to face the windshield. "I guess she likes the car?"

"I'm not sure what's going on with her. She doesn't mind the car, but she's usually asleep by now," Nicole said. It was nice that her niece wasn't upset about being stuck in her car seat for another extended ride, but she suspected the contentment wouldn't last long. "I can't tell if she's getting older and doesn't need the after-breakfast nap she's always relied on, or if she's internalizing what's going on around her and it's messing up her schedule."

"At this age, I'm leaning toward the first suggestion," Dean said. "Mostly because she sounds sincerely happy, and also because she still thinks people disappear when playing peek-aboo."

Nicole hoped he was right. The idea her precious niece was upset without the words to express it, and therefore actively forming deep emotional scars from this experience, was too much to handle.

Outside her window, the sea dropped away as they climbed the sun-drenched hill toward the neighborhood where Cari last worked. The spectacular, unhindered view of the water was breathtaking. Deep blue ripples and white-crested waves stretched to the distant horizon, flickering and twinkling with sunlight.

She checked her side-view mirror on repeat and examined every passing car for signs of the black sedan, praying it wouldn't make another appearance. Surely the driver had somewhere else to be once in a while. He couldn't spend all his time patrolling the wealthiest area of town. Could he?

The street soon leveled out, and ancient trees swallowed her ocean view. A curvy, shaded stretch of road took its place. She blinked to adjust her eyes. Pretty beams of golden light dappled the darkened asphalt before her, filtered between the leaves and branches of reaching oaks.

Houses rose from extensively landscaped lots. Sprinklers nurturing the emerald lawns.

And all around them silence reigned.

Dean slowed as their destination came into view.

The woman who'd answered the door for Nicole stood in her driveway, unloading shopping bags from the trunk of a small blue convertible coupe.

Dean pulled into the space behind her and parked. "She doesn't know me," he said softly. "Give me a minute?"

Nicole nodded, hoping the woman wouldn't recognize her in the passenger seat. She lowered the visor and adjusted her oversize sunglasses. The blonde hadn't wanted to talk to Nicole. Maybe Dean could sway her. According to Finn, the police had already been to the house, and Nicole suspected this woman knew more than she was saying. If Dean was right about unseasoned criminals being likely to crack, this could be the conversation that changed everything.

The blonde watched Dean approach with obvious appreciation, a friendly smile on her pretty face.

Dean shook her hand.

Nicole leaned closer to the open window, straining to hear their voices over the wind and subtle sounds of her SUV's engine.

"Of course," the woman said, answering something Nicole had missed.

Dean removed his phone from his pocket and tapped the screen before turning the device to face her. He studied her as she turned her eyes to the offering, presumably a photo of Cari.

"Anything you can recall would be a big help," he said. "It's been a few days, and as you might know, these things tend to become dire as time passes. You can make a difference, maybe save a life."

Nicole's throat tightened.

"You could change the future for her family and her baby daughter."

The woman looked away, attention back on her packages, avoiding eye contact with Dean.

His clenching jaw suggested he'd noticed the change, too.

"I'm sorry," the woman said, closing the trunk and moving along her sidewalk to the home's front door. "I'm afraid I don't interact with party staff. I don't have the first clue what any of them look like, and I'm only dropping these things off. I have another appointment to get to. So if you'll excuse me."

Dean returned to the driver's seat and watched silently with Nicole as the woman struggled to unlock her door, dropping the keys twice before hurrying inside.

Nicole's thundering heart beat a rhythm she felt in her temples and beneath a palm pressed to her chest. "She knows something," she whispered.

"I'm inclined to agree," he said. "She definitely didn't want to talk about Cari or that party." He shifted into Reverse and stretched an arm across the back of her seat. "You okay?"

Nicole batted tear-blurred eyes, fighting the urge to jump

out and pound on the woman's big fancy door. "When I talked to her, she said they didn't have a party."

The woman was lying.

Chapter Ten

Blakely gave a deep, groaning complaint, as Dean retreated from the driveway, still processing Nicole's words.

The homeowner told Nicole they hadn't had a party on the morning after Cari's disappearance. Two days later, she told Dean she didn't pay any attention to the staff, not that there wasn't a party.

What had she told Finn and his team?

Dean turned at the end of the block, driving deeper into the neighborhood, not ready to head home. "I'm going to pull over and shoot Finn a text. I'd like to hear how it went when he spoke with the homeowners. He should know she gave us two different stories. Everything about her body language indicated she was nervous. He'll say being approached by a stranger at home will do that, but I don't think her behavior should be written off. She didn't get twitchy until I mentioned the party."

Blakely screamed, and Nicole flinched.

"She's got to be tired, possibly hungry," Nicole said. "Maybe too warm and tired of being strapped into the car seat." She cranked the air-conditioning and rolled up the passenger window.

Dean followed her example, powering up his window as well, but Blakely's screaming continued.

The screen on Blakely's window stopped direct sunlight from getting to her, but it was still North Carolina in July.

He pulled into a small parking lot along the back side of the park where Nicole found Cari's jacket. "Do you want to get her out for a few minutes?"

"If you aren't in a hurry."

"None." In fact, everything inside him wanted to go back up the hill to the house he'd just left and demand answers until the woman caved. She had the feel of a weak link, and he knew how and where to apply pressure.

But that wasn't something he could do with Nicole and Blakely in tow.

"I'll feed and change her while you talk to Finn," Nicole said, already climbing out of the SUV.

Dean swiped his phone screen to life and dialed his brother. No reason to rush the chat with texts.

Finn answered quickly and confirmed he'd gotten the run-around from the homeowners as well. Their official statement being that they didn't have a party on the night of Cari's disappearance, but on the occasions when they had hosted events, they didn't interact with the staff. A tidy way to cover their change of story. Finn was chasing a lead to clarify, however, and that was good enough for Dean.

He disconnected the call feeling slightly better and immediately noticed the silence.

Nicole was visible in the SUV's side-view mirror, the baby no longer crying.

"It's quiet back there," he said, climbing out to join her. "How's it going?"

Nicole rocked from foot to foot, her niece sound asleep in the creamy cotton fabric of her sling. "She was dry and refused a bottle, but about two seconds in the sling and voilà.

Now I can't get back into the car. She'll definitely wake up if I try to transfer her to the car seat too soon."

Dean smiled. "How about a walk in the park?"

NICOLE LOOKED AT the expanse of lush, shaded grass. "Definitely."

He set his hand against the small of her back as they moved onto the cobblestoned path. The gentle pressure warmed her. A silly, nostalgic voice inside her wondered if this is what it would've been like for her and Dean if they'd stayed together. Would the baby in the sling be theirs? Would she have liked that? Would he?

Had he meant what he'd said to Blakely this morning? Words she hadn't been supposed to overhear. A confession of her continued importance to Dean, despite the time they'd spent apart.

She shook away the what-ifs that never led her anywhere good. "What did Finn say?" she asked instead, thankful for a reasonable distraction to her feelings.

Dean's small grin told her there was good news on the way, and her heart skipped.

"Finn says the couple denied having a party that night, and that they don't interact with the caterers when they do have a party. However, an officer working the desk recalls receiving a noise complaint from someone in the area around eleven thirty. The caller was a babysitter claiming there was a disturbance that woke the baby. She didn't have any specifics, possibly raised voices. Whatever it was ended before the call, and the kid's family returned before the neighborhood patrol car made it back around. The officer didn't see anything unusual. Finn's reaching out to the family who hired the sitter and to the patrolman on duty that night to see if one of them can shed more light. He's hoping the family will put him in touch with the babysitter as well."

Nicole smiled back. "He found a thread to pull."

Dean lifted a brow and a one hand, pointing a finger up the nearby hill. "I believe that's the back side of the home we just visited."

She followed his gaze to a distant two-story with a wrought iron fence and multilevel deck. "Yeah."

"And you found Cari's coat under a bench here."

She had. "You think Cari might've been part of the disturbance, running away from the party?"

"Maybe." Dean paused his strides and looked her over, gaze catching on her softly snoring niece. "How are you doing with her?" he asked. "I can carry her if she gets heavy. You're supposed to be taking it easy."

"I'm good. I'll let you know if I'm not."

They moved slowly through the shade, toward the home in question, each silently surveying the landscape.

Nicole tried to imagine her sister fleeing the party at night, running down the hill toward the trees, shucking her jacket to blend with the shadows.

Soon the oaks and pines formed an intentional row, and a small wooden sign in the shape of an arrow came into view. The words *Botanical Garden* were carved at its center.

Dean snapped a photo of the sign.

Nicole stared into the deepening shadows. "I didn't know the park included more than the trees, grass and benches."

"Let's see if Finn did." Dean tapped his screen, presumably sending a message with the photo before tucking the phone into his pocket. He set his hand against her back once more, and they followed the arrow onto a narrow brick-lined path.

Stone figures and bursts of greenery rose from the ground in neat patches. The trees grew sparse, and flowers bloomed in rows and planters. The babbling sound of water seemed to pull them in its direction.

A woman pushed an empty stroller at a snail's pace ten yards ahead of them. A toddler in a fairy costume trailed behind, waving a wand in one hand and carrying a juice box in the other.

If Cari were there, she would've speculated that they were looking into her future. Blakely would be that big before she was ready, and Cari would say she wished time would slow down.

Nicole's gaze fell to her niece once more.

Cari had to come home and see her baby grow up. No other future made any sense.

The fairy girl tugged the woman's shirt. "I want to see the bridge again."

The woman swept her onto her hip for a kiss. "Our picnic is over, and now it's time to go home."

Nicole's feet grew heavy, and something akin to hope twisted in her chest. She reached for Dean's hand, and he slowed. "The bridge."

"You want to see it, too?" he asked, a warm, if somewhat confused, expression on his face.

Nicole dropped his hand and dug her phone from her pocket. "Cari sent a photo of a bridge that night. I didn't think anything of it. I assumed it was part of the landscaping wherever she was, but if she ran here from the house—"

His eyes widened slightly, and he stepped closer, watching as she scrolled to the picture, then passed him the phone.

The bridge appeared only long enough for a few adults to stand shoulder to shoulder, and it stretched over a tiny stream filled with stones. Exactly the kind of thing Nicole could imagine finding in the Botanical Garden.

Dean turned in a small circle, scanning the area. His gaze

lifted to the woman and child, now significantly farther away. "Come on." He clutched Nicole's hand and headed for the pair on long quick legs.

Nicole cradled Blakely's sleeping body to her torso, struggling to ease the impact of her steps.

Dean released her hand when the woman and child took notice of their rushed approach. "Excuse me."

The woman set the child down and smiled. "Hello."

"Can you tell me if this bridge is somewhere around here?" he asked, extending the phone in her direction and cutting straight to the point. "If not here, maybe somewhere in the neighborhood?"

She frowned at his urgency, but gave the phone a look. "Oh, sure. That's the fairy bridge." Her gaze swept cautiously to Nicole, and she lifted a finger in the direction of another path. "It's at the end of the brook."

"Thank you," Nicole said, reaching for Dean once more. "Take Blakely?"

Her side burned and ached after their short speed walk. She couldn't keep up the pace with her niece in tow. Maybe not even without her.

Dean obliged without question, intervening immediately when the act of raising her arms caused Nicole to wince. She needed water and another round of painkillers, but that would have to wait until they'd visited the fairy bridge.

They excused themselves with small waves and quickly changed directions, following the sounds of water to a small pool. A narrow trickling stream spilled into a circular goldfish pond at one end. The water traveled around moss-covered rocks and over a sandy floor that began a short distance away.

"I can't believe all this is back here," Dean said, heading for the other end of the stream.

Nicole pressed a palm to her aching side. "I know. I thought the park ended at the tree line. I assumed everything beyond that belonged to nearby homes."

He adjusted Blakely in his arms when she fussed softly, then sent a hopeful look in Nicole's direction. "If I left the house on the hill and needed somewhere to hide, I'd have come here."

Her heart rate sped. She'd thought something similar on their way into the Botanical Garden, but if Cari had come here, where was she now? Nicole couldn't let herself think about what it would mean if her sister was still nearby but hadn't come home.

"Hey," Dean said, drawing her eyes to meet his. "She's not here. The lady and the kid would've seen her. This is another clue, and that's a good thing. It could bring us one step closer to finding her."

The dim glow of twinkle lights wrapped around the wooden handrail was suddenly a beacon.

"This is it," she said. "It's the same as in the photo."

Dean raised his phone and snapped a pic. "I'm sending this to Finn, along with the coordinates. He should probably get down here and poke around."

Dean held Blakely protectively in one arm as he slipped into PI mode and explored the space around the wooden structure. He photographed the collection of footprints fanning out in every direction, crisscrossing over one another on the soft ground.

His phone rang as he crouched at the water's edge, peering into the stream.

Nicole's head grew light as she scanned the larger picture, noticing the strings of unlit twinkle lights wrapped around tree trunks and limbs for the first time. It was probably beautiful here at night, when all the lights were on.

Her sister had been right here, on this spot, before she'd vanished.

Nicole's breaths grew shallow, and she bumbled to the bridge and sat. The planks were solid and sturdy beneath her, unlike her trembling body and legs.

Dean rose. "What's wrong? Are you hurting?"

Nicole concentrated on pulling oxygen into her lungs. "I needed to rest," she muttered. "That's all."

Dean snapped out of work mode, worried eyes back on her. "I can take you home. Unless you need a doctor. Are you hurting?" His attention fell to her hand, pressed against her side.

"I just need a minute. I'm okay."

"Finn's on the way," Dean said, outstretching a hand to help her back up. "He can do this. I'll take you home."

"No." The word flew from her lips like a slap.

Dean's head reared back, and Blakely's limbs flailed. He lowered his hand. "Okay," he said softly. "We'll wait."

Nicole scooted across the boards, pulling her knees closer to her chest and resting her back against a beam that supported the handrail. Something dark caught her eye between the slats at her feet. She rocked forward, then onto her hands and knees, lowering her face to the wood for a better look. Beneath her, a mound of smooth gray rocks ran along the water's edge.

Something dark and familiar rested atop the stones.

"Nicole?" Dean's voice was high and urgent. "Are you okay?"

"There's a cell phone."

Dean followed her gaze, brows lifting when he saw it, too. "Can you hold Blakely?"

She nodded, rearranging herself to cuddle her niece.

He passed the baby into her arms, then moved onto the

rocks beside the bridge. Water lapped at the soles of his shoes as he squatted and stretched an arm beneath her.

She watched between the slats as his fingers closed around the device.

A moment later he returned to her with Cari's phone in hand.

Chapter Eleven

Thirty minutes later, Dean rocked Blakely in his arms outside the SUV, mind spinning with possible scenarios to explain how Cari's phone had landed beneath the bridge. Had she dropped it while on the run?

Nicole reclined in the passenger seat, sipping from a bottle of water Finn had provided and waiting for Cari's phone to charge.

Finn leaned against the vehicle's hood, arms crossed, scrutinizing the scene at large. "No signs of the black sedan or Mikey."

Neighbors and lookie-loos had gathered in clusters on the grass, taking videos and chattering about what the police were doing in their neighborhood and at the Botanical Center.

Dean had listened for a while. The speculation ran from a murder suspect hiding among the oaks to a hunt for stolen property.

Nicole pressed the water bottle to her temple. "Is that a good thing or a bad thing?"

"Bad," Finn said. "If one of them showed up, at least I'd have the chance to question him. Or maybe the fact they aren't here means they haven't heard about this yet, which is good."

Dean agreed. He crouched slightly, peering at Nicole through the open window. "How's the phone doing?"

She pressed the button to illuminate the lock screen. "Almost five percent."

"That's enough," he said. "Let's try it."

It'd taken forever for someone to show up with a charger that worked with Cari's phone. Waiting for it to gain enough strength to turn on seemed to take even longer.

Nicole tapped the screen with shaky fingers. "It doesn't think I'm her," she said, moving the device in front of her face. They'd hoped facial recognition would assume the sisters were one and the same. Their physical similarities were remarkable to the human eye, but apparently not close enough to fool the phone. "And it doesn't know my fingerprint."

They'd expected that but agreed in advance it was worth a try.

"I have no idea what her password could be." Nicole sighed.

Finn grinned. "It's okay. Leave it to charge. Take the time to think a little longer. If you can't unlock it before you head home, the tech lab will give it a try. They're pretty good over there."

Dean felt the weight of disappointment on his shoulders. He'd hoped the facial recognition would work. He'd seen his brothers unlock one another's devices that way in the past.

"Why don't y'all head home?" Finn suggested. "I'm sure Blakely would like that. It's hot as Hades out here, and you're probably all hungry by now. It's been a day."

Nicole turned wary eyes on Dean, as if asking him to decide.

"Whatever you want to do," he said.

If she wasn't ready to leave the scene, he could probably find someone to make a trip to the nearest store for more water, food and pain pills. He could run the air conditioner in the SUV to give Nicole and Blakely a respite from the heat.

And he could play with the baby when she woke, so Nicole could take the time she needed to process their day.

Whatever they decided, he could make it work.

Finn reached through her open window and nudged her shoulder. "I promise to call if I learn anything useful. Or if I get the phone unlocked. Matter of fact, once the phone's unlocked, I'll bring it to your place, and we can go through any contacts and messages of interest. Do you know if she kept her location tracking enabled?"

Nicole shook her head. "I'm not sure. Maybe."

Dean gave his brother a nod of appreciation, then buckled Blakely into her seat. "Why don't you stop by Nicole's apartment when you leave here?" he suggested. "You can fill us in then, and Nicole can give the phone's pass code another try."

Finn patted the roof. "Will do." His gaze dropped to Nicole's tired face. "Take care. Rest. Hydrate."

She lifted her bottle of water and gave it a wiggle.

He smiled. "I guess I'll see y'all in a bit then."

The drive back to Nicole's apartment was long and silent. Dean watched every passing car for signs of the black sedan. The air was heavier. Suffocating despite the blasting air-conditioning.

And if he felt this way, he could only imagine what Nicole was feeling.

Once someone was missing three days, the odds of finding them significantly lowered. Any evidence discovered from this point forward would be polluted at best, unidentifiable and useless at worst. Time was everything, and the window for a successful recovery was closing fast.

He pulled into Nicole's designated parking spot outside her building and unloaded Blakely from the car. Her big brown eyes were open, and her face twisted into a smile. "Someone's up," he said, curling her against his chest. "Have a good rest, Little Miss?"

Nicole climbed out, one hand pressed to her side.

They crossed the lot to the building, where a moving truck had backed up to the door. A kid with floppy hair and a sweaty T-shirt kicked a stopper loose but held the door for Dean and Nicole when he noticed their approach.

"Hey, man," he said, making room for them to pass.

Dean looked him over, unease creeping along his spine. "You just move in?"

"Nah. My aunt. She's in 310 now. The family's helping her get settled. You live in the building?"

"I do," Nicole said. "Tell your aunt I said welcome."

The kid lifted the stopper from the ground and tossed it in the air, catching it before moving toward the stairs. "Will do. Nice meeting y'all."

"Hey," Dean called, hating the instinctual churning in his gut. "Was this door propped open for long?"

"Not too long. A couple hours maybe," the kid said. "Made it easier to get things inside from the truck when our hands were full."

Dean grunted.

The kid bunched his features. "Sorry, man. Was that some kind of policy violation?"

"No." Nicole reached for Dean, giving his arm a tight squeeze, clearly sensing whatever it was that had him on high alert.

"Thanks," Dean told the kid, relieving him from the conversation.

He took Nicole's hand and moved slowly toward her apartment door, adjusting Blakely in his arms. "I don't like knowing that door was propped open."

"I'm sure someone from that kid's family was coming and going the whole time."

"Maybe," he said. "But none of them would know if anyone walking inside actually belonged here."

She didn't argue, and he took the lead moving toward her apartment.

Several steps later, they stopped short when her door came into view.

The thin wooden trim around the frame was cracked, and the door was slightly ajar.

Nicole gasped, and his protective instincts went up like a cloak, covering him wholly and sending his body into autopilot.

He passed Blakely into Nicole's arms. "Stay close," he said, unwilling to leave her unprotected in the hallway, even for a minute. "Text Finn." He nudged the door open before stepping inside and removing his sidearm.

Nicole pulled the sling from her bag and slid her niece inside, then unearthed her cell phone.

The living room and kitchen were visible and empty, lit by the midday light through an abundance of windows. Each room appeared untouched.

Dean raised a flattened palm to instruct Nicole to stay put. He'd given the same silent request dozens of times when they'd dated, though typically during family baseball games.

She nodded in understanding and pressed her back against the door frame while he moved on.

He inched carefully down the hall, quickly clearing the bathroom, then Nicole's room, and finally arriving in Cari's space.

A creaking floorboard spun him on a dime, weapon raised to half-mast before confirming it was Nicole. "All clear," he said, returning the gun to its holster.

Her eyes were wide and her mouth open as she took in the scene before her. A whispered cuss broke on her lips.

"Yeah."

Cari's room had been destroyed. All Dean's work, all the tidy piles and organized rows of her personal content, were scattered. The mattress was undressed and askew. The closet's contents purged. Her laptop gone.

They'd been at the Botanical Center in another neighborhood searching for clues while Cari's abductor, or his minion, had been breaking into their home.

NICOLE SWORE AGAIN, a luxury habit most second-grade teachers couldn't afford. But—

The word escaped again.

She backed into the hallway, realizing Cari's room was a crime scene. Maybe the entire apartment was a crime scene.

Nicole's life was becoming a crime scene.

She kept moving until the kitchen came into view, then she strapped Blakely into her high chair and poured a glass of water.

Dean stayed on her heels.

She drained the glass, then poured another.

Dean crossed into the living room, relaying the details of the break-in to someone by phone. "They were looking for something," he said, pulling the black duffel Austin had brought him from its place in the coat closet. He pinched the phone between his shoulder and cheek, then retrieved a pair of blue latex gloves. "I don't know. They have the laptop. I shouldn't have left it here after what happened outside the pizza shop." He grimaced and returned the bag to the closet. "I keep underestimating the level of danger we're facing. These are motivated criminals, which tells me the stakes are big."

His gaze jumped to Nicole, and he froze. "I'm going to call you back."

He pushed his phone into his pocket and headed her way, his gaze never leaving hers.

She wasn't sure what he saw, but she felt like an alternate version of herself. Something hollow and surreal. Because this wasn't her life. She was a second-grade teacher in a quaint coastal town. Her sister was happy and healthy, a new mom who made good choices.

Nicole's eyes closed, and strong arms curved around her, bringing her cheek to rest on a broad, familiar chest. "This isn't real," she whispered, wishing she could make the words true.

Dean widened his stance, wrapping her up in him, shielding and cocooning her, then resting his cheek on top of her head. "Finn's on the way. So is Austin. We're going to dust the door and broken jamb for prints and sort Cari's room again. We'll need you to see if anything's missing. I just went through everything a couple of nights ago, so I'll be familiar. Together, we should know if anything other than the laptop was taken."

Her numb mind revived with his declaration. And another mental blow came fast and hard. "Cari was logged in to all her social media. Whoever took the laptop will have access to everything just like we did."

"They'll have to get past the lock screen," Dean said. "If we can unlock her cell phone, we can probably log her out of everything connected to her main account. The computer's lock screen should buy us some time. You're the only one who knew that password."

"Me and Cari," she said, hating all the ways someone holding her sister hostage could force the password from her. And to compound her pain, the laptop suddenly felt like her last connection to Cari. As if access to her sister's online world had been a tether.

Now that string had been cut, too.

Heavy footfalls and familiar voices echoed outside the apartment door a moment before Dean's brothers knocked. Dean released her, and an icy chill rushed over her in his absence.

Then the processing of the newest crime scene began.

Nicole and Blakely watched as the Beaumonts dusted for fingerprints, took endless photos, documented every step and eventually went to interview neighbors. Austin volunteered to knock on other first-floor doors. Finn went to find the young man Nicole and Dean had met on their way in and speak with his family on the third floor.

Dean closed the door behind his brothers, then crouched before Nicole on the recliner.

She mindlessly bounced a small stuffed bunny that had once belonged to Cari on her niece's chubby legs. Blakely giggled and kicked her feet in delight.

"Your landlord's been notified about the break-in. My brothers are going to replace your locks and repair the splintered jamb," Dean said. "They'll reorganize Cari's room before they go. We can take a look at that when you're ready."

"Sounds good." She wanted to hop to her feet and get started now, but the out-of-body sensation hadn't fully gone away, and her side was burning.

He raised a hand bearing two more over-the-counter pain pills. "You never had a chance to take these."

She took them immediately with a swig of water from her nearby glass.

"There's something else," Dean said, carefully. His tone put her further on edge.

She raised her brows, unable to voice the question. *What else has gone wrong now?*

"Given the events of the day, I think it would be wise for you and Blakely to leave the apartment for a few days. Maybe until Cari returns, but at least until the danger stops coming every time we stand still long enough to take a deep breath."

Nicole nodded. "Mom's coming in from Charleston today," she said. "She'll want to see Blakely, and I want to see her." She couldn't afford a hotel room for more than a night or two. She squinted at the man before her, turning his words over in her mind. "Are you asking me to move to the ranch?"

"No." He cleared his throat. "I thought you could stay with me."

Nicole's mouth opened, then shut without comment.

"My cabin has enough space," he said, apparently under the impression she needed to be sold on the offer, as if she hadn't been about to scream out her sincere thanks. "My address isn't listed anywhere," he pressed on. "Austin and I went to significant lengths to protect our privacy when purchasing our homes. You'll be comfortable. You're familiar with the space. I'm sure Mama will absolutely inundate us with food once she knows you're there, and best of all you'll be able to rest. When you feel like getting some fresh air, you can wander my property. Blakely can play on a picnic blanket under the trees. And I can protect you both."

Nicole didn't love the idea of leaving the home she shared with Cari, but she wanted Blakely to be safe. She wanted to stop worrying over every floorboard creak and little sound outside her window. And she didn't hate the memory of Dean's home only having one bed. Not that anything would happen if they shared it, but she knew she'd sleep better with him beside her, and having his arms around her earlier had only made her long for him to embrace her again. "Did you ever set up the guest room?"

Something like heat flashed in his eyes, there and gone before she could be certain what she'd seen. "No, but I thought we could put a portable crib in there for Blakely. You'd be right next door. I'd sleep on the couch. I'm not suggesting anything—" his cheeks darkened slightly, the blush plainly visible thanks to his morning shave "—that would make you uncomfortable."

"I know," she said. "I know you."

Their gazes locked, and the temperature rose. Her heart rate climbed for new reasons as she fell deeper into the depths of his baby blues.

Of course Dean Beaumont would willingly sleep on his own couch instead of sharing his king-size bed if she asked. That was just the kind of man he was.

But Nicole had no intention of asking.

Chapter Twelve

Nicole relaxed as they neared Dean's cabin, feeling lighter and more hopeful than she had in a few days. Dean's home would be safer for her and Blakely. And if Blakely was safe, Nicole could breathe easier, unwind and maybe think of something useful to help the Beaumonts find her sister.

She admired the familiar gravel lane of his driveway, long and narrow, lined in tall leafy trees and luxurious shade.

A large white pickup sat at the far end, parked behind Dean's big truck.

"Well, that shouldn't surprise me at all," he said, sliding her SUV into the space beside his vehicle. "My parents beat us here."

Nicole smiled as his mama started down the porch steps in their direction, arms and smile open wide. His dad followed more slowly, letting his wife take her usual enthusiastic lead.

"You ready for this?" Dean asked. A twinkle she hadn't seen in a long while danced in his soulful blue eyes.

She'd missed that twinkle.

"Absolutely." Nicole climbed out and rounded the hood, a dozen emotions pressing her forward. She'd missed his parents immensely. They were the family everyone wanted but few had. Her folks loved her, she knew, but the things they'd gone through with Cari had changed them from the people they were when Nicole was small. Her mom was distant now, thanks to the emotional walls she'd erected for her survival in the worst of times. The same walls that had pushed their dad away. And though Cari had been clean for years, their mom's barriers remained firmly in place, as had their father's absence. Part of her wondered what he would do when their mother told him about Cari as she'd promised to do. Probably nothing. It was hard knowing their family hadn't always been that way.

Mrs. Beaumont, on the other hand, seemed softer and more tenderhearted with every soul she nurtured. "Look at you," she called, engulfing Nicole in a strong, motherly hug. She smelled of lilacs and cookies. Her long salt-and-pepper hair was wild and frizzed with humidity. Her soft cheeks felt like home against Nicole's skin. "Oh. How I've missed you."

"I've missed you, too."

She stepped back, taking Nicole's hands in hers and looking her over head to toe. "Beautiful as ever. And from what I hear, every bit as strong."

Nicole swallowed a lump of grief and pride. "I'm trying. Dean's doing the real work."

His mother's warm brown eyes slid to her son. "Well, you two always did make one heck of a team." Whatever else she'd intended to say was lost as Dean pulled Blakely from her car seat.

"Oh!" Mrs. Beaumont released Nicole, heat-seeking maternal radar locked on the baby. "Sweet precious darling," she cooed, already heading her way. "Dean Beaumont, you were born for this look," she said, rising on her toes to kiss Dean's cheek as he cradled Blakely. "A-plus daddy material, right here." She patted his chest, stole a look in Nicole's direction and winked. Then she smoothly relieved Dean of his charge. "I'll take it from here. You can see to Nicole."

Nicole laughed, and Dean went to stand at her side.

Together, they watched his parents coo and fuss over Blakely, clearly in their happiest of zones.

"You want to go inside?" he asked, resting a palm against the curve of her spine.

The gentle touch warmed her heart, the scene around them reminding her of another life.

She nodded when words failed, and he led her to the door.

His folks fell in line behind them. Mrs. Beaumont carried Blakely while Mr. Beaumont hauled a slew of thermal casserole totes and grocery bags from the porch.

Thirty minutes later, the kitchen table and counters were covered in homemade foods and covered dishes. His parents had brought enough to feed an army and insisted on leaving it all for leftovers, and his brothers, who she assumed would be over soon.

Nicole sipped a tall glass of sweet tea and nibbled at an array of fruits, cheeses and sliced veggies.

Dean sat opposite her, watching with an intensity that suggested his mind wasn't on anything but her. When his gaze flickered to her mouth and neck, she was sure she could feel the press of lips there as well.

Mrs. Beaumont bustled through the kitchen, clapping Dean on his shoulder as she passed. She rinsed a teething ring in the sink after Blakely tossed it on the floor. "I'm glad you two let us know about the community forming under the highways. Lincoln and Josie delivered three dozen sandwiches that night, plus chips, pretzels, water and all the fruits I had on hand. They said those folks took everything they offered and were glad for it."

Dean dragged his attention to his mother as she hurried back to Blakely. "Nicole and I drove by there this morning and everyone was gone. Did Lincoln or Josie mention if it looked as if they were packing up?"

She frowned. "No. Josie thought we might see one or two of them at the ranch soon. She did the talking, I'd imagine."

Dean rubbed the back of his neck. "I forgot to mention their absence to Finn. It might not mean anything, or maybe it does."

"He's on his way here," she said. "I sent him and Austin messages about the food. You know they can't resist my cowboy casserole or cobbler."

Nicole sampled a fresh strawberry and smiled. The inside of Dean's cabin was more than just a respite. It was another universe, where it was safe to let her guard down, because everything was going to be just fine. And she'd needed this more than she knew.

Mr. Beaumont made silly faces at Blakely while his wife was away. He tapped her nose with one finger, making her squeal in delight, then he snapped pictures of her with his phone.

Mrs. Beaumont returned to the mix, freshly cleaned teether in hand. "You know," she said, "when things aren't going the way we'd hoped, it's important to focus on the good. This little one right here is all good."

Mr. Beaumont snapped another photo. "She looks just like Cari. Just like you and your mama, too. Look at these curls."

Blakely kicked and flailed, exercising her chunky limbs and adoring the attention.

"Will you or Blakely need anything?" Mrs. Beaumont asked Nicole. "We heard about the break-in and know you plan to stay a while. I can't imagine you fit everything you both need into that little SUV. We're happy to come back with supplies, baby gear, wine, dinner and a movie."

His dad chuckled. "Mary, let them be."

She frowned.

The older couple exchanged a long look and beat of silence, then his dad's attention returned to Dean. "Do you need help setting up the guest room? We've got twin beds in storage at the ranch."

"No." His mother cut him off with another look and an elbow. "I'm sure they can work that out."

Nicole did her best not to laugh. Dean looked absolutely horrified. A teen embarrassed by his parents.

"Nicole is taking my room," he said flatly. "We'll set up the portable crib for Blakely in the guest room. I'll take the couch. That'll keep me near the front door in case anyone drops by late, as my brothers tend to do, and I'll be able to take calls and work without disrupting their rest."

His dad nodded in approval.

His mom rolled her eyes.

Nicole decided to give him a break and change the subject. "My mom's on her way. Have you spoken with her?"

"Yep," Mrs. Beaumont said. "And speaking of guests, we should probably get back."

Mr. Beaumont carried Blakely to Dean, having been warned over dinner that Nicole was supposed to take it easy. "I'd love to stay and play with this little nugget all evening, but we've got a nearly full ranch this week, and I can't be gone too long. Who knows what Lincoln would do if one of the ranch's residents mouthed off to him or Josie."

His mother groaned. "That hypothetical kid would be better off provoking Lincoln than Josie. Otherwise he'll get two retaliations."

"If we come home to find anyone mucking stalls or doing push-ups, we'll know what happened," his dad said.

Nicole's smile widened. Lincoln never had much to say to her, but she'd always liked him. She liked Josie, too, though she was young, and they'd had extremely little in common the last time they'd met. Still, she hoped to see them both again soon.

She walked the Beaumonts to the door and hugged them each goodbye, already missing her former surrogate parents and eager to squeeze her mother the moment she got in.

DEAN PUT THE last of his mama's food into the refrigerator just before seven that evening. His brothers Finn and Austin sat with Nicole at the living room table. As promised, they'd arrived for dinner. The group had talked for hours, discussing life and Cari's disappearance in an intertwined ebb and flow. They'd gotten reacquainted while admiring Blakely and trying passwords on Cari's cell phone. The device continued to lock after each fail. The penalty time grew longer as well.

Finn drummed his thumbs against the table's edge. "If the phone's still locked when I head back to the station, I'll take it to the tech lab. Either way, we'll figure it out."

Dean appreciated Finn's words of encouragement. Nicole had been beating herself up for not knowing the password. She'd tried everything she could think of, and she was wearing down.

Finn was good at looking on the bright side. At twenty-five and relentlessly positive, he usually frustrated everyone with his silver linings. But Dean was thankful for Finn tonight. He'd kept Nicole engaged and busy, making notes of all the passwords she'd tried and lists of possibilities for when the device let them try again. Birth dates. Special occasion dates. Patterns on the keypad.

"What else is new?" Austin asked, looking bored and mildly restless as usual.

"It didn't take long to get the details on Mikey Likey," Finn said. "His real name is Michael Litchfield. He's twenty-seven and a known dope dealer with a long list of priors, though nothing big that stuck. I'm guessing he took one look at Dean and assumed he was an undercover cop. He said he thought someone might be after him, but I doubt anyone would confuse this big brother for a thug."

Dean crossed his arms, unaffected. Finn had probably meant the comment as a joke or jab, but not looking like a criminal was just fine with him.

"I spoke with Mikey's boss at Ricky Rocket's," Finn continued. "He said Mikey's a good worker, typically reliable, but he hasn't been back since being chased."

Nicole shifted on her seat, lacing and unlacing her fingers on the tabletop. "He told us we put a target on his back by showing up. I hope nothing bad has happened to him."

"Uh." Finn wrinkled his nose and forehead. "I think Mikey has done a bang-up job of painting that target all by himself."

"What did his coworkers think of him?" Dean asked. Maybe the face Mikey showed his boss wasn't the same one he showed his peers. "Any chance they had another perspective?"

"Nope. Everyone I spoke with genuinely thinks he's a good guy, even the ones who knew about his questionable side hustles. Unfortunately, no one seemed to know who he spent time with or where he went outside work."

Dean considered that, then asked the question popping into mind. "Could someone at the pizzeria be the one arranging the catering?"

"I doubt it," Finn said. "No one on staff, even the owner, has the kind of money or connections needed to fit the model we're building. The home parties are elite and exclusive. A whole other world."

Austin stretched his long legs under the table, grunting and staring at his cell phone. He'd been texting with someone off and on for a while but hadn't looked up to fill anyone in on what he was doing.

Dean had decided ten minutes ago that whatever his brother was up to had better be good, otherwise his behavior was unacceptably rude.

All he'd shared with the group so far was a thorough background check on the couple from the alleged party location. Mr. and Mrs. Tippin. Austin had gone door to door talking to the neighbors and kept a map with the feedback. He'd also dug into the couple's lives online and created a file with mostly superfluous details.

"What'd you learn about the Tippins?" Nicole asked. Her wide brown eyes moved from Finn to Austin, eager for information from any source.

"As far as I can tell," Finn said, "the Tippins have been married eleven years. Mrs. Tippin doesn't work outside the home, and Mr. Tippin sells high-end cars."

"He's a manager at the luxury automobile dealership that overlooks the sound," Austin said.

Nicole chewed her bottom lip. "He was getting into a fancy sports car when I saw him."

"Dealer plate?"

"I didn't notice. I was still hoping Cari would pop up and apologize for being late and worrying me."

His brothers grunted and nodded.

Dean leaned against the kitchen countertop, unexpectedly winded by a sudden pang of mixed emotions. He hated the reason for tonight's gathering, but spending the evening with his family, Nicole and Blakely had been nice. It'd felt good and right. He wanted to spend hundreds more evenings like these, though under better circumstances. And he couldn't help wondering if Nicole might be interested in that, too.

Finn's brows rose, and Dean realized he'd been staring.

He shook his head to indicate he'd been lost in thought. Nothing more.

"Austin found the babysitter from the phone call," Finn said.

"What?" Dean's eyes snapped to Austin's.

Austin frowned. "I just said that. Didn't you hear me?"

"No." He extended a hand in his brother's direction. "Sorry. One more time."

Austin straightened, more amused than irritated and seeing more than Dean would've preferred. As usual. "I asked every family near the Botanical Center if they were home or away on the night Cari disappeared. Eventually I found two couples who'd gone out and left their kids with babysitters. I got the babysitters' contact information and left messages. I've been texting with one of those sitters for about twenty minutes. She's the one who called to report a noise violation, and she just told me she took a video with her cell phone that night. I'm waiting for it to load. You need to upgrade your internet package."

"I live in the woods. This is a good speed."

"Mine's better." Austin's gaze flickered back to his phone. "Here we go." He rose and moved to stand beside Nicole, sharing his screen with her and Finn.

Dean went to join them.

The image on-screen was dark and quiet, save for a soft voice-over. "Look at all these cars," a woman said. "There's even a freaking valet." The video panned through a closed window, over the expanse of grass at the park and twinkle lights from the Botanical Center, then to the small lot, wholly filled with cars.

"They valeted the cars," Finn said. "No wonder no one on the street recalled a party."

"Smart," Nicole said. "No one would be at the park after dark. The lot was empty and close. This took planning."

Dean set a hand on her shoulder, lending his strength. "Do you see Cari's car?"

She squinted. "It's dark, but I don't think so. And not from this distance."

The video ended and Finn huffed. "Well, I can't wait to take this to the Tippins. Maybe they'll change their tune about that party they didn't have. Send this to me," he said, addressing Austin.

"Done."

Finn tapped his phone. "All right. I'm pushing it over to the tech lab for enhancement. If they can pick up any license plate number, or even a partial, we can try to match it with a vehicle make and model, then go poking party guests until we get what we need. We might even be able to ID one of the valets. Then I can find out who hired them." Finn pushed onto his feet. "I'm going to head back to the station and try to get this moving."

Austin followed suit. "I'm going to visit my informants. See if anyone's heard anything about Mikey."

Dean walked his brother to the door. "Good luck proving the cars at the park were valeted from the Tippins' home."

Finn offered a bland expression. "I've got this."

"I guess I'll hold down the fort." Dean itched to grab his truck keys or call shotgun, but his work was at the cabin. He had to keep Nicole and Blakely safe and comfortable.

Finn's lips quirked. "Good luck playing fort."

Austin snorted, then clapped Dean on the back as he passed into the night.

Nicole moved to his side, brushing against him as she waved goodbye to his brothers.

His body ignited at her touch, and he stepped away.

Another night alone with Nicole. Knowing she was in his bed?

He was going to need all the luck he could get.

Chapter Thirteen

Nicole woke to soft shuffling sounds outside Dean's bedroom door. A door she'd left open in case he reconsidered his night on the couch. She wouldn't have minded feeling his arms around her again. Each time he'd embraced her this week, it'd felt a little more like coming home.

She'd wondered a thousand times how he was really doing. Had he fully healed from their breakup? She used to think she had, but spending time with Dean like this had her wondering if all she'd really done was fill her time with other things. Staying busy had always been her way to manage pain. Ignore it, and it might not go away, but at least she wasn't thinking about it.

The floorboards creaked, and Nicole sat up. The world outside was dark, and according to the clock on the nightstand, it was after three. Was Dean still awake?

Soft white light was visible though the open doorway, drawing her from the bed and into the cabin beyond. Goose bumps scattered over her bare arms and legs as she left the warm blanket nest in favor of seeing Dean.

The air stilled as she walked, and tension climbed over her. For the briefest moment she feared the person she heard moving around in the next room wasn't Dean.

He stepped into view from the kitchen, and her heart fluttered. His brows rose in surprise. "Everything okay? Did I wake you?"

"Yeah," she whispered, crossing her arms over the soft cotton T-shirt she'd chosen for a nightgown. There was something nonsensically stunning about the intimacy of meeting him in the night, both in pajamas and bare feet. And her thoughts stalled.

Her hungry gaze traveled over him, eating up the sight. Pale gray cotton sleep pants hung low on his hips. His shirt clung to the angles and plane of his chest, emphasizing his perfectly lean torso.

"Sorry," he said. "Was it the light?"

She blinked, mentally rewinding the previous exchange, attempting to make sense of his question. "Oh. No. You didn't wake me." She ran a hand through her messy hair. "I meant I'm okay. Nothing's wrong. I'm just a light sleeper now, thanks to having a baby in the house." And before Blakely's arrival, a very sick and immensely pregnant little sister.

The constant anxiety that came with knowing that same sister had recently vanished only made it harder to rest.

"Do you want some tea?" he offered. "I was just putting on some coffee. I can heat water for you."

She nodded. "Okay." Her side was sore and her body fatigued, but she wasn't ready to go back to bed.

Dean went to the kitchen and pulled a bottle of pain pills from the cabinet where he kept a first aid kit and tea bags. He passed the bottle to her before filling a kettle with water and setting it on the stove.

"Thanks." She accepted the pills. Staying ahead of the pain was key for faster healing. Or at least that had been what the hospital staff told Cari after delivering Blakely.

He placed a pod in his single-cup coffee brewer, and his earlier words circled back through her mind.

"You're drinking coffee. Have you gotten any sleep?"

He offered a cautious smile. "I don't sleep much."

Her stomach tightened, knowing the reason and unsure if it was okay to ask. "Because of Cari's case? Or has it been like this since before? Since the missing boy?"

"The latter."

"Do you want to talk about it?"

Dean's expression hardened before he looked away.

She didn't blame him. This was how too many similar conversations had begun, and those chats had never ended well. Collectively, they'd led to the end of their relationship.

She stepped forward and wrapped her arms around him, providing him the comfort he always gave to her. "You know, for whatever it's worth now, more than a year too late, I'm sorry for what you went through. I'm sorry you're still going through it, and I don't know how you keep going, but I'm really glad you do."

She'd realized at some point in the last few days that investigators and law officers had to see and do things in the name of justice that most people never thought about and wouldn't survive if they did. People like Dean and his brothers dedicated their lives to protecting and serving others. But who protected them?

She hadn't when she'd had the opportunity. Dean had been hurting, and she'd chosen to walk away.

His frame stiffened for the duration of a heartbeat before he sank into the embrace.

Nicole breathed him in, absorbing his warmth and familiar scent. She could identify his soap, shampoo and fabric softener by smell alone, and for months after their breakup, someone would pass her on the street or in the store and she'd spin in search of Dean.

She reveled in the strength of his heartbeat beneath her

ear, and the way his fingers splayed across her back. One big palm skated up and down her spine, soothing and caressing. He stroked long, loose curls away from her face and over her shoulder, skimming his hand against the tender skin at the base of her neck. She shivered.

"I've missed this," he whispered. "I've missed you. Every day."

The kettle's lid rattled a warning, and Dean released her, stepping away to remove the pot from the heat before it whistled. The words *I've missed you, too* stuck in her throat, but the moment had passed. So she accepted the tea and moved with Dean to the couch, where a pillow and blanket were arranged.

His laptop and phone lay on the coffee table beside a notepad and pen. The dark video of cars in the park's small lot centered the screen.

She curled her feet beneath her, balancing the hot drink in her hands. "How do you do it?" she asked. "How do you keep going to work, performing the same job that nearly killed you? It's been more than a year since you found that boy's body, and it still haunts you. It will probably always haunt you, but you keep going."

"His name was Ben Smothers," Dean said, voice low and fighting emotion. He peered at her with tortured eyes as he lowered to the cushion at her side. "I keep going because what I do matters, and I help everyone I can. Ben was an exception, and to stop helping others because I was too late to help him doesn't make any logical sense. So I keep going, even when I don't want to, and even if I'm not sure I can make the kind of difference I hope.

"And I didn't find Ben's body. I found him. Hanging on to life by a thread. I carried him half a mile through the woods to my truck, and I drove him six miles until I found cell service, all while listening to his rattled, shallow breaths and begging the universe to keep his heart beating until I got help." He swallowed, and his cheeks darkened. "The universe declined."

Nicole's breath caught. "Dean."

He lifted a palm to stop her, jaw clenching and releasing.

She hadn't known the boy had been alive for a second of his time with him. "You never told me."

"I needed time. And you left me."

The verbal blow knocked the wind from her lungs. She'd given him three months to open up and let her back in. When he didn't, she walked out, clinging to the insistence she deserved a partner, and calling it quits because he'd fallen short of his promise on that front. In hindsight, she could see she'd really left because she was exhausted from always being the strong one for others in trauma. She'd left to protect her tired, battered heart, the same way her mom had left their dad, pulling away long before he'd asked for a divorce.

And Nicole had blamed Dean.

"I wasn't trying to push you away," he said. "I was trying to hold myself together."

She set her hand on his, bracing for the rejection she deserved. She'd stood by her sister through endless self-inflicted misery and poor choices, but when the man she'd planned to marry withdrew to process an unthinkable trauma, she'd dumped him. "I'm so sorry."

He offered a small, sad smile. "Me, too."

"I was scared, and I ran," she admitted. "But at the time, I didn't know that's what I was doing."

The floodgates opened, and truth flowed freely from her heart to her lips. Dean accepted her words, then shared his own. He confided in her about his experience on the Ben Smothers case and about the counseling he'd received afterward. Nicole confessed her fears of never being enough.

Time passed in strange lulls and spurts as they spoke, and

she begged the night to last forever. She wasn't ready for Blakely to wake and need her, for another day of Cari's absence, or for these moments of raw honesty to end.

Dean turned his palm beneath hers, twining their fingers and tugging her close.

She set the long-empty cup of tea onto the coffee table and climbed into his lap like a child, wrapping her arms around his neck and melting into him.

Dean searched her with careful blue eyes. Then he lifted a wide, warm palm to cradle her jaw.

She leaned into the touch, and he released a ragged breath in response.

Then he lowered his gaze to her lips and kissed her. Chaste and sweet, the gesture filled her heart with hope and her mind with peace.

She rested her head against his chest and drifted back to sleep, cursing her relentless fatigue.

She woke in his arms a short while later, as the first rays of sun climbed the windowsills.

Their long-overdue talk had changed everything for her, as had their kiss. She could only hope he felt the same by light of day.

"Hope." The word formed on her lips and opened her eyes.

"What?" Dean looked at her, already awake.

She pushed away, setting herself upright, mind racing and hope blooming anew. "I think I know the password to Cari's phone."

Dean grabbed his phone from the coffee table and dialed. He pressed Send, then accessed the speaker option and poised the phone between them.

"Hey, Dean," Finn answered on a yawn. "What's up?"

"I'm here with Nicole," Dean said. "You're on speaker."

"Okay," he said slowly. "What's going on?"

"Do you have Cari's cell phone?" Nicole asked. "Is it already at the lab?"

"I dropped it off last night, why?"

"I think I know the password."

Something shifted on Finn's end of the line. "Hang on. I fell asleep at the station. I'm texting the lab now to see if anyone's there. What time is it?" He groaned, apparently answering his own question. "Oh. I've got a response. Kim's already at work. Let me catch her up."

Nicole wet her lips and looked to Dean, willing her idea to be right. "Tell her to try the password NEWHOPE, use the numbers on the keypad. No spaces or symbols or anything."

"Yeah," Finn said. "Give me a sec."

Nicole's knee bobbed. "Be right," she whispered. "Be right. Be right. Be right."

Several long moments passed, and Nicole chewed her lip in anticipation.

"That worked," Finn said. "Nice job."

Dean pressed a kiss to her forehead, as if it was the most natural thing in the world, and her heart thudded with joy. "What now?" he asked Finn, eyes fixed on Nicole.

"I'm already halfway to the lab," he said.

"Now you can log Cari out of her social media and email accounts," Nicole said. "Stop whoever took her laptop from accessing anything useful." In case they made it past her lock screen.

Sounds of a buzzer and the opening and closing of doors came through the phone line, then Finn's voice, declaring himself and requesting to speak with someone named Kim.

"On it," he said a moment later. "First I need to make notes of everyone she's been in recent contact with and capture screenshots of their communication."

"Can you send some of that to us?" Nicole asked. "Maybe I'll recognize someone's name."

"Sure," Finn said. "Give me twenty minutes to get going on this, and I'll send some texts."

Her smile grew. "Thank you."

Dean disconnected the call and returned the phone to the coffee table. He peeled himself from the sofa and headed to the kitchen. "New hope, huh?"

"She learned that at the ranch." Excitement and possibility churned in Nicole's core. "Every decision is a new chance to change your life."

The moment felt pivotal. Cari's case was no longer a complete dead end. They had access to a whole phone full of leads, and Nicole nearly vibrated with the need to get started.

As if on cue, Dean's phone dinged with a new text message. It dinged again before he could return from the kitchen and unlock the screen. A third image appeared as he raised it into view of them both. Finn was sending screenshots from Cari's phone log. Then a message.

Finn: Does Nicole recognize any of these names?

Nicole scanned the names and numbers, then shook her head.

Dean: No

Finn: I'm getting called to a scene. I'll be in touch soon.

Adrenaline coursed through Nicole's chest and limbs. She wouldn't need caffeine to get her moving today. She felt ready to burst. "I'm going to call the numbers."

Dean frowned. "Maybe Finn should handle that."

Nicole bristled. "Why?" He was leaving on a case. Who knew when he'd have time to do the research needed. "I can do it. Take notes. Report back. He went on a call. I'm not doing anything."

"What happens if Cari's contacts don't want to talk to you? What if they don't realize there's a problem yet, and you cause one by alerting them to her disappearance? Then they don't answer the phone when Finn calls?"

She considered that a moment. He was right, of course, and she needed to think this through. But time was also of the essence.

Eventually, they agreed on calling Finn, both to ask permission and to request he get Kim from the crime lab to chat with them. A few minutes later, Nicole was on the line with Kim, who dialed Cari's most frequent contact using three-way calling from Cari's phone.

"Ready?" Kim asked.

"I think so."

"Okay. I'm going to start the recording, then dial Darla D."

Blakely's small voice rose from the guest room in a series of fussing sounds, and Dean moved in that direction while the call connected.

"Cari!" A woman's shrill voice burst through the line before the first ring was complete. "Oh my goodness. Are you okay? I can't believe this. What is happening? I've been freaking terrified," she ranted, sounding out of breath and possibly near tears. "Someone said you took that last job and then vanished. I've been asking everyone where you are, but no one knew. I thought you were dead. Wait. Do you need help? I can get you on my way to work. You can take my car after that if you need it. Where are you?"

"Uhm," Nicole began, unsure what to say to the woman's pure panic. A torrent of emotion choked her words.

"The newspaper said one of the party guests was killed in a robbery," she whispered. "But that's not what the girls are saying. Is that why you're gone? Do you know what really happened?"

"Who's dead?" Nicole asked, the word squeaking out before she thought better of it. Why hadn't the police realized there was a possible murder in town or that it might be related to Cari's disappearance?

"Dr. George. Cari?"

"Mmm-hmm."

Darla was quiet. "Who is this?"

Nicole debated lying, pretending to be Cari, anything to keep her on the line, but she was stuck. Darla could hang up at any moment and choose not to answer again. "I'm Cari's sister," she confessed, speaking as rapidly as Darla had a moment before. "I can't find her. I'm watching her baby, and I'm scared. I don't know what to do or who to call. You were the person she spoke to most. Please help me."

Silence returned, gonging across the line.

"Please," she begged. "I have no one else to ask. I don't understand what's happening, and I need to find her. Anything you share could make the difference in whether or not Cari comes home. I swear I won't tell anyone what you say."

The silence continued so long Nicole pulled the phone from her ear to be sure the call hadn't been dropped.

"I work at Nina's Boutique on Seacrest Avenue," Darla said, tone flat and resigned. "I'll be there all day. You can stop in, but don't act like you know me, make sure you weren't followed, and never call back. You're putting me in danger."

"She's gone," Kim said a few seconds later. "Let me know if you need anything else."

"Thanks." Nicole tucked the phone into her pocket.

Dean exited the guest room with Blakely in tow. "How'd it go?"

"Better than expected," she said. "We need to eat and get dressed. We're going shopping."

Chapter Fourteen

Dean cleaned up breakfast while the ladies took their showers and got ready for the day. So many things had happened in the last twelve hours, he wasn't sure how to feel or what to process first, but with a new lead on Cari's case, it was definitely time to hustle, so he chose to concentrate on that.

Except, even as he wiped down Blakely's high chair and loaded dishes into the dishwasher, his night with Nicole danced back through his mind. They'd finally talked the way they should have more than a year ago.

And he'd kissed her.

He hadn't intended to go for it. Hadn't meant to lose himself in the moment. It was completely inappropriate, not to mention unprofessional, of him to make a move on her, given her current emotional state and general situation. But he had.

And she'd kissed him back.

His lips twisted into a self-indulgent smile.

He'd slept better with her in his arms for a few hours than he had in months. Maybe a year. Now Finn had access to Cari's phone, and her friend Darla had agreed to meet them. It was a darn good day. The possibility of finding Cari seemed closer than it had since the moment he'd learned she was missing.

A thunderous rap on his front door sent a curse from his lips.

He dried his hands on a dish towel, glancing toward the closed bathroom door before picking up his sidearm and moving to the front window.

Austin's truck was in the driveway. Austin was on the porch.

Dean opened the door, and his brother scanned him, taking notice of the hand kept out of sight.

"Hey now," Austin said, a cocky grin sliding into place. "You planning on shooting me?"

"Maybe." Dean put the gun away and headed for the kitchen. "Why are you pounding on the door like you're here to serve a warrant?"

"I wanted you to hear me. In case you were sleeping." He stepped over the threshold and shut the door. "Where are the girls? They finally get sick of you and leave? Decide to take their chances back at the apartment?"

Dean glanced over his shoulder. "Funny. Keep it up and maybe I will shoot you."

Austin grinned. "I come in peace, big brother, and bearing news."

"In that case, I have coffee." He motioned to the table, and Austin sat.

"I found a cooperative old lady in that fancy neighborhood. She invited me in for herbal tea and those little shortbread cookies with jam in the middle."

Dean laughed, despite himself. "I knew you'd change your mind about dating eventually."

"If I was fifty years older, Myrtle wouldn't be able to get rid of me," Austin said. "Her son's a gem, too. He worries about her, so he installed cameras all around her property.

The good ones. Not the cheap stuff. She let me take a look at the footage from the night of the party."

The bathroom door opened, and Nicole appeared with Blakely on her hip. "Wait," she said, hurrying into view with a towel wrapped around her hair. "Hey, Austin. I was eavesdropping while I got this one ready." She lifted Blakely in front of her and blew against her round tummy, then cuddled her close.

Blakely squealed in delight. Her brown curls were pulled into one tiny fountain of a ponytail at the top of her head. And she wore a two-piece shorts set with a tank top. Both were yellow and covered in butterflies.

Nicole had faded jeans on with small rips and holes on the knees and thighs. Her off-white T-shirt emphasized her tan. "What did I miss?"

Dean did his best not to admire the long curve of her neck or think about sliding his fingers into the slick wet curls beneath her towel.

Instead, he motioned to his brother. "Austin convinced an old lady to give him sugar and let him see her cameras."

She wrinkled her nose. "Well, I'm glad you decided to date again."

Dean barked a laugh.

Austin made a disgruntled face. "Myrtle caught the Tippins' home and the side street to the park on those cameras. Do you want to see the footage or keep poking at me?"

Nicole slid her eyes to Dean and mouthed the word *Myrtle*.

Austin withdrew his phone from a pocket and turned it to face them. An image of the Tippins' home and driveway appeared. "What's the first thing you notice?"

"A ton of cars," Nicole said, drawn to the screen like a moth to light. "And they're all really nice. I'm just going by the emblems, but I'm pretty sure I can't even afford to think about most of these cars."

She was right.

Dean took a moment to appreciate the number of luxury vehicles. Based on the rides alone, partygoers were clearly wealthy, or at least driving cars only wealthy people could afford. Sadly, the people were too distant and pixilated to identify based on the video alone.

"This goes on for thirty-five minutes," Austin said. "Expensive cars pull up, fancy people get out, a valet drives the car away. Next car arrives. Repeat."

"Have you shown this to Finn?" Dean asked.

"Yep. He's got someone at the station running the plates on these cars." He pointed to a car being moved by the valet; it drove toward the camera before turning at the next crossroad. When he tapped the screen to stop the video, a partial plate was visible in the night. "He'll ID as many owners as possible, then give them all a call. Now, look at this." He turned the phone toward him a moment before facing the screen in their direction again. "Twenty minutes before all that, this happens."

A large panel van, like the kind that picks people up from airports, pulled into the Tippins' driveway. A dozen women in black dresses climbed out.

Cari was one of them.

Nicole covered her mouth, then fell onto a chair. Blakely made a swipe for the phone.

Austin backed it up a few inches. He froze the frame. "She's wearing that lavender jacket. And carrying her phone in this image, so we know she made it to the party, then gave up those items later."

Dean rubbed his stubbled cheek. "An all-female catering company?" All young and beautiful.

"All wearing slinky black dresses and heels," Austin added. "You know what they don't have with them? Food."

Nicole's gaze drifted to Austin, then Dean. She held Blakely a little more closely. "Maybe the food and drinks were delivered earlier. Cari can't cook. She was only there to serve."

Austin shot Dean a look, then tucked away his phone. "Finn's headed to the car dealership where Mr. Tippin works," he said, avoiding Nicole's suggestion. "He's hoping to rattle him by showing up there, maybe get some more information from him, talk to his coworkers. I'm still looking for Mikey. Something tells me he's the key to finding whoever schedules these parties, and I'm willing to bet that person will know everything else we're looking to learn."

"Mikey's still gone?" Nicole asked.

"He's probably just lying low," Austin said. "And guys like him could probably get into the back seat of a cruiser without most members of the force even knowing."

"What makes you think you can find him?"

Austin tapped his nose. "I'm a bloodhound." He stood and rounded the table to kiss Nicole's cheek, then Blakely's head. "Let me know if you learn anything else, or if Finn calls you before me. Something's definitely fishy in suburbia. It's been a long while since Marshal's Bluff had an illegal ring of some kind."

Dean followed him to the door. "Thanks for coming by with the footage." Knowing they were another step closer to finding Cari would be great for Nicole's spirits.

"Don't mention it." Austin opened the door, then paused on the threshold. "What do you think is going on?" he asked in a voice intended only for Dean. "Gambling? Smuggling? Drugs?" He mouthed the word *prostitution*.

"I can read lips," Nicole said.

Austin winced and lifted a palm in apology. "Why can she read lips?" he whispered.

"I teach second graders," she answered, not giving Dean a chance to guess.

"Half the kids refuse to speak loudly enough to be heard, and the other half are continually scheming for extra playtime or snacks. Or plotting unfunny pranks. I learned to pay attention. My sister isn't a prostitute."

Austin had the decency to look ashamed. "I wasn't suggesting she—" He cleared his throat. "I'm just spitballing ideas. Knowing what we're dealing with will help us know whose doors to knock on. No offense intended. I swear."

"Fine, but hold on." She shoved away from the table and came to a stop at Dean's side. "I spoke with one of Cari's contacts this morning. We gained access to her phone, and a tech at the station helped us connect with a woman named Darla."

He pulled his lips down and shot his eyebrows high. "Nice work."

"Thanks. Have you heard about a recent murder? Someone named Dr. George. The papers said it was a robbery?"

He frowned. "No, but I've been busy with this case since you told us about Cari."

"See what you can find out?" Dean asked.

"Sure, but have you tried the internet for local news?"

"Not yet," Nicole said. "We just learned about Dr. George, and we've been trying to get out of here to meet with Darla since I hung up with her."

Austin clasped his hands and kneaded them. "All right. Sounds like we've all got our missions today. Let's go bring our girl home."

"Deal," she said.

He jogged down the steps and climbed into his waiting truck. Dean turned to Nicole with an apologetic smile. He wished

Austin hadn't mentioned prostitution, but he was thankful to be there for her, if she'd let him. "You okay?"

She fell against him in a gentle embrace, cradling Blakely between them.

"Things are starting to move," he said. "It can feel like a lot, but it's all good."

"I know."

Dean's phone dinged, and Finn's number appeared on-screen.

"Austin's truck slowed at the end of the driveway," Nicole said, reaching for the sheer curtain.

Either he was stopping to send the message, or the brothers were receiving a group text.

He swiped his thumb across the screen to reveal the message. "Group text."

Nicole angled her head for a better look at the words.

Finn: Mikey was discovered behind the pizzeria this morning. Beaten nearly unrecognizable.

Finn: Going with him to the hospital now.

Dean didn't respond. Shock coiled in him, and he looked outside to see how Austin was taking the news.

His truck's brake lights went out, and the vehicle rolled away.

Nicole sighed deeply, regaining his attention and apparently her resolve. "Let's stop at Ricky Rocket's on the way to meet Darla. She's going to be at work all day, and I don't know how long the woman who found Mikey will be at the pizzeria."

Dean pulled his keys from the rack. "All right, but this time we're taking my truck."

Chapter Fifteen

Nicole carried Blakely in her sling as they walked along the quaint downtown sidewalk toward the pizzeria. Shoppers were out in the usual summertime droves, carrying handled bags of newfound treasures and sipping iced drinks from logoed cups with straws. The morning was balmy and overcast as the sun worked to burn away the clouds, but Nicole felt more hopeful and invigorated than hot or worried.

Blakely cooed contentedly against her, happy to be outside and in her sling, enjoying the sights, scents and sounds.

Dean stepped forward to open the door to Ricky Rocket's when they arrived.

It was still early, and the air inside smelled of coffee and something sweet. Patrons claimed a few tables near the window. Mini pizzas topped with cinnamon sugar and icing positioned before them.

Nicole moved toward the counter, Dean's hand against her back. The restaurant's interior looked the same as it had before, but unlike her last visit, the tension inside was thick. No chatter or laughter rose from the kitchen, only the sounds of running water and the occasional clang of trays against the counter.

The expression on the cashier's face was brittle but pleasant. Her lips parted as recognition dawned.

Dean opened his wallet immediately. "Two bottles of water."

She nodded, and Nicole offered a small smile.

"Can we talk for a minute?" Nicole asked softly as Laney rang up the water. "We were here looking for Mikey earlier this week. You might remember."

Laney nodded but didn't make eye contact.

"You probably heard about what happened to me that day," Nicole said. "Maybe your boss or Detective Beaumont explained our story?"

Laney gave Dean the water and a register total, then took his money. "Your sister is missing." She made change, glancing briefly at Blakely. "The baby's mom."

"That's right." The answer came easier than it had before, and Nicole hated everything that fact implied. Her mind had accepted this as reality. Her sister was missing, and that was the new normal. "This is Blakely," she said, stroking her niece's cheek beneath the eyelet sunbonnet. "My sister and Mikey are friends, and he's introduced her to some catering jobs in the evenings. She went missing from one of those assignments. We think Mikey knows who hired her and how we can get in touch with them."

The younger woman's lips parted, and her eyes widened. She scanned the dining area, then looked toward the kitchen.

"If you know something, you can tell us," Nicole said. "This is Dean Beaumont. He's a private investigator and a friend of mine and my sister's. He's Detective Beaumont's brother."

Laney looked at Dean, uncertain.

"Please. We need to find her before she's hurt or...worse." Her mouth dried with the utterance, unable to comprehend a world without her sister in it.

"I found him today," Laney said. "I work the first shift, and when I got here, he was just lying outside the door. I didn't even recognize him. His face was so destroyed. His clothes were filthy. I thought he didn't have a home and maybe he'd slept there intentionally last night. Then I noticed Mikey's car in the lot. Mikey's never here in the morning. Then I recognized his shoes." Her eyes brimmed with tears, and she blinked them back, breathless. "He didn't respond when I called out to him or when I shook him. I thought he was dead. I couldn't find a pulse. It looks easy on TV, but it's not. I was shaking and my ears were ringing. I called 911 and just sat there waiting to know if he was alive."

"You did well," Dean said, pulling the woman's eyes to his. "You acted quickly and got help. Your actions likely saved his life."

She covered her mouth with both hands, and the tears began to fall.

Laney requested her fifteen-minute break and led Nicole and Dean to a small room in the back.

They sat at a folding lunch table with mismatched chairs and watched as Laney fidgeted with a straw wrapper someone had left behind.

"Mikey always wanted to make the deliveries to the rich neighborhoods," she began. "He said they tipped better. The other drivers thought the rich people were terrible tippers, and the neighborhoods were too far away, which limited the number of deliveries they could make. So it all worked out. One night when we were closing up, Mikey told me a customer gave him a business card and invited him to be a server at a fancy party. Afterward, he said they paid him in cash for the work, plus he made good tips and the homes were like nothing he'd ever experienced. Too fancy for words."

Dean shifted forward, resting his forearms on the table. "Did he mention the customer's name?"

"No, but he called the company Rising Tides. It sounded too easy to me. Too good to be true, and that usually means sketchy. Mikey thought you were one of the rich guys from the company."

Nicole fought a smile. Dean's brothers liked to tease him for being a little higher maintenance than they were. For using product on his beard every fall. For knowing the difference between Carhartt and Calvin Klein and for wearing less of the former than the latter.

Dean slid his eyes in her direction before returning them to Laney.

"That's why he ran," she said. "He called me later to let me know he was okay."

"Did he tell you anything else?" Dean asked. "Anything you remember will help."

Laney gave a humorless smile. "Mikey was always recruiting, looking for more women to serve at parties. He said the candidates had to be young and clean up nice. They also needed to keep their mouths shut, but he swore the pay was worth it. He tried to get me to go to meetings where he claimed additional information would be provided. I got the impression those meetings were interviews that gave the higher-ups a chance to choose who they wanted. The whole thing icked me out. Until I graduate and the student loans come due, I make enough here to get by."

"Do you still have that address?"

"I think." Laney scrolled through her phone.

"Did you tell Detective Beaumont all this?" he asked.

She pressed her lips together, looking sheepish. "No. I didn't know this was relevant. I was shocked by the guy holding a knife to you," she said, addressing Nicole. "He stabbed you when you had a baby in your arms. Who does that? I needed time." She passed her phone to Dean. "This is it, but you didn't get it from me."

He accepted the device, then removed his phone from his pocket.

"I don't know what Mikey told whoever beat him, but from the condition he was in, he probably confessed it all. Whatever that is. I don't think I would've survived it. I don't want to find out. You know what I'm saying?"

"Of course," Nicole agreed. Laney had been smart enough to stay out of all this. She didn't want to drag her into it now, when she was willing to try to help.

Dean took a photo of Laney's screen, presumably to avoid evidence of Laney's communication with him. For her protection.

Nicole kissed Blakely's head, the reality of Cari's situation becoming clearer. All those wealthy people had arrived in fancy cars. And one of them was using Rising Tides as a way to take advantage of young people in need of easy money. Maybe even exploiting those same people. Because who would believe Mikey or Cari over the supreme elite?

She nearly laughed at the pretention and naive presumption. Obviously anyone running on that mindset had never met her sister, or experienced the Beaumont family on a mission.

Someone somewhere was about to get an education.

DEAN BEEPED THE doors to his truck unlocked, then opened the passenger side for Nicole. He helped her remove Blakely from the sling, then tucked her into her car seat in the extended cab. Nicole seemed to be in less pain today, which was a good sign of healing and a massive weight off his chest.

Once everyone was buckled in safely, he took a beat to mentally explode over the audacity of some rich locals taking advantage of struggling youths. Why were so many people absolutely awful?

"Thinking about this company, Rising Tides?" Nicole

asked. "And how they intentionally drew young people in and exploited their need for money?"

He blew out a breath. "Yep."

She stroked a gentle hand down his arm, pulling his gaze to meet hers. "I've only been following you around for a few days, so I'm not saying I know what it's like to be you, but I think I'm beginning to understand the toll a job like this could take on someone."

He frowned, unsure where this was going.

"Before this week, I'd only seen the bits you showed me. The victories. The joy of a tough case closed. Families reunited. Bad guys busted."

He dipped his chin, wondering if she was about to pass judgment. Maybe point out something he could do better. And he knew there was plenty of room for corrections. This week had been a trial on every level. He normally worked alone. He never had to do his job while trying to keep someone else safe, definitely not two people, never a baby. Normally, it didn't feel as if the whole world was waiting for him to fulfill his promise to bring someone home safely. "It's not usually like this," he said, preparing his defense.

He started the engine and unlocked his cell phone. It was time to go. Check out the address Laney had given them. This conversation could wait.

"I should've been more patient with you before we broke up," she said.

"What?" Dean turned back to face her, chest tightening. That hadn't been the blow he'd anticipated.

"I didn't see the whole picture," she said. "I was focused on myself when I should've been focused on you, and that wasn't fair. You're always thinking of everyone else, and I let you down. I'm really sorry."

His heart swelled, relieved and grateful for words he didn't realize he'd needed to hear. They'd spoken at length the night before, but this confession meant everything. He unfastened his seat belt and reached for her, emotion tugging at his heart and squeezing his lungs.

She smiled as he closed the distance and kissed her. Her lips were soft and yielding; they parted easily as she slanted her mouth to his. Last night's kiss had been chaste and accepting, a seal on all their shared confessions. This kiss tasted like dreams and promises.

This was how things were meant to be. Him and her. Facing things together.

He longed to take her straight home. He wanted to tangle his body with hers and lose himself in her for days. Until life forced them up for air.

Blakely babbled, then squealed behind them, and Nicole broke the kiss with a laugh.

Her fingers curled against the back of his neck, tracing the hairline. She released him reluctantly, and he righted himself behind the wheel.

Unable to erase the goofy smile on his face, he focused on his phone screen. "Let's get this address plugged into the truck's GPS, then I'll forward it on to Finn. We can do a quick drive-by to check the place out before we go see Darla."

"Is Finn still at the hospital with Mikey?"

"Probably not," Dean said, checking the time on his watch. "There wouldn't have been much to do there. I'm guessing he's at the car dealership questioning Mr. Tippin by now, unless something else came up." He tapped the address into the display on the truck's dashboard and waited while the navigation system set a course.

The street grid zoomed and turned, setting a blue arrow to represent their current location and a red pin at their destination. The ocean took up half the screen. "Looks like we're headed for the coast." But not the rougher, industrial part of town. They were going to the section of Marshal's Bluff that looked like downtown, but every price tag had an extra zero. An area Dean sadly frequented during divorce and cheating-spouse cases.

He supposed that made perfect sense.

"Dean," Nicole said, leaning forward and extending a finger toward the navigation's display. "That's the car dealership."

Chapter Sixteen

Finn was on his phone outside the dealership when Dean pulled into a space beside a pair of cruisers.

"Wow." Nicole unfastened her seat belt, gaze fixed on the scene outside. "Two cruisers and a detective. Were they all here before we called?"

"Must've been," Dean said. It'd only taken them a few minutes to make the trip from Ricky Rocket's. He doubted the officers could've beaten them, unless they'd already been en route.

He settled the truck's engine and climbed out, taking a beat to make silly faces at Blakely, before freeing her from the car seat.

Nicole appeared at his side, her sling in place around her shoulder. "I've got her," she said, opening the fabric for Dean to tuck in the baby.

Finn approached next, his cell phone out of sight. "Mr. Tippin wasn't at his home when I paid a visit, and according to his employees and coworkers, he hasn't shown up here, either," he said. "Given the way this case seems to continually circle back to him, I'm going to assume the cause of Mr. Tippin's absence is directly related to Mike Litchfield's assault, and he's lying low."

"That sounds about right," Dean said. "Why the extra men? You find something?"

Finn looked toward the building, its floor-to-ceiling windows at least thirty feet high. Several vehicles inside were arranged in a semicircle while others were elevated on pedestals at different heights.

"As it turns out," Finn said, "several of the cars caught on that video Austin tracked down were purchased here. Most were sold by Mr. Tippin."

Nicole rocked gently as she stood at Dean's side. "What does that mean?"

It was a good question, one Dean had been puzzling through as well.

"We don't know yet," Finn said. "That's what we're here to find out. Come on inside." He moved slowly toward the building, speaking as he walked. "We're trying not to disrupt the business day more than necessary, assuming Mr. Tippin acted alone. Though to be honest, all these people are suspects until I can figure out who was or wasn't involved."

Dean passed his brother and grabbed the door for them to enter.

Men in suits and women in heels gathered at desks, watching the officers interview their coworkers. A couple with a double stroller peeked inside a giant SUV, discussing the benefits of style over the practicality of a minivan.

Framed photos of the staff lined a wall outside a series of offices overlooking the sales floor.

Nicole stopped beside Mr. Tippin's photo and turned to stare.

"That's him?" Dean asked.

"Yeah."

The man was in his late forties in the photo, dressed in a suit and wearing a charismatic smile.

Finn knocked lightly on the wall and angled his head toward the nearest office, directing them inside. "We're waiting for a judge to provide a search warrant so we can get a look at company files. Right now our evidence of Tippin's involvement is circumstantial, but we're trying to change that."

"Did you run a background check?" Dean asked.

Finn frowned. "Obviously."

"And?"

"Cleaner than half the Beaumont brothers."

Nicole chuckled, and Dean smiled, despite himself. He and his brothers hadn't always been who they were now.

"No priors," Finn continued. "Not even a traffic ticket. He and his wife are model citizens on paper."

Nicole stepped away from the brothers, always in motion when Blakely was in her care. She made a circuit through the room, looking carefully at each framed photo on the desk and bookshelves. "Any idea who runs Rising Tides, or if that's even a real company?"

"No, and it's not registered with the North Carolina business bureau," he said. "That's as far as I got, but it's on today's agenda."

"What about the death?" Dean asked. He'd given Finn a complete rundown of their talk with Laney on their ride over. He didn't expect his brother to have answers yet, but the question was still worth asking. If Finn needed extra hands or eyes, Austin could step in.

"That's interesting," Finn said. "I reached out to the officer who made the initial report on the body and crime scene. I was on the line with her when you arrived. An older male doctor named George Maline was found inside his car with a deadly amount of painkillers in his system. His wallet was emptied, but his Rolex was still on his wrist. And the car was worth more than my annual salary. I don't know how much cash had been inside his wallet, but I'm guessing the watch and car were of higher value."

Dean bobbed his head. "Staged robbery."

"That's my guess," Finn concurred. "Though initially it was seen as an overdose. An autopsy indicated habitual use of the same prescription."

"An addict," Nicole said. She'd heard of doctors getting hooked on pills and writing themselves prescriptions to keep the medication coming.

Finn nodded.

A female officer appeared in the doorway. "Detective?"

Finn lifted his chin in acknowledgment. "On my way."

The officer left, and Finn offered Dean a fist bump before waving goodbye to Nicole and Blakely. "Stay in touch," he said.

"Back at ya," Dean echoed.

HALF AN HOUR LATER, Nicole climbed down from Dean's truck for the third time in less than three hours, feeling the stretch and burn of her healing side, and the minor exertion of carrying Blakely in a sling all morning. The possibility of finding her sister felt closer than ever before, and she couldn't bring herself to ask for a break. She and Dean had stopped for smoothies after visiting the car dealership, so she could change Blakely and give herself a little boost.

"How are you doing?" Dean asked, beeping the truck doors locked and meeting Nicole outside Nina's, a small clothing and jewelry boutique near the bay.

The lot was full of mostly fancy cars, and the traffic predictably heavy given the season and perfect southern summer weather.

"I'm getting nervous," she admitted. "I don't want Darla to change her mind about speaking with us, and part of me wonders if she's really in there, or if she just said she would be to get us off the phone."

Dean slid an arm around her shoulders, tucking her against his side and dropping a kiss on her head. "Whatever happens, whoever's in there, or isn't, we've got this."

She exhaled a load of unwarranted panic. "Okay."

"Finn's following leads in a bunch of directions now. Anything we learn from Darla is going to be icing, but it's not the cake."

Nicole nodded, and they began to move.

Dean's arm loosened around her, but he kept a hand on her lower back, maintaining physical contact. "Remember not to ask for her," he said. "She doesn't want us to let on that we know her. She must think she's being watched."

He opened the etched-glass door, then followed her into the air-conditioned shop.

Racks of pastel tops and floral dresses were gathered around a table featuring straw hats, beach bags and flip-flops. Similar displays fanned out in both directions, showcasing jewelry, novelty items and socks. Headless mannequins on tabletops were dressed for a night on the town.

An exit sign hung over a hallway on the back wall, beside a small checkout counter and fitting rooms. A petite redhead folded clothes near the register, eyes darting repeatedly toward the front door.

"Welcome to Nina's," she said, tracking Nicole and Dean with her gaze. "Anything I can help you with?"

Nicole searched for the right words to identify herself without causing trouble, unsure the woman at the counter was even the one she'd come to talk to. "I'm looking for something for my sister," she said. "I brought her daughter to help me."

The woman stilled. She scanned the empty shop, then

lifted one of the tops she'd been folding. "What do you think of this?"

"Cute."

"Is your sister your size? I can set you up in a fitting room. You can try it on and see what you think."

Dean reached for Blakely. "Why don't I hold the princess while you do that?"

Nicole nodded anxiously, freeing her niece from the sling, then unhooking the material from around her shoulders and passing that to Dean as well. "Thanks."

Dean nodded toward the dressing rooms, and she moved slowly in the redhead's direction, feeling strangely uncertain, as if this might be a trap.

A tall blonde in platform sandals dragged a rolling rack from the hallway beneath the exit sign. She smiled at Nicole. "Finding everything okay?"

Nicole nodded. "Yep. Thank you." She stopped at the counter and selected an olive-green tank top from the stack. "May I try this one?"

The redhead straightened, a pile of similar tops strewn over one forearm. "Sure." She headed for the dressing rooms, and Nicole followed.

Her oval black name tag contained a single word in gold script letters.

Darla.

She knocked on a fitting room, then unlocked it and held the door for Nicole. "If you like that one, we carry it in multiple colors. Blue and red are both popular." She removed the top two shirts from the pile on her arm and handed them to Nicole. "Let me know if I can get you anything else or if you need a different size."

She stepped out, and the door swung shut, leaving Nicole alone in the wooden cube.

"I think you'll like the red one," Darla said, her voice projecting into the little room.

Nicole raised the item in question, and a slip of paper floated out, drifting to a stop on the bench beside a full-length mirror. "I'm trying it now," she said.

Her heartbeat raced as she collected and unfolded the paper. Her hands trembled as she read the words.

Destroy this message. Buy one of these shirts. Meet me out back.

Nicole tore the paper into bits and shoved them into her pocket, then gathered the tank tops and let herself out.

Dean leaned against the wall outside the fitting room, waiting.

"I'm going to get this tank top," Nicole said, heading to the counter. She set the green and blue options aside and pushed the red one toward the register.

The blonde met her with a smile. "Just the one?"

"Yes, please."

Nicole paid, glancing repeatedly at Darla, who didn't make eye contact again. Then she followed Dean out, passing the redhead without further comment.

Back inside the truck, he looked to Nicole, brows high. "What happened in the fitting room?"

She pulled her sunglasses from the cup holder and slid them over her eyes, still shaky from the bizarre encounter. "She gave me a note. We're supposed to meet her out back."

His lips quirked slightly as he started the engine. "Nice work."

"If I haven't expressed it before," Nicole said, voice wobbly, "I am not cut out for this. I don't know how you stay cool all the time. I'm a wreck, and nothing even happened in there. The most intense situation I can handle on a daily basis is a classroom full of eight-year-olds."

Dean grimaced. "I wouldn't survive a day like that."

She smiled as he piloted the big truck through the crowded lot and into a small alley behind the retail establishments. The lane was probably only accessed by delivery trucks and trash collectors with any kind of regularity.

He parked near a dumpster and cut the engine.

Nicole stared at the back door to Nina's, waiting for Darla to appear.

Minutes ticked by, and she didn't show.

Nicole fixed a bottle for Blakely, then watched the clock as the baby drank.

Fifteen minutes passed.

Then twenty.

Dean scanned the area on a slow visual circuit. "She might have to wait for a scheduled break."

"Then why didn't she tell me when that was?"

"She was scared," he said. "Probably not thinking clearly. I could see her uncertainly in every movement from across the store. Fidgeting, darting gaze, rushed speech. A preoccupation with the front door, as if she suspected she was being watched."

Nicole's skin crawled. "You think she was being watched?"

"I didn't see anyone, but the lot's full and traffic's heavy," he said. "My main focus was on you. As for Darla, I think she wants to talk or she wouldn't have asked us to wait out here, so as long as you and Blakely are comfortable, I say we—"

The back door to Nina's opened and Darla appeared with a small bag of trash.

Dean climbed out and closed the truck door with a barely audible click.

Nicole rushed to do the same.

Blakely was asleep and stayed that way as Nicole moved her from the car seat to the sling.

She met Dean at the truck's grille.

Darla was frozen near the dumpster, the small bag dangling from her fingertips.

"Do we approach her?" Nicole asked.

"No."

"What if she changes her mind?"

"She's come this far," he said. "Let's be patient a little longer and see what happens."

Nicole chewed her lip, knowing he was right, even if the need to act pulsed wildly through her veins.

Darla shook her head a few times, then tossed the trash into a dumpster and started moving toward the truck, a look of resolve on her thin face. "I only have a minute," she said quickly, "so I'm going to talk. You can listen, but you can't come back here or call me again."

Nicole nodded, biting her tongue to stop the tidal wave of questions.

"I'm leaving work early. I told my boss I'm sick, which isn't a complete lie. I don't know where Cari is." Her voice cracked, and her expression crumpled into distress. "I have to work a party tonight and pretend as if everything is fine so no one suspects I'm ready to crack. Dr. George is dead and my friend is missing. Things are definitely not fine, and I don't know what to do."

Dean opened his wallet and offered her a business card.

She took it. "What's this?"

"It's a ranch outside town that helps people in need and provides a place to stay while folks get through tough times. The people there will help you. They can keep you safe."

She wrapped her arms around her middle, clutching the card in one hand. "I have to keep up appearances. I think they're watching me. They know I was close with Cari and probably suspect I'll go to the police, file a report and tell them where she worked last."

"We've already done all that," Nicole said.

Darla's eyes widened. "This is why they look for people without family ties. If something goes wrong, they can keep us quiet, but not outsiders, cause y'all don't get it."

"Get what?" Nicole asked, forgetting her orders to be quiet and listen.

Darla rolled her eyes and shook her head again. "I've got to go."

"Wait! We asked about Dr. George," Nicole said.

She paused. "Was it murder?"

Dean nodded. "That's what it looks like now, thanks to your tip."

Darla swiped a tear from her cheek. "Good. He was a nice man. He deserved better than he got."

"If there's anything you can tell us, it could stop something like that from happening again," Dean said.

Nicole watched his gaze slide meaningfully to her and Blakely. The unspoken message loud and clear. Maybe, if they were lucky, Cari wouldn't turn up dead and pumped full of drugs like the doctor. Classified as another former user who backslid. Not worth the investigation.

Darla checked over both shoulders. "Okay. Here's how it is. The ladies are just eye candy," she said, shifting foot to foot as if she wanted to run. "We dress up and serve partygoers drinks and hors d'oeuvres from trays. We're paid to mingle and be nice. The guests are mostly rich men. We're allowed to stop work and be alone with guests anytime we want, but we don't have to. The hosts spend all night trying to get guests to invest cash in the company and buy high-end cars. If that doesn't work, they blackmail them with images taken during the night, usually of the men with servers who don't look like servers. We're told that this is all acceptable because the money is used to keep the business going, which means more jobs for us. If the men like the servers, they sometimes offer them nice white-collar jobs at their offices, or make them personal assistant at their massive homes."

She swallowed, looking a little ill. "That's all I know. Except that once in a while, if one of the guests complains about a server, she never comes back. I assumed in the past that meant she was fired. Now I don't know."

"Thank you," Nicole said. She looked to Dean to be sure they had enough information.

He nodded. "I meant what I said about the ranch. I can call ahead and let them know you're coming. They're good people."

"No one's good people," she said, then she turned and jogged away, bypassing the shop and slipping into the shadowy space between stores, heading for the main parking lot out front.

Nicole watched her go. "Should we follow her home for her safety?"

Dean considered. "Maybe. I don't think she'd notice my tail, but if she's right about being watched, that person likely would notice. I don't want to make things worse instead of better."

Nicole's heart leaped as another thought crashed into her mind. "We should've asked where the party was tonight." She grabbed Dean's hand and started for the alley.

Darla was on the sidewalk out front when they entered the walkway between buildings.

The rumble of an engine rose on the air as Darla stepped onto the little parking lot road outside her store.

Nicole fell still as a squeal of tires and streak of blackness collided with Darla, throwing her small body up and over the hood. She crashed, lifeless, onto the tire marks left behind by the sleek black sedan.

Chapter Seventeen

Dean scrubbed a hand over his hair, stunned and gut-wrenched by the horrific scene before him.

A young woman was dead, and he hadn't been able to save her. He'd raced to her and performed chest compressions until the first responders arrived, but he'd known it was a work in futility. He'd just kept hoping he was wrong.

Nicole sat several yards away now, in Dean's truck, beneath the shade of a tree. Tears tracked down her cheeks as she entertained Blakely with a stuffed pony.

Half the available Marshal's Bluff police force was visible in the space around the tire tracks and collision site. Thankfully, the coroner had been efficient at the scene and quickly removed Darla's body from public view. A report would be available soon, but Dean didn't need anyone to tell him what had killed her. He'd never forget those details. What he wanted to know was who.

Members of the strip mall's security team assisted officers in interviewing bystanders. A few had glimpsed the event from start to finish, but many more had seen or heard the car as it raced away. Security footage from the stores was already under review.

Finn moseyed in Dean's direction, surveying the area as

he made his way to the sidewalk. "Well, this has been a long and increasingly awful day."

Dean dropped his hands to his sides, then braced them on his hips, aching to be useful in some way that would end the reign of terror in his town. "Any luck identifying the car or driver?"

"Maybe. Security footage confirmed the make and model match the sedan that tailed you. There's front-end damage now, so the owner will be looking to get that repaired. We've already contacted all the local body shops and provided a heads-up. If a car fitting that description comes in for work, they're to accept and keep it, then notify the police. We've also got the dealership's garage under surveillance, since so many threads are already leading back there."

Dean grimaced, unsure how useful the surveillance team really was. Officers had been watching Mikey's home and work, but that hadn't stopped him from being beaten nearly to death outside the pizzeria. All it took was a few minutes of distraction, accidental sleep or a changing shift for something to go irrevocably wrong. "How's Mikey doing?" he asked, fearing whoever had hospitalized him and killed Darla might want to finish the job.

"He's stable now," Finn said. "Swelling's coming down in his brain and on his face. The internal bleeding was stopped, and the rest of his injuries are cast and bandaged. He's got a few broken fingers and ribs. Fractures on both hands and his clavicle. He put up one hell of a fight from the looks of it. Austin's with him and keeping me updated after each set of rounds."

Knowing Austin was with Mikey went a long way toward easing Dean's concerns. "Have you learned anything more about Rising Tides?"

Finn blew out a long, weary breath, looking a decade older

than his years. "I think the whole thing was a front. My best guess is the investment money goes straight to some offshore account. There's no evidence of any company by that name in North Carolina, and the handful of similarly named businesses in other states are either defunct or have legitimate storefronts with specific purposes. One in California is a surf shop. Another in Maine sells boating and fishing equipment. In this town, on the other hand, it seems the name was just made up for the sake of hiring clueless workers and duping investors." He squinted against the sun, frowning deeply at the growing crowd of curious onlookers. "The Dr. Maline robbery case is being reopened as a murder investigation."

Dean's brows twitched, surprise and approval swirled in his mind. "That's good." And fast. Things involving the legal system didn't typically happen this quickly, but given the circumstances, he was glad to hear the powers that be were cooperating.

"A brief look into Dr. Maline's financials revealed monthly cash withdrawals for the past seventeen months. He'd all but eviscerated his funds about a month before his death. Assuming those withdrawals were blackmail payoffs, whoever had been the recipient likely burned him when the well ran dry. No reason to leave a man with nothing to lose alive. He might've finally gone to the police."

Dean grunted, hating that Cari had gotten involved with this group, whoever they were. His fear for her life grew exponentially with each passing second.

The gruesome thoughts were likely on Nicole's mind as well. His attention returned to her and Blakely. He couldn't help Cari yet, but he could take care of her daughter and sister. "I'm going to drive the ladies home," he told Finn. "It's hot, and this has been a terrible day."

"Stay in touch," Finn said. He offered his fist, and the two exchanged a short series of taps that had become a private handshake when they were younger. The gesture was surprisingly comforting now. A reminder that the Beaumonts got through everything that came at them. And they got through it together.

NICOLE CURLED ONTO the sofa at Dean's place that night, legs pulled up to her chest, chin resting on her knees. She'd soaked in his tub after Blakely went to sleep; fatigue and steaming water had slowly cleared her mind and relaxed her tense muscles. She'd never forget the things she'd seen that afternoon, but a long bath and the cool night air were working wonders to keep her mind still and calm. For that she was immeasurably thankful.

Dean had opened the windows, thinking the night air would help her sleep, and she couldn't disagree. Something about the gentle breeze drifting through the curtains was incredibly soothing to her nerves. And she suspected Dean missed being outside.

Cari's disappearance had kept him on the job nonstop for days, when he'd normally have gone fishing or hiking or spent time on the family ranch. He was an outdoorsman and a cowboy by nature and nurture, not someone who could be cooped up long without going stir-crazy.

He'd been living outside his comfort zone for Nicole without a single complaint.

"Thirsty?" He appeared barefoot before her in pale gray sweatpants and a white cotton T-shirt, a glass of cold water in each hand. His brown hair was dark and wet from the shower. Familiar scents of his soap and shampoo sent a tingle down her spine.

It was beyond unfair that the sight of him still did that to her. She missed him in ways she couldn't begin to describe.

"How's your side feel?" he asked, scanning her as he passed her a drink. "Can I get you anything for the pain?"

She set her glass on the coffee table, then she lifted the side of her shirt to reveal her fresh bandage. "It's healing. No signs of redness, swelling or infection, and I hurt less today than yesterday. I took more painkillers while you were in the shower."

"May I?" he asked, lifting a hand toward her raised shirt.

"Yeah."

He drifted careful fingers along the exposed skin of her side, brow furrowed, expression tight. "I hate that this happened to you."

"I know." She shivered at the sensation of his touch, wishing he'd come closer, take her into his arms and make her forget about the ugliness of their day.

His Adam's apple bobbed, and his eyes flashed with heat, as if he'd somehow read her mind. He pulled his hand away and straightened, allowing her shirt to fall back into place. "Did I hear the phone ring while I was in the shower?"

She nodded, embarrassed by her need. Thankful he couldn't read her mind. "Yeah. Our moms called. Mom made it to the ranch and had a late dinner with your folks. She wanted to see Blakely tonight, but she'd already fallen asleep, so I told Mom about our day and promised we'd come for breakfast in the morning."

"Sounds like a plan. I'm glad she made it."

"Me, too." Nicole's stomach clenched at the thought of seeing her mother. She missed her terribly, and felt guilty for putting her off, but it'd been a long week. Nicole had to be the strong one whenever her mother was upset, but she couldn't do that tonight.

"I was thinking," Dean said, his voice soft and casual. "It might be best to leave Blakely at the ranch tomorrow instead of taking her with us again. Truthfully, I think you should consider staying there, too. It's the safest place for you both, and having you there will be an incredible comfort to your mother."

Nicole turned on the cushion, dropping her knees and facing him. "What if I want to stay with you?" she asked. The unintentionally deeper meaning lowered her voice.

Surprise flickered over Dean's expression, widening his eyes and lifting his brows for an instant before he hid it away.

She wanted to stay with Dean long after Cari was found and this nightmare ended. She wanted to make up for leaving him when she should've been there for him, and she wanted to make up for lost time. Because since the moment she'd first met Dean Beaumont, her heart and soul had belonged to him and him alone.

"If you stay with me, I'll protect you and care for you as long as you want to be here," he said.

Her heart thundered and her breath caught.

A look of torture tightened his jaw. "We should probably talk about some things when this is over and Cari is home," he said slowly. "Emotions are high right now, and you're going through more than anyone ever should. I don't want to add to that. And I don't want to make assumptions. I just want to be here for you."

Nicole inched closer, struggling to find her voice. She wanted him to make assumptions. To make a move. To read her mind.

She wanted him to want her. "You don't mind me being here?"

"No." Dean's voice was low as he lifted her hand in his and pressed her palm against his chest. "You've always been right here."

A small gasp parted her lips as his eyes searched hers.

Slowly, he erased the remaining distance between them, cupping her face in his hands and guiding her mouth to his. The press of their lips and tangling of their breaths sent a rush of bliss from her core.

Memories of a thousand shared moments like this one whirled in her heart and head. Dean was her safe place. Her emotional haven and physical comfort. He was her perfect match in every way, and she wanted him back, body and soul.

"Dean," she whispered, head falling back as he dragged his mouth down the column of her throat. "Touch me."

He wrapped big hands around her hips and lifted her onto his lap, her thighs bracketing his. Rough palms slid beneath the hem of her shirt, long fingers curving over her ribs. The pads of his thumbs brushed the sensitive undersides of her bare breasts, and she was never so thankful to have skipped a bra with her pajamas.

Dean's deep moan of pleasure quickly became a growl as the material shifted higher, exposing her fully. His hungry gaze climbed to meet hers, and she smiled.

A curse slid from his mouth as he splayed one hand across her back and lowered his lips to one taut nipple. He teased and lavished her with nips and sucks until a deep ache formed between her thighs.

The cool night breeze arched her back and pulled her skin into a cascade of goose bumps. A delicious contrast to the heat of his hands and mouth. And Nicole wanted more.

She tugged restlessly at his shirt, desperate to remove the barriers between them.

He released her, reluctantly, and freed them both of their shirts in seconds.

Then he dragged the pad of one thumb across her kiss-swollen lips, then studied her bare, flushed breasts with reverence. Indecision warred on his brow.

"Dean," she whispered, gripping his chin and locking him in her stare. She slowly rocked her hips against the hard length of him. "Take me to bed."

His hands were on her backside in a heartbeat, gripping her to him and rising in one fluid movement, taking her with him as he stood. "Are you sure this is what you want?" he asked, voice husky with desire, eyes patient and kind.

"I want you," she answered. "Only you. Always you."

His mouth twisted into the smug, satisfied grin she loved, and his mouth met hers once more as he carried her to his room.

Chapter Eighteen

Nicole woke the next morning wrapped in Dean's arms. His long, lean body was pressed to hers. Their legs tangled beneath a single sheet. Fresh summer air drifted through his bedroom curtains.

"Morning," he said, trailing kisses over her forehead and temple, cheek and jaw. His arms tightened gently, gathering her closer.

She twined their fingers and nuzzled against him. "I don't want to leave this bed or this room," she said. "Or this moment."

He rolled her onto her back and hovered over her, dotting her nose and each corner of her mouth with more light kisses.

She squeezed her eyes shut, pushing away thoughts of a new day and the troubles awaiting them outside the blissful bubble.

Dean gathered her wrists in his hands and stretched her arms above her head. His eyes skimmed her body, and he lowered his mouth to her shoulder.

Maybe she could ignore the day a little while longer.

His phone rang, and he lifted his face to frown in the device's direction.

She smiled while he seemed to consider whether or not to answer.

Eventually, he sat back on his heels, taking the sheet with him. His eyes skimmed her fully exposed body. "Life is truly unfair."

"Truly," she agreed.

The phone rang again, and he reached for it with a sigh. "It's Mama."

Blakely fussed a moment later, and Nicole grabbed one of Dean's shirts on the way to soothe her, dressing as she went.

No more life in a bubble.

Blakely was awake in her portable crib, kicking her feet and cooing at dust motes on sunbeams when Nicole arrived.

"Hello, sweet baby girl," Nicole said, pulling her niece into her arms. "I bet you're ready to get changed and have a little breakfast. What do you say?"

She combed Blakely's hair into its usual tiny ponytail on top and selected a flowing A-line tank top with spaghetti straps and layers of lavender ruffles that emphasized her round little belly. Paired with matching stretchy bike shorts, she was the definition of adorable.

Nicole was sure Dean's mama was calling about breakfast. Her mother was likely eager to see her granddaughter, and Nicole couldn't make her wait a second longer than necessary. She also agreed with his declaration from the previous night. Blakely would be safer on the ranch than staying with Dean and Nicole. Too many people were getting hurt now. She couldn't allow her niece to become one of them.

Nicole raked a brush through her thick waves and pulled them into a ponytail. She dressed in jean shorts and a faded Marshal's Bluff Athletics T-shirt. The outfit was cute and comfortable, which was perfect, because assuming the last few days were anything to go by, there was another long day ahead. But at least, whatever came, she would be with Dean.

"Nicole." Her name rose on his voice through the air, and

the fine hair on her neck and arms stood at attention. She gathered Blakely to her and hurried in the direction of the sound.

"Yeah?"

His expression was hard, and he held his cell phone on one palm. "I've got Finn on speaker. She's here," he said, glancing at the device. "Go on."

Nicole's muscles tightened and her stomach coiled. Was this the moment she learned Cari had been found, and she wasn't okay? Were they too late, like Dean had been while searching for eight-year-old Ben Smothers?

"Morning, Nicole," Finn said. "I'm just providing an update. No real news just yet."

Her shoulders drooped, and she heaved a ragged sigh. "Okay," she croaked. "Thank you."

"I secured a warrant to search all records at the auto dealership," he said. "That hit-and-run motivated the judge, so I'm taking some officers with me to get started right away. Also, one of the men working in the garage lied about where he was on the night of the party, which garnered my interest. A background check came back dirty. Criminal past, gang affiliations in Charlotte, and no friends I could find among his coworkers. He worked exclusively on all Tippin's cars, and Tippin's clients' cars. The clients asked for him by name when they needed service, which wasn't company policy, more like grace offered to the dealership's biggest seller. Now that we've established a relationship between the two men, we're looking for the mechanic. His name is Joseph Knolls. We think he might also be the driver of the black sedan that hit Darla and chased you guys."

Nicole watched Dean's face for clues on how to interpret Finn's news, but Dean's expression was flat. "What does this mean?" she asked. Bigger questions mounted with each new heartbeat. Would they find Cari when they found Knolls?

Did they know where to look? What exactly had the man's criminal past involved? Was he violent? Did he hurt women?

"It means I think this is the lead we needed to break the case. I think Knolls knows where the Tippins are hiding and what happened to your sister."

Dean pulled the phone closer to his mouth. "We're headed to the ranch to see Nicole's mom. She made it into town last night. Where will you be in an hour or so?" His gaze lifted to meet Nicole's.

"Likely at the dealership. Give me a call when you leave the ranch. And Nicole?"

She looked to the phone. "Yeah?"

"We're getting close."

THE BEAUMONT RANCH was a few miles outside town, located on more than one hundred acres of land passed down through the family for generations. From what Nicole had been told, the place was even larger once, but fringe acreage had been sold off in parcels over the years, especially during hard times, to keep the ranch up and running. Other portions had long ago been given to extended family members as wedding gifts, but those plots had been sold and resold to owners who likely had no idea the family who'd originally owned them was still thriving next door.

Dean turned onto the long gravel lane that led to the ranch. His family's name was branded into a massive slab of wood fastened to the wrought iron gate. Nicole's lips curved into a smile as they bounced along the gently pitted path toward Dean's childhood home.

Their mothers rose from rocking chairs on the wide wraparound porch, heading for the steps before the truck was parked. Both women wore jeans and tennis shoes with untucked T-shirts and tired smiles.

Dean stopped the truck in a wide space meant for turn-arounds, and Nicole climbed out, suddenly desperate to get her arms around her mother. She hoped she wouldn't be disappointed that Nicole had let something bad happen to her sister.

"Honey!" Nicole's mom pulled her into a tight embrace, tears streaming. "I'm so sorry you've been going through this alone," she said, stepping back to look into her eyes. "I should've been here."

"I wasn't alone," Nicole said, hoping to put her mom's concern at ease. "I've been with Dean, and his brothers are helping every day. You came as soon as you could. How are Grandma and Grandpa?"

"Fine." Her mom sniffled, shame and guilt clouding her face. She was otherwise beautiful and lithe with the same dark curls, brown eyes and dusting of freckles as her daughters and granddaughter. In many ways it was like looking into a mirror for Nicole, except there were creases on her mother's face that hadn't yet appeared on her own.

"I love you," her mother whispered, snapping Nicole's gaze back to hers. "I don't say that enough. Spending all this time with my parents has made me realize a few things. One of those is how much I love you girls. Another is how much I relied on you when things were tough with Cari, then the divorce, and that was wrong of me." She slid her soft palms to Nicole's cheeks. "I'm sorry for every moment you felt abandoned by me, or as if you needed to be strong for me. That was never your role to play."

Tears blurred Nicole's eyes, sliding hot and fast over her cheeks as she hugged her mom again. She hadn't known how much she'd needed to hear those words until they were presented. "I love you, too."

Blakely squealed with glee, and the sound broke them apart. Nicole's mother laughed nervously, then kissed her cheek and turned to Mrs. Beaumont, who'd collected Blakely from her car seat.

"Lucky grandma," Mrs. Beaumont said. "You only have two girls, and you already got a grandbaby. I've got five boys," she said, tossing a mischievous look in Dean's direction. "And not a single one of these." She nuzzled her nose against Blakely's neck, causing a sharp squeal of delight. "It doesn't seem fair."

Nicole's mom pulled Blakely into her arms with gentle care, as if she were the most precious thing on earth.

A tangible connection to her own missing child.

Mrs. Beaumont clapped her hands. "Hope y'all are hungry. We've been cooking all morning." She looped one arm through Dean's and the other through Nicole's. "Let's go. There's plenty for everyone."

Nicole's mom followed, snuggling Blakely tight.

Dean stayed at Nicole's side throughout the meal, a hand on her back, fingers grazing her hip or curled over her knee beneath the table.

As if the connection they'd made last night had meant as much to him as it had to her. And just for the moment, she let herself hope.

Chapter Nineteen

Dean took Nicole's hand as they left Blakely and their moms on the porch after breakfast. He didn't miss his mama's prideful, cat-that-ate-the-canary grin as she watched him reach for Nicole. And he hadn't been able to quash his echoing smile as Nicole accepted his touch, folding their fingers easily together.

Nicole's reunion with her mother had been hard on her; it was written on her face beneath the smile. In the set of her jaw and pinch of her lips. She'd likely internalized Cari's situation as her fault somehow, though she logically knew better. That was any decent sibling's cross to bear. An unspoken, deeply rooted acceptance of responsibility. Dean had been glad to hear her mom tell her this situation wasn't her fault, but the words hadn't stuck. Nicole had been the strong one in their family for too long, and it would take time to ease that burden.

He could also see that walking away from her hurting mother right now was hard. Her every instinct probably told her to stay and provide comfort. And leaving Blakely was one more heart-wrenching choice. Cari had asked Nicole to care for her baby. But the weight of the week had taken its toll, and Dean knew she needed space and time more than she needed to continue giving bits of herself to others. So he ushered her along, hoping she wouldn't change her mind.

Everyone needed a break and a safe place to recuperate.

He wanted to be that place for her.

She was silent as they buckled up inside the truck and pulled away from the ranch.

Soon Dean navigated the desolate country roads on autopilot. His mind was back in the homey farmhouse kitchen his mama adored. Sharing a meal with Nicole and her mom had been a more emotional experience than he'd anticipated. They'd shared dozens of meals like that one in the past, often with his father and brothers as well, but everything had been different this time. Not just the specific circumstances, but the fact that their time together was limited. If he didn't convince her to give him another chance, he could lose her for good. The possibility twisted his gut.

Beside him, Nicole unearthed her phone and tapped the screen. A minute later, Cari's voice arrived through the speaker. Nicole replayed the video her sister had sent for Blakely on the night she'd disappeared.

"They're all wearing black dresses," Nicole whispered. "Just like Darla said." She turned to face him, and her gaze heated his cheek. "If that guy would run her down in cold blood like that, in the middle of the day, outside a store, what's he been doing to my sister all this time?" Her voice cracked, and he reached for her again.

"Hey," he said, covering her free hand with his. "We're going to find her."

"How do you know?"

He didn't, and statistically, things didn't look good, but Cari was tough and resilient. Those qualities would serve her well. And he wasn't willing to break Nicole's heart as long as there was still room for hope. "You heard Finn this morning," he said instead. "He's close. So we're going to hang in there just a little while longer before we start letting panic sound the alarm bells."

She nodded and broke their connection to wipe beneath her eyes.

Dean pressed the button on his steering wheel to make a phone call, shaking off the nonsensical sting of rejection. "Call Finn."

"Calling Finn," the automated female voice responded.

Nicole played Cari's video again, her sister's happy voice sounding against the background of fellow waitstaff chatter and the echo of closing car doors. "She's got the frame so tight on her face, I can't tell where she was," Nicole complained. "We saw a shuttle drop her off at the Tippins' place. This is somewhere else. Where?"

"Hello, brother," Finn said, his words arriving through the truck's speakers. "How was breakfast?"

Nicole looked to the dashboard. "Hi, Finn," she answered.

"Breakfast was good," Dean added. "Any news?"

"Hey, Nicole. Nothing solid yet, but my gut says something's about to give."

Dean grunted, feeling much the same, but unsure why, specifically.

"What are you guys up to?" Finn asked.

"We're just leaving the ranch," Dean said. "Where are you?"

"Headed back to the dealership. I just left tech services. They're deep into Cari's phone. She didn't have tracking engaged, so they're concentrating on her contacts, recent communication and social media connections."

"Nicole's watching that good-night video Cari sent Blakely," Dean said.

As if on cue, Nicole's fingers curled over his arm.

A single glance in her direction told him something had happened. Her eyes were wide, her lips parted. She'd paused the video and held the phone near her ear. "You okay?" he asked, unsure what he'd missed.

"I think I hear an alarm," she said.

Dean frowned.

"What?" Finn asked.

Nicole held her phone closer to Dean's and played the video again. "Ignore Cari and listen to the other girls' laughter."

Dean's foot eased off the gas, attention hyper-focused on the background noises.

It was barely there, but it was something. A buzzer?

"What is it?" Finn asked. "Play it again."

Nicole moved her phone toward the dashboard and played it again.

"That's the drawbridge alarm," Finn said. "Change of plans. Meet me down there. I'll call Kim in tech and tell her to isolate the sound in case we're wrong, then I'll ask if they've found anything else on the phone to suggest Cari spent time in that area during the days or weeks before her disappearance."

"There are a lot of warehouses near the water," Dean said. "Would be a good place for the servers to meet up and catch the shuttle."

"Agreed," Finn said. "Nice work, Nicole. See y'all in a few."

The call disconnected, and Nicole flopped back in her seat, hugging her phone to her chest.

They zipped along the outskirts of town toward the bay, taking back roads to avoid stoplights and traffic. The silence between them was charged with anticipation, and their fingers were twined on the seat between them. Whatever happened, they were in this together, and he'd be here for her however he could. For as long as she'd allow him.

The pretty rural scenery quickly morphed into the battered gray of the waterfront, where fields and farmland were swapped for business parks and concrete. Clouds blocked the morning sunshine, reflecting their dreariness onto the water.

They slowed when the drawbridge came into view, and an unpleasant sense of foreboding slithered into his core.

Beside him, Nicole played the video again.

They drove through every parking lot and alley within earshot of the drawbridge alarm, searching for Cari's missing car, or a reasonable place to stash it. Someplace the servers would meet up and wait for their ride. Maybe even a sign with the words *Rising Tides*.

The truck crawled past a row of triple-stacked shipping containers along the waterfront, waiting to be moved or packed. A motionless barge floated just offshore.

"Look," Nicole whispered, turning the phone to Dean. She'd paused the video again and zoomed in on the space above Cari's shoulder. The edge of a rust-colored building or possibly a shipping container. The tip of a blue streak visible. Maybe the work of a street artist or more of the area's abundant graffiti.

The containers beside them showed no signs of spray paint.

"What is it?" he asked, unsure what to make of the unidentified corner.

"Train car?"

It only took a moment for Dean to process the words and perform a smooth three-point turn in the narrow alley. Then they were headed north, away from the drawbridge by another block, moving swiftly toward the tracks.

His phone rang, and Finn's name appeared on the dashboard screen.

Dean pressed the button to answer.

"I've got something," Finn said, foregoing a greeting. "A picture sent to Cari from several weeks ago had a geotag. Looks like it was taken at a warehouse near the train tracks."

Dean exchanged a look with Nicole, who'd gone still at his side. "We're on it," Dean said. "Meet us there?"

"Already on my way."

The call disconnected as a pint-sized metal building with several parking spaces and roll-up garage doors came into view. The structure was across from the tracks and positioned in the shadows of multiple larger buildings.

The black entry door had two words painted on the security window.

Rising Tides.

NICOLE SHOOK AS she jumped down from Dean's cab, unsure what to say to whoever was inside the building. Would the people here run away like Mikey had? Would they lie like the Tippins? Or try to hurt her and Dean the way the driver of the black sedan had hurt Darla?

Dean met her at the truck's hood and reached for her hand.

Something in the unseasonably cool air and mass of ominous clouds set her intuition on high alert, making her doubly glad Blakely wasn't with them now.

They paused before the door, and Dean tried the knob. When the knob didn't turn, he rang the buzzer.

No one answered, so he knocked.

Then he pounded.

"Hello?" he called.

Nicole jumped at the sudden, deep and authoritative boom of his voice.

He grinned down at her, then released her hand. "Stay right here."

He jogged the few feet to his truck and came back with his lock-picking tools. "Finn's on the way, so I have to hurry."

Nicole watched as he selected two pieces from the small leather pouch, then got to work.

A moment later, Dean turned the knob, and the door opened.

He raised an arm in front of her before she could step inside. He tipped his finger to his lips, warning her to be quiet. "Hello?" he called, projecting his voice inside.

The deep tenor echoed through the cavernous interior, and a soft shuffling sound returned on the breeze.

Nicole raised her brows. Was someone hiding inside? Was Cari tied up and held captive?

Dean stepped forward, tucking Nicole behind him. "Marshal's Bluff Police," he called.

Nicole gave his arm a reproachful shove. Impersonating an officer was a major offense.

He shrugged, then took her hand and moved inside, leaving the door open behind them.

Several silent steps later, the short, narrow walkway opened into a vast, dimly lit space. The shuttle from the video came into view several yards away. The same ride that had delivered Cari to the Tippins' home.

Beside it stood Cari's car.

The sound of an approaching vehicle outside the open door sent Dean against the wall, pulling her with him. Together, they waited, motionless and watching the lot outside.

A moment later, Finn's cruiser pulled into the spot beside Dean's truck.

He climbed out with a frown, then marched inside, head shaking at the sight of them. "What are you two doing in here?"

"Door was open," Dean said, straight-faced and voice level.

Nicole averted her gaze.

"Uh-huh." Finn glanced back at the door's knob and dead bolt, frown deepening. "What'd you find?"

"This is as far as we got," Dean said, "but there's a lot to see so far."

Finn followed them to the end of the hall, and his gaze jumped to the vehicles on the warehouse floor. "Cari's car?"

Nicole nodded, still shocked by the vehicle's presence. She hoped it was a sign they'd soon find Cari as well.

She moved with the Beaumonts as they closed in on the parked shuttle and car.

A small office with a large window looked over the wide-open floor. A desk, computer and filing cabinets were visible through the glass.

Finn called dispatch as they walked, reporting the findings and requesting his team's immediate presence.

Nicole's heart thrummed with anticipation, and Dean's grip on her hand tightened in response. Someone had busted the driver's-side window, scattering fragments of glass over the warehouse floor.

Dean dug his phone from one pocket and accessed the device's flashlight app. He shone the beam into the car.

There weren't any signs of Cari or her things inside. Only Blakely's empty car seat.

Finn tucked his phone away. "The team's en route. Try not to touch anything." He pulled a set of blue gloves from his pocket and passed one to Dean. "We're going to have to share." They each pulled a glove over their right hand.

"I can look through Cari's car," Nicole suggested. "No glove necessary. My prints are probably on everything in there already."

"It's still a crime scene," Finn said. "You can look, but try not to touch. Use your phone's light. Take pictures, make mental notes. Talk to the team when they get here about anything that strikes you as odd or wrong."

Finn turned toward the office thirty feet away. "I'm starting in there."

Dean hovered, staring into the thick line of shadows against a nearby wall, then scanning the warehouse from top to bottom, paying careful attention to the catwalk overhead and a door on the rear wall. "When the team arrives, they'll break up and check every inch of this place. I'd say this is ground zero."

Nicole trembled.

Dean gave the larger scene another cursory look. "It's a clean warehouse. Probably just used to store the transport vehicle and possibly the waitstaff's cars while they're at a gig. It shouldn't be too hard to find out who owns or leases the space. And any evidence uncovered here won't have been exposed to the elements or a lot of people, which means the findings will be less contaminated."

His phone rang, and he turned it over in his hand while Nicole peered into the car. "Hey, Austin," he said. "Get down to the tracks by the drawbridge."

Nicole's spirits lifted by a measure. The Beaumonts were circling the wagons. They were closer to finding Cari than they'd ever been, or at least finding the person responsible for her absence. Finn and Dean were on-site already, with Austin and members of the Marshal's Bluff PD on the way.

Lights flipped on inside the small office across the large space, where Finn opened filing cabinet drawers and riffled through the contents.

Dean moved back toward the small hallway and open warehouse door. "No," he said. "We're on the north end."

Nicole circled to the other side of the car, keeping both Beaumonts in her sights, then she opened the passenger door, not wanting to disturb the broken glass.

She illuminated her phone's light and squatted outside the open door, peering under the passenger seat for clues.

The distant creak of metal turned her head as a heavy hand clamped over her mouth. The oddly familiar scent, which she now recognized as motor oil, lodged in her nose, and a knife pressed against her throat.

"If you want to see your sister alive, you're coming with me," he whispered, already pulling her away from Cari's car and into the shadows.

Chapter Twenty

Dean gave Austin directions to the little warehouse tucked among the much larger ones, keeping one eye on Nicole in case she needed him. Seeing her sister's car had likely upset her more than she let on, but he didn't want to press. There was much work to be done.

She rounded the silver compact to the far side and opened the passenger door, crouching low. The light from her phone flashed on. Maybe she was truly inspecting the vehicle, but Dean suspected it was her way of gaining a little space as well.

Austin arrived a moment later, taking his time to climb down from his truck and meet Dean at the open warehouse door.

Cari's car door was still open, Nicole still out of sight as he led Austin to the small office on the opposite side of the warehouse.

Dean itched to go to her when she didn't pop up to greet Austin. He stared at the car, willing her to call to him, not wanting to intrude.

"Y'all are going to want to take a look at this," Finn said.

Dean and Austin pushed through the office door in single file.

Finn was on the phone with a smug grin. "Send a tow

truck," he said, one finger pointed to a set of computer screens on the corner of the desk.

A black-and-white image of the Charger that had hit and killed Darla sat in a parking lot monitored by the camera. The same car that had chased him, Nicole and Blakely.

The satisfied look on his brother's face spread to Dean as well. He poked his head through the doorway to the area beyond. This was a good enough reason to interrupt Nicole.

He projected his voice into the cavernous space. "Nicole!"

"I wonder why he didn't he park the car inside?" Austin asked. "If he brought it here to hide it, why leave it in the lot?"

Dean stared into the warehouse that suddenly felt much larger and more ominous than before. The absence of movement and absolute lack of response from Nicole echoed all around them. Then he dragged his attention back to the security monitor.

Joseph Knolls hadn't pulled his car inside yet, because they'd arrived and interrupted him.

Nicole appeared on the small screen, being dragged across the lot at knifepoint.

NICOLE'S CHEST ACHED with every ragged breath, the knife scraping at her throat as they moved through the rear lot. She longed to scream, to fight, to let him cut her throat right there and take her chances at survival when emergency responders arrived.

But her abductor had mentioned Cari.

He knew where she was, and though she might already be dead, and he could be a liar, there wasn't any choice to make. If there was a chance that leaving with him meant seeing Cari again, she had to go. Because maybe she could help her.

She squinted against the assaulting outdoor light and struggled to keep pace with her attacker.

Trickles of wet heat rolled over the column of her throat. Sweat or blood, she wasn't sure. The knife was sharp, and their jagged, uncoordinated movements could easily send the blade into her skin. It'd happened before.

He lowered the knife to adjust his hold on her, and she nearly doubled over in relief. "Drop the cell phone. Now."

He pressed the button on a key fob, unlocking the doors of his car, and yanked the phone from her stiff wooden fingers when she didn't comply. Then he shoved her toward a familiar black sedan.

Her stomach pitted and lurched.

It was the car she'd seen kill Darla, the front light still broken from where her body had collided with the plastic. Images of the hit-and-run sent splinters of ice through Nicole's veins as he opened the driver's side-door and shoved her inside.

"Move," he barked. "Get into the passenger seat." He locked the doors and took up position behind the wheel.

The car peeled backward before she could get seated, and in her side-view mirror, three outraged Beaumonts raced into the lot too late, guns drawn.

The man beside her snickered. He wore baggy jeans and brown work boots, mostly unlaced and dark with oil. A gray T-shirt underscored his scowl. He appeared to be in his late thirties, with a scar running across his forehead and through one eyebrow. Heavy acne scars marred his cheeks.

She would never forget his face, and she committed every detail to memory in case she lived to describe it.

The needle on the dashboard climbed with their increasing speed, and she worked to fasten her seat belt before he jammed the brakes and threw her into the windshield.

He tore around corners, taking a nonsensical path away from the warehouse and waterfront. Making it harder for anyone to follow.

Then they were on the highway, flying over the bridge and looking down on the section of town where they'd just been.

A line of police cruisers stormed the area below, lights blazing.

But she was already gone.

"Are you taking me to my sister?" Nicole asked, forcing the words up a shrinking windpipe. Fear, trauma and distress lightened her head and tilted the car beneath her.

He didn't respond.

She tested her seat belt, unsure what he might do to her while driving and not wanting to find out. She rested her palm over the button to unlatch her restraint, guarding it as she spoke again. "Are you taking me to Cari? Are you the one who took her from the Tippins' house?"

His jaw tensed, the only indication that he'd heard her. A suggestion she'd hit a nerve.

"Please tell me about my sister," she asked, carefully. "Is she okay? Where did you take her? Is that where we're going?"

"Shut. Up." His teeth snapped over each word, lips curled back in a snarl.

Nicole bit her tongue, stomach clenched and toes curled in terror. She watched the passing exit signs and the clock, calculating the amount of miles and minutes that passed.

Too much and too many.

Memories of Darla's confession rushed into her mind, along with the Tippins' absence. If the car salesman was the leader of this crime ring, was his mechanic just the muscle? Was it possible the man beside her was also a victim somehow? Maybe being blackmailed, too? It seemed possible that Knolls could be a pawn in Tippin's awful game.

She could only imagine what kind of information Tippin must have on someone to make them do the things Knolls had done.

"Does Mr. Tippin make you do this so his hands stay clean?" she asked. The words were out of her mouth before she thought better of them. "Does he force you to do his grunt work while he and his wife run off and hide?" Days' worth of anger, frustration and fear attached themselves to each syllable, making her tone unintentionally snide and condescending.

"What did you say?" His face jerked in her direction as he raced along the highway, yanking the steering wheel left, then right with barely a glance. The Charger flew in and out of lanes, barely missing a hatchback and cutting off a semitruck.

Nicole's hands curled around her safety belt. She straightened in her seat, prepared for the inevitable crash and hoping she'd survive it. Though surviving seemed unlikely at 120 miles per hour with nothing but pavement, large moving vehicles and a concrete divide to stop them.

"I'm no one's errand boy," he seethed. "We're partners. He couldn't do his job without me. I'm the one who makes everything possible."

"By everything you mean the blackmail, abduction and murder?" Nicole asked, all sense of self-preservation having gone completely out the window. Anger welled in her. If death was imminent, she at least wanted one answer. "Where is my sister?" she screamed.

He cut through multiple lanes, cruising at top speed to an off-ramp and earning a series of outraged honks from drivers behind them.

"I should've asked where Mr. Tippin told you to take her," she said, tired of being the victim and desperate to hurt him in some small way for all the pain he'd already caused her. "You don't need to lie to me. The police have already seen the files. Talked to everyone at the dealership, too. Darla and Mikey told us you're nothing more than a henchman and an underling, Joseph Knolls." She spoke his name with emphasis. If he'd been surprised she knew Tippin's name, she suspected he'd be doubly shocked to know his gig was up, too.

A grease-stained hand flew out to connect with her temple, and her head slammed into the passenger window before her world went black.

Chapter Twenty-One

Nicole's eyes opened to a thunderous sound. Sharp pain spiked in her head and neck. Her ears rang and stomach coiled. Then the ground fell out from beneath her.

"Wake up," an ugly but familiar voice demanded, catching her before she rolled out of the car.

Above her, light lanced her eyes. Beneath her, the hands of her attacker gripped and tugged, dragging her into the day. Before her a cavernous opening loomed.

It took several seconds for her addled brain to recognize the location as a storage facility. The noise that had awoken her was likely the sound of the heavy door being rolled upward.

Now, Joseph Knolls shoved her toward the stacks of boxes.

She struggled to make sense of the situation. He was supposed to take her to her sister. "Cari," she choked, the voice not sounding like her own. "Where's Cari?"

He pushed hard against her shoulders, thrusting her toward the nearest wall before retreating and rolling the door down behind him.

A moment later, sounds of the car's engine grew distant and disappeared.

Bits of light filtered in around the door, and a small, narrow beam flashed on. The soft glow climbed her noodle legs and trembling chest.

"Nicole!" Cari's voice cracked and warbled in the darkness. "Cari!"

Her sister appeared, barely more than a silhouette, flashlight in hand. Her thin arms wrapped around Nicole, embracing and guiding her through the boxes to a small camp near the back. A pop-up chair with a car logo emblazoned on the material stood beside piles of identical stadium blankets with the name of the car dealership where Tippin and Knolls worked.

Tucked away together in the little nook, Nicole hugged her sister long and hard, afraid to ever let go. "I can't believe you're here. You're alive. Did he hurt you? What happened?" She pressed a palm against her throbbing temple and found a knot the size of an egg. That wasn't good.

Cari directed her to the pop-up chair and helped her sit. Even in the dim light, it was easy to see she was filthy and gaunt, her face and arms littered with bruising, some marks much darker than others.

The pungent smell of sweat and urine registered belatedly, and Nicole stifled a gag.

"I'm okay," Cari said. "But you're bleeding."

Nicole touched her head again, still processing the new circumstances. Had her sister been locked alone in a dark storage room in the southern summer heat all this time? Did she have access to water? To food? What had been Knolls's plan? To leave her for dead?

Her stomach twisted at the thought, and she pressed her lips tight.

"Your throat," Cari said softly.

Nicole shook her head, then winced from the pain. The knife had cut her, but it wasn't deep. "It'll heal."

Cari nodded, eyes filled with tears. "Nicole—" She inhaled a ragged breath, then set one hand on hers. "Where's Blakely?"

"She's safe," Nicole said quickly. There was so much to tell Cari. So much she needed to know. And so many questions Nicole had for her as well. "She's at the Beaumont Ranch with Mom."

"She's safe?" Cari asked, voice wobbling and face bright with relief. "Mom's here?"

"Yeah. Everyone's looking for you. And they're close to finding the guy who left us here, but I don't know when they'll find this place. I don't even know where we are."

"It's a storage unit owned by the car dealership where Mr. Tippin works," Cari said. "All this stuff is old. Like by a decade. I've been through most of it. I doubt anyone other than him even knows this place exists anymore. Everything in here still has the old logo I remember from commercials when I was little."

Nicole scanned the dim, sweltering space. "Tell me what happened. I've been looking for you since the morning after you went to work that catering job and didn't come home. The Beaumonts have been helping."

Cari lowered onto the piled blankets and began to sob. "I'm so sorry. I knew better than to keep taking jobs with Rising Tides, but I was trying to save money before you went back to work. I kept thinking I could turn everything around, make up for all my bad choices. And look at what happened. I'm so foolish."

"This isn't your fault," Nicole said, pushing away from the chair and joining Cari on the floor. "It's not foolish to want something more or better for you and Blakely. People like the ones running Rising Tides shouldn't exist in the world. This shouldn't have happened. You should be able to take evening jobs and not have to worry about getting involved in a black-mail ring just by being there."

"You know about that?"

"We knew everything," Nicole said. "Except how to find you."

Cari grimaced. "The money was really good. Easy. Quick. We met at a warehouse by the water, left our cars there and took a shuttle to the events. The other women told me it was so the valet wouldn't have to park so many extra cars. So the neighborhood streets wouldn't be as packed with vehicles. And so we could drink a little if we wanted and not have to drive right away. I think Tippin and Knolls just wanted an extra measure of control."

Nicole wrapped an arm around Cari's narrow shoulders and tugged her near. She wondered how many times Cari had replayed the story in her mind since being locked in here. How many times she'd wished for someone to tell. Someone to help her sort out the unthinkable.

"I think some of the women slept with party guests for extra money," Cari said, darting a glance in Nicole's direction. "I just wanted to go to college and make something respectable of myself. I wanted Blakely to be proud of me. For you to be proud of me."

"You are respectable. You don't have to try. You're good and worthy. Your past is in the past, and I am proud of you," Nicole assured. "Always, and no matter what."

Cari wiped freshly falling tears. "We were constantly offered champagne, especially on the shuttle. I guess it was supposed to loosen us up. I never had any. I'm probably overly cautious, but I avoid all substances. I know I had a problem before. I don't want to go through that again. In hindsight, I think there was something in the champagne."

"What were the parties like?"

"Sometimes servers paired off with guests and left the party for a while. The rest of us just mingled. We carried trays with finger foods and drinks. I made a lot of small talk and pretended not to have any friends or family. It seemed dangerous to tell anyone anything real. At the last party, a new guy got a little handsy, and I noticed the shuttle driver, Knolls, was watching. He tipped his head in the guy's direction, as if I should accommodate him. That was the end for me. I knew I couldn't keep working those parties. I didn't belong there. So, I excused myself to use the bathroom, grabbed my jacket from the kitchen and headed out the back door."

Nicole held her sister tighter, and Cari's head leaned onto her shoulder.

"I walked to a park behind their house, at the bottom of a hill to call for a ride. I sat on a bench and ordered an Uber. The app said the nearest car was nine minutes away, and I saw the twinkle lights in the trees, so I walked over there to kill some time and get out of the open, in case someone from the party noticed me. A few of the guests and servers were on the patio by the pool."

"That's when you found the bridge," Nicole said.

"I loved it. I sent you the picture because it was so perfect. Blakely would love it."

Nicole could hear her sister's smile in the words. "We found your phone there."

Cari shuddered. "I heard people talking nearby when I took the picture. The flash went off, and I startled them. Apparently the conversation was top secret, and Knolls came looking for the cause. He was so mad when he saw me. First I shut down the handsy party guest, then I left without telling anyone. He was yelling and wild-eyed before he got near me. I freaked out and ran. I dropped my phone but there wasn't time to get it. It hit the bridge then fell through the slats. When he caught me, he wanted to know what I heard. He wanted my phone. He thought I took his picture and recorded something I shouldn't. I thought he'd kill me, so I lied and told him I hid the phone. I dropped my keys in the process and didn't even notice. He was mad about that, too."

"You were smart to get out of there. You didn't belong, and you made good choices when it counted. I'm really proud of you for every one of them."

Cari tipped forward, hugging her knees to her chest and releasing her sister. "He comes here every day to try to convince me to tell him where I hid my phone."

She'd used the word *convince*, but based on the bruises covering her sister's frame, she'd really meant Knolls tried to beat the truth out of her.

And she hadn't told.

It explained why Joseph Knolls had been circling the Tippins' block. He was looking for Cari's cell phone. Trying to eliminate evidence of his crimes.

And he'd had to break into her car at the warehouse, because she'd lost her keys in the foot chase.

"He thought I was the persona I'd made up," Cari said, her tears dry and voice distant. "So he tossed me in here, said I was a junkie with no one who loved me, and if I didn't tell him what he wanted, he'd leave me to die alone and no one would even notice."

Nicole's temper flared as she kissed her sister's head. "No one has ever been more wrong. Everyone is searching for you, and when he comes back tomorrow, we're going to be ready."

Chapter Twenty-Two

Dean paced his parents' kitchen the next morning, while his brothers and father ate as if they were headed into battle and this might be their last meal. Dean couldn't even think about eating. He'd watched the man who stabbed Nicole drag her into his car and peel away. Knife to her throat this time.

The car that'd killed another young woman had been sitting outside the warehouse where he was the entire time, and he'd never even thought about walking the exterior perimeter.

Worse, a seasoned criminal and killer had been right there with them, probably watching and listening, waiting for Dean to let his guard down. And that hadn't taken long.

He and his brothers, along with members of the Marshal's Bluff police, had scoured the city, eventually finding the group of homeless who'd relocated without warning several days before. They'd gotten wind of trouble afoot after Mikey was attacked, and they'd wisely taken themselves out of the cross-hairs. Unfortunately they didn't have any information about Joseph Knolls.

Dean had been forced to call it a night when he'd dozed off for a moment behind the wheel and realized he was no longer useful to anyone. In that condition, he was a danger. So he'd gone home, where of course, he wasn't able to sleep.

He'd tossed and turned on his bed, the scent of her trapped in the fabric of his sheets and pillows. Images of her alone, terrified, injured or worse had pulled him awake each time his exhausted mind and body dared relax. He'd given up before dawn and made coffee.

Finn had called soon after and ordered him to the ranch for breakfast. The whole crew had been there when he'd arrived, and Mama was already cooking.

Mrs. Homes and Blakely were sleeping.

Dean's heart broke for the older woman and her grandchild upstairs. He couldn't imagine the pain of knowing both his children were missing, both in the hands of a killer.

"We tapped the landlines of Mrs. Tippin's siblings and Mr. Tippin's brother," Finn said, shoveling grits into his mouth by the fork load. "Mrs. Tippin called her sister. She used her cell phone, so we were able to get a location on the couple. State troopers are en route to collect and return them. They were halfway across the state at a resort spa. We brought the sister and her husband in for questioning last night."

Dean's gaze shot to his. "You're just telling me? What did they say?"

Finn placed a hand between them, palm side down, as if suggesting Dean relax. "We got them out of bed and brought them to the station in separate cruisers." He smiled. "It took all of five minutes for the husband to realize this was about his in-laws. He had no problem answering our questions. His wife was slower to cooperate, but it didn't matter. Her spouse had already told us the Tippins wanted to meet for lunch somewhere outside town and borrow cash. He'd said no, and that had caused a marital spat that lasted until they went to bed. He was still worked up about it when we spoke."

Austin set his fork on an empty plate and swigged his coffee. "They probably wanted cash so they could avoid making any bank withdrawals or using their credit cards. I'm guessing they never thought about the police tapping phone lines."

"We were lucky so many of their relatives still have landlines," Finn said.

Dean scrubbed both hands through his hair. "How long until the Tippins arrive?"

Finn checked his watch. "Any time now."

"Let's go." Dean grabbed his truck keys. "I want to talk to them."

Lincoln rose from the opposite end of the table, a warning in his small smile. "Hold up now. I don't think you should get anywhere near those folks."

"Why not?"

Lincoln's smile grew. "Oh, I don't know. Maybe because you'll say the wrong thing, threaten someone you shouldn't, or knock this Tippin guy into next week and get sued. Potentially lose your PI license."

Dean scowled, forcing his hands over his hips and willing himself not to lash out in his mama's kitchen. "Well, I'm not staying here, if that's what you're suggesting."

Finn wiped his mouth and stood, facing Dean. "How about you promise not to threaten or punch anyone, and I let you sit in the observation room and watch from behind the mirror while I talk to each of them?"

Dean glanced at Lincoln, then met Finn's gaze with a nod.

Austin carried his plate and cup to the sink, then kissed their mama's cheek. "I'm going with those two. Sounds like they're planning a party."

Lincoln made a *pft* sound and sat, returning to his meal. Apparently he wasn't interested in a trip to the police department. That was probably for the better. The last few times he'd been there, he was under arrest.

DEAN AND AUSTIN took seats inside the observation room and watched as Finn interviewed the Tippins. It didn't take long for Mr. Tippin to crack. His wife seemed genuinely confused about everything she was asked, and Dean got the feeling she was left out of quite a bit when it came to her husband's side hustle.

Tippin, on the other hand, started talking as soon as Finn dropped Joseph Knolls's name and said he'd traded information for a lesser sentence. Tippin turned red, then gave up everything he knew about the man who seemed to act as the crime ring's muscle.

According to Tippin, violence was forbidden, but Knolls couldn't seem to help himself. He called him an unhinged miscreant and gave Finn a number of ways to contact the man in question. Including the name of Knolls's girlfriend, whose home he occasionally shared.

The door beside Dean opened, and Finn entered the observation room with a manila file folder in hand. "Uniforms are picking up the girlfriend."

Austin clapped Dean on the shoulder. "Closer every minute."

Maybe so, but Nicole had been missing all night. Cari had been missing for days, and their abductor had less and less to lose by killing them.

Finn's phone buzzed. He checked the screen, brow furrowing. "The uniform picking up the girlfriend called dispatch. Apparently she and Knolls are on the outs and she's already talking. Knolls makes daily trips to a storage unit in Elizabeth City. She's been tracking his cell phone in case he was seeing another woman."

Dean pushed onto his feet with a jolt of fresh adrenaline. "Let's go."

NICOLE SLEPT AT her sister's side, waking at every small sound, afraid Cari would disappear. The small cut on Nicole's throat had scabbed. Now it itched and burned. The goose egg on her head continued to throb, but her head hurt slightly less, until she moved. Her empty stomach moaned with discomfort, as did the muscles in her neck, back and shoulders.

Cari whimpered in her sleep.

According to her sister, someone had delivered a jug of water and flashlight a short while after Knolls left her at the storage unit. The door had rolled up far enough for the items to be inserted, then the door was closed. Nicole wasn't sure if that had been Tippin or his wife, but she didn't think for a second it had been Knolls. He was far too callous to care.

Anticipation bounced and buzzed in her system as she awaited his return. She and Cari had made a plan before falling asleep. Cari was too weak and sore to fight, but she was sure she could run. When the door opened today, they'd be ready.

Meanwhile there was still hope that Dean or Finn would find them first. Maybe it wouldn't come to that, and Cari wouldn't have to run. She hadn't eaten in days, and her water jug was empty. She was petite, but Nicole couldn't carry her, at least not very fast or far.

Facing off with a cold-blooded killer wasn't something either of them was up for, but an even more worrisome thought was that Knolls might simply never return. And no one would find them.

The low rumble of a car's engine straightened her spine.

Cari sat upright beside her.

They exchanged a look and put the plan into action. Cari turned her flashlight on and set it on the floor. Then they tiptoed silently toward the door and crouched behind a row of boxes, praying Knolls wouldn't spot them immediately.

The barrier rolled up with a thunderous racket.

The sky outside was fire. Bright flames of orange and red against a distant gray horizon.

Sunrise.

"All right," Knolls called, his voice low and rough. "Wake up. Your little friends crossed a line. They took my girl to the station. Now I'm going to send their girls to the emergency room. But y'all won't be surviving the experience." He skulked past the boxes where they hid, too tunnel-visioned to bother looking around. As expected, he headed straight for the light, attention fixed on the back of the unit. "No one messes with me like this. No. One."

Adrenaline coursed through Nicole's system as she gripped Cari's hand. And they ran.

Fresh air crashed over them in a tidal wave, and Nicole's lungs seemed to expand fully for the first time in hours, devouring the cool, sweet oxygen. The dewy air met her sweat-slicked skin, invigorating and pushing her ahead.

"We should take the car," Cari said as they ran past, ducking into the next row of units. "He might've left his keys in the ignition."

They'd had this talk last night, but Nicole had insisted they just run. They couldn't afford to waste time, and if he had the keys with him, those lost moments could ruin their escape. Every second was too precious; it wasn't worth the risk.

Cari had agreed, but as they dashed passed the parked car, she looked and sounded uncertain.

A Godzilla-worthy roar echoed through the morning air, peppered with cuss words and the sounds of bursting boxes. He'd realized Nicole and Cari were gone.

The ominous sound of a low chuckle that followed made Nicole's blood run cold.

Joseph Knolls knew they couldn't have gone far, and he was up for the game.

They'd unintentionally invited a predator on a manhunt.

Chapter Twenty-Three

Nicole and Cari ran down the next aisle of storage units, moving in the opposite direction the car had been facing, hoping to find a way out.

Cari panted beside her, struggling to keep up. Her bare feet slapped against the ground. The high heels she'd worn to the party had been left behind for practicality.

"I've got you," she whispered. She checked over her shoulder to see her sister nod as tears streamed over her cheeks. The pain in her expression was undeniable. Her battered frame was thoroughly covered in bruises and cuts, all visible in the daylight.

She'd hidden how badly she was hurting, and Nicole's heart ached at the sight of her, but they had to keep going.

"We can do this," she promised. "Just keep your feet moving, and we'll be okay. We can do anything together."

She scanned the space over Cari's shoulder, then turned forward once more, surprised their captor hadn't yet followed.

Was he still searching the unit for them? Had he given chase in the wrong direction?

The sound of a car's revving engine stopped Nicole in her tracks.

Cari doubled over, catching her breath.

Images of Darla's gruesome death returned like a freight

train, and suddenly the road they traveled between storage units felt more like a rat's maze than an escape route. If Knolls came for them by car, there'd be nowhere to run.

Tires squealed, and Nicole's heart banged wildly against her ribs.

The Charger spun into view, smoke rising from its tires as they painted a patch of blackness across the asphalt. Then the car stopped suddenly, facing them head-on and separated by half the length of the long row of storage units.

Knolls torqued the engine, and the car's frame tilted with barely tamped power.

Cari screamed, and Nicole turned them back the way they'd come. "Run!"

DEAN WAS IN his truck and on the highway before Finn and his team could pull themselves together. The moment they had an address on the storage unit in question, he was out the door. Austin's truck was in his rearview, and Dean's chest tightened with pride and appreciation. He had no idea what he'd find when he reached his destination, maybe nothing, or maybe his worst nightmare. Either way, he was glad once again to be a Beaumont. Things could've gone differently for him and his only biological brother, Jake, but fate had delivered them into a family his childhood mind hadn't even known to ask for.

Austin was here, and he'd have Dean's back, whatever came. He was probably also the only thing capable of stopping Dean from ripping Knolls into pieces if the man was anywhere within reach when they arrived.

Sounds of a racing engine broke through the quiet morning air as Dean took the final turn toward his destination. A black Charger spun into view atop the nearby hill, braking to a rocking stop at the end of one set of storage units.

Dean raced up the incline toward the Charger with Austin on his tail.

The car waited, shifting in place with each rev of its engine.

Austin broke away, circling the units while Dean headed toward the Charger.

The car broke forward with a scream of tires, and Dean's heart plummeted.

At the end of the aisle, two fast-retreating figures were running for their lives.

NICOLE WRAPPED HER arm around her sister, slowing her pace to help Cari, as if they could escape the car. "Run!" she yelled again, as the Charger launched forward.

They were almost at the end of the row.

The distant sound of sirens teased her ears, but even if help was on its way, it wouldn't arrive in time to save them.

Cari cried out as Nicole jerked her around the corner and against a roll-up door in the next row.

She couldn't keep running, so they needed another plan.

"Press your back against the wall," Nicole said, throwing an arm across her sister's middle to hold her in place. "When the car makes its turn, it won't be able to hit us here. It'll have to back up and reposition. We can run again when that happens."

Cari nodded, face red and eyes closed, narrow body trembling against the orange door.

As predicted, the Charger appeared in the space of a heartbeat, spinning at the end of the lane, but it didn't stop as Nicole had expected. Instead, it flew past, the sound of another engine on its heels, and the sirens growing louder.

"We're not alone," Nicole panted, relief filling her eyes with hot tears. "We're going to make it."

Dean's truck swung into view then barreled past, chasing Knolls and his amped-up car.

Nicole's hair fluttered in the wake of the vehicles.

Another roar broke Nicole's reverie, and she started at the sight of a pickup racing toward them from the opposite direction. The truck's driver waved frantically through the open window.

"Austin!"

She tugged Cari's arm, and her sister's body slumped forward, collapsing onto the ground.

The truck was beside them in a second, the door opening as she fell to her sister's side.

"I've got her," he called, closing the distance in a rush. "Get in."

Nicole obeyed, trusting him completely with their lives. She threw herself into the truck's cab, and he passed her sister onto her lap like a child before jumping behind the wheel once more.

They'd cleared the end of the aisle and made a turn toward the exit when the Charger reappeared.

The black car flew at them, seemingly determined to collide head-on in the space running along the end of all the rows.

"He's going to kill us," Nicole whispered, holding her sister more tightly and knowing it wouldn't be enough. Cari needed a safety belt they didn't have. And they all needed a miracle.

Austin smashed the brake pedal and jerked the shifter into Reverse, tossing Nicole and Cari forward then back in two sharp moves.

The Charger came faster, eating up the space as Austin piloted them away.

Nicole's heart wedged into her throat, attention fixed on their predator and unprepared to die.

A flash of black on black exploded before them in a teeth-rattling boom!

The Charger flew sideways, shattered glass bursting into

the air as the car spun and bounced, end over end, on the asphalt before crashing to a stop against a telephone pole.

A smashed black truck was left in its wake. Front end annihilated. Airbag fully deployed, blood splattered over the ballooned material.

Dean.

THE DAYS FOLLOWING Dean's collision were touch and go. Nicole moved into the hospital waiting room, much to the dismay of some hospital staff. A thorough exam of her head had confirmed she wasn't concussed, and after an IV of fluids, she'd been released for home. Dean and Cari hadn't been as lucky.

Cari had gone home the next day, after a night of observation and a long line of tests for internal injuries and broken bones. She'd been severely dehydrated and in desperate need of sustenance as well as fluids. The emergency room doctors had cleaned and bandaged her wounds, then admitted her. Their dad had finally responded to their mom's calls on the matter after Cari had already returned home.

Dean had gone straight to surgery.

Nicole set up accommodations in the waiting room beside Mrs. Beaumont and several seats continually occupied by the Beaumont brothers. Even Jake, an ATF officer and Dean's biological brother, had traveled from Memphis to be there.

By the time Dean moved from the ICU to a semiprivate room a week later, it was fair to say a good chunk of the staff was glad to see him and his entourage moving on.

Now, just three weeks later, Dean was on the mend in big ways. The room was filled with balloons, flowers and enough food to feed the entire medical staff, plus a whole slew of loved ones. Per the usual.

"Everything's looking as it should," an older male doctor said, smiling warmly at Dean's chart. "You're healing at an incredible rate, no doubt thanks to this group." He tipped his head at the multitude of bodies around him. "Sometimes love really is the best medicine. Keep it up, and I think you'll be on your way home in the morning."

Nicole squeezed his hand, heart swelling and silent prayers rising. They'd all survived. They'd all healed. And soon, they'd all be home.

"Tomorrow," Dean repeated, deep blue eyes locked on hers.

Nicole raised the penny on her necklace into view. Emergency room doctors had found it in his pocket following the crash. A small heart shape had been punched through the coin, and she'd slid her favorite chain through it, keeping the talisman close to her heart while Dean healed. He'd carried her heart with him a long while, and she was ready to return the favor for as long as he'd allow. She rubbed the coin between her thumb and first finger, a habit she'd formed these last few weeks. "I can stay with him for the next few weeks while he heals," she told the doctor, "or at least until he's cleared to drive again."

"Lucky me," Dean said, lips curling into a playful smile.

The doctor gave some basic care and follow-up appointment information, then took his leave.

Cari moved to Nicole's side, Blakely dozing in her arms. The bruises from Cari's time in captivity had healed, but the emotional trauma would be there for a while. So she and Blakely were moving to Charleston with their mother and grandparents. She needed a soft place to land while she got the counseling and rest she needed.

Saying goodbye was something neither of them was prepared for, so they didn't mention her move more than absolutely necessary. And Nicole did her best not to think of how empty her apartment would seem without them.

Nicole rose from her chair to kiss Blakely's cheek and slide her arm around Cari's back. Cari's head tipped instantly to rest on Nicole's shoulder.

"So," Cari said. "What are you waiting for? I'm leaving soon, in case you haven't heard."

Nicole wrinkled her nose. Cari and their mother had just arrived. She craned her head for a look at her sister, but Cari was speaking to Dean.

"What am I always waiting on?" Dean asked. "Finn."

"Who's waiting on me?" Finn appeared in the doorway, dressed in a gray suit and blue tie.

"I am," Dean said. "It's about time."

Mrs. Beaumont waved a hand at Dean, then greeted Finn with a kiss on his cheek. "You look so handsome. Did you see any social workers at the courthouse today?"

Finn slid a sidelong look at his mama.

Nicole smiled. Cari laughed. Finn had been in love with a social worker once. Everyone had loved her, and Nicole never did get the whole story on that, but she hoped they'd find their way back to each other one day, the way she and Dean had.

"Court went well," Finn said, changing the subject and clasping his hands. "Joseph Knolls will be going to jail on two counts of murder, Darla's and Dr. Maline's. Two counts of kidnapping, assault, blackmail, all of it. The Tippins are both getting jail time, though Mrs. Tippin will likely have the bulk of her sentence suspended. Her husband, however, will be spending a long chunk of his time behind bars. All their assets are being seized in conjunction with the blackmail scheme, so when they get out, they'll have a lot of rebuilding to do. All in all I'd say justice was served. How'd your morning exam go?" he asked Dean.

"I get out tomorrow."

Nicole's mom moved into view, her phone raised as if she

might take a picture. "I have my folks on a video call," she said, turning her screen to pan the room.

Dean waved at the camera. "Hey, Mrs. and Mr. Dupree."

"Hello, Dean," her grandmother called.

"What?" her grandpa asked.

Nicole's mother turned the volume down and smiled. "Okay. All set. Go on."

Nicole frowned at the suddenly still room.

Even Lincoln, though perpetually silent, had moved to stand near the hospital bed with everyone else.

"Nicole," Dean said, drawing her eyes back to his.

Something in his tone sent goose bumps down her arms. "Yeah?"

"I planned to take you to our spot at the coast," he said. "I had a picnic in mind with something from each of our best dates. Photos from the county fair. Wine from that vineyard you love. Mama's apple pie."

Nicole returned to her seat, reaching for his hand. "We can still go."

Couldn't they?

Dean smiled. "I'd like to think there are hundreds of picnics in our future. Maybe fifty or sixty years' worth."

Nicole smiled.

Mrs. Beaumont pressed a tissue to the corner of each eye and latched onto her husband's arm.

Nurses gathered outside the doorway.

When Nicole's gaze slid back to Dean, he held a small ring box on his palm.

"Nicole Marie Homes," he said, tugging her closer to his side. "I've got something I've been meaning to ask you."

Shock stole her breath as she admired the thin gold band and glimmering solitaire.

"Will you accept this ring as a promise of my love?" he

asked. "Will you wear it always, knowing it represents my heart in your hands?"

Tears of pride, honor and love raced over her cheeks. "Are you—" She faltered, checking the warm smiles all around her, then the tear-filled eyes of the man she loved. "Are you asking me—"

"I am begging you to be my wife," he said, humbled and smiling before her.

And Nicole said yes.

* * * * *

LAST CHANCE
INVESTIGATION

TARA TAYLOR QUINN

To the men who made and have preserved the sanctity of my most special place on earth: my grandfather, Walter Wesley Gumser; my father, Walter Wright Gumser; my older brother, Walter Wright Gumser, Jr; my younger brother, Michael Scott Gumser; and to my husband, Timothy Barney, who not only gets that I need to spend time there, but is as eager to do so as I am.

Chapter One

The glint caught her eye. Watching as it bounced along the river's narrow flow, Kelly Chase felt a kinship with whatever was riding away down the river. And when it swept into a natural logjam on the opposite bank, she related to being stuck, too.

Caught by the natural beauty of the remote northern Michigan wilderness, Kelly continued to watch the stuck glint bobbing up against the water-weathered logs and sipped from her coffee. She'd been sitting at the old wooden table for over an hour. Had watched the sun rise through tall kitchen windows rising from the low counter, and from beside them through the open back door that left only mesh trimmed in wood between her and the outside.

She'd been listening to the water rolling along. Watching it skip its way to somewhere else.

And there was that glint. Once free, and then stuck.

On her property.

Right there with her.

Like her.

Three days before, she'd rolled in through the gate, and up the dirt-path drive dug into a forest of pine trees, in a car she'd rented at the nearest airport—three hours away. Had planned to return said vehicle the next day. She'd had a return ticket to Phoenix booked, too.

She'd been planning to call a Realtor that first day. Put the cabin she'd inherited from her paternal grandparents on the market, pack up anything meaningful and get the hell out of Dodge.

But there she sat.

Drinking coffee.

Watching glints.

Three days into a two-week hiatus, the majority of which she was supposed to be spending on a beach with wave sounds and sunshine for company. And vacationing strangers as background noise.

She'd call the realty office in Idlewood as soon as it opened. Have someone come out to the cabin.

Avoiding the nine-mile trip into the closest town altogether.

She hadn't been back since the day she'd left for college. No point in revisiting dead ends.

She'd sign the realty agreement right there at her own table, lock up and head out. Get a room close to the airport for the night.

Jump on a flight back to Phoenix in the morning, and still have ten days to lie incognito on some sand somewhere.

Without seeing even the outskirts of the small town where she'd grown up.

Idlewood would applaud her choice.

Or at least one member of the police force would.

Yep. She just had to wait for the realty office to open.

Sip coffee.

And…

The glint moved again. Bobbed a little higher and—broke free! Continuing its downstream dance. Maybe it would land on a beach. The thin branch of the river that ran through the property—her property for the past six months—emptied into Lake Michigan forty-five miles away. The lake had a lot of sandy beaches.

She'd barely finished the thought when the glint stopped again. Caught, this time, by a larger logjam on her side of the stream.

No.

Kelly stood.

She would not be caught.

With that thought, she grabbed jeans, a tank top and underthings from her suitcase and went in to shower. The stall was small. Square. Metal. Sixty years old. As a kid, when she'd been forced to leave her mother behind and spend a couple of weeks every summer with her father's parents at the cabin, she'd sometimes close her eyes, standing under the water, and knock her shoulders against the walls, creating the sound of thunder.

Once, when she'd been allowed to bring a friend with her for one of the two weeks, she'd had Jolene stand just inside the bathroom and flip the light switch back and forth really fast, making lightning.

At the time, the activity had seemed like a game.

The expert psychiatrist in her wondered—as she stood under the spray, closed her eyes and knocked her shoulder into the wall—if her childhood self had really been expressing the storm raging inside of her.

Fighting the sense of being trapped...

Kelly shut off the water. Grabbed a towel and was dressed in less than a minute. She had a call to make.

In the kitchen she grabbed her cell off the table, slid her thumb up to open the screen—and glanced outside.

The glint was still there.

So tightly trapped in a log joint that it was barely bobbing.

She found herself outside without making any kind of formal decision. On her way down to the water.

Freeing the glint was all that mattered.

Doing so would free her from the place, the nearby town, the whole damned state, once and for all.

Her gaze firmly locked on the glint, she strode with purpose. Let it call to her. Until she was so close, it was no longer just a glint she saw.

But, rather, a small canning jar with a partially rusted metal lid.

Someone's trash?

Glancing over the meadow she owned on the other side of the river, and up into the mountainous hills beyond, she frowned.

No one lived up there. Or owned a place anywhere near her upstream.

Angry now that a squatter or illegal camper was not only hanging out where they shouldn't be, but was polluting the beauty, she stepped carefully down to the bank and onto the sturdiest portion of the logjam. A tree trunk from an elm that had fallen too many years ago to remember.

From there a couple of slippery steps took her to her goal.

And, jar in hand, she managed a few more paces back to dry ground.

That was when she saw the folded white paper shoved haphazardly inside the small wet glass container she held.

CHOPPING WOOD WAS good for the soul. His dad had told him so many times over the years. And his grandad had, too. Levi Griggs didn't have much hope for any spiritual part of himself. He needed the wood.

He could live without heat during the summer. No way was he going to ask Betsy to do so. In her younger days, the old girl could take whatever the Michigan outdoors handed out. At seventeen and some months, she was losing muscle tone—and a tolerance for the early morning cold.

Urgent barking from behind him, coming closer, heading up the drive toward the road, didn't stop him. Bets might have outgrown her life expectancy, but the Jack Russell terrier didn't much care. She wasn't done yet.

Whoever dared to come near their property would get the message that they weren't welcome.

Axe to center, the crack, even split. Satisfaction followed, and he lifted another log, standing one end on the trunk he used as a base. Yeah, he and Betsy, they made a good team...

The thought, and his next swing, were interrupted by the sound of an engine coming up the drive. Standing, axe still in hand, Levi rounded the line of pine trees behind which he'd set up shop—mostly for the shade—and looked to see who'd dared to trespass on his leave of absence.

And risk his irritability. His family—even his extended family—knew better than to descend without a text.

Unless the intruder was the uncle who was the sheriff, and also his boss, and had arrived in his department-emblazoned truck.

Tossing his axe head into the ground, leaving the tool standing, handle up, he wiped his hands on his jeans and headed over.

Determined to fend off any advice his uncle might be set on giving.

He'd extended his leave as a decorated detective in the bureau of the River County Sheriff's Department because he'd thought it best. He didn't need anyone trying to convince him otherwise.

At six-three, Sheriff Martin Reynolds could be an imposing figure. Unless you'd grown up being tossed into the lake by your mother's younger brother—and having him right there to rescue you back out again.

At thirty-one, Levi took himself down a step when he read the steely look on his boss's face.

The sheriff's lack of greeting increased Levi's sense of foreboding as he took the phone his uncle handed over and gave it a cursory glance to see the crinkled piece of white paper depicted on the screen.

"What is this?" he said, holding the phone out to his uncle with a frown. "Some kind of attempt to shame me back to work?" he asked. "Remind the guy of the fifteen-year-old cold case he finally solved too late, getting one of his junior detectives, his own cousin, almost shot in the process?" He threw a lethal look at the man he respected more than just about any other. "You trying to remind me that I'm driven to be a cop? That I take cases like dogs take bones and won't give up until I solve them? Because it's not going to work."

The man didn't blink that Levi noticed. The sheriff just watched him.

Being under a microscope pissed him off when he was in a happy frame of mind. In his current state...

His uncle hadn't taken the phone back, which seemed pertinent enough that Levi glanced at it again.

Took a closer look.

Help Me

Two simple words. He'd seen them before. Way more times than he wanted to count. Written with various substances. Including, once, blood from what turned out to be a pricked finger.

But they'd been a bit smaller. More concise. In line. Written by the same hand.

He'd never seen that particular note before. "What is this? Some kind of sick joke?" he asked, shoving the phone back at the man who stood over him by a good three inches.

"It came in this morning."

No way. The case was done. Over. Two months ago. Victim dead. Perp dead. Tilly almost shot.

"How?"

"Called in by a citizen who found it."

"Where?"

"Floating down the river. Same kind of small canning jar."

He shook his head. Glanced at the phone, wanted another look, but didn't ask for it. Didn't need it, either. The photo was already emblazoned on his brain.

"Probably caught in a logjam or against the bank," he said. "With last week's rains, the river's up, current broke it free."

And the bigger handwriting?

Maura Allison had been panicked there at the end. With good reason. Desperation drove people to bigger actions.

If she'd been in a hurry...

On the verge of getting caught...

"The jar hadn't been in the water more than a few days. At most." Martin's grim expression said as much as his words. "The lid...looked like it had just come out of the cupboard. No rust. The glass...very little residue. I dropped it off with Forensics on my way here, so we'll have the confirmation soon, but I know what I know."

Levi had no doubt that if his uncle thought the jar hadn't been hanging around outside somewhere for two months, he was right.

Which only left one other option. "Some sick prick's pranking us. Or, more likely, me."

Martin's gaze narrowed. "You willing to take that chance?"

What the hell? "We got him, sir," he said then. The sheriff had arrived on official business. Levi addressed him as the boss he was. If Martin needed reassurance, Levi had it to give him. In boatloads.

"She wrote the notes. He killed her. I killed him. Took a bullet in the process. I was there. We got him."

"Are you willing to bet a life on the fact that there isn't anyone else up there?"

There wasn't. No way. He and his team had searched every mile of those hills that had river access over a period of years. Every time a new note showed up.

And until that past spring, had come up empty.

"The fiend admitted to doing it."

"I know." Martin nodded. "I have the report. I'm saying, what if there's a copycat?"

The case had been all over the eastern Michigan news. Some sick dude could have gotten the idea to try to hold a woman captive for himself.

He liked the prankster idea better. Tried to convince himself to go with that.

Felt Betsy sit next to him, leaning against his leg, as he looked at the phone again. His girl always knew when he was agitated.

And pushed him to do the right thing. Damn her.

"I need my weapon back," he told his boss. He had his own gun, but if he was going back to work, he'd need his department-issued tools. "And someone to take me to the exact spot the jar was found. And I need to speak to the person who found it…"

His brain was spinning as he spit out orders. Something he normally reserved for his team—and his own internal dialogue.

"Yeah, about that…" Martin was still frowning, but the

steeliness was gone. Replaced by something that looked very much like concern. Maybe even compassion.

If the sheriff thought he was going to come lay a new note on him, and not give him the lead…

Throwing out a heavy dose of steel in his own look, he said, "What?" His tone more challenging than he'd ever used on the man before.

Martin's look didn't lose the…whatever it was. If anything, the expression grew, fanning out to lines around the man's eyes. A tilt to his head.

What? Had he had some complaint against him? The shooting had been cleared the day it had happened.

"The spot where it turned up… The person who rescued it… You won't need any help getting to either."

Holding his stance, Levi frowned. "Why?"

"Because Kelly Chase found it, Levi. She's at her grandparents' place. Right on the middle branch of the Locke River."

The Locke River. The source of fifteen years' worth of the same notes.

Yeah. He knew where the cabin was.

And if his uncle hadn't been standing in front of him, Levi would have taken a seat.

Right there in the grass of his massive front yard.

Chapter Two

She'd planned to call the Realtor as soon as the sheriff left. Rather, as soon as whatever deputy he'd sent out had left.

Preferably one she'd never met before.

She had been expecting to see someone she didn't know.

Instead, answering the old wooden front door of the small cabin to Uncle Martin had been…a surprise. Sending a wave of shock clear to her heart.

She'd heard he'd made sheriff a couple of years after she'd left. Her mother had told her. Right before Kelly's mom had married the high school principal who'd been such a good friend to both Kelly and her mom, and the two had moved to South Carolina.

No way had she expected the county sheriff to show up— in person—at her door. Most particularly over a note in the water.

Granted, the idea of it, reading the words, had been off- putting. Worthy of a phone call to the county sheriff's office.

But…to stand there face-to-face with a man she'd once been certain would be family to her—who she'd loved as she had the rest of Levi's family…

He'd been polite. Distant. Not friendly. But not unkind.

And all business.

Acknowledging that he knew her by calling her by name.

But that was it. No *How've you been?* or *I heard you'd inherited your grandparents' place.* No small talk at all.

He'd been there and gone in less than two minutes.

Leaving her...

Lost?

Made no sense.

She'd planned to leave without seeing anyone but a stranger who'd list her place. Why would the fact that the sheriff only gave her two minutes bother her?

For an expert psychiatrist to still be contemplating her emotional state an hour after the man left wasn't good. Instead of doing business with contracts at her kitchen table, she was walking the bank of her property. As though she'd find answers there.

Which also made no sense. She had her answers. Had had them for years. Had acted upon them and had built a successful, fulfilling, rewarding and sometimes downright exciting career. With friends who were more like family to her than her own mother and stepfather.

She loved her life.

The truth of the thought, the rightness of it, settled upon her. Just as...

Was that another glint?

"It can't be," she said aloud, even as she was running for the shed outside the front door, bursting inside to grab an old fishing net and head back to the bank just upstream from the cabin. Splashing into the knee-high frigid water in capri jeans and tennis shoes, she barely felt the cold as she saw the glint again and homed in on it.

And captured it in her net.

Shaking—not so much from cold, although she felt the ache of it in her wet limbs—she hurried to the cabin, dripping net and all.

The back screen door fell closed behind her with its usual spring-induced slam, just as another sound came to her attention.

And a different glint.

The sun on the bumper of a shiny black truck pulling up out front.

She wasn't ready for visitors. Didn't want any.

Dropping her net in the big old hip-level kitchen sink, she grabbed a towel for her legs, shaking her long blond curls out of her face and over her shoulder as she slipped out of her tennis shoes.

The front door was locked. She didn't have to answer a knock.

Quickly closing the larger door over the screen in the back, she locked it, too. Glancing at the netted jar in her sink, she went barefoot to the bedroom off the kitchen and retrieved her grandfather's .22-caliber hunting rifle from the corner where it had been living ever since she could remember.

She'd loaded it the day she'd arrived.

Not into shooting, she hadn't intended to use it, but old habits died hard. After that summer when a bear had come down out of the hills for water, no one was ever in the cabin without the rifle loaded and in the corner.

And two notes in one day?

She'd read the first one, thinking as she'd opened the jar that she'd latched on to some kid's time capsule or something. Wasn't touching the second now that she knew prints were an issue.

The way Sheriff Reynolds had just taken the jar, heard what she had to say, nodded and left, she'd figured he hadn't been any more worried about her glint than she'd been.

But maybe…

Glancing at the jar again, and at the front door, she wished her phone wasn't all the way over on the kitchen table.

She'd be in view of the window by the front door if she went to retrieve it.

The cabin, as remote as it was, and on such a large portion of fenced private land, had always been so safe.

But what did she know? She hadn't been there in nearly thirteen years.

Hadn't read a word about the county, the river, the town since, either. Once she'd stopped the slew of letters she and Levi had been sending, ending them once and for all, she'd cut Idlewood, River County and all memories associated with either off from her heart. And her mind.

Surely, though, if there was some creep on the loose, the sheriff wouldn't have just tipped his head at her and driven away.

No matter how much he might hate her for breaking his nephew's heart.

The truck had stopped. Engine off.

But she hadn't heard a door shut.

Gun in hand, she hunkered down and made a dash for the kitchen table, staying down between it and the cupboard behind her. Even if the owner of the truck came around back, she'd hopefully be at least partially hidden from view of the kitchen windows.

She almost dropped the gun when a knock sounded on the front door.

Oh Lord, please go away.

Moving around the edge of the table, hitting her butt on the stove as she passed, she reached up with one hand to slide her phone down to her. Was holding the rifle, crouching and trying to type in the pass code for her phone's security with one hand, intending to dial 911—even knowing that she could be dead long before any law enforcement would reach her out there. Movement out of the corner of her eye stopped her long enough for her to glance up.

And see the face peering in from the windows lining the couches just feet away from her.

LEVI HAD SPENT the entire drive out, and a few extra minutes parked by the cabin, preparing himself to be face-to-face with Kelly Chase again.

Schooling himself not only to show no reaction—but to have none.

But how in the hell did a guy not react when, after having received a note with potentially deadly associations, the woman he'd come to question didn't answer her door?

And then, to see his Kelly—a woman who, at twelve, had stood up to her imposing, rich, important father and told him he wasn't nice and she didn't want to see him anymore and was going to tell the judge—cowering barefoot on the floor with a rifle barely held by the butt, under one arm, while she fooled with her phone…

No way he couldn't feel something when she looked up and saw him standing there. Watching her.

He hadn't expected a flash to the last time he'd seen her… also barefoot, and naked in all other parts, too, the night before she'd left to go to the fancy Arkansas college where she'd won a full-ride scholarship.

It had been the first time either of them had ever had sex…

Jaw dropping, she stared at him.

Was the first to move, heading toward the front door before he'd taken a step.

At least he'd kept his mouth closed.

The fact that she hadn't, pleased him.

That he was noticing any of it, didn't.

Kelly Chase. She was really there.

He moved slowly toward the door, pulse rate up. As a kid, he'd been eager just to be in her presence. And as a man, unbelievably hungry, hard, from one glimpse through the window of the woman she'd grown into.

Hungry to hear her voice.

An urgent step turned him toward his truck instead of the front door.

He had to get out of there.

And he remembered the photo that his uncle had sent to his phone.

The case.

Giving himself a mental slap, he got to the door in a few broad steps. Meant to step past the beautiful blonde holding it open to him. To get right down to business.

A quick glance in her direction, to make certain he didn't touch her as he swept past, stopped him.

Her gaze was...open and searching his. Just as it always had.

He was glued to it.

She moved.

And his lips met hers.

LEVI.

Kelly's entire body came to life, as she fell against him, kissed him hello. Right up until her brain caught up to her natural reaction at seeing him, and she pulled back.

"Oh my God, Levi, I'm so sorry," she said, appalled at her behavior. "I can't believe I..."

Shaking his head, he stepped back. Looked her up and down, his hands folded one on top of the other in front of him, covering his fly.

No need. She'd felt the reaction.

"It's good to see you, Kel," he said, his voice deeper, but still Levi.

His body...wow. Broader, more muscled. Still six feet of dark-haired hunk.

"That uniform looks good on you." And it hit her. He wasn't there to see her.

Martin had obviously told him she was in town. She'd been trying not to let herself wonder if he would. To think about Levi.

His uncle had spoken with him. About the note. She'd been peripheral. Hence, the uniform.

"You're here about the note," she said then, pulling her own years of professionalism around her. Psychiatrists, even ones who were partners in a nationally renowned firm of experts, didn't wear uniforms.

But if she'd known she was going to see Levi Griggs, she'd have put on something a bit...more...than old capri jeans and a T-shirt.

Her bare toes felt exposed. Their nakedness embarrassing her.

She moved to the end of the table by the kitchen cupboard. He stood at the end by the front door.

"What did Martin tell you about them?"

"Them?"

"The notes."

Plural. She'd only told Martin about one, but they knew there was a second?

They knew who'd planted them, then? And he'd come running?

Oh God, had it been him? Messing with her?

He'd pulled a prank or two in the past—high school boy stuff—but never on her.

Wow. Her brain was scrambled. Running all over the place, with him standing there. She'd promised herself...

What?

That she wouldn't see Levi.

And yet in three days' time she hadn't managed to make one phone call? Or sort through and pack up any of the cabin's contents.

Were the notes his way of getting back at her? Getting her attention?

Had Martin been in on it?

"Notes." She made herself focus. "As in plural. You know about the second one?"

She'd kissed him.

He'd kissed her back.

Didn't mean anything.

Old times' sake.

She'd been shocked, seeing him stand there. Had had no time to prepare.

He'd known he was going to see her, though.

And had kissed her back...

Was he there to...?

"What second one?" His tone sharper, Levi came closer to the table.

Confused, she told him, "You said notes." And then, "Why are you here, Levi?"

He continued to advance, and she stood her ground. "What second one?" he repeated, a new urgency to his tone.

A stillness about him, the steely glint in his eye, turned him into a man she didn't know. One who commanded her to get her mind out of high school and join him in the present.

"I found a second note," she told him then, motioning toward the sink. "I didn't touch anything this time," she added, and he moved with a quiet swiftness and lifted the fishing net.

"Where?"

"It was floating downstream. Just like the last," she said, slipping her feet back into her wet tennis shoes, ready to head outside with him if need be.

But it was bothering her. "Why did you say notes?"

Net held suspended above the sink, he looked from it to her, his expression as grave as death. "Martin didn't tell you."

Obviously. "He was here all of two minutes. Took my statement, the note, and left."

"You don't follow River County news."

"No." The admission was painful. Because she knew what it was telling him. When she'd ended their relationship, she'd cut the town they'd grown up in out of her life as well. "My mom told me when you graduated with your criminal justice degree and joined the sheriff's office," she added, wanting to make him feel better somehow, even while knowing she never could.

That particular news had been from more than ten years before. Over time, her mother had settled into her small South Carolina town and lost touch with Idlewood.

"These notes…" Levi nodded toward the jar hanging in the net he held. "The first one showed up nearly fifteen years ago."

Horrified, and fully focused then, too, Kelly asked, "The first one? How many are there?"

"Until today, twenty-seven in total. They'd come in spurts, and then there'd be months, even a couple of years once, without any."

"Who's sending them?"

He seemed to flinch. His elbow pulling into his side, and Kelly went to work without even meaning to.

"What's going on, Levi? What happened?" She was trained to notice the tells.

Her work with Sierra's Web, the private firm of experts

she and her partners formed, had taken her into some of the country's darkest places. Exposed her to dangerous minds.

They'd helped solve historic cases, had saved a lot of lives. If Levi needed help that she or her partners could provide, there was no way in hell she was leaving.

Chapter Three

"The case was mine," Levi told this grown-up version of the woman he'd planned to marry. He knew what she did, of course. Knew about her firm.

And needed her out of town so he could remove the distraction of finding himself face-to-face with the love of his life and focus on what he did well.

Instinct told him that laying it out up front would get rid of her quicker than if he left her to dig for facts on her own.

And what she'd find…he'd rather she hear it from him.

The unvarnished version.

"Over the years, I became a bit obsessed with it."

"Wait…you said the case *was* yours? It isn't anymore? Why? Whose case is it now?"

Kelly's questions. He'd forgotten how they would come at him in numbers. Constantly. Always looking to understand every nuance. From spawning fish to how a movie made him feel.

And she hadn't just wanted to know. She'd wanted to know why.

Martin should have taken the note to someone else.

"The case is closed," he told her. "I solved it. Two months ago."

"Well, but…" She glanced at the net he held. Reminding

him to lower it back to the sink for the few minutes more he'd be there.

"'Well, but,' indeed," he told her with a sigh. "I'm hoping what we have here is a prankster."

"And if it isn't?"

"Then we're looking at a copycat." His tone was grim.

"You're sure this isn't still part of——"

He cut her off with a quick shake of his head. "Robert Yardle, an uneducated man from Hairwin, kidnapped a woman, Maura—a runaway from a foster home in Cadillac—nearly a quarter of a century ago——"

"When we were just kids," Kelly interrupted. "Hairwin's only fifteen miles from Idlewood."

He nodded. "He'd been holding her captive up in the hills, in a rustic, one-room place he built, ever since. The scumbag built an enclosed cage out of fencing that led from the house to the river so she could bathe, do dishes and laundry. The cage segued off to a garden, too, where she grew vegetables and canned them. When he left to go to work, or into town to buy supplies, he chained her up inside. Maura started hiding canning jars with notes in them in the laundry and would send them off when she was washing clothes."

"What about in the winter?"

The question didn't surprise him. Kelly had always caught on quick. "Right, the notes only came during the spring, summer and fall. During the winter Yardle would haul water up to a huge tub for her to use for both laundry and bathing. She'd bathe first, and then wash their clothes. There was a pump for dishwater." He could talk all day about the atrocities he'd seen. Kelly had always been able to do that to him.

Had a way of pulling things out of him without even trying.

He didn't have all day.

"Somehow she figured out how to make a homemade flare.

Used things like salt substitute and maybe cooked banana peels with crushed egg whites with other stuff for fertilizer the best we can tell, shaved something made of copper down to powder, cooked it together with some common plastic, we're not sure what all. Loaded it into tubes of cardboard. Forensics didn't have a lot to work with. This past year, she started sending up the flares anytime Yardle was gone.

"The day we found her, I led a team up, expecting to get her out and take Yardle in, but he'd set booby traps in the woods around the place, holes filled with cans, covered in leaves. One of my team members stepped in one, alerting him." Enmeshed in his real world again, he was going to get it all out, answer any question she could ask so her curiosity would be satisfied, take her statement, collect the evidence and be done.

She'd been in town three days, according to his uncle. And hadn't contacted him. If not for the note, likely wouldn't have. The message in that was clear.

"A young deputy saw Yardle, raised her gun and ordered him to put his hands up, but he pulled a gun on her..."

"He shot one of your people?" Her horror was so... Kelly. She lived life big. Always had.

"I managed to deflect the bullet," he said, then finished. "I shot him, but not before he pulled his trigger and killed Maura."

So there she had it.

"Wait, you deflected the bullet by shooting him? If that happened, how did he shoot Maura?"

Her perception had always intrigued him. He'd missed it.

But wasn't going back.

"I deflected the first bullet. Then shot him, but he'd already killed her."

"You saved your deputy, giving him time to kill Maura," she summed up.

"Yep."

"How'd you deflect the bullet, Levi?"

He was done talking. Pulled a small section of his shirt out of his waistband, enough to show her the ugly pink-and-purple scar, and leaving that piece of shirttail loose, ignoring her gasp, grabbed the net.

A glance out the window told him he remembered the branch of river that ran through the property accurately, had already noted the logjams. If he needed more from her he'd have one of his deputies call.

"Levi! Where are you…? You can't just… Levi Griggs, do not walk out on me."

He heard the familiar note in her voice. How did a guy remember the sound of his woman's hurt after so many years? Paused a step.

Remembered that she'd walked out on him—and would again—and headed for the door.

"I WANT TO HELP." Kelly blurted the words to Levi's disappearing back as he reached the front door.

He paused, but let himself out.

"Levi!" She ran after him. "Please." When he stopped a second time, she ran around in front of him, standing between him and the passenger door of his truck. "My firm and I… we've got a forensics expert, and a state-of-the-art lab that departments from all over the country tap into…and I… I do personality and psychological profiles, including some forms of handwriting analysis…"

She sounded desperate.

Because she was.

No justifiable explanation, just fact. She couldn't let him simply walk away with his bullet-damaged side and his dead victim and new notes and…

That kiss.

It wasn't going to fade into distant memory without some kind of real closure. The kind that came through understanding, not by way of a Dear John letter sent from a confused, grieving college student.

"The notes," she blurted then, when, though he hadn't moved, he hadn't given any hint of relenting. He wasn't even looking at her anymore. Had his gaze pinned somewhere above her right shoulder. "You said twenty-seven in fifteen years and now two in one day? And if it's a copycat, how does that work? Someone being held captive is trying to send notes to get rescued? It would have to be someone newly caught, right?"

"Or someone caught anytime in the past fifteen years that the case has been in the local news."

"So someone from around here."

His gaze narrowed as he looked at her.

"And for two to show up in the exact same place? What are the chances of that? I can actually have that answer for you fairly quickly. I'd just need to get some facts to Glen—our scientist and forensics expert—you know, like water depth, wind speed. He can get an aerial view of the river and he could probably tell us the chance of something floating to the exact same spot…" She was halfway spitballing on that one, supposing, but she'd seen Glen work similar feats of magic.

"Unless," she continued, "and this would be my guess for the moment…the person knows I'm here and is deliberately dropping the jars in the water not far upstream so that they're pretty much guaranteed to hit me. Maybe, if we hike a little bit upstream, we'll find one or two that got caught in the rock hole."

A bend just upstream that had a big bank of rocks that she used to play on as a kid. When she'd had to spend her couple of weeks at the cabin during her high school summers, Levi had driven out almost every day…

His gaze narrowed.

"Or maybe you'll find evidence along the bank. Since both notes are showing up here, and the jars don't look weathered, it's reasonable to think they've been dropped in the water close by. Maybe even early this morning. And since there aren't a lot of river access points around here, it would be easiest for you to set up base here."

She'd keep going for as long as it took.

"If I could get a look at the other notes, I might be able to tell you if there are any psychological similarities, the pressure put on the writing implement, or not, that kind of thing. Denotes state of mind of the author."

"We know Maura wrote the other notes. She's dead."

"But if there are similarities, it could support the suspicion that someone else is being held captive." She took a step closer to him. Was heartened when he didn't back away. "For all we know, someone's out here right now, Levi. Close by. Trying to reach out to me."

"This isn't random, Kel," he said then. And the shortened use of her name not only sent a spark of warmth through her, but told her that he was softening to her idea, too. "The canning jar…same size…"

"There are only two basic sizes, right? But I agree. It's not random. Someone needs help. Someone who knows about the previous case. Which likely suggests…someone from around here, right? Someone who would have read local news?"

"The story went a little wider when we solved the case," he said. Then nodded. "I need to get this to Forensics, but I'll think about what you said. And if you're sure you're okay with it, I'll have someone out here this afternoon, checking out the property just upstream of your cabin…" He broke off.

"On second thought," he continued more slowly, heading back toward her front door, "I'm going to stay put. Call for people to come out. I don't want you out here alone with the possibility of a kidnapper on the loose."

His words struck fear in her again. Similar to what she'd felt when she'd first come inside. Like someone really was close by. Watching her.

Someone who needed help?

Or the criminal who was holding captive whoever had put those jars in the water.

With a nod, she led the way back inside.

Two notes in a few hours meant someone was close to the river. And not far from Kelly's property. Maybe even on her property. With deputies canvassing the area, hopefully there'd be a rescue yet that day.

And she'd have a little bit more time with Levi.

He was why she'd been unable to call the Realtor. Funny how things could be hidden in dark places for years and suddenly become crystal clear.

She had business with Levi. She just hadn't wanted to have business with him.

The need to clear things with him had been lingering in her heart, her subconscious, for years.

She needed to try to explain to him why she'd done what she had back in college. To let him know that the problem had been all her. That, though it had been done to him, the breakup hadn't been about him at all.

To let him know how very much she'd loved him.

To apologize.

And…maybe…to be able to kiss him goodbye?

One last time?

Chapter Four

Knowing the area as well as he did, Levi had teams scouring Kelly's grandparents' property and the surrounding hills within an hour.

He was having the evidence brought out from the previously closed case as well. Being the nephew of the sheriff had its advantages.

Because he was lead on the case, and was running teams via a map on Kelly's table and radio, he held back close to the cabin.

And to Kelly.

Just until he could be sure that there wasn't some crackpot abductor lurking outside her door.

He still wasn't ready to believe there was anything to the notes. They must be someone's idea of a sick joke.

But after Kelly had started talking about the situation, bringing up all sorts of things he hadn't yet let himself think about—because he'd been too busy thinking about seeing her again—he wasn't willing to risk her life to his own wishful thinking where the strangely delivered messages were concerned.

Nor, once he got his damned head out of the past and focused on the job, could he stomach the idea that another woman was being held captive and he was doing nothing about it.

Even if the eventuality was a long shot.

He had to be sure.

While he waited for teams to check in, he was casing the immediate vicinity of her property. For his own comfort, mostly. He had to be certain that Kelly was safe.

From what he'd read about Sierra's Web over the years, she and her partners had taken on some pretty big cases, earning them enemies in the criminal world. For all he knew, someone could have followed her to town, heard about the case involving Locke River and was using the information as a means to an end they didn't yet know about.

To get Kelly's attention?

Make her look like a fool, to discredit one of the seven partner experts? Or her specifically?

A lot was missing from that scenario, but it was odd that notes were suddenly ending up at her family's place when not one other note in the previous fifteen years had been found in that area of the river.

Because Maura had always dropped them in the same place—the only part of the river she could reach from her cage of fencing.

"Hey, Levi, come look at this." Kelly's voice reached him from a hundred yards away. She'd insisted on searching with him. He'd made certain that, while she was always in sight, they weren't within easy talking distance.

There was the case—and nothing else—between them.

Nothing more to be said.

He'd lost himself for some minutes there, upon first seeing her, but he'd come back into his right mind.

He headed over to where she was standing, in a meadow of chest-high ferns with trees along the bank several hundred yards down from the cabin. His teams had started farther upstream and would work their way down.

Leaving the area immediately downstream to him.

They'd crossed the stream in waders from the shed, leaving them hanging on a tree branch by the bank. He told himself that any sense of satisfaction he was getting out of the transpiring events came from being back to work after a two-month hiatus.

His family, including Uncle Martin, had been right. He'd needed to get back in the saddle.

"Someone's been here," she said, pointing to a patch of broken ferns, lying flat, in the midst of the forest of them.

Doing a quick visual sweep of the area, Levi saw nothing that proved a human being had been present in the area. No litter, certainly. But no trail leading to or from the spot, either. "Probably a deer bed," he said aloud.

"Levi Griggs, you know as well as I do that deer beds are circular in nature. This is the shape of someone sitting." She pointed to the center of the disturbance and then to two other smaller spots a couple of tall ferns beyond. "That's where the feet were," she said. "It's clear that whoever was here was deliberately hiding, leaving as many ferns undisturbed as possible, so as not to disturb their cover."

There was sense in what she said. He was still feeling the "Levi Griggs" she'd just doled out on him, for the second time that day. Full naming him.

She'd been the only person, other than perhaps his parents when he was little, who'd ever dared to call him out that way. The only one who'd ever gotten away with it.

He focused on the ferns. "Could have been a smaller animal. And her babies," he told her, sharing what he suspected they were seeing.

She shrugged. "It could also have been a person," she said.

"Maybe someone who's scared, hiding out…someone who'd purposely tried to not be seen by walking so carefully they didn't trample down a path in the ferns."

"With access to canning jars?" He asked the question even as another possibility occurred to him. Maura could have hidden the jars, along with paper and writing implements, someplace Yardle wouldn't find them.

Down by the river?

Levi had ordered that Maura's cage be taken down. Thankfully a law preventing any structures close to the river had supported his demand. The rudimentary cabin, along with a hundred acres of woodland, was in probate. Turned out it had been in the Yardle family for generations, Robert being the last of the bunch. Because it was wilderness, with no roads leading to it, the land's deed had just contained a long series of coordinates with names being passed down from one generation to the other. None of it was computerized.

Half a mile downhill there'd been an old dirt path, allowing hunting access to another property. Yardle had used that road to access his place. They'd found a tunnel dug out of the hillside where he'd parked his truck.

A team was already headed up the hill to check out the Yardle property. Pulling out his radio, he asked them to tread carefully. They were on the lookout for any sign of current or recent habitation. Something they'd already have been doing.

Could be they had a squatter in the area.

Or someone who'd followed the news of the Yardle case had grown curious, set out to find the property and had copycatted the dangerous old man.

Could also be that the only thing their current situation had to do with Yardle was the story in the news. And that someone was watching Kelly.

"Let's get back to the cabin," he told his ex-fiancée then. For no other reason than because he wanted her inside.

WATCHING AS LEVI sat at her table, taking calls and making notes on the map in front of him, directing searches, Kelly had to check herself.

Someone was in trouble. She couldn't possibly be enjoying herself.

And yet…while she was gravely concerned, a part of her felt better.

Used to keeping vigilant track of her own mental health—she knew way too much about such things not to check in with herself—she noted the odd lift within her, and moved past it.

Not having planned to stay, or have company, she didn't have a whole lot, but offered to scramble some eggs she'd purchased from a roadside stand after she'd left the highway on her way to the cabin the other day.

She'd grabbed some red potatoes and vegetables, too. "Or I can do an omelet," she told him, needing to do something besides stand around and stare at the man working in the intimate space she'd shared with only herself over the previous three days.

Levi's nod was more the shooing away of an irritating fly than a buy-in, but she set to work immediately. He loved vegetable omelets.

She used to get a buzz out of cooking for him. And was trying not to think about some defenseless person being held hostage close by.

"You'll let me see the evidence when it gets here, right?" she said as she chopped a green pepper on an old wooden cutting board, with a knife that had been around when she'd been a kid. There was something comforting about that.

The sameness.

The history that kept a building alive even when those who'd owned it were gone.

When Levi didn't answer, she said, "If you need to, we can make it official, sign a Sierra's Web contract, with the fee being waived. We take on many cases pro bono, and since this one involves my property…"

"Your grandparents' property, you mean."

Levi's sharp tone had her turning around, knife in hand, frowning at him. "No. Dan died several years ago. Willa just passed away in December." Kelly hadn't seen her paternal grandmother in a couple of years. She'd never been particularly close to either of her father's parents.

Which was what made the whole current situation, them leaving her the place, so odd.

"Wait." Levi was frowning. "You trying to tell me you bought this place from your dad and uncle?"

She shook her head. "Dad got the mansion in Grand Rapids. Uncle Harley got the place in Florida. The money was split between the two of them. And I got this place."

He of all people would understand the stupendousness of the move.

He watched her for a few seconds, then asked, "What about your cousins?" Uncle Harley's kids. Two boys and a girl. All older than Kelly. And not particularly interested in having a little kid from the backwoods town trailing around with them.

She shrugged. "I guess they get what's left when Dad and Uncle Harley die. I was cut out of Dad's will years ago." There'd been no big scene. Just a letter.

She'd been relieved.

The last thing she'd wanted from the man who'd had zero husbandly or fatherly abilities was his money. He could donate it all to his constituents for all she cared.

The Chases had always been generous to those less fortunate than them. It was part of their image, part of who they were.

It took her a second, standing there with chopping knife suspended, to realize that Levi was staring at her.

When she met his intent gaze with a raised, questioning brow, he slumped back in his seat. "You own this place," he said. Seemingly deflated somehow. Depleted, maybe.

"I thought you knew," she told him. Martin hadn't questioned her being there.

He shrugged. "You know how it is out here. Places sit vacant for decades sometimes, crumble to ruins. With the vast, wooded acreage...surrounding government land...the sheriff's office is only out here if we get a disturbance call."

The cabin didn't have a mailbox. Or trash service, either. As long as the taxes were paid...

But...she'd come to town certain that Levi would know... that he'd kept tabs...or someone would have told him...

As though she was that important. Twelve years after she'd dumped him.

Oh God, she wasn't more like her father's family than she knew, was she? Viewing herself with such importance.

Willa had had a good heart. She'd loved Kelly as best she could. Mostly, though, Kelly had been an obligation to her grandparents. A need to keep up appearances of an active, congenial involvement in the life of their youngest grandchild.

The result of their son's brief rebellion when he'd been denied the partner position he'd wanted in his father's law firm upon graduating and passing the bar.

Levi's gaze had warmed some. With a hint of the personal connection she'd sensed when he'd first arrived.

"You're here, vacationing in your own cabin..."

The way he said the words, as though they were good

news…had her heart stopping for a second. Until she felt the emotional stab inside her.

He thought she'd come home. Just for vacation, but…

She shook her head. "I'm here to sell the place." She told him the truth, right up front. Something she thought he'd already ascertained.

Not the selling part, obviously, since she'd made no moves toward that end. But he'd known her better than anyone. And would certainly expect her to sell.

He blinked. Nodded.

And had become a stranger again. The lead detective on a case he didn't believe warranted more than a cursory investigation.

Feeling a loss of something she knew she hadn't even had, Kelly had to bite back an immediate urge to blurt out that she hadn't called the Realtor yet.

Because she was going to make the call.

And no matter how conflicted she felt right then, seeing Levi again, she was still the same woman who'd written to him to break off their relationship. Would make the same choice, if she had to do it over.

For the same reasons.

Though, in her more mature state of mind, she hoped she'd do him the respect of handling the breakup in person.

If she had it to do over again.

Chapter Five

She'd inherited the cabin. Had owned it for six months.

No reason he should have known. No business of his.

Levi still felt poleaxed.

By a life that continued to make less and less sense to him.

"Will you let me see the evidence?" Her question was much more pragmatically spoken the second time around.

"That's why I'm having it brought out," he told her.

Aside from anything personal, Kelly Chase came with one hell of a reputation. And while his gut was telling him that the notes she'd found were little more than a prank in very poor taste, he didn't trust those instincts as much since Tilly had almost been shot. The internal doubts, combined with the insights Kelly had already thrown at him, were enough for him to at least give the expert-witness psychiatrist a chance to have a more thorough look.

So that when she left town to go back to her high-profile life, he could feel as though they'd finished whatever business lay between them.

Get on with his life before it passed by without him.

"You could have sold the place without a visit." Not smart for him to make something out of that. But the fact remained. Right there on the map in front of him. Blurring his vision to the routes his teams were taking.

Her lack of an immediate explanation had him looking over at her. Her back to him, she'd stopped chopping. Was just standing there holding the knife.

His radio crackled and he listened to the report that the first full grid had been searched, with nothing found. He told the team, consisting of one deputy and four civilian searchers, to head back to town.

Placed a large red X over their portion of the map in front of him.

The smallest area, it was also the least likely to have been used for any kind of hiding out or secret living. On top of being immediately behind Kelly's property, the area was not only visible from the river, but it was also flat, open ground with the least amount of vegetation.

Still, it was one down, four more to go.

"I'm here because I need to pack up some things," Kelly said, placing her knife in the sink. She moved to the eggs she'd scrambled with milk in a bowl, carrying them over to the pan heating on the stove, saying, "The heater is great for the summer, but in the winter, the bedrooms are frigid. And the pipes are drained because water freezes in them."

Same as most of the random cabins set in the miles of wild land between Idlewood and the highway down to Grand Rapids.

Still, some crankiness inside of him wanted to push her.

To get a rise out of her?

Or some kind of admission that wouldn't burst out of her, no matter how much he egged her on, because it didn't exist?

"You could have paid someone to pack the place up. Have the stuff shipped to you. Or put in storage until you could get to it." *Admit it, you wanted to come back*, he silently challenged.

Sprinkling vegetables on the bed of flat, cooking eggs, Kelly shrugged.

He let the unspoken dig lie there in the silence. Festering.

"Much cheaper to do it this way," she finally said. "I can leave most of the stuff right where it is, as it is, and sell it with the place."

Yeah. Good point. He needed to let it go.

Wasn't in the mood to do much of anything but get under the woman's skin. She had brought him out there…kissed him…made him concerned for her safety…

"I can't imagine there'd be anything here worth the trouble to you," he said, patting himself on the back for coming up with the thought, right on time.

Kelly's spine straightened. Others might not have noticed the small tell.

She wasn't the only one with expert status in their field.

"It wasn't like you ever came out here of your own accord." He twisted the knife a little.

To the contrary, she'd hated being forced to spend those two weeks every summer with people who didn't feel like family to her.

They'd always been kind, though. He remembered her saying so. And recalled his own experience with her father's parents.

Being nice was something he most definitely was not doing. Reining in his lowest self, Levi took the deep breath he needed to apologize, just as Kelly shoved the pan over to a back burner on the small electric stove—one of the first models made—and walked into the bedroom just beyond. A room that, with two full walls of windows, had once been an enclosed porch off the kitchen.

He heard some rummaging. Dragging. What sounded like trunk fixtures being opened. And a minute later she reappeared.

"You want to know what I was coming back for?" she asked him, her eyes like glints of steel as her gaze bored into him.

"This!" she said before he could even nod, holding up a small stuffed dog with a white body and long black floppy ears. "This is what I wanted."

His gut froze. He'd given the dog to her to keep her company during her time at the cabin. To remind her that she had unconditional love.

His.

"And this," she said, reaching behind her and turning up one of his old T-shirts. She'd said she was going to sleep in it.

"And I want the stupid picture over there of the dogs playing poker. It always made me feel good as a kid. And the quilt my great-grandmother made. Willa's mother. I remember her tucking me in with it one night. I'd been crying, afraid of the spiders that were going to get me in the dark. She told me a story about a mama spider watching over children that slept, only touching them to caress them. She rubbed her hand against my cheek to show me what *caress* meant."

Had he been the mean young boy she'd made him feel like, Levi would have slapped his hands against his ears, telling her to stop.

Instead, he listened, giving her his full attention, a solid gaze. And when she fell silent, standing there holding the stuffed dog and T-shirt, he said, "I'm sorry."

"I'm sorry, too," Kelly told him, her gaze so intent, he was pretty sure they weren't talking about packing up her cabin anymore.

Turned out, while he could try to force more from her, packing-the-cabin talk was all he had to give.

Everything else had been said, and buried, long ago.

STARING AT TWENTY-SEVEN NOTES, all protected by evidence bags, laid out across her table, Kelly heard the rumble of voices outside her front door. The teams had completed their searches. Turning up nothing.

No sign of habitation. No footprints. Nothing that could explain the notes that had shown up in Kelly's portion of the Locke River. Levi had had a couple of his deputies take a look at the broken ferns across the river and just down from her backyard.

Neither of them thought the smashed greens looked like a deer bed, further mentioning that generally, when a deer bedded down by the stream, there'd be a thin trail nearby, leading down to the water.

With waders they'd borrowed from Kelly, they'd walked a half mile of river, in both directions, looking for any sign of disturbance at the water's edge, and found none.

They didn't report to her. She'd just heard the first summary as they'd come out of the water and she'd shown them the nails for hanging wet waders on the back porch.

They'd continued their discussion after joining the others out front, but Kelly had the impression, based on expressions and the little bits and pieces she could make out, that, at the very least, the jarred notes she'd found made everyone uncomfortable.

And from the frowns and shaking heads she could see, the straight faces, no one had any good theories as to the notes' source.

Filled with agitation, with the adrenaline that kept her working hard every day, Kelly tuned out everything around her and became a part of the notes taken from the evidence box. She absorbed not so much the words, but the ways in which they were written. The way words were arranged. The order in which they'd come in.

Levi's reentry into the cabin jerked her back to reality. Brake lights filled her front clearing as cars waited their turns to leave the premises via the single, two-dirt-track road that would lead them through her acres of pine forest to the county road—also dirt, but tended dirt with two full lanes—that would take them back to the state highway into town.

Assuming he'd come in to tell her he'd be heading out right behind the rest of them, she didn't give him a chance.

"Were you serious about wanting my professional opinion?" she asked him. He'd get it, either way, but a perverse, maybe personal, part of her wanted his buy-in.

"Absolutely. You find something?"

"It doesn't work that way, Levi. What I do, it's more drawing conclusions based on what's in front of me, not finding proof that a crime was committed like you do."

"Understood." Suddenly looking all powerful to her, approaching her in full uniform, with the gun and other police paraphernalia at his belt, he said, "Show me what stands out to you."

Those seven words, so simple, basic, tripped up her heart. It took her a second of staring at the evidence spread around her to right herself and treat him like anyone asking for her expert opinion. "I think that someone else, someone tied to your previous case, is still out there," she said, giving him the bottom line first, as she would any other law enforcement or attorney.

Unlike most cases, her heart pounded as she heard her words aloud. Right then, somewhere close by her, someone was in trouble.

Needing her. Whether the victim knew she was there, trying, or not.

That tamped-down ground…no matter what the others thought… Kelly was convinced someone had been watching her place. Watching her. Knew she was there.

And was reaching out…

Levi's shaking head didn't deter her. Not even a little bit. Rather, his sign of rejection spurred on her need to rescue the victim.

If the police weren't going to keep looking, Kelly could be the person's only hope.

But she was getting ahead of herself. Letting emotion slow her usual process.

"See these notes?" She pointed out the first few that had arrived fifteen years before. "They're simple, one or two words. A mostly hopeless cry for help."

He was studying the notes she'd indicated. Kelly took that as encouragement. "As they progress, they tell you more. Maybe not literally, but look at the word choice. The order. Instead of 'help me' and 'help' you have 'I need help' then later, 'I'm trapped, I can't get out.' The victim—Maura, you say—she was gaining power in her own belief that she'd be saved. Or at least gaining power in the knowledge that if she didn't help herself she was going to die in that cage."

Which, sadly, was exactly what had happened.

"There's that old saying, what doesn't kill you makes you stronger. In a sense, that's what happened here. The longer she survived, the stronger she grew in her attempt to help herself. In her belief that she had to."

There was more to it than that. Glancing at Levi, she tried to determine how much to give him at a time. Or whether to change tactics.

He was listening. But what he was thinking…she had no idea.

A fact she didn't like. She'd always been able to tell, at least a little, whether he liked something or not. From food to a friend she'd introduced him to, or even a movie they were watching.

"You're telling me that whoever wrote these notes is a new victim?"

Because they'd just said, "Help Me."

He was listening.

"Not exactly, but rather a victim who's new to the concept of asking for help. Who's just begun to try to get help."

"Say there is someone being held captive out there," he began and nodded toward the windows over the sink, looking over the river and up into the hills, "isn't it possible that the person is just getting straight to the point? Maybe he or, unfortunately, probably she, didn't have much time."

"Of course that's possible. Psychological profiling, which is basically what I'm doing here, isn't an exact science."

But it was a valid one and she wasn't going to lose him yet.

Moving away from the notes for a second, she stood in front of the pictures of the jars the notes had come in. "What did you think about these?" she asked, pointing to jars numbered eleven, twelve, thirteen, nineteen and twenty-three.

"They're more weathered than the others," he said. "Forensics confirmed that they'd been in the water longer. The logical conclusion is that, like with your logjam, they were held up by a natural blockage in the river."

"Or they could have come from another source," Kelly said. "What if there were two prisons, not just the one you found?"

"You're saying you think Yardle had more than one woman up there?" The horror in his voice spoke to her heart. He was giving her the benefit of the doubt.

As did all of her clients, or they wouldn't have hired her. Not once had someone's buy-in made tears spring to her eyes.

"It's possible, but that's not necessarily where this leads me. The original twenty-seven notes were clearly written by one person," she said, stating what had been immediately obvious to her. Handwriting tells alone gave her that. Word spacing—spaces between each word as well as margins left on the page—were also identical.

She paused long enough to point out both facts to him.

"But what if he kept Maura in two different places? One further upstream. Further back in the hills…"

Frowning, he glanced toward the map he'd left folded at the end of her table.

"You said he'd been holding her for twenty-four years, but the notes started fifteen years ago," she continued, before she lost him to geography.

"Right."

"What if she had a child, Levi? It makes sense, doesn't it? Yardle took her up in the hills to be his wife. It says so in your report. And it's not like she'd have ready access to birth control, or the ability to hold him to some kind of rhythm method…"

His face ashen, he looked at her. "You're telling me you think someone's been living up there alone for the past two months? Having just lost both parents?"

She shrugged. But pointed to the two new notes. "It's clear that these notes were written by someone much less educated than Maura. The way the letters are written, it's as though the person had to really concentrate to get them right. See the various little juts in the letters? It's as though whoever was writing them paused along the way. Like they were copying them."

"Maybe tracing them?"

"From a rudimentary school lesson in writing," she said, nodding. "I'm assuming you found nothing at the Yardle place that indicated someone had been schooled there? There's no mention of anything like that here." She held up the evidence log.

"When it turned out Yardle owned the place legally, our warrant was only for things that pointed to him holding Maura captive—the crime we were proving. Post facto. He was killed the first time we breached the premises."

"Is there any chance we can get in there again?"

"With *your* testimony, I'm sure we can," he told her. She didn't miss his inflection on *your*. Her reputation alone could get them another look.

She was busy feeling good about that when he added, "But this is all just conjecture, Kel…"

With a hand on his shirtsleeve, she pulled him to the end of the table. "Look at the squiggly at the end of the *e*, Levi. And the way the *L*'s are always capitalized."

There were four notes there—just a sampling. Any of them would have worked.

He froze.

"Whoever wrote today's notes…had access to the ones previously written," he said then.

At the very least. She believed the current writer had been taught by the previous one, but decided she wouldn't push Levi too far.

She needed his help.

His resources. And he needed hers, whether he knew it or not.

"If you can ship jars eleven, twelve, thirteen, nineteen and twenty-three—maintaining chain of command, of course— overnight them to Glen, his people could let us know, maybe within hours, if there are major differences in the water they were housed in. If they can pinpoint particulars, it might give you a starting point within the hills to begin a search…"

He didn't nod. But he didn't say no, either.

"The team could likely prove whether the five jars came from the same access point. And if you send along one of the others, you could prove that the cage you had taken down was the access point for most of the jars, but not those five."

She'd spent the past eleven years of her life making miracles with her Sierra's Web partners and their teams of experts. Never had it been more crucial to her that someone know that.

That Levi know.

She hadn't broken it off with him to live in a big city and get rich. She'd done it because she'd discovered her life's purpose.

Maybe, if he could see her in action, she'd at least be able to help him understand.

And not hate her so much.

Chapter Six

Levi wasn't just a lawman standing there getting a report from a person respected in the field of criminal psychology.

He was a man getting caught up in the professional passion exuding from his ex-girlfriend. There was nothing sexual about it. But he felt Kelly's presence in parts of his body that shouldn't be active when a guy was working. His groin, of course. But running through his entire system, too.

Like she was in his blood.

He hated to stop the flow.

But couldn't let himself get caught up in it, either. Like her, he had a job to do.

"Photocopies of a couple of the notes were printed in one of the news stories about the case," he told her. "These similarities you talk about. They could have come from someone bent on copycatting this case for reasons of their own." He had to point out the facts.

Not let emotion snowball them into rolling down the wrong hill.

Beyond that, for as long as she was in his jurisdiction, he had to keep her safe. He was pretty sure she wasn't going to cooperate, to make that feat easy on him.

"You sound like you have a theory," she told him. "Something you've already discussed with your deputies, I'm guessing?"

He'd been that obvious?

"You're good at what you do, Kel," he told her, not even trying to hide how impressed he was with the woman she'd become.

Course, he'd been just as flummoxed by the woman she'd already been, too.

"So good, in fact, that we could be looking at someone out to get *you*." He didn't want to scare her, per se, but needed her to be concerned enough that she'd get out of town.

Or, at least, into safer accommodations in Idlewood, with an escort out to the cabin to do whatever it was she needed to do there.

"That makes no sense, Levi," she told him with what sounded dangerously close to a scoff.

"Oh really." He took a step closer. "You have any rancorous court cases coming up?" he challenged, hoping she'd deny the possibility.

Her pause increased his dread.

"An expert-witness psychiatrist isn't called to court unless there's serious contention," she told him. "But I do a lot of other things, too. Just recently I worked with a woman who'd witnessed something horrible when she was three years old and at thirty-two, after another tragedy, she started having nightmares. Through cognitive interviews, I was able to help her find freedom from what haunted her."

He nodded. Impressed again. Wanting to know more. And shutting down the want. "What if someone knew their only hope was to undermine your testimony?" He pushed her right back where he needed her.

"What if they've been watching you, hoping to find anything they can to discredit you?"

"An upcoming court case would simply hire another expert," she told him.

"What if it was a case that's already been heard, and the only hope is to discredit you, then?" he asked. He wasn't the only one who'd come up with the possibility that she was the target.

"Maybe the case is up on appeal, request for another expert witness has been denied because there's already been a valid one, and the request appears as nothing more than a stalling tactic?"

He could come up with half a dozen other scenarios he'd rather not think about.

"Okay." She nodded, crossed her arms over her chest. "What if?"

"Your firm doesn't come cheap. I'm guessing someone with money, who's been irretrievably hurt by your testimony, has hired someone to find dirt on you…"

Her arms tightened. She frowned. And his heart started to pound. "You know of someone, don't you?"

"No," she said. Looking him in the eye. "It's just, what you just said, it hits a little too close to home regarding another case we handled…"

That rock in his gut grew. Aware of the gun at his side, Levi wanted to grab it, and her, and get them out of there before…

"I wasn't involved," she told him then, her tone oddly soft. As though she knew…

"A client who'd been charged with a plethora of white-collar crimes…he'd been found not guilty, but hired us—the entire firm—to prove, after the fact, that he'd been framed. He didn't just want to be out of jail—he wanted his freedom, his life back. Anyway, someone had gone to incredible lengths to follow this guy, to find one smear in his life and turn it into a blackout…"

It was his turn to nod.

And to hate the friends of hers who'd been able to give her so much more of life than he'd ever have been able to do.

"I'M NOT NEGATING your theory here, Kel." Levi's words bothered Kelly more than she wanted them to. She didn't believe for a second that someone had gone to such lengths as to follow her to Michigan, and read local news, to figure out a way to get at her.

But Levi's opinion…she'd always known she could respect that. Hearing from one of his deputies during the donning of waders just how decorated a detective Levi had become only strengthened what she knew about him.

But she had to get him on another track.

The notes weren't about her.

"How would anyone discredit me here?" she asked him, figuring her best hope in convincing him to give more serious consideration to her theory was to use his own logic against him. Someone who was desperate might try to kill her, but to copycat a crime by sending notes down the river in jars?

"By getting you to do exactly what you're doing. Using your skills, your talent, to convince the cops that solved the crime to reopen it. Get a judge to sign a warrant. Get the sheriff to allocate manpower. It's bound to get in the news. It's not like all that much of interest goes on in Idlewood. Or River County, for that matter. And now, here's this nationally renowned expert witness claiming that there's either a bigger crime than just one man, Yardle, with one woman, Maura, or that the man had more than one woman held captive. Someone who's, what, suddenly two months later deciding to ask for help?"

She opened her mouth to offer an explanation, but held her tongue long enough to hear him out.

"He plays it out as long as he can, letting it get as big as it can get, and then suddenly some anonymous proof shows up that it was all a hoax—and you're left with egg on your face."

"I don't care about my face."

But she got where he was going with his little story. Her credibility could be argued in court over such an occurrence.

"So, what, you think we should just ignore the notes?" Because she wasn't going to. She was a free citizen, on her own property. She might not be able to get jars to Glen, but on her own, she could do whatever the hell she wanted to do.

The bravado lasted all of two seconds. No part of her wanted to continue forward without Levi's help.

But she would. Because that was who she was.

She'd proved that when she'd broken up with him.

As they both well knew.

His gaze met hers, and she held on. Hearing the silent communication between them loud and clear.

"I think that you should find accommodation in Idlewood for the time it takes you to get your business done, and then head back to Phoenix. Let me do my job here."

"You're going to go looking for a prankster who's out to discredit me?" she asked. And then, "Wouldn't it be easier for you to do so if you had access to my files? Knew what cases I've worked on, and have coming up? That's your subject pool, right?"

She wouldn't give them to him. Some of them she couldn't, due to patient confidentiality, but even the court cases she could disclose, due to her testimony being public knowledge, she had no intention of sharing. Doing so could expose Sierra's Web in a bad light and she'd die before she'd do that.

The work they did, the reasons they did it, was way too valuable.

"That would be helpful, yes," he told her. Then added, "We

aren't going to ignore these notes, Kel. Nor are we only going to be looking at you."

Kelly. My name is Kelly.

"But it strikes us all as unusual that both notes showed up, in the water running through your property, right when you happened to be around to find them."

"There could be others, caught upstream, or further down, that just haven't been found yet. We're talking miles and miles of uninhabited land that this river runs through. And even where it runs through properties, like this one, most of the time the places are deserted. It could be months before anyone found them. The reason that two of them have shown up here is because I saw them," she said. "I retrieved them."

But she didn't disagree with him, either.

"And if you need more of a reason than that," she said, "I have one of those, too. Because, like you, I found it strange that there were two. Within a few hours of each other..."

Eyes narrowed, he watched her. "I'm listening."

"It has to do with the psychology of a captive, Detective," she said, putting up defenses against his "Kel" in the only way she could come up with at the moment. "Say Maura did have a child, or, even, that Yardle had two women up there. Chances are, either way, the second was younger than Maura. Looked up to her. Was dependent on her."

"How do you get that?"

"Because Maura was the first, she'd be the most experienced. She'd coach any others on how to deal with Yardle. And, if she had any heart left in her, she'd likely comfort them. And take comfort from doing so."

She wasn't trying to convince him anymore. If he wanted to run with his own investigation without her, that was fine.

He was stopping her from trying to help a victim in the hills.

"Now, take this victim. Say this is a child of Maura's, as

that's unfortunately the more likely scenario. The child had no education, except what she could give. Has lived in captivity since birth. Being fed and cared for solely by parents, who, by the way, are the only people this child has ever seen."

"You think the victim is young, then?"

She shrugged, shook her head. "Not necessarily, but it's possible. Maura was up there twenty-four years. We might be looking for a twenty-three-year-old adult. But one who, in many ways, is childlike. The victim could be much younger, though. With both parents suddenly gone, and with no outside world, at the very least this person is hugely frightened. Maybe can't even speak well. Growing up or living with Yardle, becoming aware of Maura's death, the younger person would be mistrusting of everyone. Then I show up. A woman all alone who sits and drinks coffee…"

No. Stop. That was too much.

Clearing her throat, she continued. "I think it's obvious that whoever we're looking for knew Maura sent those notes. And I'd wager a bet that that's why they're being sent."

"You really think there's another shack somewhere up there? Another person living in a cage down to the river?"

She shook her head. "I think whoever is up there is free," she told him. "And watching to see what happens with those jars. If I'm right, we'll get more."

His frown showed immediate displeasure. "You aren't seriously suggesting you're going to sit here and wait."

She had ten days left of her two weeks.

To save a life?

Hell yes.

She'd make herself available in case someone trusted her enough to come out of hiding.

"I'm going to stay here and enjoy some time off, while going through things and packing up the stuff I want to ship home," she said, staring him down.

Home was Arizona.

Not Levi.

"I THINK WE'RE dealing with someone who has more animal instincts than human ones," Kelly said, meeting Levi's gaze, as though asking more of him than he was prepared to give.

And knew he might be giving anyway.

"The handwriting…it's not just the jaggedness of it, but the different-sized letters, the slant of the words. It's like a person who never learned fine motor skills."

In five minutes, she'd given him more than he'd ever have had on his own—if she was right. There was a strong possibility she was on the wrong track.

But what if she wasn't?

And if she was…could he really just leave her sitting out there while some criminal with an axe to grind set out to ruin her credibility?

Or worse.

If the guy had enough money, a hired gun could do a whole lot more than leave notes.

Maybe that was the plan if the note-leaving didn't get her to act in a way that could be perceived to be irrational. Taking up a cause she believed in, convincing others to do so, when said cause didn't even exist, would be a great defense against her testimony during an appeal—but only if it worked.

And if it didn't?

She'd talked about a sophisticated white-collar crime setup—what if someone ran out of time, got desperate, had his hired gun kill Kelly and leave her in such a compromising situation that her life's work would be discredited?

Maybe Levi's thinking was far-fetched.

And maybe not. She lived in a world where clients had enough money to buy off people to get what they wanted. And their enemies, equally so.

Every one of his deputies had reached the same conclusion he had. On their own. They'd all been part of the note case, if not over the years, then at the end. They all found it disturbingly odd that two notes had shown up in one day in the same place. And that Kelly had seen them.

As though they'd been planted right when she'd been able to notice them.

She'd admitted sitting in front of the windows, with her door open but for the screen, that morning. It was how she'd seen the first jar.

A glint, she'd called it.

And the second jar, she'd been outside, openly visible.

One guy, Officer David, a man Levi wasn't altogether sure he liked, had even suggested that Kelly had planted the notes herself.

As a way of getting Levi's attention.

Levi wished. Not really.

Giving himself a mental shake, he knew he was going to regret his next words. But found no right choice other than to utter them.

"I'd like to join forces with you, Kel," he said, looking her in the eye. Needing her to know that, no matter what, she could trust him.

Her wide-eyed look, the small smile filling her face, gratified him for the second it took him to continue. "On a couple of conditions."

"Okay." That was it?

What the hell! Where was the fight?

"Don't you want to hear what they are?" Was he really disappointed there was going to be no battle? No way to release the repeated waves of emotion washing over him where she was concerned?

"Of course. But I'm in, Levi. I can't walk away, believing as I do that someone is out there needing my help. And I absolutely don't want to handle this alone. I know I'm not equipped to successfully manage everything that could come at me."

"You're afraid I might be right, aren't you? That someone is out to discredit you." *When had he become such a jerk?*

He entertained the question.

But he knew the answer.

The day he'd received her letter telling him that she wouldn't be returning to Idlewood. That she'd found a different life, one that suited her, and that she couldn't marry him.

"I'm not perfect, and you've presented a viable possibility."

Wow. Honest in spite of his attempt to goad her. Vintage Kelly. The woman was going to drive him over the edge.

Twelve years after she'd dumped him.

Well, he wasn't going to go over easily. He had his own life that was worth living. At least the past hours had brought him back to that much.

"You don't ever go down to the river, or out of the yard, alone. You don't even go to the shed without letting me know you're doing so. And…you make up a bed in the room furthest from the one you're using."

"What!?" She looked…shocked…maybe a bit ready to fight…then shocked some more.

"Until we figure out what's really going on, I'm staying here with you. That's my deal, Kel, take it or leave it."

Might be viewed as inappropriate—okay, highly so—for an ex-lover to force his former love to spend the night with him in a remote cabin. But accusations of impropriety were worth maneuvering if it meant he could make sure Kelly Chase stayed alive.

He knew she could trust him.

Whether she trusted him or not, she'd said she'd agree to anything.

Turning her back, Kelly walked away from him.

Chapter Seven

In one of the two original bedrooms in the cabin—both of which had one very small, very old window, a bed and a single dresser that barely fit the space—Kelly was rummaging through a bottom dresser drawer when Levi came in through the thick thermal curtain that served as a door.

"What are you doing?" he asked, seemingly peeved that she was calmly going about the business at hand.

The man had a right to be angry with her. She'd promised him a lifetime and a few years later, robbed him of it without a chance to even talk to her about it. To defend their plans.

"I'm doing what you told me to do. Making the bed," she told him, nodding toward the plastic-covered mattress. Protection from mice that took up residence in the cabin during the off-season. "While I don't know the exact measurements between the porch room, the bedroom off the kitchen by the back door, or this one off the living area by the front door, I'm guessing it's about the same. And this one is closest to the bathroom."

Down the hall from the front door. An addition that had been added the year she'd been born, or so she'd been told.

"You're not sleeping in the porch room." His tone made it clear that there was no room for argument.

"Yes, I am," she responded, as though he'd just misunderstood. "It's the room I stayed in as a kid. It's where my stuff is. And the only room where I'm not claustrophobic."

"The room is two walls of windows, Kelly. Anyone out there can watch you all night long. Shoot you while you sleep."

He was trying to scare her.

It worked.

"Then put down the shutters," she said, hating the idea, even as she offered it. But if it kept her out of the small dark rooms that had always scared her as a kid...

"We can put them back up every morning," she added. She'd do it herself. At dawn. The porch room had been a huge boon to her emotional health over the three days she'd been there. Since she wouldn't be the owner of the place much longer, the days she was there were the last she was going to get. "Besides, you said the room furthest from yours," she told him, pulling sheets and pillowcases out of their protective cover, and starting to tuck the corners of the bottom sheet under the mattress. "The other room shares a wall. I'd hear you snore all night and that wouldn't be good for either of us."

She used to tease him about his snoring. But it hadn't bothered her. She'd taken comfort from the rhythmic sound the few times they'd fallen asleep together on the couch in either of their family homes.

And once, on a blanket up in the hills he was currently there to investigate.

When he walked out without another word, Kelly continued to dress the bed.

Wearing a smile on her face.

DINNERTIME LOOMED. ALONG with almost four more hours of daylight since Michigan summers didn't see dusk until well after nine.

Levi's parents sent a text saying they were picking up Betsy.

And nothing else. He'd asked Martin to see to Betsy when he'd called his boss to let him know the status of the case.

None of his elders had mentioned a word about Kelly Chase to him.

While he welcomed the silence, it left him wondering if they thought he'd lost his mind. Maybe because he wasn't sure he hadn't.

What in the hell was he doing, staying at Kelly's cabin with her?

And yet, how could he not when the obstinate, single-minded, albeit way too kind for her own good, woman refused to leave?

Kind to others, that was. Turned out, not so much to him. A Dear John letter?

After all their years together, the closeness, the talks, that last night of lovemaking, she breaks up with him from out of state with a damned letter?

He'd saved the cursed thing until he was done for the day, had opened a beer, looking forward to Kelly's epistles about school, her classes, her friends. The highlight of his world. But had opened it to find apologies and the end of life as he'd grown to believe it would be…

He'd arranged to have the note jars sent overnight to Arizona, as Kelly had suggested. And to have a deputy pick up a list of things from his place. Was just heading out to meet the department car he could see through the trees, on its way up the drive, when Kelly jumped up from the table.

"There's someone across the stream, in the brush," she said, pointing as she headed for the door.

"Wait." He grabbed her shoulder, holding her back.

She stopped with a glance at his hand on her, but there wasn't time to react. "You stay here," he told her. "I handle the danger. That's the point of having me here…"

He was out the door before she could argue. If she followed him, at least he'd be the front-runner. Keeping her behind him meant keeping her safe.

Hand poised, ready to get his gun, he moved quietly in the direction Kelly had pointed, and saw what she had. Movement in the brush. Could be any number of members of the wild animal population making their homes in the hills beyond, coming down to get water. He didn't want to scare anything off before he had a chance to identify it.

Careful to keep his torso hidden from any chance of the lowering sun casting his shadow, he stepped as he'd been trained to step, ball to heel, making no sound. Drawing closer.

But didn't even make it as far as the bank on his side of the river, before brush moved in a quick trail away from him and into the woods. Not waiting to get waders, he traipsed into the thigh-high water, rather than heading downstream a bit where it was shallower, and using branches to pull himself up, climbed quickly onto the opposite bank. His target had seen him, knew he was in pursuit. There was no longer reason to hide his presence.

His body, though, he kept behind trees, looking out and darting from one to the next, until he lost sight of the moving brush.

Whatever had been there had either outrun him or just vanished. He took his time getting back, studying every inch of the ground he'd followed. He'd seen the deputy's car coming up the drive. Knew that Kelly would be protected back at the house.

And they needed evidence.

Deer tracks. Shoe marks. Something. He looked overhead as well. Could have been a buzzard, except for that disappearing trail of moving brush as the intruder departed.

A turkey maybe? A rafter of them? They were commonly out during the summer months.

He saw three raccoon nests.

And...a couple of porcupine quills.

The brush movement had seemed larger than a porcupine would make. Their location made sense to the flight-from-position he'd witnessed.

Back at what he'd determined was the original movement site, Levi conducted a thorough sweep of the area. To no avail.

And headed back across the river, downstream at knee height, taking the weight of the water much easier than he withstood the weight of dread he felt.

He wasn't his usual impenetrable self with Kelly Chase around. He needed her gone. And she wasn't going until they had some answers about those notes.

The last case had taken fifteen years to solve.

He couldn't see himself lasting fifteen days on the current one.

IF NOT FOR Deputy Donaldson arriving at her door, Kelly would have gone with Levi. She'd agreed to his stipulations. He'd agreed to join forces with her.

Not shut her down.

As it was, the young deputy, after unloading a couple of boxes of food supplies and dropping a large duffel on the bed she'd indicated to him, had stayed with her, talking to her about Sierra's Web. It hadn't taken long for word to get around, apparently.

She'd rather have questioned him about Levi. Or, better yet, just have him open up about his superior on his own, but Levi was heading back across the stream before that could happen.

She knew before he reached them that his trek had been unsuccessful.

And wasn't all that surprised.

She'd already put away the grocery items he'd had sent out—some had to be refrigerated—and as soon as he came back from walking his deputy out, she went on the attack.

"You scared whoever it was off." She wasn't going to be nearly as calm if it happened a second time. "If we're dealing with a child, or a young woman, or even a childlike adult, you aren't going to get anywhere playing the big bad cop out to get bad guys."

She hadn't meant to belittle what he did, and cringed inwardly at the words. But didn't take them back.

"This person obviously saw me here. Has probably been watching me for a couple of days." Oddly, even hearing the words aloud didn't scare her. Not in her scenario of what they were in the midst of.

"We've been building a rapport. I can feel it. That's why the second note was sent. Because I collected the first one. It's like the first dance." She needed him to understand. "Right now, the reaching out is at its most fragile stage. If we blow things, there might not be a second chance."

And she couldn't bear for someone to be locked alone in the wilderness until they eventually perished.

Or froze to death.

Yardle and Maura had died in the spring. Summer was relatively warm enough, even if the nights got chilly.

But come fall—and winter—unless whoever they'd left behind knew how to provide heat—that person was not going to make it through the winter.

"If someone in the state I suspect this person is in starts to feel desperate, someone else could get hurt," she told Levi—purposely hitting him where she knew he'd feel it. She needed him on board, not working against her, as he'd just done.

"A person afraid of other humans could easily be driven to break into a home where there was heat to survive. And anyone who happened to be there would most likely end up as collateral. Out of fear, not anger or hate."

And she had to make it clear. "From what I'm building here," she said and pointed to the pile of notes, both previous and current, "I don't think we have a criminal yet. But we might create one if we don't let this person come out willingly. And approach someone who seems safe."

She wasn't the one in danger. Levi needed to understand that or all could be lost.

And there was another side to that. "If this person thinks I'm a safe place, and you get in the way, you could be in danger."

Until she knew more about what they were dealing with, about who, she couldn't know the extent of danger anyone who interfered might be in.

"If you ignite a fight or flight instinct at the wrong time, when this person can't flee…"

"I found some porcupine quills right at the spot where you first saw the brush move."

He suspected a porcupine?

"They don't shoot their quills as legend says, but when they feel threatened, they tighten, readying for attack, and if they back into something, their needles are pushed out by the toughened skin."

He was giving her the kindergarten version. Her grandfather had taught her all about Michigan wildlife before he'd ever let her out on the property, and up into the hills, on her own.

"There was no other sign of an intruder, Kel. Not a single discernible shoe print. And when it ran, it stayed beneath the top of the brush. The only way a human could have stayed that low was to be on hands and knees. You really think this person could, on all fours, outrun a grown man in excellent physical shape?"

She wanted to point out that he was recovering from a gunshot wound, but she'd seen him, through the kitchen window, when he'd taken off in pursuit across the stream. And petulance didn't agree with her.

"If we're dealing with a person who's lived life more like an animal than a human, someone raised in the hills, or if we're dealing with a child, the disappearing act seems feasible to me," she told him. "And I'm guessing Yardle didn't provide his captives with shoes. Bare feet aren't likely to leave tracks in the brush."

When he didn't immediately shoot a comeback at her, she knew she'd at least convinced him not to argue with her.

And hoped that meant he was one step closer to seeing the truth in her theory.

Chapter Eight

Levi wasn't great with sitting around doing little in the best of times. With Kelly Chase around, he'd set himself up for certain failure.

He'd keep her safe. But end up sending himself over the edge.

Just as she'd been when she'd sent him her letter, she was certain she saw all, understood all and knew what was best.

"Can I ask you something?" he posed as they sat at the table after sharing the spaghetti dinner he'd already prepared that morning for his evening meal. The deputy had brought it over with the other supplies.

Had it really only been a matter of hours since he'd been in his yard chopping wood?

Coordinating and implementing a major search, even one using the civilian volunteers the sheriff's department had on its roster, was all in a day's work to him.

Going over evidence, reviewing a closed case. Ditto.

But traveling back twelve years, speeding forward to the present, heading back again, coming forth—that would make any guy's head spin. At least in his book.

Kelly finished reading the basic summary Levi's department had collected on Yardle's family history, several pages of which she'd already perused, before she glanced over at him.

"Of course. Ask away." Her agreeability had enamored him in the past. Present day, it just made him peevish.

"When you're working a case, do you keep an open mind?" He'd meant to phrase it as a request that she do so.

"I look at all sides, if that's what you're asking. But I'm trained to understand the human psyche, Levi. People hire me to tell them what I think, on a professional level, based on the evidence I'm given. Not to keep my mind open to new evidence that might present itself at a later date."

Not quite what he'd been asking, but close. She'd just put him in his place without really having to do so.

"If you're asking if I'm able to amend my opinions, with new evidence, then, yes. Absolutely."

Her gaze held his. He couldn't look away.

And didn't seem capable of preventing the small grin that split his lips, either.

DARKNESS WOULD BE falling soon. Kelly helped herself to a glass of the wine she'd purchased on her way to the cabin. Offered one to Levi because it was the polite thing to do, but wasn't surprised when he shook his head.

He'd always been a beer guy.

Still, things changed.

She sure had. More than he'd probably ever know.

She'd just finished Maura's dossier. Taken from addicted parents at the age of two, put in foster care, the woman had been passed from home to home for various reasons, none of which included any misbehavior on her part, and, when she got word, at fifteen, that she'd again be changing homes and schools, she'd run away.

No one had heard from her since, until Levi brought her home.

In a casket.

He'd taken a bullet trying to save her life, and while he hadn't been able to keep her alive, he'd found her. And had killed her captor.

He was a good man. A great man.

The best.

And that was saying something since she knew three other unbelievably wonderful men. Her partners in Sierra's Web.

He'd wanted to know if she could keep an open mind. Or rather, wanted her reassurance that she wasn't completely discounting his theory on what was happening there at her place with the copycat notes appearing.

And if he turned up new evidence that put a different light on the situation, she'd definitely take a new look.

At the moment, she felt pretty certain she was on the right track. For whatever reason, someone had noticed her over the past three days and was reaching out to her.

The being in the brush...close enough that she could see the movement...that was just too much coincidence for her.

Even with telling herself that it made sense that an animal could be there, coming down to the stream for water.

But not once in eighteen summers of visiting that cabin, eighteen years of hearing stories about things that had happened when she hadn't been present, had she ever heard of an animal coming down to the stream in broad daylight, much less with the scent of human beings around.

She didn't bother mentioning the thought.

Levi was itching for an argument. Even if it was a debate about Michigan animal life.

She didn't blame him.

Much.

Or maybe she did, a little.

Her way of handling their breakup might not have been the best where he was concerned—but it could have been. How much harder would it have been on him to see her sobbing as she walked away from him? Or he from her?

Because it had broken her young heart to let him go.

In the twelve years since, while she'd certainly dated, she'd never been in a long-term relationship. No other guy had ever come close to filling the huge void Levi's loss had left in her heart.

But he...

Watching him do a perimeter check as she sipped from her glass, listening as he lowered the shutters around the entire cabin, not just her room, locking them down, she started to burn a few angry flames of her own.

She'd wanted him to get on with his life. Honestly and wholeheartedly had wanted that for him.

But for him to do so, and then still be so angry with her...

"Can I ask you something?" she shot at him as he came back into the cabin, closing and locking the front door behind him. She could see from the door's curtained window that he'd turned on the outdoor floodlights.

No one was going to get close to the cabin without being fully exposed.

Too bad they were too far out for internet service, other than her phone's hotspot, so security cameras had never been added to the place.

He was taking his time answering. Had tossed his flannel shirt in the door of his bedroom, leaving him in the jeans and T-shirt he'd changed into after his trek through the river.

He'd lost the detective paraphernalia at his belt, too, other than the gun.

He probably slept with the thing.

Was it wrong of her to get a little bit hot at the thought?

After grabbing and uncapping a beer, he sat at the table, slouched down in his chair and said, "Ask away." As though he'd taken the time to ready himself for whatever she was about to throw at him.

Readying himself to deflect her was the vibe she was getting from him.

"Why are you so angry with me?" It wasn't the question for which she needed an answer. But getting him to admit the anger mattered in order to get what she was after.

"I think you know."

"I think I do, too," she acknowledged, watching his fingers peel at the label on his bottle of beer. "But I'm keeping an open mind..." The dig was unlike her, but she felt justified in delivering it all the same.

She'd been taking them from him all day, and it wasn't her fault a note in a canning jar had turned up on her property. Or that, when she'd read the cry for help, she'd felt compelled to call the police.

Nor was she to blame for Martin turning the case over to Levi, for that matter. Or for Levi accepting it, either.

"A letter, Kel? After six years of being together, you didn't have two days to fly out and back? Or even give me the decency of a phone call?"

Yep, she'd been right about the reason for his disdain.

And she deserved it.

Except...

"You stole my first kiss when we were twelve," she told him, keeping her tone conversational. "You told me how we were meant to be, me and you, and that we had to fight for each other, to keep us together, no matter what. But the first time we're facing a breakup, you just instruct me to return your ring and walk away, figuratively speaking, of course, since this was done by mail."

She hadn't meant to be so wordy. One sentence was all that was supposed to have come out.

He'd been sipping from his bottle, and as she'd started her tirade, the bottle had frozen midair, halfway between his lips and the table.

A full thirty seconds after she'd stopped talking, his bottle hit the table with a loud crack. The emotion-filled look in his eyes wasn't sending love her way. She wasn't sure what it was sending.

"You aren't going to sit there and tell me that if I'd fought, you'd have capitulated," he said, as though he'd never been more sure of anything in his life.

And he had her. She shook her head.

"But you wasted no time in getting over me, Levi." She delivered her endgame. "Which just proves that I was right to end things. You were able to move on, just like I'd hoped you would."

Hoped was pushing it. She'd needed him to be happy.

But when her mother called and told her that he was seeing someone, then just a few short months later he was engaged, she'd known she had to be happy for him.

And in her heartache, had known a small measure of relief, too, to know that she hadn't made a horrible mistake and ruined his life, just so she could live the life she'd been certain she was meant to live.

Twelve years later, she was certain she'd made the right choice, in terms of her own life's journey, too. She was where she was meant to be—a vital part of a vital firm that did vital work.

When he said nothing—didn't even try to deny that he'd replaced her almost immediately—she found that she had no appetite for the fight.

Her anger had come and gone. Holding her glass, she stood.

"I just think that your anger toward me isn't altogether fair," she said then, looking over at him.

And when he looked back, but said nothing, she told him she was turning in for the night.

She made her bathroom stop, noticed his shaving bag on the counter—opposite side of the sink from her own larger toiletry and cosmetic pouch—did her business quickly and prepared herself for war as she headed back out.

The table was empty. The adjoining living area the same.

Kelly walked through without stopping, swinging the porch door closed behind her.

LEVI SLEPT SURPRISINGLY WELL. Other than missing Betsy's weight on his feet, he couldn't remember a time in recent years when he'd been so comfortable.

Old beds had a tendency to feel that way, he told himself as he lay awake, just before dawn, and realized that he'd spent the best night he'd had since being shot.

He'd set his phone to wake him every two hours.

Had done cabin and perimeter checks.

But hadn't lain awake even a full minute after falling back into bed.

He'd have thought, with Kelly Chase just yards away, he'd have been chafing to get to her.

Maybe, after getting through the slog of seeing each other again, he'd finally reached a state of being completely over her.

The thought held right up until he passed her in the hallway on his way to the bathroom. Already dressed, in a pair of black what-looked-to-be stretch jeans, with a white tight-fitting short-sleeved shirt, she wished him good morning, as though meeting that way was a regular thing, and then just kept right on walking.

Unless he was going to run behind her like some kind of needy puppy dog, he had to continue on his way. Which, of course, he did. Only to be swamped by the steam from her shower, the fresh ocean scent of her body wash—a scent he knew only because it said so on the bottle in the tiny shower. If he hadn't so badly needed a cold come-down-to-earth massacre of skin, he'd have foregone the need to step on the wet shower floor she'd just vacated.

And took the fastest shower in his personal history when he started to picture her body as it had been, in there, only moments before.

So much for being over her.

If his body's reaction—even with frigid well water beating at him—was any tell, he was anything but over the one woman he'd never been able to get out of his system.

Chapter Nine

Kelly had the shutters up, held in place by the posts that went from the heavy, roof-tiled shutter to a block on the house, and coffee made in the few short minutes it took Levi to shower and finish his ablutions.

She needed the enclosed intimacy of the cabin to disappear. Wanted to be at the table by sunup, in case her newest client was watching for her, and had a raging headache that would only be soothed by loads of caffeine.

Unlike the first three nights she'd spent at the cabin, she'd hardly slept all night. With Levi getting up every two hours, even if she'd started to relax, she'd hear him and get het up all over again. While she'd told Dorian and Savannah, the two of her partners who'd seen her off at the airport in Phoenix, that she was sure she was over Levi, she'd clearly been wrong about that.

There'd been good reason her brain had told her not to venture into Idlewood, risking a chance to run into him. If only her psyche had also given her a clue as to the tragic state of her heart, and her body, where he was concerned.

How did one burn with wanting for someone she'd only slept with once?

And hadn't seen since the summer after high school graduation?

With no answers readily available, other than the obvious—

she had to get herself under control and make her escape as soon as possible—Kelly didn't even glance Levi's way when she heard him behind her.

"Coffee's hot, cups are in the cupboard directly above the maker," she told him, her gaze on the meadow directly on the other side of the river. Wishful thinking on her part that whoever needed her would magically appear, let her approach, respond well, and they could wrap everything up in time for her to catch a flight home yet that day.

But she let herself go with the thought anyway.

Right up until Levi sat perpendicular from her, taking the seat at the end of the table, placed a notepad in front of him and said, "We need a plan of action."

Without waiting for a response, he wrote on the pad. "First," he said, "I need to know how soon your partner thinks he can get us evidence on those jars. If we're lucky he'll be able to lift fingerprints off the two new ones."

"Even if he does, you won't find them in any database, Levi," she told him.

"I might, if based on your theory that someone just needs our help, the person is a runaway who was kidnapped like Maura was…"

She should have thought of that. Sipped more coffee. "It's three hours earlier in Phoenix," she said. "I'll call Glen later this morning. Since he has to wait for the shipment of jars to arrive, there's no point in dragging him out of bed."

Looking back at his pad, writing again, Levi said, "Second, I need what you can give me of your Sierra's Web case files, Kel." Before she could object, he held up a hand. "I know there are protocols and protections. Just give me everything you can. Any case that isn't protected, and for those that are, if you can give me basic facts, not names or places, just things to go on so I can get a picture of this guy…"

As tired as she was, she had to acknowledge that, on the off chance he was right, they had to be prepared. "I'll get right on it," she told him.

"Third," he said, pen to paper as he spoke, "I'd like you to accompany me to the Yardle place. I'm clearing it with the sheriff, and as soon as we get a warrant, I want you to go over the place with me. Professionally. Doing what you do."

Her gaze shot up to his. He was giving her credence. Suddenly infused with some energy, she sat up straighter. Nodded. "Absolutely." Her mind began spinning with things she should look for, signs of cohabitation. Either two women in captivity, or a woman and child...

Levi's people had been up the day before, looking for signs of habitation, but he'd look deeper. She instinctively knew that about him. When it came to his responsibilities, Levi seemed to have a photographic memory—whether for homework, or remembering every little detail of something that mattered to her. He'd notice if anything looked different from the photos he'd seen after the case was solved.

Didn't matter that he'd been in the hospital, and then recovering, so hadn't been able to do the actual canvassing of the place himself. He'd have put every detail to memory. She'd bet her life on that one.

"And fourth." He put his pen down. And, picking up his coffee mug, sipped from it, watching her over the rim.

"I didn't replace you, Kel. I moved on, just like you mandated that I do. Because that's what you were doing. I knew what I wanted. A wife and kids and a life here in Idlewood. Her name was Jen. It didn't take her long to figure out that, while I was fond of her, good to her, I wasn't in love with her. She stuck with me until she met someone who was in love with her. I caught them in bed together. The divorce was quick and amicable. I was invited to the wedding."

Wow. Her mother had left town by then. She'd heard at some point that Levi was divorced, had passed the basics on to Kelly, but hadn't known any details.

Levi hadn't replaced her.

He'd moved on.

There was no reason the distinction should matter. The things that separated them, that made them not meant for each other, still stood there, big firewalls, between them. She stared out at the meadow, her eyes scanning the bank. The water.

No glints.

"And five." Levi's words brought her gaze back to his. "Who was he?"

"Who was who?" Kelly's immediate frown, her seeming total confusion, didn't fool Levi. Even though she'd learned over the past decade plus to hide her thoughts, he'd known her then.

No way she'd have just thrown away the life they'd had before them. Not unless her heart had been completely taken over by someone else.

"Obviously there was someone else." He told her what he'd figured out after days of reading her letter over and over. "Your life is led by your heart, Kel. He had to have been someone who took your breath away so fast that you couldn't live without him."

Words she'd once said to him.

Open-mouthed, she stared at him. Figuring he'd make it easy on her, getting it all out there without her having to say a word of confession, he continued. "You knew if you came to see me, I'd figure it out. Same thing for a phone call. I'd hear it in your voice."

They'd been that close.

"You thought you were sparing me, letting me think it was just you, your life, who you'd discovered yourself to be. You didn't want to hurt me worse by letting me know some other guy meant more to you than I did."

When her jaw clamped shut, and her gaze shuttered, Levi almost wished he'd kept the truth to himself.

Except that there it sat, in the air between them. Stifling them both.

Preventing them from giving their total focus to finding the whack job who was out to get her before she pressed her theories so far, he wouldn't be able to keep someone from the news getting ahold of them.

And, in the end, making her look like a fool. Perhaps ruining her entire career. Or worse.

Even in the unlikely event that she was right, they'd need total focus to find, in tens of thousands of acres, a hunted woman who'd been warped by who knew what atrocities, or a woods person who'd been raised to stay hidden.

His phone rang before either of them had a chance to change the subject.

They had the warrant to take her up to Yardle's cabin.

They had no more time to sit around and talk. They had work to do.

And maybe that was for the best.

She'd found someone she'd loved more than him.

The guy's name wasn't going to do him any good.

IT HAD BEEN a long time since Kelly had been on any kind of a real hike. Walking with Dorian up a mountain path in the middle of Phoenix, one that wound delicately around the mountain, was nothing like traipsing up slippery dead leaves with twigs and brush. If she had to bet, she'd put money on the fact that Levi's quick pace was meant to show her up.

Which meant she couldn't let it.

And didn't really need to. She could keep up. She just didn't have a lot of air and fortitude left over for conversation. Not that she wanted any.

She'd been shocked when Levi had accused her of leaving him for another man. And yet, as she climbed—keeping her eyes constantly scanning for any sign of movement or life around her—she could understand how Levi had reached the conclusion he had. In her mind, the idea was ludicrous and she hadn't seen him going that way with it. But when he'd laid it all out for her, she got it.

Their perspectives both held logical possibility.

The reminder came at a critical time. Levi was a great detective. She needed to pay more attention to his perspective on those notes. If someone were out to ruin her, there was no better way to do it than show her as someone who could be so easily led astray into a fantastical theory of someone no longer in captivity living of their own accord as an animal in the woods.

Seeing her at her cabin.

And sensing by, what, osmosis, that they could ask her for help?

She knew who she was, what she did—someone trapped out in the woods wouldn't have that information.

They'd headed out early enough that the summer sun hadn't yet risen high enough to warm the air, but with the forest of trees towering around and above her, it wasn't like any of the warmth was going to reach her as long as they stayed in the woods.

But it wasn't the heat she was worried about, as she picked up her pace, keeping her closer to Levi. Whichever scenario she went with to explain the notes, Levi's or hers, there was every likelihood that she was being watched.

That they were being watched.

"If someone *is* using the Yardle shack, you need to let me

talk to them before you pull a gun," she said softly, walking on a flat patch of ground beside him. "Assuming the person looks lost, confused, disheveled or under eighteen," she quickly amended.

"Got it, Doc."

His words, seeming to carry a grin in them, made her smile. Was it possible she and Levi could find their way to a truce?

Maybe even become friends?

Stay in touch now and then?

The thought turned her grin into a smile. That lasted on the inside until the rudimentary home was in sight. With a finger to his lips telling her to be silent, and a flat hand telling her to wait, Levi bent low and approached the shack without making a sound, while she stood still.

More than a little nervous, watching the area all around them.

When one minute became two, with Levi out of sight, Kelly started to worry. She'd heard no gunshots, no scuffling or voices. Surely he hadn't walked into a trap that had quietly taken his life.

But if she went to investigate, maybe she'd lose her own the same way.

They'd lost cell phone service half an hour back. Levi had prepared her for that eventuality. Just as he'd forewarned about her current situation.

If he were to be rendered incapable, by any means, she was to run, and keep running, taking the quickest route with cover to the river, and dial Martin as soon as she had service.

He'd made her put his uncle's personal number on her speed dial.

She'd taken it all in, repeating it back to him as he'd demanded, programmed in the number, all to appease him.

Certain that he'd crossed the line into overkill.

But standing there alone in the woods, with more than a thousand acres separating her from any sign of civilization...

And then she heard it. The birdcall. A whip-poor-will. In Michigan, they generally sounded in the woods during summer evenings. And it wasn't two calls. Silence. Two calls. Silence.

She was hearing Levi's version. He had an owl call, too. Had entertained her on summer nights calling birds, and having her listen for them to respond.

He was calling her.

But what did it mean?

She was to leave if there was total silence. He'd have told her if his birdcall was a sign to go for help. A much better plan, now that she thought about it.

The call came again, and she listened carefully, moving slowly in the direction from which she thought it was coming, keeping cover in the woods as she did so.

If he was certain no one was nearby, he'd have just called her name.

If he was able to birdcall, he must be okay.

But maybe he had someone in sight? Someone who was under eighteen? Or looked as though they'd been living in the woods...

Moving as swiftly as she could while remaining as soundless as possible, she circled around to the back of the shack, her gaze focused on the building and small clearing around it. They'd approached from the hillside, and what she spotted as she saw the view in front of her both stunned and stopped her.

The cage to the water had been removed, but the metal posts cemented into the ground—clearly what had held the fencing—still remained, and led a clear, half-mile path down to water flowing below. She'd pictured the shack in a valley between hills, with access to the river similar to her own. Instead, Maura had had to traverse that steep path with loads of laundry? To bathe throughout most of the year...

The whip-poor-will sounded again, closer now, and Kelly turned. What had felt like long minutes of standing still, had only been a second or two, and she was back on track. Turning toward the birdcall. Moving forward as the call sounded again, and again. Almost continuously, with her going in circles, thinking she was getting close, but not seeing Levi.

She was looking outward, watching for a sign of movement from him, thinking he was leading her to their victim, took a step and lost her balance as the ground seemed to give way. And then, with her foot landing on something solid only an inch or so down, righted herself almost immediately.

"Kel..."

Was that Levi? Whispering to her?

Spinning, her eyes wide, she searched everywhere with no sign of Levi.

Was she losing a grasp on reality? Too caught up in being back in Michigan? Selling the cabin? Seeing Levi again?

Thinking he was whispering to her?

"I'm down here," he whispered again. Her foot moved beneath her. Not enough to unbalance her.

Just enough for her to glance down.

And see Levi's fingers wrapped around her tennis shoe.

"Levi?" she whispered back, following his lead.

"Step off me," he said then. The urgency in his voice was apparent. Moving immediately, she dropped to her hands and knees, thinking he'd found a tunnel into and out of the house.

But...

He hadn't been in the house...

"Oh my God, Levi? What happened? What..."

"I stepped on what at the moment seems to be Yardle's

idea of a land mine," he told her. "Took a step and slid down a rabbit hole."

Heart pounding, she stared down, saw only darkness. And the tips of his fingers.

"My foot's on some kind of root," he said then. "If it gives, I fall. I have no idea how deep this thing goes. I need you to get to phone service as quickly as possible, watching your back, and get help."

Her head shook before he'd even finished. "I'm not leaving you, Levi. You could slip. The root could give way. Quit wasting time and tell me how to help."

He didn't move.

"I mean it, Levi Griggs," she hissed softly. "You work with me or I…"

"Tie this belt around your ankle and the trunk of a tree about five feet out from here," he shot up in a hoarse whisper, barely giving her time to grasp what was going on as his belt flew up at her. "And be careful, while we've had teams out here multiple times now with no problem, we have no idea what this hole is for. There might be another. More importantly, someone could be watching."

She caught the belt with one hand. Amazing considering she was shaking so badly. Then, putting pressure down before she actually took steps, carefully walked off what seemed to be five feet. Belted herself to the tree, and then lay down exactly where she'd walked, stretching out so that she could get close enough to the small hole in the ground in order for him to hear her. "Okay."

"Good. You're already lying flat. Stay that way, Kel, and lower your arms down. I'm holding a root with one hand. I'm giving you my free one first. I'm going to grasp your forearm, and need you to grasp mine. If you can bear the weight, we'll repeat the same for the second arm. The root at my foot might give way when I let go with my hand. As long as you can hold me steady, giving me something solid to hold on to, I think I can climb up the dirt…"

She'd bear the weight. Even if it pulled her arms out of their sockets. She was not going to let Levi suffocate down some hole while she went for help and someone made it up there with equipment to dig him out.

"Just be careful. I don't know if we're alone up here…"

"And you didn't want to find that out with me up here un-protected, right, Detective?" she said, forcing a saucy tone to her voice. She would be his rock, not his crumbling cake.

"Guilty," he told her as she felt the first hard tug on her right arm. "Does that hurt?"

"No." Her muscles were straining…more than she'd have thought possible. She wouldn't call it pain.

"Give me your other hand."

She'd already set it down to him before he got the words out.

And as she held on, closing her eyes to visualize his suc-cessful attempt to save himself in an effort to stave off the burning pain in her arms, she'd never been more afraid in her life.

Chapter Ten

He could feel her arms trembling. Knew he was hurting her.
And dug his feet into the earth surrounding him. Adrenaline
pumped through him in waves as Levi got one elbow up on
level ground, laying his arm flat. Still holding both of Kelly's
arms securely, he didn't allow himself to look at her, to read
the pain on her face, as he fought to get one more step up so
that he could let her go.

"I've got you." He wasn't sure he heard the words or imagined them, but went with them as he dug the toe of his boot
into earth and used his freed elbow to push into the ground
to push his body upward. He was there, his second elbow
aboveground, as the dirt beneath his lower foot gave way and
he started to slide.

"No," he said through gritted teeth, and pushed with his
steady elbow, felt the tug come from Kelly's smaller arm
grasping his trapped limb. Once. Twice. As his boot scrambled for another hold, he felt a weed under his elbow. Crushed
against it for all he was worth, and got his shoulders aboveground. He hung there, arms and shoulders out, one foot on a
root that he prayed was solid.

"Don't stop now, Detective." Kelly's voice was sexy, taunting. "You know how you hate to get close and have to quit."

He got the reference immediately. She was describing the

sex life they'd shared for all but one night of the six years they were together. They got close, real close, inventively close, but always quit before he actually entered her.

She tugged, and he scrambled toward her and was lying on his stomach with only his legs hanging in the hole. Sweating profusely. A little scraped up.

And afraid to look at Kelly. To see the damage he'd done.

She might have broken his heart, but she'd saved his life.

And for that, he would always love her.

LEVI INSISTED THAT they each have a long stick in hand, poking the ground in front of them before each step as they made their way back down to her place. And he went first, having her step directly in his path, as a secondary safety measure.

She understood.

Just wished she could get him to believe that she was fine.

Yeah, the muscles in her upper arms were shaky. Her forearms ached, and already bore bruises from his grip on them.

She didn't give a whit about any of that.

She cared about not ruminating on the deep, tight hug he'd given her after he'd unfastened his belt from the tree and they'd both stood up.

Strangers who'd just lived through what they had would have done the same.

"How long do you think it'll take for your team to get up there with scopes so we can get in the cabin?" she asked as they neared her land and he threw his stick off to the side.

"An hour or two to get up there, another hour to clear the area. I'll have them mark a direct path on the way up."

"You don't honestly think Yardle made traps all the way out of the hills," she said. She understood his caution where getting them both back to her cabin safely was concerned.

But they still had a job to do.

"No," he admitted. "But I'm not letting you back up there without taking every precaution."

Because his genuine worry for her warmed her heart, she didn't argue further.

"We knew about the booby traps with the cans," he said as they put on the waders they'd hung from a tree, and made it back across the river to her place.

"To alert him if anyone got too close to the cabin," she replied, repeating what he'd said half a dozen times on their way down.

The hole he'd fallen into had shaken him.

In a way she'd never seen before. Levi had been truly scared.

The idea not only frightened her, but it tore at her heart, too.

"But why the hole? Why had he tunneled such a deep hole? And how? It's not like he could take equipment up there."

She heard him repeat the question to Martin when they were safely back in the cabin and he called his boss.

Why or how a demonic man had created a hole in the ground didn't concern Kelly nearly as much as how Levi had happened to step into one.

Pure chance?

It seemed certain.

And yet, she'd had an eerie feeling as they'd been leaving the shack's clearing. As though someone had been watching them.

Had been watching all along.

But she decided, rather than lose credibility, to keep the sensation to herself.

THERE WERE A total of six approximately twelve-foot holes in various spots all around Yardle's shack. Sinkholes, technically.

Except that from what Levi was told by the experts who'd

surveyed for him, the holes had been created by well drilling. Where there were no wells.

The single well that served the shack's one pump had been put in a hundred years ago—before Yardle's birth.

The new holes were no more than twenty-five years old. There could have been a path cleared up to the place decades ago. The first well had been drilled somehow. Yardle could have had equipment up on his property as a young man and no one would have known the difference.

Any sign of a road would have grown over long before he and his teams had been up in the area.

Could be that the man had been drilling to find a new well source. Except that every place he'd drilled would have made a great well, and he'd neglected to put one in.

"You think he was creating sinkholes to use as threats to Maura in case she ever got out and tried to escape? She wouldn't know there were only six. She could assume the shack was surrounded by them. That there was no way out," Kelly said as they sat at her kitchen table, eating sandwiches he was pretty sure neither of them wanted. His stomach felt like lead. She had barely touched her lunch.

"You need to eat," he told her, still concerned that she was in more pain than she was letting on. "I'm not taking you back up there without some energy from this food." At the moment, peanut butter.

A much easier topic than the one she'd just put forth. Because he did believe, wholeheartedly, that terrorizing Maura was exactly what Yardle had done. With the cage, sinkholes and probably other horrible things they'd never know.

"What were you doing when you stepped in the hole?" Kelly's question came softly as she took a bite of sandwich.

The quick mental flash that followed her quiet question came out in easy communication. "I thought I saw something move. Fall from a tree maybe. There was something glinting on the ground."

"Like what?"

He'd just heard his own words. The flash was gone.

"I have no idea. Probably nothing."

"Or something meant to get you to step where you did." Kelly's words came just as softly as the previous ones, but hit him loud and clear.

"You can't possibly think that what happened up there was a direct attack on my life?"

"If someone thought you were preventing them from finding safety with me, absolutely."

He shook his head. Didn't buy it. More likely, whoever was after Kelly was seeing success with every piece of bait she took, and was going to play this out as long as he could. While the location of Yardle's shack hadn't been in the news, the man's name had been. Anyone with patience and enough motivation could find the Yardle family plot in old records. And with some work, figure out the coordinates up on the hill.

Kelly was watching him.

"Then why let me leave?" he challenged her.

"My first guess would be that, other than the traps and means Yardle used, whoever is left up there doesn't know what to do to get rid of a threat. The report says law enforcement confiscated all possible weapons and ammunition as part of the crime scene."

Levi did not like her words. Didn't like anything about the situation that was quickly turning into more than a jar with a note.

He hated that he couldn't refute what Kelly was telling him. Even while he remained fairly certain that she was wrong. But what scared him most of all was that she truly seemed to believe what she was saying. And thus believed that while others could be hurt, she was in no danger at all.

AT LEVI'S REQUEST, a couple of deputies accompanied the two of them back up to the shack in the hills. With the hike being more than an hour one way from her place, they didn't make it back until midafternoon. Other than answering a question or two about her work, and her and Levi's experience that morning, she remained silent throughout the trek. Concentrating on holding back from the three men. Ostensibly to not intrude on their shop talk.

In fact, she wanted to be seen as apart from them. Separate. A woman alone who would be approachable when she was on her own.

She just had to find a way to lose her ex-fiancé bodyguard long enough to be approached.

And in the meantime, to appear as unalarming as she had while sitting all alone at her cabin contemplating life for three days.

On her current mission to Yardle's place, that meant that in addition to conducting a psychological assessment based on the interior of the shack, she had to be the overseer of personal space.

The protector, making certain that the men with guns didn't damage or overly disturb what might be the only home someone had ever known.

They were just minutes away from the site, by her calculations, when a thought occurred to her. If she was dealing with a captive, how would that person have known where to shoot a berry with a slingshot, or drop something from a tree above—or whatever other means of making it appear as though something dropped on the ground—in the exact place where the sinkhole had been?

If the purpose for those holes was to create fear in whoever lived inside the cabin, to keep them from wandering were they to escape locks and cages, then said person wouldn't know where the sinkholes were.

Unless Yardle had loved the child born to him. Had taught said child how to escape in the event of emergency...

The thought, while somewhat chilling, also gave her hope. If the child had grown up with love, albeit in a very twisted and disturbed situation, there was more hope for an eventual transition to a healthy future.

Or...she had to admit the more likely possibility that Levi had just been unusually unlucky to have stepped in only one of six places on the property where he could have fallen in.

"FROM THE MOMENT he brought her here, Maura was taught that she was beneath her abductor, not just sexually, but in every sense," Kelly said as she slowly walked around the small space inside Yardle's shack. At her request, the two deputies who'd hiked up with them remained outside.

It had been an easy request for Levi to grant, since that had been his plan all along. No way was he going inside with her without backup watching the area around them.

"See the beds," Kelly continued softly. "One is not only shorter than the other, but lower to the ground."

He'd noticed as much in the photos he'd seen. Had figured it had to do with the tree limbs that had been used to create them.

Or the amount of old clothing that had been handstitched together to form the mattress that held the crumbled leaves inside for cushioning.

"He taunted her with things withheld from her," Kelly continued, pointing up toward the ceiling. "Those high shelves, with no counter space between them. Something he could reach, but she could only see. My guess is she'd be rewarded with whatever was up there for a deed well done."

She stopped, but he saw the shadow cross her face.

"Or punish her with whatever was up there to remind her what would happen if she misbehaved," he said. Kelly saw a lot of bad stuff in her job. He was just beginning to realize how much. No reason she had to shoulder it all alone.

Her shrug told him he'd gotten that one right.

And he was reminded of the hug they'd shared after she'd pulled him to safety. She'd held on so tightly.

Because she still cared?

He couldn't help wondering.

But couldn't make anything of it, either. Because they'd had their breakup. They'd both thrived.

They weren't meant to be.

But her focus, the way she let the room speak to her... He glanced around. The couch had been moved from the original photos—something he'd noticed, and mentioned, when they'd first walked in. It was a foot closer to the tree trunks and limbs that served as a table.

Could have happened the day before when his team had been up there searching the place.

He agreed with their assessment, though. There wasn't any obvious sign of habitation over the past couple of months. And he said as much to Kelly.

"If Yardle kept anyone up here under his strict control— and it's fairly obvious that he did—it's believable that whoever is left behind will continue to conduct each day in the same manner. Sameness gives a sense of safety. And if it's all they know..."

More of her head stuff.

It made sense. But it was like she was writing a story, not solving the mystery of notes in a jar. He didn't have time for stories. He needed answers, the case done and Kelly safely on a plane to wherever she was headed next.

Chapter Eleven

Levi had said the couch had been moved. And...the sameness of daily activity... Kelly went to the couch, looked at the wall. The floor.

Noticed nothing. When Levi came up close, looking over her shoulder, she moved on. Closeness to the man who'd lit her hotter than any other—most particularly after that hug—was a thing to avoid. Not a debatable point.

But moving furniture...

At the end of what she believed to be Maura's bed, she pushed with her thighs, but the thing didn't budge. Bolted to the floor somehow? Or, because it was made of solid wood, just too heavy?

Her knee brushed the mattress. Reminded her of making Levi's bed the night before. The thoughts that had run through her mind as she'd touched the sheets that would be holding his body...

A mattress moved. How else would one change the bedding?

Pulling the smaller mattress away from the wall, Kelly stared. "Levi..."

Anyone investigating a crime scene with both the victim and the perp dead wouldn't think much of small marks on a crudely built wall—if they'd even seen them. They wouldn't have had to remove the mattress to check under it. All they'd have had to do was look up when they scanned under the bed. And even if they had...

"What?" Levi asked, standing at the opposite end of the bed from her.

She pointed to the small marks going against the grain of the wood. All in twelve separate little grids. And the rudimentary tip—the end of a porcupine thorn—sticking out of one of them.

"Months of the year," he said, his focus intent.

"And the tip is in the fourth mark of the fourth grid."

"April fourth. The day Maura died. She kept track of the days she was here...for twenty-four years."

"She wasn't giving up," Kelly said. "She had something to live for, Levi. I'm telling you...there was someone else up here. After twenty-four years of captivity, especially having been taken so young, and without a previous loving home to remember—Yardle was her family. He was all she had. And he provided for her—no matter how disgustingly. And in spite of the fact that he was brutal to her, too. Natural instincts would have her give up hope of change. Give in. Accept. Even fall in love with him. There'd be no motivation or motive, either, for keeping a count of the days. One was the same as another. It was the life she knew. But this...such a diligent count of days that she knew the date the day she was killed...it's like I said, she had a reason, other than just herself, for trying to get out."

"She had a child," Levi said, and she wanted to believe that he was finally seeing the bigger picture, but knew he could just be repeating the theory she'd already shared with him. Drawing conclusions from where he knew she was headed.

"Or someone else, besides Yardle, to live for. Some reason for time passage, or awareness of time, to matter."

"Could just be that she wanted to know when to expect changing seasons," Levi offered.

"Or to know when her period was coming," Kelly offered. "So that she could prevent pregnancy."

And that was why it was important to talk things through, she reminded herself. Maybe Levi was right. She was pushing too hard to prove her theory, rather than observing all sides and drawing professional opinions with an open mind.

"Obviously she started keeping time pretty much from the day she arrived," Levi offered then. "She'd had to have done so to have an accurate date twenty-four years later."

"Or she somehow got word of the date along the way and then kept track…"

Deflated, Kelly realized that while the discovery gave them a bit of insight into Maura, it didn't really shed any light on their current situation. It could mean that Maura had something to live for besides Yardle. But they had no way of knowing if it did.

The biggest impact the calendar had was that it had given Kelly a heads-up on her own bias.

And made her wonder, too, if the reason she'd lost sight of it, even for a day, was because she'd been driven by a subconscious need to put defenses up against Levi. And so she had needed a theory separate from his. Something to keep them apart. On opposite sides of the fence.

That theory pleased her least of all.

"THERE'S A BLANKET MISSING." Levi hadn't wanted to feed Kelly's obsession with Maura's story and someone left up there as collateral, needing her, but neither was he going to treat her as anything less than a professional.

"What?" She stared at him.

Pointing to the end of the bed, he said, "There was a blue

quilt there. It was odd to me, a quilt, in the midst of all of this stuff made out of whatever Yardle could get off the land up here. We figured he probably stole some stuff—like the garments used to make the mattresses, and clothes throughout the years..."

His voice trailed off as instincts kicked in. Someone other than his people *had* been in the cabin—most likely whoever was out to get Kelly—and he'd just found his clue.

Crime scene photos, taken before and after all evidence had been collected, didn't lie.

A stolen blanket, to ward off summer night chills up in the hills, fit a hired gun forced to spend time watching Kelly, leaving clues that would keep her mind spinning.

Was he feeding the perp information, helping him, by involving Kelly in the investigation?

If he didn't, she'd be out there on her own. A far worse prospect.

"It makes sense," Kelly replied. "If someone left behind was missing Maura they'd take comfort in her quilt. You're sure it was on this bed?"

Grabbing his phone, Levi scrolled back two months, pushed a photo and showed it to her. Hoping he wasn't also helping to put a knife in her back.

She'd already seen the crime scene photos. Would have certainly looked them up again as soon as they returned to the cabin.

He'd memorized every inch of every photo during his first week of recovery. Had gone over them far too many times since, too. Including the fact that the end of the couch had been underneath the big ugly knot on the wall.

Kelly turned a complete circle, looking over the entire space—reminding him of a time they'd been at the beach and she'd spun around with her arms out. He'd asked her what she was doing, and she'd just smiled at him. And told him she was soaking up the happiness.

He didn't want to ask what she was soaking up at the moment.

And looked down. To the floor by the couch. From his current angle, there was a darker line along a board in the floor. With the boards' roughness, having been laid, but not sanded or coated, so long ago, it was hard to see, period, but from where he stood...

He walked back over to just below the large knot. Pulled his knife off his belt and bent down.

"Well, I'll be damned," he said a minute later. He'd pulled up a single board, a smaller one, maybe eight inches in length, clearly cut to fit to the wall. Was staring down into a small, boarded-off area lined in some kind of plastic? Part of an old tarp maybe.

"It's empty," Kelly said, stating the obvious. "And you said the couch was moved," she continued. "Maybe this is where Maura hid the extra jars she managed to hide away without Yardle noticing."

She'd missed her calling. Should have been a fiction author.

"Or where Yardle hid the gun he used to kill her," he pointed out.

What bothered him was that...

"You said the couch was moved." Kelly finished his thought as though she'd been in there reading it.

Yep. That was it. "Probably just got bumped by one of my people up here yesterday," he answered, repeating his earlier thought.

"If someone like Maura, whether it be a child or another woman, had accessed the spot, they'd have moved the couch back." Kelly's words brought his gaze from the spot in the floor to her—a bit of a travel since he was still down on his haunches. "Clearly the place was meant to be a secret. One they'd be afraid to expose. Continuing the practice would be a natural way to maintain a feeling of safety."

She'd just jumped away from supporting her theory. From thinking that they'd found a recently accessed spot where Maura's jars could have been hidden.

"Yardle's gone," he pointed out. Testing her? "You keep saying this person is afraid, but the cause of the fear is gone. They'd have to know that by now."

"But if you've lived in fear for years, just because the source is gone doesn't mean the fear is. The mind works in its own way, Levi. For all this person knows, Yardle told someone about what he was doing and they're living in fear that that person shows up. I've seen the mind go into all kinds of tunnels over the years. If, as I think, we're dealing with someone who's been kidnapped, held captive and abused for a long time, or worse, someone who was born into captivity, then you can't count on this person to exhibit rational behavior. Their life has taken a turn most of us can't even imagine. Their actions aren't necessarily going to make sense to you or me."

She had him again.

"To you, they might," he told her, taking several pictures of the hole in the floor, from various angles, before covering it back up.

"You think I'm not in my right mind?" she asked, sounding affronted. He couldn't tell if she was teasing him or not.

Which bugged him. Meeting her gaze, his completely serious, he said, "No, Kel, I think you're that talented."

The surprised look on her face, followed by a serious nod, told him he'd pleased her.

Not his job. Or, he hoped, his intention.

He'd simply stated the truth.

From one professional to another, she deserved it.

And from one professional to another, he added, "Let's head out. We haven't found anything that's getting us anywhere."

He didn't know if he was relieved, or disappointed, when Kelly didn't argue with him.

THE HIKE BACK down out of the hills was mostly conducted in silence. As if by previous agreement, everyone kept their distance from each other. And did a lot of intent looking around.

Kelly hoped that if someone was spying on them, it was clear that no one had taken anything out of the cabin. Thankfully new phone images wouldn't be something on her victim's radar.

Everyone, including herself, watched carefully for any sign of a piece of the missing blue quilt. Levi had shown the image to both of his deputies before they'd started the trek down.

Kelly didn't expect to see any sign of the blanket. It would be wherever the victim was hiding out. For all she knew, it was being carried back to the cabin every night, but taken for security out into the hills during the day.

In cases like the current one, all she could do was give educated guesses and hope that she was close enough to the truth to be able to help.

As soon as she had cell service back, her phone buzzed a message.

A missed call.

From Glen.

She dialed him back immediately. Once she and Levi were alone in the cabin, she relayed the conversation. "The new jars are a match for some of the previous ones."

Which meant very little. "They're made by the same manufacturer," she clarified. "According to Glen, they're the most common, can be bought at pretty much any place that sells canning jars, and at yard and junk sales, too."

That news hadn't surprised her. Levi, sitting at the table with the cup of coffee she'd poured for him, nodded. Lifted his ankle to rest on the opposite knee. While he seemed relaxed, she could almost feel the energy radiating off from him. And knew his mind was working.

She almost hated to give him what else Glen had told her. Afraid he'd fly off with his theory and leave her, and hers, in the dust.

Her gut was telling her not to quit this one.

"He got a fingerprint from inside the edge of one of the new jars." She delivered the news she was bound by professional courtesy to share. "And from both of the notes. It wasn't in any database."

Which kind of blew a little hole in his hired gun theory. Most people with enough money to pay someone to do dirty work, and who would actually hire someone, didn't go for amateurs. But they'd go for a professional who'd been good enough to not get caught. Someone who'd never been arrested and wasn't in the system. At the very least, someone who knew better than to leave fingerprints.

Levi watched her, his gaze intent again, as though he knew there was more.

"Based on the fingerprint ridge density, among other things, Glen says we're most likely looking for a male, six feet or so in height," she finished.

And that fact pretty much blew her own theory to smithereens.

"WHILE THERE'S A marked difference in male and female ridge densities, there's also overlap." Levi told himself his statement was offered strictly for the case, not because Kelly looked so bothered by the news she'd just delivered.

"That's what Glen said," she offered, nodding. Her expression a bit less strained. And he wondered if her tension had been more because she'd thought he'd use the information to cram his theory down her throat than because she was bothered by the news.

And shook his head.

"What?"

Keep your mouth shut.

"Nothing." He gave another shake of the head to emphasize the weight behind the delivery.

"Levi…"

That look in her eyes…it pulled at him.

"This lack of trust between us," he blurted out. "It's hard to take."

"Yeah." She didn't look away. He needed her to look away. "Kind of criminal in and of itself, huh?" she asked him softly.

In the same tone she'd asked him about what had made him step into that hole earlier that morning. It was almost soothing. As though coaxing things out of him, and…

"I'll be damned," he said for what seemed like the hundredth time that day. "You're working me."

"What?"

Her immediate frown made him a little uneasy, but he forged forward. "You and your cognitive interview stuff, your mind reading… You're doing your stuff on me…"

"Oh really?" The glint in her eye wasn't one he'd seen often in the past. But he knew it. Didn't much care if he'd made her angry. He wasn't all that happy with her, either.

"And exactly what reason would I have for, as you put it, *working* you, Levi Griggs?"

Yeah, well, he obviously didn't have it all figured out yet.

"Besides, what would it matter if I was?" she asked then, arms folded across her chest. She wouldn't be doing that if she knew how the position pushed her nipples up on the tops of her forearms. Like they were on stage.

Her words hit him a second later. "You're admitting to working me?"

Now, that he hadn't expected. Was a tad bit intrigued.

"No, I'm not admitting to anything as devious as working anyone," she told him, clearly peeved again. "You even asking the question is not only insulting beyond measure, it's also just plain beneath you, Levi. What reason could I possibly have for working you?"

He'd already left that question unanswered. Pretty much said he didn't know. Or wasn't planning to share.

"What is it that you think I want out of you that you don't want to give?"

"Nothing."

"Then what point would I have for working you?"

Throwing up his free hand, Levi set his coffee cup on the table, about as frustrated as he could ever remember being. "Okay, okay," he told her. "I surrender."

"Well, I don't accept your surrender," she said, still sitting there all puffed up. And out. "You seem to think that I trick people into saying things they don't mean. Or that aren't true."

"I don't think that, Kel." But replaying the past few minutes... "I can see how you'd think that, but it wasn't what I meant."

"Then what did you mean?" she asked.

He wasn't getting out of it.

"I hate that you're so good at getting me to give up things that I wouldn't admit to..." To...to... What was the end of that sentence?

She sat there. Clearly ready to wait as long as it took.

He sighed. "See, you're doing it now."

"Doing what? I'm sitting here waiting for you to finish your sentence."

"To anyone but you," he threw at her. She'd asked for it. He'd given it to her.

"Oh." Expressions chased themselves across her face. Nothing akin to anger. More like…softness. And sorrow. Her arms tightened around her. Pushing her a little further into the stage-light zone.

Since she wanted honesty… "And I wouldn't sit like that if I were you, at least not while I'm sitting here." His gaze went clearly to her breasts. And he nodded toward them, too. Just to make certain she got everything he had to say on the matter.

She glanced down. Back up at him.

And dropped her arms.

But not before she'd given herself one last push up.

Clearly for his benefit.

He just wasn't sure if she was egging him on or flipping him off.

Chapter Twelve

Kelly didn't tell Levi she was going out on the back porch. He was sitting right there. He could see her turn her back to him and leave.

She needed space.

Away from him. From herself, too, though that was a little harder to accomplish.

Sitting in one of the two matching white wooden rockers she'd pulled around from the shed the day she'd arrived, she pushed gently with one foot, swaying herself as she'd done so many times as a kid. Taking comfort from the sound of the stream flowing just yards away, from the cool air, the blue sky and the trees seeming to keep her private and safe. From the sounds of birds, and the breeze rustling tree leaves now and then.

Closing her eyes, she tried to absorb it all into her spirit, her soul.

She'd hated being made to stay at her father's family cabin for two weeks every summer. But she hadn't hated the cabin. Or the time she'd had there with her friends. With Jolene. And Levi.

She and Jolene had lost touch by the time they were in high school. Jolene had moved away. Had gotten into cheerleading. And partying.

And Levi...

She'd had some good times with her grandparents, too. Since she'd hated her father—Willa and Dan's son—she thought they'd made certain that he was never at the cabin during her time there.

As she'd gotten older she'd realized that that particular choice had been his. Oliver Chase hadn't wanted to be a father. Hadn't been good at it. And hated to look like a failure more than just about anything. Kelly had only been seven when her parents had divorced, but knew that her father had blamed her mother for everything.

He'd met Kelly's mother during a week's vacation at his parent's cabin—had had fun hanging out with a girl completely unlike his usual dates, from a backwoods town that was as different from his way of life as he could get. He'd been rebelling against his parents, who'd insisted that he come home, rather than summer in Paris. When Becky ended up pregnant, they'd forced him to do the right thing. To marry her. Threatening to cut him off if he didn't.

But Becky Chase had refused to leave Idlewood and her ailing father. Her friends. The only life she knew. And Oliver had been equally reluctant to introduce the completely unpolished girl to his Grand Rapids society friends. For a long time they'd stay apart during the week, with Oliver only coming home on weekends. And then he hadn't even done that.

Willa and Dan had always stayed in touch with Kelly, though.

And they'd seen to it that their son paid more than the state minimum for alimony and child support.

Hearing Levi moving around inside, Kelly opened her eyes.

What was it with her? So many trips down a lane that held all the memories she'd purposely left behind.

Not to run or hide from them, but because they no longer served her. She no longer needed them.

She heard a chair scrape... Levi must have gotten up to get something and sat back down. The thought of him had her nipples tingling, and she shook her head.

The man was an enigma. She couldn't analyze him out of her.

Wasn't even sure she wanted to try.

They weren't suited. Not in real life.

But, God, what a bright spot he'd been.

And, being honest with herself, still was. In the moments that they were sharing.

Knowing that such thoughts were only going to get her into trouble, Kelly glanced back down to the water. Watching the constant flow of life, traveling from there to somewhere else. Taking away cares and sorrows.

And happiness, too?

Water sustained life. And life didn't come with just one or the other—happiness or sorrow.

It just flowed. From one day to the next. One year to the next. Bringing what it brought. Taking what it took.

And...there. *Oh my God.* Standing, Kelly ran down toward the water. Bobbing there, in a miniforest of reeds, at the bank right in the middle of her yard, was another jar.

Almost as if it had been left there?

Bending down to pick it up, she could hardly breathe. Her heart pounded. And as she began to straighten, her gaze landed directly across the stream. Not far from the ferns she'd seen move the day before.

She didn't see anything unusual. Didn't hear anything but nature.

But was certain someone was watching her.

Calling out to her.

Waiting for her to get their message.

She just wasn't sure anymore if it was someone out to get her.

Or someone who needed saving.

Help Me
You

As he stared at the note Kelly had brought in half an hour before, Levi's blood burned in his veins. If anyone tried to harm even a fingernail on that woman's body, he was going to…

Deputies were on their way out to search the area. Levi had already been over the immediate acreage on both sides of the stream.

Had found nothing.

But he hadn't expected to.

The guy was good.

Clearly, he knew the area and was at home in the woods.

"How does a six-foot guy move around out there without leaving any marks in the area?" Kelly asked.

Six-foot guy, based on Glen's assessment.

"If he grew up in the woods…" he said, thinking about someone like himself, who was trained how to travel without leaving a trace.

Kelly nodded. "I've been thinking the same thing," she said. "What if Maura had a boy? Who's now maybe a teenager and big like his father was?"

"Or a big girl," Levi allowed.

They were possibilities.

But he needed her to face the more likely scenario. "Or we could be dealing with a hired gun who's from upstate Michigan. Someone known to those who hire guns…"

A third new note had appeared. They couldn't fool around for another second about that.

"Kelly, you have to accept that it's possible someone dangerous is out there gunning for you."

She didn't flinch, but her lips tightened. He prepared for a fight because he wasn't backing down anymore.

You.

He didn't need to glance at the note again. That one word would be forever ingrained in his brain.

The chills that had shot through him the second he'd read it…

"I know."

He glanced at her. Could read the fear in her gaze.

"We can leave now, get you to Idlewood…"

She shook her head, and while he was disappointed, he wasn't surprised. "If there is someone out to get me, right now they're just trying to discredit me. If they wanted me dead, I would be."

She was probably more right than not about that. She'd been at the cabin alone for three days. No one in town had even known she was there.

Anyone could have surprised her, killed her and left her there to rot. At least until her friends started looking for her when she didn't return.

While the thought left him feeling sick and cold inside, it was also at that moment a comfort. If someone wanted Kelly dead, she would be.

For a time, she was of more use alive.

Unless the plan changed.

"I'm still really strongly convinced that we're dealing with a victim, Levi, not a criminal for hire. Or any kind of criminal. I'm guessing he's out roaming the hills during the day. Probably looking for food. Maybe he saw me and I appeared safe to him. We have someone who's desperate and doesn't know what to do. And the only way he knows how to get help is to send notes in jars."

He had to grit his teeth not to argue.

But the detective in him knew that he had to keep her theory on the table right alongside his own. He didn't like it as much. Didn't buy into it the same way she did.

But he had no proof against it, either.

And a lot of what she said made sense.

The adrenaline pumping through him made it hard to sit and have a conversation, period.

He needed to be doing.

To be taking down the threat—or, if Kelly was right, rescuing the victim.

"We can't discount that it's another woman," he told her. "Ridge density aside, amino acids tell more conclusively the gender of the fingerprint bearer. Has to do with the difference between male and female sweat."

He'd taken a fingerprint class the previous year.

"Glen did mention that he hadn't gotten any viable amino acid sample. I thought that had to do with ridge density."

He shook his head. "The acids decompose over time so they can't lift amino acid from all fingerprints, and some produce such a small amount of acid, it would take less time to decompose. The technology is evolving all the time, but it's not a given that every fingerprint is going to tell you that it's male or female. It also depends on the powder used to lift the print."

Way more than she needed to know. Giving a rundown of the class he'd taken was lowering his testosterone to a more manageable level.

She was looking at the note and jar on her table.

"We'll get this off to Glen today," he said, before she could ask.

And was rewarded with a Kelly smile reminiscent of the past. Reminding him of things he'd done just to get that beauty bestowed upon him.

The flowers he'd purchased with money he didn't have to spare, the love notes he'd written, the sodas he'd bring her when she was home studying. The sentiments behind the flowers, the sodas, the words in the notes had been real.

He'd been besotted with Kelly Chase from the first day he'd met her. A fate that had grown deeper and more intense with each of the next six years they'd shared.

But those little things he'd done to express the state of his heart—those had all been done just to be the recipient of that fool-making smile.

"WE CAN'T AVOID the changed message on that note, Levi."

The first twenty-seven notes had varied in message as the years had passed. "Please help me," or "I need help." One had even said, "Find me up here." They'd all been strictly about the victim begging for themselves.

"What's to say?" Levi asked, avoiding her gaze. "You think it's your victim, asking for only you to help. Because this person trusts you. Or, at the very least, isn't as frightened of you. And I think the *you* is directed at you as well, but for a different purpose. This guy is trying to get you to further entrap yourself, to do something more outrageous, like getting the state police involved or something in looking for Yardle's missed victim, all to find out you were believing in a hoax."

"I'm being targeted," she said then, letting him know by the tone in her voice and the look in her eye that she wasn't altogether comfortable with that fact. "It's clear, with this third jar." She shivered inside as she said, "It was like the person was here, on my property, to lodge it in those reeds so it wouldn't float away."

"I agree," he told her, offering no sympathy. Because he wanted her scared. So she'd leave the premises and let him take over.

And what…have another fifteen years pass?

"If I'm right, I leave here, and we could be sentencing someone to years out there alone. It's pretty clear that if this person doesn't want to be found, they won't be. Look how many times you all looked for Maura. And you've already done a full canvass of these hills this week, and no one saw anything."

His gaze locked on hers. He didn't argue.

"If I'm right, the criminal is dead and gone, Levi. You killed him."

He nodded. His pinched chin told her how much he hated having to give her that much.

"And if you're wrong, someone who is targeting you, almost certainly with criminal intent, has been on this property since yesterday afternoon." When he'd searched the water and the banks.

Her skin crawled, but she didn't blink. "I know."

Levi sat back, as though he was done with the conversation.

"There's something else," Kelly said. Until they knew which of their theories was right or wrong—and they could both be wrong—safety lay in being open and honest.

"This note…psychologically…is very different from all of the others."

He sat forward, intent again. "How so?"

His clear interest, the energy flowing from him suddenly, amped up her adrenaline, too. He wasn't blowing her off. Or listening out of courtesy. It was like her opinion carried weight with him.

And it was going to fit his theory, too.

"This person isn't just asking for help. This is someone

with enough sense of self—of power over self—that he's is-
suing demands."

"He doesn't want help as desperately as Maura did?"

She shrugged. "He might. Or she might…" Kelly had to
keep in mind that if they had a victim, they could still be female.

Someone else Yardle had kidnapped.

Levi's team had an entire list of women who'd been reported missing and hadn't been found in the past twenty years,
up until Yardle was shot. She'd seen the list in the report.
They'd been looking for any kind of pattern—any location—
that the missing women had in common. Some had been runaways, some had simply disappeared without a trace.

And there were women, like Maura, who'd never even been
reported missing.

Kelly looked at Levi. "This note carries more of a sense
of authority than Maura exhibited," she said. "Maybe a sense
that he has some power over his life. Which could have grown
simply from being loved unconditionally by Maura, could be
his size, might be that Yardle treated his own child differently,
gave him more respect and freedom, than he did Maura. Could
just be an ignorant confidence that the wish would be granted.
Or, if we're dealing with another runaway, as Maura was, it
could simply be a decision that if it's not me who offers rescue, this person isn't going to come out of hiding. That they'd
rather live as they are than risk having someone else get ahold
of them. They could just be desperately afraid that someone
else is going to treat them as bad or worse than Yardle did."

"Or, he could be a hired gun who's playing you."

Yep.

"Or someone with an axe to grind against Sierra's Web,"
he added. "I've been going over the lists of cases you had sent
and I see potential for a lot of angry people. Any number of

them might want to make Sierra's Web pay by discounting the expert status of the partners."

Alarm shot through her anew. "You think that I might not be the only one targeted?"

"I do."

She picked up her phone.

"I'd like to speak to the partners as a group, if I may," Levi told her. "As the lead detective on this case, and due to the fact that the case could just be a starting point for targeting everyone else…"

She nodded again. Dialed the office. And set up a time for all the partners to have a video call, from wherever they happened to be, later that evening.

And then she panicked for an entirely different reason.

Levi would be, by video, coming face-to-face with the catalyst of their broken engagement. And he didn't have a clue.

Chapter Thirteen

Levi heard a truck pull in while Kelly was still on the phone with Sierra's Web. Handing off the plastic bag containing the newest jar and the note—which had only been handled through the hem of Kelly's shirt and then plastic gloves—he asked for a full report from the deputies who were searching the area once again. A car of searchers had pulled up behind the truck. And more were parked in different areas around the various lanes, most private, leading up to the hills.

If nothing else, his people were going to know the woods in the area so well, they'd be more likely to notice if anything was amiss.

While he felt better, knowing there were trained officers all over the place—many whom he'd helped train and trusted implicitly—Levi was still on edge.

He had a potentially life-threatening situation developing and didn't actually know anything about what was happening except that he had some copycat jars and notes.

Supposition could only go so far.

It wasn't going to save Kelly.

Not if he couldn't figure out what was going on and stop it before something catastrophic happened.

As had been the situation with Maura. Yes, he'd finally solved the case. He'd gotten his man, all right.

But not in time.

Which was one of the reasons he'd been loath to go back to work. How did you feel good about a success when you watched an innocent, tortured woman die?

How could you even bear to listen to people congratulate you, to have local news stations want to interview you, when all you could see was the panicked look of a woman right before she lost her life?

Then there was Tilly... He'd made a major mistake there, taking his young cousin with him on what he'd hoped would be a moment she'd remember forever—being a part of saving Maura's life—only to have Tilly almost end up just like Maura had.

His cousin had quit the force. After talking about being a cop since she was a kid in elementary school.

Not that he blamed her.

He blamed himself.

And now... Kelly. He could not let her be hurt. Even if he had to hold her hostage in a safe house himself to keep her from harm...

Whoa. He reined in his thoughts as he entered the cabin. He couldn't force any adult into a safe house. Least of all Kelly Chase.

But...

"Levi?"

She was standing at the back door, looking out, and he hurried over, standing just behind her, thinking she'd seen something, was watching it...

"Yeah?" he asked, his gaze scouring the yard until he realized that Kelly was watching him. Her face turned over her shoulder. Just inches from his chin.

He backed up so quickly his butt hit the refrigerator. So, he opened it. Pulled out a bottle of water. Uncapped it and drank half before pulling it away from his face.

Giving him time to get back to being the decorated detective he was.

Instead of the damned jilted lover he'd been.

Who still happened to care one hell of a lot for the woman who'd ditched him.

Albeit, against his will.

As he lowered the bottle, Kelly was right in his line of vision. Par for the damned course. In her jeans and short-sleeved shirt, those long blond curls hanging around her shoulders, one strand even taunting him as it lay against her right breast.

There was no mercy for him.

"There was no him," she said, her tone nothing like he'd heard since he'd seen her again. She sounded young...vulnerable.

And his gut wrenched. Needing to...what? Rush to her rescue? Because of a tone of voice? Had he gone completely over the edge?

"I don't get it," he said. Was she finally seeing that her theory was less plausible than his?

Now that she saw that her entire team could be at risk, she was realizing how much was at stake?

Leaning back against the corner of the countertop, she was staring at the floor. Chewing her bottom lip. Her tongue ran over the bite. And then she looked at him.

"You asked his name," she said, both hands braced behind her on the counter.

No, no. *No.* He had a job to do.

Deputies out right then, surrounding her property and beyond. Working for him.

He had to...

What?

Go over evidence another time.

Wait.

He was in wait mode. Until he had something more to work with.

Grabbing a glass, Kelly headed for the refrigerator. He could stand there and let her hand touch him as she reached for the handle behind him.

Or he could move.

Pulling out a chair, he sat.

Heard her pour liquid into her glass. Saw the glass—with tea—land on the table. And didn't look beyond it.

He didn't want to know.

Earlier...he'd asked...

"I shouldn't have asked, Kel. I was out of line. It was a long time ago and doesn't matter."

He'd make certain it didn't matter one way or another. Somehow.

Get a lobotomy. Cut his heart out.

"It was a fair question," she told him, that tone still in her voice.

"My partners... The meeting you requested... They...all know about you."

Stunned speechless, Levi stared at her. Telling himself not to make too much of that revelation, even while he was doing a mental celebration dance.

Right up until he realized that her college friends knowing about him had not stopped the breakup.

And knew it was time to grow up.

Be done with the past, once and forever.

"It's all in the past," he said, sitting forward, both arms on the table, with his water bottle between them.

He should bread and fry the fish he'd caught early the previous morning. Back when he'd thought it would be just him and Betsy for dinner. Right before he'd made dinner and then went out to chop wood...

"We had a communications class together." Kelly's words, not so vulnerable, but still different, held him in place. And listening.

Her gaze was aimed at the table, toward the finger she had running up and down along a wood grain. He watched her.

Couldn't look anywhere else.

"I'd already been struggling. I had this pressure inside me...the classes I was taking, the things I was hearing about, and seeing... I needed to do something. Living in Idlewood, being only a mother...felt...stifling."

Her words were bricks. Each one hitting him harder than the one before. He listened then because he had to know.

"It wasn't about not loving you, Levi." She glanced up at him, but quickly lowered her gaze again. "Dorian and Savannah, they held me, literally, on nights when I couldn't stop crying for grieving over losing you..."

What the...?

He sat back. Frowning.

"I just... And then...well, first...this class where we all met. We were a team and our semester assignment was interpersonal communication. We had to engage in it. See where it took us. Learn from it. Good or bad. We were given different topics, sometimes to just discuss. Sometimes to write about..."

He needed her to get on with it so he could start to breathe again.

"I talked about my struggles. We all did."

"All seven of you." He'd read the dossier of the Sierra's Web partners.

She shook her head. "There were eight of us."

Eyes narrowed, all detective suddenly, he waited.

"We got super close. And stayed that way after the semester ended. It was like all of us, in our own way, and for different reasons, had been struggling, and needed each other. Like it was somehow meant to be."

His gut took a hit with that one. He swallowed.

"The following semester, we were all supposed to meet up at the end of our break, to spend a few days together just the eight of us. Except one of us didn't show up."

The way her chin tightened, he knew. Wanted to stop her.

"Sierra," he guessed. Sierra's Web. Eight friends. Seven partners.

"When we all started talking, each of us had noticed different things that were off about Sierra—and when we put them together collectively, we knew she was in some kind of trouble. We went to the police, but they called her father, who said there was no need for a missing person report. Said that Sierra often went off on her own. But then classes started and she still wasn't back."

Without thinking, Levi reached out a hand to cover her almost desperately moving finger on the table. Wrapping his fingers around the side of her palm.

"We went to our professor, who knew a cop…"

He knew what was coming. And couldn't save the day.

"Our information solved the case, but they were too late. She'd already been murdered. If they'd only listened to us when we'd first gone to the police…"

Kelly finally glanced up. Met his gaze. And he knew.

He'd never had a chance.

"Losing Sierra, but also being a part of fighting to find her…the way we all used our individual talents… We knew," she whispered. And then said, "I knew. I'd lost a part of my heart, but I'd found myself, Levi. The only way I was going to feel whole, complete, alive, was to hone the skills I'd been given to an expert level, and spend my days trying to help prevent what happened to Sierra. Or, at the very least, helping people who are going through trauma, or who've been through trauma, to find their missing pieces." She stopped. Sucked in her lips. Swallowed. "I could do that in a small private practice, to some degree, but with all of us and our combined skills...what we'd managed to do by working together..."

That time when she looked up at Levi, and shrugged, he nodded back.

Finally understanding why he'd received his Dear John letter.

Kelly hadn't stopped loving him. Their love just hadn't been enough for her.

Knowing that brought another truth home. Strangely, without bitterness.

Kelly had made the right choice.

LEVI'S HAND HOLDING HERS...focusing on that touch...had helped Kelly finish telling her story. For so many years, she'd grieved. For him. For herself, too.

"I guess I'm more like my father than I ever knew," she finally said to him. And added, "I hate that so much."

"You are nothing like your father, Kelly Chase." Levi's words, the way he kept holding her hand, even after she was done giving him the information he deserved to have before meeting with her partners, gave her an odd kind of strength.

One that came from within as much as from without. Generally she only found inner strength from herself. Didn't understand.

Figured she was just overwrought.

The tension...believing she had a victim she could save... not sure that she wasn't being set up, as Levi thought...knowing her partners might also be in danger...

She couldn't lose another one of them.

Levi's affirmation that she wasn't like her dad meant far more than it should have done, but if anyone would know, he would.

He'd been there.

Her current friends had not.

"We...just went through a really tough time this past year," she told Levi. "Dorian had been kidnapped. We thought it was because of a case...so when we meet tonight, everyone is already going to be able to tell you every case they think could be involved...turned out it wasn't one of our cases with Dorian, but..."

He nodded. Squeezed her hand.

And still didn't let go.

"Your dad is all about himself, Kel, about keeping up appearances at all cost. About needing to be liked for what public regard can do for him, not because he cares about others. He cares about having money because of what it can do for him. You're none of those things."

She wanted to point out that her father had done a lot of good things. But her throat was too tight to speak. Tears blurred her eyes.

Levi's hand moved against hers and she turned hers over, grabbing at his in case he was going to let her go.

Neither of them could hold on. Not forever.

But for the moment...

"My partners...they've said similar things over the years," she told him. "You know, doing what they do, they've each looked into him in their own way...but you..." She held Levi's gaze. "You knew him."

And he'd known her, too. An important part of her that no one else would ever know.

That mattered.

"Your situation with Sierra," he said then. "It's like mine with Maura."

Such simple words. But the way he was looking at her. The gentle shake and then squeeze of her hand.

He was telling her something big.

He was suffering over his inability to save Maura. To the point of struggling with who he was and what he did.

Just as she'd agonized over the inability to save Sierra.

They shared and understood the unbearable pain of knowing that you were too little too late.

She and Levi might not be meant for each other as lifelong partners. As husband and wife. But they were meant to be partners for some extraordinary times in their lives.

To share things that struck them to their cores.

They weren't supposed to be together forever.

They were soulmates meant for specific moments.

And, for that, she was thankful.

Chapter Fourteen

Levi didn't cook fish. Kelly offered to bake the trout as she'd been taught to do by her grandmother and Levi got back to doing what he did best.

Investigating.

Kelly's talk about her life, about using her skills to do big things, living her life to the maximum capacity, had made sense to him.

In a way, after his disastrous marriage—a rebound from losing Kelly—he'd done pretty much what Kelly had done. He'd become the best at what he was good at.

And spent his life helping others.

He liked knowing that.

And was ready to get back to it. Even when the notes were explained, and Kelly was out of danger and traveling around the country on assignment with Sierra's Web, he was going back to work. Solving crimes was his purpose.

Leave was over.

And yeah, as much as he hated to admit it, his family had been right on that one. Just as Kelly had been right to break up with him.

Clearly, emotional stuff wasn't his strong suit.

He needed to stick to the things he got right. Detective work. Investigating.

So thinking, Levi pulled out the crime scene photos he'd brought for Kelly to look at. Spread them over three quarters of the table. And then added the ones that had been taken the day before by his team up at the cabin.

If he was in the office, he'd have them up on a big screen. Could click through them. Enlarge them. Highlight specific spots.

But he knew how to peruse evidence the hard way. Had grown up helping his uncle whenever he could talk his father, who'd been the mayor of Idlewood at the time, into letting him do so. Being an only kid had advantages. It had also made it easier for his protective father to keep tabs on him.

One thing they'd agreed on, though, was Kelly Chase. The old man had fully approved of Levi's choice to date the daughter of the town's kindergarten teacher.

Trying not to be so aware of Kelly moving around the small, L-shaped kitchen counter as she worked, Levi verified, once again, that he'd been right about the movement of the couch.

And the missing blanket.

Comparing photos from the past with those from the day before, he noticed a few other discrepancies. Minor things easily explained by the deputies being in the house.

A ripped burlap bag that served as a curtain over the window in the cabin door had been moved slightly to the left, leaving a small portion of the window in view from the inside of the cabin.

Any of the people in and out of the door could have done it.

As could some hired gun squatter who'd been keeping a lookout.

He looked for marks of someone standing or sitting directly below the small window, but with the rough plank floor, which always appeared dirty, he couldn't distinguish one mark from another. None appeared to be new dirt tracked in—and even if they had, the new smudges could be from any of the shoes that had traipsed through the woods to get to the shack.

Including his own. Although, he'd had Kelly knock the dirt off her shoes before she'd entered. And had done the same himself.

His people were all trained accordingly.

Every one of them had, at one time or another, gotten caught up in the important stuff and forgotten minor details, himself included.

And...wait.

He picked up a two-month-old photo. Stared at the bottom left, rear post of what they all assumed was Yardle's bed. The bigger bed of the two.

Grabbed another photo from the previous evidence collection, showing another angle of the back post of the bed, just as background—who cared about bedposts? And then, Levi pulled out his phone. Enlarged the digital version of the photo he held.

"Can I have your phone?" He didn't even look up as he saw Kelly's phone appear on the table. Lock screen bypassed. Grabbing it, he quickly pushed buttons, cast photos from his phone to hers, enlarged them until only the bedpost was on-screen.

And then picked up two photos he'd been studying from the day before. Partially because they'd been taken of the area where he'd come potentially close to death that morning.

The baling twine used to tie the logs together to make legs for the bed...a layer of it was missing from the newer photos. The bedpost was still tied, but not as thickly. The patterning was different. Crisscrosses didn't overlap the same.

"Look at this," he said, his gaze firmly glued to the photos. He was onto something. His gut was telling him.

"What?" Kelly stood so closely beside him, her arm touched his as she bent to look at their phones side by side.

He felt her. Liked her there. But kept his focus on the photos. Whether she saw it or not, he knew he'd found something significant.

"The rope is different," Kelly said within seconds. Because she was looking at versions where the rope filled the entire screen.

"Right, now look at this." He handed her an outdoor photo from the day before.

Taking the printed photo over to the light, she studied. Frowned. Studied some more. And then shook her head.

"Look at the tree, Kel, third one in on the cluster in the upper left."

She squinted. Pulled the photo closer.

He handed her the magnifying glass he'd dropped into the evidence box when they'd cleaned up earlier.

"It's rope."

"Baling twine," he qualified. "Same as the bedpost."

"I don't even know how you saw this. It looks like part of the tree."

He didn't know how he was able to pick out odd little anomalies, either. Maybe the same way she figured out people.

Didn't much matter.

"I need to get back up there."

"Tonight?"

It was almost six. They had the call with the other Sierra's Web partners at seven, four o'clock Phoenix and California time—though that could be rescheduled. Darkness hit close to ten, but up in the hills, with the trees blocking light, it would be earlier.

As much as he hated to wait, he knew that it was stupid

to do otherwise. "First thing in the morning," he told her. "I mean that literally. As soon as morning hits…"

"You know I'm coming along, right?"

He didn't bother fighting her. He couldn't hold her hostage. She wasn't in custody. She was a professional who'd been on the job for more than ten years, attending crime scenes all over the country.

Who was he to think he could hold her back?

"I know that this means something," he said, instead of answering her question.

"Someone besides your deputies have been up at that shack since Yardle and Maura were killed."

That, yes. But…

"Why would someone have a rope hanging up in a tree?"

She looked at the photo again. "Look at the trees, Kel. See how lush they are at the top. So thick with branches that you could practically lay down and take a nap…"

"But the trunks are practically bare," she said slowly. "You think someone scales the tree to keep a lookout?"

Pretty much exactly what he'd been thinking. "You'd have to have a good arm, to get the rope around that branch," he said, assessing the photo again. Listening to his instincts. "Maybe scaling the trunk was difficult and the rope was attached for easier, or quicker, access in the future."

"Definitely would be easier coming down if someone could hold a rope and scale…"

They were on the same wavelength. It felt damned good.

"Another woman…or Yardle's possible son," she continued, studying intently.

As though, if she looked hard enough, her victim would appear in the shadows.

Letting her know how to make contact.

And conduct the rescue.

"Or a hired gun on the lookout," he had to say. To keep her constantly aware of the danger she was in. Even if he was wrong, and someone wasn't out to get her, specifically.

If she was right and a victim needed her...she'd be walking into a potential minefield of mental illness.

Something she was far better trained to deal with than he was.

And a valid, professional reason to have her along in the morning. And to keep her close at all times.

"Are you going to have deputies meet us up there?"

Because she was going, he wanted to do so. But knew he couldn't waste any more manpower, to go over the area yet another time, without more than a rope to go on.

Knew, too, that if Kelly, his Kelly, not the professional woman she'd become, wasn't going with him, he wouldn't even consider calling in extra help.

Knew how it would look to those who worked for him, those who looked up to him, those who watched out for him. To his uncle. Who'd tell his parents.

"No, we'll go alone," he said, acting like the professional he'd become.

And leaving behind, once and for all, the besotted boy he'd been.

KELLY FELT AS nervous as a schoolgirl when she sat next to Levi on the couch that evening, with her laptop propped on books on the coffee table in front of them, making them both visible to the camera. She'd turned on her hotspot. Had brushed her hair and changed into a fresh blouse, too.

She was attending a meeting at the office, not hanging out in her family cabin. Even if her attendance was via video.

Mostly, she'd felt the need to freshen up before sitting so close to Levi.

Her unexpected case of jitters had nothing to do with the man sitting so close to her. The warmth in her nether regions, however, could be attributed to that.

"What's got you going?" Levi asked, his tone almost teasing, as they waited for the meeting to begin.

"I'm just waiting."

"Your knee's bobbing and you've checked your fingernails six times since we sat down."

"You count how many times I look at my fingers?"

"It's a gift," he told her, sounding more... Levi...than he had since he'd first arrived on her doorstep. "My ability to notice things," he added.

So, okay... "I'm nervous about the two of you meeting," she said.

"The two of us? Me and who else?"

"You and my partners," she clarified, watching the line circling in the middle of the screen as they waited for the host to begin the session.

That would be Hudson. Their computer expert.

"You afraid I'll embarrass you?"

His question, so serious, had her turning to him in shock. "Oh God, no, Levi!"

"You said they know about me." He shrugged. "Maybe they see that you fell for a backwoods simpleton."

Anger rose up so fast she didn't see it coming. "Don't you ever, *ever* say anything like that to me again," she said. And then, hearing her voice, sat back against the couch. Watching the screen again. Thankful that her partners hadn't just observed the atrociously out of character moment.

"I'm sorry," she said, filled with an anguish she didn't understand. "I just...for a second there... It's like you were accusing me of being my father." But that wasn't really it. He'd already told her she was nothing like the man who'd fathered her. "And I can't believe that you'd think, even for a second, that I'd think of you that way. Or that I'd ever, in a million years, be embarrassed for having loved you."

She heard Levi take a breath. Tensed, awaiting his response.

Tried immediately to relax because he'd notice her tension.

And was disappointed when Hudson's face suddenly popped on-screen.

SHE'D TOLD HER partners she'd loved him. She'd intimated as much earlier, but the validation, just as he was going into a meeting with the six geniuses Kelly loved like family, all experts in their fields, gave Levi back some of the confidence he'd lost the second Yardle shot Maura.

Success should do that for him.

Not a wayward emotion.

Still, sitting next to Kelly, knowing they were aware how much he'd meant to her, gave Levi a sense of equality that had him at the top of his game. He gave facts. Answered questions. Made suggestions. And when he said that he'd need a list of all cases that could potentially have angered someone to the point of putting any or all of Sierra's Web's partners at risk, all six faces on-screen nodded.

So much so that he chose to tell them about the baling twine he'd noticed, and Hudson and Glen both asked him to forward them the photos to see if they could glean anything more before Levi and Kelly set course for the shack compound again in the morning.

He received a hearty round of thanks, too, as they were all disconnecting. Along with several pleas to take care.

Without detecting a single note of doubt in any tone, expression or word.

Kelly leaned forward to click to leave the meeting as soon

as goodbyes were said, while the faces of her friends still filled the screen.

"That went well," he said, wanting to glory for a minute in the successful cohabitation of old life with new.

"Uh-huh." Her agreement couldn't have been more tepid—and still signal any kind of like thinking.

"What?" he asked, turned to search her face. A feat made more challenging by the fact that she wasn't looking at him.

"If I'm at all on my mark, I say that I'll be getting a text within the next…"

Her phone binged.

"And…" Kelly said.

It binged again.

And didn't he feel like a fool, thinking the meeting had gone so well.

"What's the problem?" he asked, not sure he wanted to know. Figuring he didn't need to know. As long as they co-operated on the case, and Kelly got out of there safely, with any victim brought out if indeed there was one, then nothing else mattered.

Not Kelly's friends' opinions of him, at any rate.

She was too busy reading from her phone screen to answer him.

Figuring that in itself was his answer, Levi sat forward on his way to standing up.

Her arm, phone in hand, swung his way, landing at his chest.

He glanced down, felt the nudge against his chest as her hand shoved the phone at him a second time.

Eyebrows raised, he watched her for a second. Couldn't get her to meet his gaze.

So he did the only thing left to him.

He took the damned phone.

Chapter Fifteen

"'I see now why no other guy adds up,'" Levi read aloud.

Dorian's epistle.

Kelly might have cringed if she had any cringeability left where he was concerned.

"Glen just asked if he's why you're still alone." Levi was voicing Savannah's message, his tone deadpan. As though reading a report.

He hadn't looked at her.

He wasn't leaving the couch, either.

"Glen's a whiz in the lab, and tends to see life in terms of black and white, provable and not provable, as well," she said, as though they were discussing the weather.

When a third ping came, she grabbed her phone.

Read what Mariah wrote, and shoved the cell into her back pocket.

"You aren't going to let me see it?" Levi asked, sitting back as he looked over at her, their faces only inches apart.

"No."

"Why not?"

"Because."

"Because why?"

What were they…twelve again?

"Because I'm choosing not to do so, Levi. Let it go."

"Now I have to see it, you know." The teasing tone…one she recognized from long ago. One she'd forgotten until she heard it again. It lit a fire in her. Liquid flame, coursing through her. Pooling in pertinent places.

"Let me see it, Kel." He used a different tone on her. More adultlike. Less forceful.

It had the same exact effect.

"Why don't you want me to see it?"

"Because it's none of your business, Levi."

"It is if it's about me."

It was about him. Oh God, it was about him.

"Who says it's about you?" Her mind scrambling, she sat there, like a zombie held in the grip of something far more powerful than any muscles and strength she had to fight it.

"Then why not let me see it?"

"I do have other things going on in my life that have nothing to do with you, you know." Was she purposely egging him on?

To what end?

The idea that she was purposely teasing him, and was still sitting there next to him, excited her, too.

It was like she'd been possessed by some young, naughty side of herself that she'd left behind. Forgotten about.

A young woman who'd been denied.

But she really didn't want him to read Mariah's message. The child life specialist saw too much. And not only in children.

Mariah spent her life in tune with the emotional aspects of young life. With needs that couldn't be expressed.

Levi moved beside her. Leaving her to her stupid game? Disappointment flooded her.

Until he made a sudden dive, was over top of her and taking possession of the phone that had been lodged in her back pocket.

She felt the device slide away from her butt.

Grabbed for it and caught his hip as he jumped up and away from the couch, opening her phone.

He could sit there and swipe and punch all he wanted. She wasn't giving him the password to her lock screen.

Arms crossed over her chest, she stuck her chin up and waited. Ready to take him on, hand to hand, foot to foot.

Mouth to mouth if it came to that.

She wasn't giving up Mariah's message.

He stood there, staring at her phone. So long it took her a second to realize he was reading.

"How did you…?" Jumping up, she grabbed for her phone.

With a quick jerk of his hand, he held it up and away from her.

With a wad of his shirt in one hand, she stood on his foot and reached up for her phone.

He looked at her.

And she froze. He was no longer smiling.

Or playing, either.

"She thinks you're still in love with me."

She had no response. Until it occurred to her to ask, "How did you know my password?"

Still on his foot, holding his shirt, she watched as his mouth opened, and then her gaze was captured by his as he said, "I'm good at what I do, too, Doctor. I watched the pattern of your thumb when you punched it into your phone."

His blue eyes seemed to bore into her until nothing mattered but them. She didn't care what he knew.

Or what the future held, either.

All she cared about was right then, right there.

Feeling what she was feeling.

With him.

HE DIDN'T APPROVE.

Not of a single thing he was thinking. Or feeling.

But when Kelly rubbed her pelvis up against his hard-on, he didn't give a damn about self-approval.

He cared one hell of a lot about her, though.

And how she'd feel if they did something she'd regret.

She wouldn't trust herself around him.

He didn't want to be that guy.

He wanted to kiss her, though. So much it hurt.

His head started to lower.

Just a kiss. That was it…

Thought fled as his lips touched hers. And then devoured her. Nothing like the greeting she'd given him the day before.

Full of hunger, of want and need and danger, he sucked her in, felt her tug at him and just wanted more.

Wrapping his arms around her, he pulled her fully to him, both her feet on both of his, as close as he could get her.

The slimness of her waist, the softness of her lips, her cushy breasts against him, all were in direct contrast to the strength of her grip as her arms around his neck held his face to hers.

As they broke for breath, a coherent thought came through. He had to pull her arms down. Get her away from him before they blew what they had.

But when she kissed him again, starting with tongue this time, he couldn't remember what they had.

He only knew what he'd lose if she let go of him.

And so he embraced her back, taking her weight upon himself, holding her up, drank in her sweet scent and tasted from her hungrily.

KELLY COULDN'T BREATHE. Didn't care. Levi. The scent of woods. His wetness and warmth. She absorbed it all.

And caught a glimpse of herself.

Standing on the feet of the man she'd left behind, throwing herself around him, all over him, inside his mouth.

She stepped back.

Felt his arms fall away. Shivered with the chill their loss left behind.

"I apologize," she told him. Embarrassed by herself.

With a glance up at him, standing frozen exactly where she'd left him, staring at her like he'd been hit in the head, she said, "I swear to you, I have never before in my life come on to a man like that. I've never even…"

Known she could feel that kind of hunger. Much less act upon it.

So much for having her act all together. Being sure of who she was and fulfilling her promise to make the most of her gifts and…

Sucking in air, she hiccuped. Felt a little like crying, but mostly…her blood still burned.

"I want you, Levi." The words flew free. And she felt better for them.

Their truth took away the sting.

"It's you. Something about you…"

His eyes seemed to burn into her.

"You make me feel things no one has ever been able to come close to…"

He didn't turn away. Or take a step forward.

He was still hugely turned on. The evidence was obvious.

He'd put the shutters down all around the house before their meeting, just in case it lasted into dark. The feeling of being shut in so completely with him was an aphrodisiac more potent than nudity or alcohol.

"Can we do this?" she asked him.

"Oh, we can do it, Kel. I think that much is obvious. The question is, what happens afterward?"

She nodded. "It might be hard, parting ways…" The understatement of her life. But also something she was completely certain would have to happen.

He blinked. His head tilted. And he said, "You think we can have sex here, now, and when it's done, remain friends?"

Another surge of desire shot through her at the question. At the implication.

"You want to remain friends?"

"I do."

"I do, too."

And there they stood. Like two dogs in heat. Staring at each other.

"In my professional opinion," she started. And then stopped. "Scratch that. No way can I hope to have an objective view on this one…"

"So, in your personal opinion…" He let his statement trail off…begging the question.

"In my personal opinion, I can't imagine a future without you as my friend." She spoke directly from the heart. "Now that I've seen you again…now that I know I can talk to you, be a part of you, without the life we'd originally planned, but, rather, as the people we are…no way I see me ever being okay without staying in touch."

His eyes closed for a long moment. She'd said too much. Had gone too far.

She'd had to. The truth was the only thing that would let any kind of future between them work.

"I want that, too, Kel."

Her gaze shot back up to him as he finally spoke. The words falling softly upon her, sending soft tingles through her body.

"We both know it would have been wrong for us to marry,"

he said then. "Our needs, outside of our love for each other, were too different."

"I know." And was so relieved to hear him so calmly admit that he did, too. "I was afraid we'd end up resenting and then hating each other. I couldn't bear it if that happened."

He nodded. "And now?" he asked.

She smiled. "Remember how awkward it was the first and only time?" she asked, posing her own question instead of answering his.

With a shrug, and a grin, he said, "Mostly I remember worrying I'd never hold on long enough and would embarrass the hell out of myself and disappoint you, too."

"It hurt," she told him.

"I know. I felt horrible—my body had never known such euphoria and you were hurting."

"I knew euphoria, too…once we got through the tough part."

"If I'd had a bit more experience, I'd have been able to make that easier on you."

His words flooded her panties. And her mind with wanting to know exactly how he'd have gone about doing that. And she said, "You want to show me how?"

"You're sure?" His gaze had an intensity she didn't recognize…all grown up and yet, somehow needy, too.

"I think we owe it to our younger selves to get it right, don't you?"

She took a step forward. And then he did, sliding his arms beneath hers, around her, and pulling her up against him.

"Oh God, lady, you have no idea how badly I need to pay that bill," he nearly growled against her mouth right before he devoured her lips with his own.

LEVI THOUGHT EXPERIENCE, maturity, would make the second time he took Kelly Chase into his arms to have sex more about pleasing her, about his own slow build, than the nervous, almost desperate sense of trying to hold on he'd known the first time.

He was wrong.

Completely, all the way, off his mark.

He held her all of ten seconds before he heard her moan, and knew that his time was near.

"I'm going to screw this up," he said, hearing the pain in his voice.

Her chuckle made it worse. Even when she pulled away from him, he thought he might spill inside his pants, right there in front of her.

Instead, he watched, mesmerized, as, with trembling fingers, she opened the top button of her pants, got the zipper down and then struggled to get the tight, stretchy denim over her hips.

She needed help.

He had to help her.

Got the pants down, held them for her to step out of and then tossed them. When he stood, he didn't even have a chance to look at the gorgeous beauty he'd exposed because her head was in the way, bending over the button at his fly.

No way he was going to be able to bear that one.

With a crude word and a quick flick of his wrist, he had his fly undone, and his penis free, ready to explode.

She moved then, pushing him back against the TV table up against the wall and, just as he started to explode, slid herself on top of him. Catching every drop of the love she'd created within him.

And, somehow, he managed to do it for her, too, he realized as he felt her convulsing around him.

Twelve years of wondering and in less than ten seconds, it was done.

"I didn't wear a condom," he realized, far too late.

"I'm on the pill," she told him. "It's a cycle thing."

And then she smiled. A womanly, brand-new-to-him expression of temptation, desire, kindness and intent.

"You want to come to bed, Detective, and show me what else you can find to bring out the naughty in me?"

Levi had no words left.

Giving her the only response he could find, he picked her up and hauled her off to investigate every inch of the woman he'd always known belonged to him.

Even if she was only his for the night.

Chapter Sixteen

Kelly's body was a little tender in spots as she showered the next morning. Gentle reminders of the glorious hours she'd spent, before sleeping deeply and peacefully next to Levi Griggs.

As close as they'd been, they'd never spent the entire night together before. Certainly never slept in a bed together.

Oddly, the situation had felt completely comfortable. Nice. Not the least bit awkward.

And when morning came, she'd woken as he was quietly leaving the bed, and the next time she'd seen him he'd been dressed in his uniform.

Not a mistake, she figured.

Yes, they were going on an official check that morning. He was on duty. But it was more than that. He'd officially been on duty the day before when they'd been up in the hills. He hadn't had his uniform on then.

She got the choice, though. He'd been establishing the boundaries.

They weren't new lovers starting a relationship. They were work associates who happened to be old friends who were enjoying some extracurricular activity by mutual consent when off duty.

And while she wished life could be different for them, she

was glad to know that she didn't have to worry about hurting Levi this time around. She could let her heart flow freely with him in it.

Without the dread, the constantly building pressure that she was going to hurt him.

And if she got hurt?

The question came quietly as she dried herself off and pulled on the fresh pair of black stretch jeans and a white fitted short-sleeved shirt with black lace flowers on the front.

She'd promised herself, after having to let Levi go the first time, that she'd never ever put herself through that grief again.

She didn't want the thought on the table. She was going to stay until she found her victim. Or Levi found her stalker.

And no matter how much she'd pay later, there was no way she was going to deny Levi, or herself, anything he wanted with her while she was there.

She met him in the kitchen, finishing up the cup of coffee she'd made when he'd come out of the shower. Putting her own empty cup, which she'd carried out from the bathroom, in the sink, she grabbed a couple of bananas and apples, handing him one of each. They'd said they'd eat fruit for breakfast on the way.

Tucking the banana in his shirt pocket, he checked his gun. Headed for the back door. And stopped.

"You okay?" he asked, his gaze not quite impersonal as he looked at her.

She looked back. "Yeah, you?" She didn't let the smile grow on her lips, but she knew it was shining from her eyes.

"Oh, yeah." Two simple words, but the look in his eyes, the tone in his voice…she was wet all over again.

Then he opened the door.

And they went to work.

THE EARLY-MORNING HIKE was just what the doctor would have ordered had Levi had the guts to talk to Kelly about the quagmire of emotions churning inside him. He'd just needed to be outside. To exert.

Before they crossed the stream, he had himself in line. He was a cop protecting a potential woman in jeopardy. And by the time they reached the Yardle clearing, he was all business. Keeping Kelly close enough to grab, throw to the ground and cover with his own body if danger presented, he watched every leaf, both dormant on the ground and moving in the breeze. Every twig. And was careful to avoid the markings designating sinkholes.

They both knew where they were headed, and didn't speak as they made their way to the site of the emergency they'd experienced together the previous morning.

Levi didn't shudder as he kept a safe distance from the sunken ground, but he wasn't thrilled to be back there, either.

Turning his attention to the group of trees a mere ten yards away from the site of the near disaster, he held Kelly's arm, keeping her close to his side, as he pointed upward.

And there it was, right where he'd known it would be…a doubled-up piece of baling twine, knotted securely around a lower tree branch about nine feet up.

"You can barely see it," Kelly said softly, as though she thought someone might be listening to them. "The way it blends with the wood and the bits and pieces of old leaves and loose dying bark."

He heard her, but his attention was on the rope. On the branch that held it securely. Gut sinking.

"I can't believe you even noticed it," she continued. "From a photo, no less. I'm here and I'd have walked right by it."

He heard the nervousness in her tone. Noted it.

But had a sick feeling that wasn't going away. Measuring

the distance from the rope to the ground directly beneath it—land that was also covered by a bed of fallen foliage much like the hole he'd stepped into the day before—he pushed with his boot. Moving aside the sticks and twigs, built up from years of natural shedding throughout the woods. But thicker in that spot?

Wind blew, and areas with a barrier—say a group of trees—would become collection spots.

He continued to push aside the dead growth, hoping he was wrong.

"Levi?" The way she'd drawn out the word gained his full, immediate attention.

"What?" She was looking in the direction of the entrance to the hole from the day before. He'd already made a thorough visual check of the spot. Nothing had been disturbed since they'd left it the day before.

"If someone heard us coming yesterday…someone who knew where the sinkholes were for defensive measures…he could have climbed up that rope. You said you thought you saw something drop. He could easily have thrown something from that branch and hit the area you were searching."

He glanced from the branch to the hole. Knowing she was right. A stretch. Still, possible.

He had a much bigger concern pushing at him.

Wasn't going to say anything until he knew…

Just kept digging at the ground with his boot. The softness beneath the debris was not good.

He could still be wrong.

But knew he wasn't. Bending, he grabbed a thicker fallen piece of branch and started digging.

Kelly watched. Saying nothing.

If she suspected what he was doing, looking for, dreading, she didn't say.

And didn't ask.

A shallow foot down, his log scraped a long solid piece of not-dirt. And not rock, either.

He should have brought a team with him.

And what if his "rope" had turned out to be a thin dead branch with some browned offshoots on it?

"Is it a deer bone?" Kelly's whisper shot fear through him. She shouldn't be up there. He didn't want her anywhere near...

She wasn't his to want. Or to order where to be. She was a professional working the case.

"No," he told her. "It's human." And he had no damned radio. No one nearby.

Another pass with his branch, and he could see enough to know that bones were attached to bones in the way they would be if they'd been buried still covered with flesh. He was digging up a skeleton.

If he left the area, he could come back to find the body gone.

He couldn't send Kelly back alone. Would lose evidence before he risked her going on an hour-and-a-half hike with someone on the loose.

Probably the stalker.

"This body has been here a while," he said.

"Yardle was keeping more than just Maura up here, like we suspected." Kelly's low tone, while clearly saddened, gave no indication of panic.

It hit him, then...she was every bit the professional he'd expected her to be when he'd officially attached her to the case. One who'd been present at many crime scenes.

That wasn't her first dead body.

"I'LL STAY HERE with her while you go get help." Kelly couldn't look away from the shallow grave. It wasn't the first she'd seen. Not even the tenth.

Sierra's Web had worked a serial killer case a few years back and had used her skills to profile the perp.

But this one…felt personal.

Ridiculous, considering that she'd been in other parts of the country when Yardle had been terrorizing at least one, probably two and possibly more women.

But though the man was dead, his reign of terror wasn't over. Kelly had never been more certain of that fact than she was in that moment.

"I'm not leaving you up here alone." His tone brooked no refusal. Arguing wasn't going to change his mind.

"Because you know there's someone still up here. Another victim."

"Maybe. But if you have a stalker, then this body has nothing to do with him. We've just helped him stumble onto another juicy piece of whatever story he's going to present about your lack of credibility. Or he'll realize that with the discovery of a body, you won't look so over the edge after all, and then his method of operation changes and you'll meet with an unfortunate accident in the woods."

"Like falling down the hole you stepped into yesterday," she said, frowning as she looked at him. She could see it.

Didn't want to.

But Levi was damned good at what he did. She had to pay attention.

"I want you to start taking pictures now," he said, keeping his voice low. As though he was aware of the possibility that they might be overheard. "Keep taking them, nonstop as I carefully unbury the body. I'm not going to touch any of the debris covering it, and I need you to be sure you don't, either. We'll get full skeletal photos, then cover the body back up and get down the hill far enough to get service and call for a crew and the medical examiner to come up and remove the body."

She used his phone. It was a department issue with a much better camera, and she did what she was told. Moving around to get every angle, she photographed every bone, every clog of dirt he moved aside with his log, taking full shots while standing and, squatting with him, close shots, too.

As he uncovered the junction to the legs, he said, "She's female. The pelvis is thinner, less dense, the bone is wide, oval…"

Kelly's phone hand dropped to her lap for a moment. She'd assumed…but her stomach still sank when she heard the confirmation.

The woman, whoever she was, deserved to be known.

To be rescued.

No way was this body going to spend eternity on Yardle land.

She resumed her photo taking.

DUE TO THE nature of the Yardle case—and to the fact that it had been all over the local and state news—an autopsy was going to be conducted immediately. Two medical examiners, from both county and state, happened to be in the area and went to the crime scene.

Preliminary thoughts, shared by both, were that the woman had been no more than mid-twenties. She'd been dead less than three months.

And had died by hanging. Something Levi had already figured out.

Before he'd uncovered the top half of the torso and had seen the rope still tied, lying limply around the woman's neck bone.

He'd heard Kelly telling one of her partners in a phone call that he'd noticed two different abrasion marks on the tree branch where they'd found the original twine.

Along with the nooselike knot in the rope still attached to

the tree, that second, ropeless abrasion was how he'd known to start digging.

The impressed tone of her voice, almost like she was bragging about him, but most definitely as though she respected him, was one of only two good things about the first half of that day. The second was that Kelly had made it back to her cabin safely.

By early afternoon, they were alone at the cabin, having a late lunch of leftover baked fish and the last of the fresh vegetables he'd brought with him. The radio connecting him to the team up on the Yardle property sat on the table beside him.

"This might not have anything to do with the current situation," Levi had to tell her. "Most likely it does not."

"It does if she died after he did," Kelly said, sounding more emphatic than ever. "If there's someone else up there, keeping women hostage..." She had an energy about her...almost a frantic kind of determination...that worried him.

"If that's the case, we need to be more careful than ever, Kel. He could want you, too." The thought had been digging at him all morning. "I want you to move into Idlewood. Just until we figure this out."

She shook her head. "Are you and the others going to leave it alone?" she asked. "You going to stay out of harm's way?"

He didn't bother responding.

"I'm what's bringing this person out, Levi. Whether it's a woman who's all alone and abandoned, one Yardle didn't kill, or a child left behind, or some demented fiend who's out of women and wants me...we have to end this. If I go, and I have a stalker, as you think, he'd just follow me to Idlewood. Or elsewhere. Maybe use another case to try to discredit me. You want to send me out into the world to start this all over again?"

She was good. Too damned good. And he continued to hold his silence.

"And if there's another man out there, and I go, he may kill whoever is trying to get to me. Things would go quiet again. For months. Or years. A girl could silently disappear and you'd never know she was up there."

He pushed his plate away at that one.

"Or if, as I suspect, we have someone who's emotionally fragile asking for help, and I go, we could be sentencing an innocent victim to an eventual slow and painful death up in the hills alone."

He nodded. Met her gaze, and had to ask, "Why are you so sure you're dealing with a victim?"

The body had upset her; it hadn't unhinged her. At all. She'd been calm through the entire process. She'd told him about the serial killer case, and a few others where she'd been present at graves or autopsies on the way down from the hills. Dealing with perps, using her expertise to expose them, wasn't foreign to her.

And yet, in their current situation, she continued to avoid acknowledging the possibility that a perp was there.

She'd finished slowly chewing the bite she'd just taken. Swallowed it down with a sip of tea. And then met his gaze. "It's the little things, Levi," she said. "Just like you noticed the twine change on the back bed leg, the abrasion on the tree… I notice things like an extraheavy dot on a note. Like someone was uncertain, even writing it. Afraid. A perp doesn't show fear. Not when he's trying to lure someone into his trap. He's generally overconfident then. Turned on, pumped up, excited about the plan, about the prize he's on his way to getting."

Her words resonated. But he asked, "What if it's a stalker who knows the nuances and is purposely laying a trap for you?"

"It's a possibility," she told him, meeting his gaze directly. "But if we quit now, after this person, whether a victim, a stalker or another kidnapper has made contact, and it's not a stalker, is that a chance you want to take?"

His gut hurt. Like when he'd first read the Dear John letter she'd sent him. "We could be dealing with another Yardle, Kel," he said, his gaze imploring her on a very personal level. "You could be his next victim."

She nodded. Held his gaze, and with quiet conviction said, "And you'd find me, Levi."

Chapter Seventeen

Levi spent a lot of that afternoon either on his radio or on the phone, getting reports and giving orders. A rush had been put on a DNA sample taken from the skeleton they'd found that morning. If the woman was in a database, they could know her identity within hours.

In the meantime, Kelly was helping him scour hundreds of missing person and runaway reports going back ten years—assuming that, like Maura, Yardle took them young. They calculated a maximum age of twenty-five for their current victim.

They didn't have hair color, but they had height, bone structure and a quick computer composite that Glen provided based on the photos she'd sent him of the skeletal head.

"Taking a younger child fits the psychological profile," Kelly told Levi in one of his brief free moments. "She'd be less able to provide for herself, afraid of being caught, of being in trouble, possibly of being sent back to whatever she'd been running from. A child, even a runaway teenager, is more vulnerable than an adult, which makes her more easily conned in the first place and then more malleable once he had her. If she's a runaway, she also has less hope of anyone looking for her, which makes her more prone to trying to please and fit in." She looked him in the eye as she said the last part.

There was no way she could leave any potential child up in those hills...

His phone rang, and, still holding eye contact with her, he answered. His lips thinned, and he thanked the caller. Asked to be kept posted and hung up.

"That was the coroner's office. There were indentations in her wrist bones congruent with having been kept bound for a period of time. And on her neck, indicating a hanging. And...she's been dead less than two months." His last, harsh statement clogged the air between them. "Butyric fermentation, a means by which they measure decomposition, is not yet complete, which happens around the fiftieth day. Some of the insects and fauna, in the dirt and on the body, both dead and alive, are being sent to a lab for further confirmation. Grass, for instance, decomposes at different rates depending on species."

His completely empty tone brought tears to her eyes. She understood, so well, the feeling of helplessness that came with not knowing your enemy well enough to stop him.

"We don't know that there's still a captor up there, Levi." Not that it would matter to him in the moment. "She might have hanged herself."

His gaze, steely and...moist, too...met hers.

"I know that means you missed her before, but she wasn't a criminal, and if she didn't want to be found, chances are, you weren't going to find her." She had to press on. "And this is why it's so important that we let whoever is trying to reach out to me do so. What if there's another one up there? One who didn't want to die? Who didn't feel completely hopeless? One who is right now hoping that I'm going to be able to help?"

"There's more, Kel."

"What?"

"She'd given birth."

Heart pounding, she stared at him. "Are you telling me there's an innocent little child up there?" Either alive...or not?

He shook his head. "It wasn't recent. Probably before she ran away. Or maybe why she did. And that's assuming Yardle only took runaways. If not, he could have kidnapped her from a park, school, even her home. Regardless, if the child is still alive somewhere, they have just lost their mother. We need to find out who this woman is. To bring closure, either now or future, to a now-motherless child."

"It narrows our search," she told him, all business, because it was pretty clear to her that that was what he needed from her at the moment. "I can get Hudson working on scouring every database, running comparable searches for known missing women in the five-state area around us, who'd given birth. And another one to weed out those who had never given birth. He can search state birth records and..."

She was babbling. Levi knew darned well what Hudson, and every other expert in the field, could do.

And they'd still have far too many names and faces to go through to try to get a match. As soon as they had a narrowed-down list, ground crews, either sent by Sierra's Web or local police, would start visiting the homes of those who'd reported loved ones missing, sharing the sketch with them. Any possible recognitions would be followed up with requests for DNA to match with that of the body Levi had found.

He was watching her. She rearranged some photos. Was starting to sweat a little.

Eventually, when the tingling at her nerve endings grew too fierce to deny, she looked over at him. "We can't rule out the fact that she might have been held captive for a number of years already when Maura was killed, that she gave birth while in Yardle's possession and we have a child up in those hills," she said, sharing what she'd feared from the beginning.

"Who could be trying to reach out to you. A woman," Levi acknowledged. "Maybe the only woman they have seen since Maura's and the mother's death. The only other woman this child has *ever* seen."

She saw the worry in his gaze. Felt tears fill her eyes. And nodded.

LEVI SAW THE writing on the wall. Kelly was their only real shot at finding the note writer. And none of them—not the sheriff's department, not the state police, not any local law enforcement, not Sierra's Web and not him or Kelly—were going to rest easy until whoever had put those jars in the water was found.

Whether whoever was out there knew that they'd found a body that morning was an unknown that bothered him. Would the discovery cause an escalation in the case?

Remain undetected?

Or was it simply unrelated?

And Kel…

As a detective, he needed her to be an active part of the investigation. Front and center.

And as a man with nonprofessional emotional involvement, he needed her hidden away in a safe place.

The former was going to happen. There was no question there.

Which left him scrambling with what to do about his far too personal feelings where she was concerned.

He knew there was no future for them. Not in terms of a marriage-type situation. He wasn't setting himself up for heartbreak a second time.

But she'd offered friendship. A potential lifetime of it.

And he was fairly certain he was going to accept that commitment. Had already pretty much done so.

In the dark moments when he wasn't kidding himself, he knew she was too much of a drug to him for him to ever willingly walk away.

He'd take whatever crumbs she had to offer.

Which left him to learn to deal with caring deeply about someone whose life work sometimes involved putting her life in danger. The irony of that one, considering what he did for a living, was not lost on him.

The department had taken dogs up into the hills with them, after the body had been exhumed, but no other bodies had been found. Not in the clearing surrounding Yardle's place, and not five hundred acres out in any direction, either.

Levi was taking that as a win.

Aerial surveillance had been sent up as well, to get an idea of any other possibly unknown habitations farther up in the hills, but with the denseness of trees, all fully bloomed with greenery, nothing had shown up.

But another note did. Levi knew it the second he heard Kelly's chair scrape back against the floor in one swift push. She'd been facing the opened back door, watching the water. By the time she'd made it to the door, he was at her back, grabbing for the fishing net he'd insisted they leave out.

It wasn't there. Because a lot in the day wasn't going easily.

"Hey, where's the net?" he called, hurrying after Kelly as she ran downstream.

"Hanging from the wader hook by the rocker," she called, clearly following something in the water. He wasn't about to leave her out there to head back up to the cabin, so he left the net behind and reached the bank just as he saw what she had.

Another glint in the water. Bobbing downstream.

Because he was wearing boots, he went in after it, just as it reached a shallower area in the water. With a rock bottom.

Using the pulled-out tail of his uniform shirt, he grabbed

the small jar, with a piece of white paper inside, identical to all of the other jars they'd collected in the past three days. And stood there, with water rushing over his calves, turning to get a full 360-degree view. Looking for any movement. Any sign that someone was watching the jar's retrieval.

And saw nothing.

Not even a leaf swaying in the breeze on that completely quiet late afternoon.

You HeLp

The note was written in the same hand as before. The letters running on a downward spiral, with a few upward jumps, just as before. And the *L* was capitalized. "You see that really dark spot where the curve of the *p* stops?" Kelly pointed to it. Levi, who'd been standing right next to her as he'd carefully, and with latex gloves, opened the jar to look at the note, bent closer. Their faces were almost touching.

With all the tension racing through her, that small feeling of warmth next to her cheek was a standout moment.

A calming one. She glanced over to see him studying the note, and got back to work herself, but with more inner strength than she'd had seconds before.

"That indicates heightened emotion," she said.

"Fear?" He bent even closer to the note.

"That. Or could be frustration. Any emotion, really, that is spiraling at the time the note was written."

Levi stood. Gave her that pinpoint stare. "Excitement?" he asked.

And she knew instantly where he was going with the question. A stalker who felt that he was close to his mark, ready to cash in on whatever plot he'd planned, one who was purposely re-creating broken-letter penmanship, could still show some of himself in a dark imprint. "Yes."

He nodded, and she was surprised when he didn't press the admission any further.

Instead, he walked to the back door, looked out and then approached the table again, frowning.

"When was the last time you saw the fishing net?"

"Today."

"When?"

"When we left to head up into the hills. Why?"

She turned toward the kitchen window, through which the net would be partially visible. Didn't see it.

Went to the door, looked out.

And saw the empty hook.

LEVI COMMANDED HIMSELF to remain calm. He'd seen the net as they'd left that morning as well. And had no photo memory of seeing it as they'd returned.

Having just found a body, and being on the phone, he hadn't paid attention to what was or wasn't hanging on a hook as he'd entered the door. He'd scanned the yard for danger, had entered the cabin first to make certain no one was there. Other than that, he'd been too concerned with getting the right people up to the Yardle property before someone removed the body they'd found.

If someone was watching them, watching Kelly, waiting for a chance to discredit her, the body's discovery could have provided what seemed like a gold mine.

No body when crews got to the scene, with no sign or proof that anyone other than Levi and Kelly were even up in the hills—other than the damned notes that kept appearing— would raise a lot of questions, at the very least.

And someone out to discredit an expert didn't need proof.

He'd only need to be able to create enough doubt to weaken Kelly's credibility.

But there had been a body in a shallow grave when his team arrived.

Because...

"Someone was here." Kelly finished his unspoken sentence aloud.

Levi was already on the phone. Verifying that none of his people, including family members, had been by the cabin to see them that morning.

When he hung up, Kelly was still standing by the door, staring out.

"Of all the things here, why take the net?" she asked. "It was my surest way to retrieve the jars. To get the messages."

"Chances are you have another in the shed. You can also just get another." He was doing her victim's thinking aloud, because he knew that was where she'd go first. And, as he followed that route, added, "If you're living off the land, it would sure come in handy for fishing."

"Yes, but..." She shook her head. "The notes should be the most important thing, if what they want is for me to get the messages."

"You're assuming your victim knows you used the net to get the jars. And you haven't every time."

Turning from the door, she glanced at him, eyes wide-open. And serious. "You think it's the stalker, the hired gun, ramping up his game, don't you? He's letting us know he's right here, stealing a net off our porch. He's trying to push me over the edge."

He couldn't stand the lack of confidence in her expression, the sudden slump in her shoulders. And he couldn't deny that he'd had the thought she'd just expressed. That it made the most sense to him.

"It could also be that some random hiker is out for a day-long journey from somewhere, following the river, saw the net and helped himself."

"Right." She nodded. Moved back to the table.

And when they arrived, she focused on the images of faces that Hudson sent—looking for any similarities in the skeleton they'd studied—while Levi coordinated with police departments in five states to get feet on the ground to check in with those who'd reported the various young women missing.

What had taken days or weeks for him to accomplish with his own resources was happening almost in the minute with the help of Sierra's Web.

Kelly spoke with Glen. Reported that the new jars had definitely been dropped at a different point in the river and had traveled through some varying terrain, based on sediment coming from all of them.

While Levi was busy coordinating efforts, Kelly made dinner. Rice bowls with chicken and veggies and a barbecue ranch dressing. Something new to him.

He'd liked it.

She'd kissed him when he'd told her so.

But she'd looked outside right afterward. As though she suspected someone was out there. Watching her.

Watching them.

He couldn't reassure her on that one. He thought so, too. Made many trips around the clearing that surrounded her cabin. Headed upstream, and down again, just before dusk.

If he didn't find some merit in Kelly's steadfast conviction that they were after a victim, he'd have insisted they move the investigation headquarters into town.

And knew that doing so wouldn't guarantee that Kelly would move with him.

When it was lighter inside than out, putting them on display, he lowered and locked all of the shutters on the cabin. And closed and locked both doors, too.

He made sure her grandfather's .22 was loaded, and slid it behind the back edge of the stove right outside the porch bedroom door. No matter where she was in the cabin—other than the bathroom—that gun would be within feet of her reach.

When all else failed to ease the strain in her expression, he pulled her into her bedroom and covered her back with his arms.

Giving her every ounce of strength and support he had as he joined their bodies, silently promising that they'd be similarly together during every second of whatever lay ahead of them as the investigation unfolded.

She might not spend the days and nights of regular life in his arms, but for the moment they had each other, and he wasn't going to let her down.

Chapter Eighteen

It was just a fishing net. And Kelly felt violated. Someone who needed help shouldn't steal from their proposed helpmate.

And yet, to someone desperate, trying to survive in the woods with very little, a net to catch fish could seem like the difference between life and death. A way to hang on for a little while longer.

Most particularly if one's hope for an eventual rescue was growing.

The net was nothing fancy. She could replace it at minimal cost. Maybe her victim knew that, figured she wouldn't miss it.

And maybe that missing net was a warning that she was a sitting duck. That she'd be caught if and when her stalker chose to grab her.

The chances of it having been stolen by a random hiker weren't even on her radar.

With Levi's arms around her, and her body satiated from the workout they'd given each other, she got some sleep.

But was awake when she felt her short-time lover slide out of the bed at dawn. They'd left a light on in the hall leading to the bathroom, giving the entire cabin a small glow, and she watched unabashedly as he rounded the bed and took his tight naked butt out into the kitchen on his way to the bathroom.

Loving him, respecting him, admiring him—and knowing that, once again, she had to choose between being true to who and what she was, or being who Levi wanted her to be.

She had to live authentically.

Could not live a lie.

With that thought, she was up and dressed in under a minute, and out the back door. He didn't want her out without him.

Last night's note. "You HeLp."

All evening those words had cried out to her. They'd been there the second she awoke. Her victim was crying out for her.

That indentation on the curve of that last letter meant that whoever was there was getting desperate.

Because of so many people around, Kelly knew.

The discovery of the body, once her victim knew…no telling what that would do to her.

Worse yet if her victim was a child and that body belonged to their mother. No telling what a child raised in the woods—and with Yardle—would know or think about death.

The note they'd retrieved the night before could be the last…

No way could she ignore what her psychological profile was drumming at her.

While it was light outside, the sun hadn't yet come up over the woods on her property, leaving the world around her slightly dusk-like. Quiet. Serene.

Moving swiftly away from the cabin, she headed to the edge of the clearing surrounding it, listening to the water as she drew close and then walked along it.

Upstream.

The source of the notes.

Listening for a louder splash or rushing sound that would denote a foreign object in the water. Like a body crossing through it.

Or standing on the edge of it.

She moved slowly, as though taking an early-morning stroll, as she'd done the three mornings she'd thought herself completely alone in the world out there. But she didn't try to hide the sound of her approach.

The entire idea was to lure out whoever needed her. To make contact. Even if it was only a glance, a smile, across the river for now.

Just enough to give her a clue as to what she was dealing with so she'd know how to proceed—what kind of help to offer.

And enough to let her victim know that she got the message. The help had to come from her.

Most importantly, she needed whoever was out there to know that she was willing to comply. She was there.

Alone.

Ready to help.

While she wasn't moving softly, her steps along the bank weren't making all that much noise. She could hear the wind rustling through the leaves in the trees. Listened for the early-morning call of birds, but didn't notice any.

Figuring the stream was drowning them out, she continued on, determined to go as far as it took to find whoever needed her.

Levi would worry. The text she'd sent him had been…too much like the breakup letter for her not to know that he'd be hurt.

If he came to find her, she was kicking him off her property. Closing it off to law enforcement.

A huge call, she knew. And maybe not a smart one.

But if she had a victim, and couldn't follow the edicts to tend to the situation alone, then she'd have to do what was necessary to ensure that she could do so.

Branches scraped at the skin left bare on her arms in her short-sleeved top. Knowing she wasn't going to be walking around clusters of growth, but rather forging through them so she didn't lose sight of the water, she should have put on a long-sleeved shirt.

Busy looking at the water, she missed a root on the ground and stubbed the toe of her tennis shoe so hard, she lost her balance. Had to grab a tree to right herself.

And with the twist the movement caused, caught a glimpse behind her.

Movement.

Color.

She'd seen color?

As in a shirt.

Made out of the blue quilt that had gone missing?

And high up on the tree. A little over her head.

Someone that much taller than her?

Not a young woman small enough for Yardle to force into compliance? Or a child?

Heart pounding, Kelly wasn't sure what to do.

Did she let her pursuer catch up to her?

Keep walking and pretend she hadn't seen someone so she still appeared as a safe harbor?

Or hightail it back to the cabin, screaming the whole way, so Levi would know the stalker was there, and she needed help?

And then it hit her.

Levi had a blue cotton shirt. She'd seen him lay it out with a pair of jeans the night before. He'd laid them on the dresser in her room closest to his side of the bed.

In the event he needed to jump into them with little notice.

He was following her?

After the text she'd sent?

Angry, hurt, panicked because it meant she was going to have to send him away, Kelly turned and continued moving slowly upstream. Trying to figure out what to do.

With Levi behind her, any chance that her victim would show herself had just dimmed to pretty much nothing.

Her attempt to gain trust by being out alone had just become the opposite—evidence that she couldn't be trusted to come alone.

Glancing behind her again, just too mad to pretend she didn't know Levi was there, she saw nothing but stillness.

Except...out of the corner of her eye...movement. In the woods, not by the water. She couldn't see anyone. There was no body. Hadn't really been one earlier. Just that flash of blue.

But it was drawing closer to her.

Levi wouldn't do that. Would he?

Unless he knew she'd made him.

And her victim—why leave the water chosen as the means of communication?

Turning in a circle, she took in her surroundings. Saw movement again from the woods. Drawing closer to her.

And her stomach clenched. Deeply. In pain.

She had to get back to the cabin.

If her victim was in the woods, playing cat and mouse, they'd just had their first session. She'd made herself accessible, alone, by the water.

And if it wasn't her victim, she could be in imminent danger...

The last thought propelled her, full speed ahead, running through the brush and the trees, not stopping to look behind her, or to listen for sounds in the woods.

If Levi was out there, he'd won. Scared her so much she'd just blown her first shot at meeting her victim.

She was a psychiatrist, not a law enforcement officer. Or a

bodyguard. She didn't have the training to take on a six-foot-tall being who was stalking her in the woods.

A hundred yards from the cabin, she slowed to a stop.

Damn.

She'd let fear cloud her judgment. Hoped to God she hadn't just lost the only chance to help whoever was out there.

Walking the rest of the way to the clearing around her cabin, she listened for sounds of Levi, making his way out of the woods behind her.

Feeling sad, and lost—and confused with herself. She'd never lost her professional insight on a case before. Not ever.

In the clearing, she glanced toward the cabin—shutters raised—and stopped when she saw Levi standing inside, at the kitchen sink, a coffee cup in hand, watching her walk up the yard.

His shirt was blue. Dark blue.

Nothing like the splash of blue she was sure she'd seen.

Tears filled her eyes. Because the morning had been awful.

And because Levi hadn't disrespected her after all.

IT TOOK EVERYTHING Levi had to stand at the kitchen sink in Kelly's cabin and watch her come walking out of the woods.

When she drew close enough for him to see the scratches on her arms, he slammed his coffee cup to the counter and tore out the door.

"What happened?" He glanced at her, toward the woods from which she'd come, and back again. Over and over.

She shook her head, but one look at her face told him that the morning hadn't gone as she'd hoped.

Had she been crying?

"Kelly. This is Detective Griggs speaking. I need to know what happened."

With a glance at him, she nodded, and headed up the cement steps from the bottom of her yard up to the small porch that ran along the back of the house, to the door.

Adrenaline pumping, he took another glance around them, and then followed her in.

"What happened?" he demanded again, as soon as they were both inside the door, watching as she moved to the cupboard, pulled out a coffee cup and poured from the almost empty pot. He'd been ingesting the black liquid one swallow after another since he'd come out of the shower and read her text.

Standing right where he'd been when she finally reappeared in the yard. At the kitchen sink, looking out.

Possibly losing her to some fiend, and helpless to do anything about it.

Reminiscent of the past.

The similarity was not lost on him.

He needed Kelly alive and well. Whether he was standing next to her or living on the other side of the world.

Taking her cup to the window, she stood, back to him, looking out, much as he'd been doing for most of the past hour. Seemingly unaware of the blood dotting her arms like periods at the ends of sentences. The scrapes were thin—the blood there, but not dripping.

"I screwed up." Her words shocked him. He'd been expecting…different.

Danger. A realization that there was no victim.

Not *screwing up*. Concerned anew, he joined her at the counter, side by side, her staring out, him watching her. "Can you explain that?"

"I saw movement, Levi. Someone was there. I'm sure of it…"

Completely alert now, staring outside, surveying with the

eye that had solved many cases, he asked the first question he'd ask any witness. "What'd they look like?"

A shake of her head wasn't the answer he'd been after.

"I didn't actually see anyone. Just…movement. It was behind me. I'd tripped, and was twisted as I righted myself. There was a flash of blue…"

The kill-or-be-killed tension inside of him relaxed a notch. "You say the movement was above you?"

"Yeah. The person, if there was one, had to have been at least six feet tall."

"How sure were you that it was a person?"

"At the time, a hundred percent."

"What changed your mind?"

She turned, leaning her butt on the counter, held her cup, but didn't sip. "I don't know," she said. "I got scared… I panicked… I ran."

Thank God. "All good things, Kel," he told her. "Your instincts kicked in…"

"Fear kicked in." She sounded equal amounts of disappointed and disgusted with herself.

And he had as much need to engage as he had when he'd thought her life had been in immediate danger.

He still wasn't sure it hadn't been. Had to get outside. Look for footprints. Newly broken twigs.

But first… "At its core, fear is an emotion meant to keep you safe," he said, realizing how inane it was to be telling a psychiatrist about emotions.

"I know." She took a sip of coffee. "I'm just not sure that my gut was telling me I was in danger, or my imagination was. I could have been on the brink, Levi. Maybe this would all be rounding up right now, except that the whole six-feet thing… My mind got away from me…"

He didn't believe it. She wasn't panicked. Or showing any

signs of irrationality born of panic. "How so?" The question was all detective that time.

When she glanced at him, her gaze filled with sorrow, he didn't understand.

Until she said, "I thought it was you, checking up on me. Not trusting me to do my job and be smart about it. Then, after thinking about you I was suddenly thinking that it was the stalker you keep saying is out to get me. I got scared, Levi. It wasn't rational thinking, or a true awareness of danger."

He replayed her words again, silently.

She'd seen the movement, the flash of color, and only then been afraid?

Urgency pumped through him.

"I'm sorry," she said.

"For what?"

"Doubting you."

He shook his head. No time for such nonsense. "It was fifty-fifty, whether or not I was going to follow you," he admitted. "Tell me again, do one of your close-your-eyes cognitive things, and tell me what you saw, Kel."

Her mind had been thinking completely rationally at the time of the sighting.

"Movement higher than my head. I was sure it was a person, but I don't know why. The flash of blue. A shirt, I was sure. Again, nothing to back that up."

"You don't need to back it up," he said, irritation born of the belief that someone had been out there, in his tone. "Please," he tempered himself. "Just continue."

"That's it...except...no, a little bit later, I'd gone further upstream... I thought I saw him again. In the woods, this time. And closer to me." She looked up at him. "That's why I ran."

"Because if he was coming closer, you needed to run," he told her. "The movement you saw, could have been the wind.

The blue, a patch of sky seen from an odd angle because you were righting yourself. But if it was a person, you did the absolute right thing, Kel. I get what you were doing. I get why. As a cop, a detective, I agree that it was the best next step to finish this thing. But you aren't going to do anyone any good if you don't trust your instincts."

His gaze bored into her, hard. He had to know that...

"You want me to trust my instincts," she said.

He nodded. "You didn't screw up."

"You aren't just saying that." She wasn't asking.

"No."

"Okay."

Brows raised, he held her gaze. "Okay?" He needed confirmation.

"Okay."

"Then are you okay to get back out there? Because if you *were* being followed, by a nonvictim, we're losing precious time."

"You want me to go with you?" She seemed surprised. Not the least bit put out by the suggestion.

"Yeah. You know what you saw and where you saw it."

"I'm ready." She headed toward the door.

And he had to add, "Besides, there's no way in hell I'm leaving you in here all alone."

She grinned at him. Kind of laconically.

And he grinned back.

But only for the seconds it took for them to get out the door.

After that, he was all cop.

On duty.

Both investigating, and protecting.

Chapter Nineteen

Levi found what might be a trail consisting of a few spots of tamped-down earth, starting from Kelly's own trail, made by her early-morning walk along the bank, and forking off at the spot she said she'd seen the movement. She'd remembered the tree, had pointed it out to Levi, before he'd even gotten close enough to find the trail leading from it.

The quasi path he found rounded back toward the bank up-stream, if he connected the loosely laid dots of broken ferns. Probably from moving quickly to follow Kelly, Levi proposed.

Had she continued forward, he suspected someone would have been ready to confront her another few hundred yards up ahead of her path.

Her victim?

Or someone else who was clearly up to no good?

If it was a victim, why not just stop at the cabin and speak with her?

Why follow her, and then forge ahead to cut her off when she was too far from the cabin for Levi to hear her cry for help?

The answer, of course, was obvious to her. If it wasn't her victim, it was someone up to no good.

And the bend in the river where someone had obviously

sat for a time had been in one of the deepest, most rapid parts of the river in that region.

But if it *had* been her victim, the move made sense to her. They'd have wanted to be far enough away from the cabin, from others, that they couldn't be heard. And would have wanted to get ahead, and keep watch, to make certain that no one else came up with her.

All of which she'd explained to Levi.

He hadn't been in a listening kind of mood. He'd nodded. Grunted and called in the morning's event to his uncle, asking, once again, for people to comb the woods surrounding Kelly's cabin. He'd spent the next two hours canvassing the perimeter of the building, from the clearing to a few hundred yards in the woods.

Needing a break, a chance to find her calm, Kelly had taken an hour off to stand under a hot shower. Blow-dry her long hair.

To dress in clean jeans and a button-down shirt, wanting her scratched arms hidden. The damage wasn't bad. Would be barely noticeable in a day or so. She just didn't want the constant reminder of the early-morning walk.

She needed to put it behind her.

To concentrate on what she could still control.

She was going out again. Whether Levi liked it or not. She suspected he knew as much.

But she'd be smart about it. Have a plan that she talked over with Levi—because he was her current on-site business partner—before she embarked.

Glen called to confirm that the current notes had been written with the same type of substance. Some form of charcoal. She told Levi about it the second he came inside midmorning.

"The notes were all written with something akin to a charcoal pencil that artists use."

He stood there in jeans and his blue T-shirt, a shirt that made the pure blue of his eyes even more vibrant than usual as they appeared to see right into her.

Because he was Levi, she didn't mind. Didn't put defenses in place. And couldn't be bothered at the moment to analyze the realization, either. Her skills were fully occupied trying to help someone else at the moment.

"Glen says that they're homemade. Testing the charcoal, he's sure they're from oak trees." There'd been plenty of them around Yardle's shack. But the hills were filled with them as well. "He described the process. You put thin, pencil-or larger sized pieces of wood into an airtight fireproof container. Like maybe a vegetable can from the grocery store with the lid securely attached, or any metal container. Artists apparently often use paint cans because the lids are easy to securely re-attach." Not pertinent to her victim. There'd been no sign of anything having been painted up at Yardle's place. But she wanted Levi to know every detail in case something reso-nated. "You punch some holes in the container," she contin-ued. "They let the gasses out. You put the can in a fire, even a small campfire, for a couple of hours, and you've basically got homemade pencils."

Standing by the couch, looking out the window, he turned to her. "He thinks Yardle made artist pencils?"

"Of course not, he thinks—"

"I know." Levi shoved his hands in his pockets. "Maura obviously did it. And maybe by accident. Picking up a piece of burned twig, it could have marked her skin and she took it from there. It makes sense. But that still doesn't tell us if we're dealing with a victim, a child who was born into victimhood or someone out to smear your name by getting you to lead Sierra's Web and law enforcement on a wild-goose chase."

"Except that we found a body."

"*I* found it," he told her, frowning.

That look. The standoffish way he was standing. Looking over her shoulder, not at her. The odd emphasis on the *I*. They all put Kelly on alert.

"What aren't you telling me?"

"Martin thinks if the stalker is any good, he's going to know, or find out, about our past. Add to that the fact that I'm staying here…and suddenly I, the key investigator on the original case, find a body in the hills to substantiate what the stalker knew was just him all along. He started a farce, and I find a body that could make the farce look…not so fake."

"Unless it's completely unrelated."

"Right, but either way, I'm either in collusion with you, helping to protect your reputation by producing a body I just happen to suddenly realize is up there. Or…"

"Or?"

"I'm helping the stalker discredit you in a bigger way."

"That makes no sense. Why involve your department, and Sierra's Web, if…"

She broke off, stared at him.

He nodded. "The bigger I can make it look, and my doing so is all driven by my need for revenge, the harder you—and possibly Sierra's Web—falls. Even if I'm not being paid off, not involved in the subterfuge at all, the stalker just has to make it look like I am to get his job done."

"So, what are you telling me? Martin's pulling you off the case? You're leaving and sending someone else to stay here with me?"

Or worse. He was leaving her out there all alone? Forcing her to either abandon whatever victim might be there, or remain in a potentially dangerous situation in the middle of the woods, miles away from anyone else?

Her mind slipped into high gear. "We've got a plethora of

bodyguard experts working for Sierra's Web," she said then. "I can have someone here by this afternoon."

Hands still in his pockets, Levi watched her. "You've made your decision, then. You want me to go."

Her brows came so tightly together, they impaired her vision a bit. "My decision?"

"Martin and I discussed the situation and determined that the choice had to be yours."

She didn't get it. "Why mine?"

"I know I'm not duplicitous. As does Martin. We both know that this has something to do with my Yardle case, even if we're not sure how much is a copycat and how much is truly connected. We both agree that, given my fifteen-year history with Yardle, with Maura, with the way he worked, with the hills themselves, I'm the best man to see this through. But because I could be perceived to be complicit here in a plot to discredit you, I have a motive because of the way you dumped me in the past, and there are a slew of witnesses who can attest to the fact that my dealing with that wasn't pretty—you have to be the one to determine if you're willing to risk whatever fallout there could be with having me associated with you. Here. At the cabin."

His expression, his stance, didn't change. Everything inside of her did.

"There is no question, Levi. I thought you were leaving me."

"I'm not the one who does that."

It was a low blow. Speaking to the unresolved, heightened emotions flowing between them.

"But I understand why you do," he continued before she could find a response she wanted to actually own. "I tend to be overly protective of those I, um, care about. And I'm not quiet about it. I wanted you, the person you were, but I wanted to keep you safely in an Idlewood box where my uncle and I, together with a great department, kept a lid on criminals. If you'd come home after college, I'd have slowly, unknowingly, unintentionally snuffed your spirit."

Her mouth fell open. She stood there, staring at him, completely shocked. What he'd just said… She'd never put it consciously into words…but he'd just described how she'd felt after her first month away.

"What?" he asked then. "You think I don't know that I had a tendency to think I was your protector to the point that you weren't free to make your own choices without fear of upsetting me?"

"I was never afraid of you, Levi Griggs. Not for one second. You would no more try to force me to your will than you would blow up this town." The words burst out of her like a gunshot. Fiercely. Filled with fire.

His jaw visibly tensing, he rocked a bit on his feet. She could see his hands clenched into fists in his pockets.

He hadn't tried to stop her from leaving Idlewood to accept the scholarship she'd won. He'd supported her choice. Told her he was proud of her. Nor had he fought, even with a single sentence in his response, her need to break up with him.

She hadn't been afraid of upsetting him.

"I was afraid of hurting you, Levi," she whispered. "I still am."

HE WAS AFRAID of someone else attacking Kelly. And she was afraid of hurting him. What a mucked-up pair they made. Levi paced the cabin, hating the inactivity, the lack of evidence to lead them closer to their note writer, in spite of all of the feet on the ground in the hills.

They'd found a body. But they couldn't find anything that led them to a few jars floating down the river.

And now someone had been following Kelly? And then hurried around to set a trap for her? He was sure to the core of his soul it had happened that way. Every instinct he had was screaming at him that there was a man out in the woods fixed on Kelly Chase.

Yet there he stood, powerless. Drawing a blank as to what to do next.

The guy was getting closer to her. Getting bolder.

Because Levi was there and he was afraid that they'd catch him? Send him to jail, definitely, but also, in the process, expose whoever hired him? Which could, depending on the person's contacts and finances, give him trouble in prison.

Kelly had talked about a sense of growing desperation in the last note. She'd been referring to the victim in her theory. But when applied to his suspect—that morning's near disaster struck a chord of fear in him.

The stalker was getting desperate. Either to tip Kelly over the edge in some obvious way, or to just help her into a seemingly accidental death.

A shove at that bend in the river...she could easily hit her head on any of the rocks on the way down, tumbling into water in the midst of the swift current...

He shuddered.

Had to get himself under control or be of absolutely no use to her.

The only good he could find was that if the stalker was getting more desperate, there was more chance he'd make a mistake. That's all Levi needed...one mistake.

Like the tamped-down growth in various spots in the woods, leading to the river.

The guy had shown his intent.

And nearly left evidence that would allow Levi to prove it.

As things stood, it could be argued that a larger animal had made the trail in the woods. A deer that was running off—the way they jumped and landed—could have done it.

If not for the seeming coincidence of the trail starting exactly where Kelly had first seen movement, with blue, and ending at that precarious bend in the river. No deer would seek the spot as either a crossing point or a drinking spot.

Facts that seemed to fit too closely to be coincidence would not get him a conviction in court. But they told Levi a story that he knew to be true. They were his warning that he was running out of time.

Martin called late morning, just as Levi and Kelly were cooking and cutting veggies for a chicken-and-egg salad for lunch. They'd been working mostly in silence, moving around each other as though they'd choreographed it.

She'd probably say they were that much in tune with each other. He knew he was just being mindful of keeping his space.

In the bed at night, he could lose himself in the smell and feel of her. During the day, his job to protect was the only thing on the table.

She'd been peeling boiled eggs when the phone rang. She was drying her hands, watching him, as he hung up.

"They got an ID on the body," he told her, maintaining her gaze, wishing he could hold her as he delivered the news. She'd always been one to feel things so deeply. Her own stuff. But the distress of others, too. "A family in Indiana recognized the picture last night. A DNA match came through half an hour ago. Her name was Robin McKinney."

"Oh my God." Kelly sank to a kitchen chair, her gaze never wavering from his. "Who...what—"

"She was fourteen the last time her foster mother saw her. She climbed out her bedroom window in the middle of the night. Left a note saying she'd met someone who loved her, and not to look for her. The state did, of course. The case has been open all these years."

"Until last night."

He shrugged. "Or this morning." When the confirmation came through.

"There was evidence that the girl had met someone on the internet. They think she was in Ohio first, and eventually made it to Michigan. Someone recognized her photo at a homeless shelter in Cadillac five years ago. The case went completely cold after that."

"Cadillac." Kelly's gaze grew dark. "The same place Maura was last seen until the day Yardle shot her."

He nodded.

"How old was Robin when he got her?"

"We don't have any way of knowing when he got her, Kel. But she was sixteen at the last sighting in Cadillac."

Sixteen. He'd already asked Kelly to marry him by the time they'd turned sixteen. They hadn't told anyone, of course. They'd been so young.

But he'd known she was the only one for him.

She'd sworn he was it for her, too.

Sixteen.

Too young to know.

Right up Yardle's alley.

Chapter Twenty

Kelly couldn't get Robin McKinney off her mind. She ate some lunch because she knew she had to. Because there was another Robin wandering the hills outside her window—maybe even in her own woods at the moment—needing her help.

She had to keep her mind focused. Compile all that she knew of Robin, and of Maura, reread all reports regarding both women and figure out how best to reach a possible third young woman.

Perhaps one even younger than Robin.

And the person she'd seen that morning? Could very well have been a young woman. Levi had been right. She'd been bent, slightly twisted when she'd seen the movement. Her perspective had been skewed.

She'd seen the movement, though. The memory was clear. And the blue. Maybe a patch of sky between the leaves. She didn't think so.

She'd tried to get a sense of a spot on the tree behind which the person had moved, but got nothing. She knew the ground, the way the trunk had had two protruding roots. The tree had been the widest in a grouping of three. And she knew the river—the tree had been right across from a rocky embankment where she used to catch frogs.

Nothing farther up on the tree itself.

Which all agreed with Levi's assessment that her sense of height had been skewed by her own position.

Once again, his input helped her do her job.

Kelly sat at the table after lunch, reading and rereading everything she knew about Yardle's two known victims.

Took notes.

She looked at pictures of both.

Dark haired. Small boned.

Easily manageable, in a physical sense.

She jotted down impressions as they came to her. The way things were escalating, she might only get one shot at bringing her victim out of those woods and she needed to know everything she possibly could to win enough trust, in the space of maybe only seconds, to succeed.

First and foremost, there could be no hint of any use of force. Of any kind. Not physical, certainly, but not psychologically, either.

The woman needed to feel as though she was in control of her life.

Which meant Kelly could absolutely not be out walking around with her grandfather's .22 in her hands.

The hills and meadows and woods had been home to the victim. She'd exhibited an ability to remain hidden, knew where and how to hide, and she'd managed to stay alive all alone in the wilderness. They had to assume that she'd be aware if Levi, or anyone, was following Kelly—watching Kelly—as Kelly approached.

She and Levi were going to have to come up with some guidelines by which she could alert him if she was in trouble. Text was the obvious first course of action. Unless, like that morning, she'd thought her life was in immediate danger.

She'd been in fight-or-flight mode and clearly had not felt up to the fight.

Maybe, as Levi stated, she'd made the right move.

She didn't think so.

He'd finished up dishes and was out chopping wood for a fire they didn't really need, when she heard voices in the yard.

A deputy she'd seen from a distance but had never met before—a redheaded woman who looked attractive even in uniform—was commanding Levi's full attention.

The way he leaned toward the woman, bending his head to her, sent a shot of jealousy through Kelly's veins, shooting waves so high they almost drowned her.

She'd given Levi up more than a decade before. He was free to entertain any woman he wanted. He'd been married.

Kelly knew all that. She just didn't ever let herself think about it.

But seeing him there...the way the woman looked up to him...

Urgently. The woman's expression held an intentness that bespoke a critical need for action.

And Kelly was out the door.

LEVI HEARD THE back door open, and motioned Kelly over.

"This is Annie Williams," he told her, nodding toward the deputy he'd worked with a few times. "She and her brother are both deputies with the River County Sheriff's Department. Annie just found some footprints about an hour's hike upstream from here, tracked the coordinates the entire way. I'm heading up to take a look and think you should come along just in case."

In case he found her victim and needed her, yes.

But more in case her stalker saw him leave in that direction, had left the prints purposely to draw Levi away from the cabin, so that he could gain access to Kelly alone.

The missing fishing net had been a clear warning that the man was close. That he could walk right up to the cabin without being seen.

That he was confident and getting more bold.

The missing net followed by the morning's near miss...

Levi couldn't let himself dwell on that one. He had to stay one hundred percent professionally focused.

With Annie guiding them, they made it to the site of the footsteps inside the hour. Dennis Troutman, a deputy on loan from a neighboring county who'd been standing guard over the area, shook Levi's hand and reported that there hadn't been more than a bird chirp in the couple of hours he'd been on watch.

Levi heard the man, but then after the brief greeting, he was on the ground, studying a heel print in a slightly muddy area on the bank. And then, farther up, what looked to be a heel with maybe a big toe.

"These are adult," he said, an educated guess. "We'll need Forensics out here to get some molds."

Dennis was on his radio immediately, delivering the ask.

And Kelly, who'd been silent and walking slightly behind him and Annie most of the way, knelt down beside him.

"The heel is deeper down there." She pointed to the first track. "This one almost looks as though there was only partial weight on the foot."

"I thought so, too," he told her. And then had to add, "Unfortunately, there's not enough here for me to have any idea if the print is male or female."

Her nod said too much to him. She didn't need a print size. She believed the print to be female.

"If the stalker was out there this morning, he'd have to

know he came close to getting caught. He'd know we'd be calling in another search party. He'd be eager to get out of the area. Probably took off his shoes and waded upstream long enough to avoid any possibility of being tracked by dogs, and then got out, here, and..."

"What?" Kelly asked. "That's what I was trying to figure out. Where did she go from here?"

She.

The rock in his gut hardened at the confirmation that no matter what evidence turned up, she was going to find a way to make it fit her victim theory.

Even if it got her killed.

Kelly was up and walking around the area. "It's loose dirt here," she said. "How would a wet foot leave two prints, and then nothing?"

It was like the person had been scooped up by...

Not finishing the thought, Levi stared upward. His gaze glued to a particular branch in the tree, part of a thick cluster of trees, next to the footprint. A broken twig?

Without another word, he was at the trunk of the tree, skimming up it, loaded belt and all. His gun, radio and knife didn't slow him.

"Levi?"

He heard Kelly's voice. And then nothing but silence below him. Didn't take his sight off the branch he was aiming for. And when he arrived, just as he'd suspected, hoped, he saw another broken twig. One branch led to another. Completely on task, Levi followed the trail until it abruptly ended. Glanced down, to check for footprints on the ground, and found himself four trees over from the trunk he'd climbed.

The deputies were back by the print, watching him.

Kelly was right underfoot.

Nodding.

"SHE KEEPS HERSELF safe by traveling in the trees as much as she can," Kelly said as soon as they headed back to the cabin alone.

The deputies were staying in the area until someone could get up to make a mold of the partial prints.

"Or, he's woods savvy enough to know how to avoid tracking dogs. The way you suddenly turned and ran this morning, he has to figure that you saw him…"

They debated the point and then revisited everything else they knew about the case. Kelly felt better on the trip back, having Levi to herself, and that upset her. Jealousy, a sense of ownership, had no place in her dealings with the detective.

Then she thought about the fact that she only had him for a few days, told herself that she was just being protective of the short time they had together and gave herself some slack.

She wasn't forgiven. But she was understood.

"We need to come up with a game plan for my next trip out," she told him as they neared the cabin.

He didn't want her to go. She knew that.

She was going anyway. He knew that.

They'd agreed to work the case together and she had no doubt he'd help her. Just as she'd help him, follow his edicts implicitly, if it turned out that his theory was right.

It was as simple as that.

THEY DECIDED IT would be best for Kelly to wait until morning to head out alone. Most of what she saw as contact efforts had come in the morning. They'd had searchers out all other times of day over the past few days and no one had seen anything, so it made sense to believe that whoever was out there moved most during the night or early-morning hours.

He'd refused to support her being out at night by herself. Or would have, if she hadn't allowed on her own that she didn't feel comfortable out after dark. She wouldn't be able to see, or assess key expressions and body language in the dark. Nor could she hope to distinguish anyone up in a tree. Animals roamed at dark.

He'd had to smile as that little factor slipped out her lips. And after sticking out her tongue, Kelly had grinned back at him.

They'd debated plans over a dinner of loaded scrambled eggs. One of his specialties. Turned out Kelly spent so much time on the road that she didn't cook all that much. The knowledge saddened him. She used to love to cook.

"What?" she asked, when he sat with that thought.

He shrugged. Didn't want to get into it. Saw no point.

"You think I'm a loser for eating out all the time?" she challenged, her chin in the air.

"No!" Try as he might, he couldn't find one damned thing about Kelly Chase that he'd post in a loser category. And Lord knew, he'd given it many shots over the years. "If you want to know the truth, it makes me sad."

Her brow rose in what appeared to be genuine surprise. "Why on earth does that make you sad?"

There was no good reason to go into it. Except that she wasn't about to let it go. "You loved coming over, helping my mother cook, sitting down at a table filled with family…"

He stopped. She'd also hated that she didn't have a family of her own to sit down with. It had always just been her and her mother. Even for holidays.

And the times with her father's family, she'd never felt like real family.

I'm always on the outside looking in. He remembered her words from long ago. That time had been after Thanksgiving with his family. But she'd mentioned summers with her paternal grandparents during the conversation.

"I just pictured you with your own family," he said. "It makes me sad to think of you alone."

"You're alone." He heard the defensiveness in her tone, and figured she had, too, based on how taken aback she looked, right before she relaxed, and smiled. "Besides, I'm not alone," she told him then. And his gut sank.

She had a guy in her life? But she…

And they'd…

"My Sierra's Web partners…we really are family, Levi. I wish you could meet them in person—you'd see. From that week we lost Sierra, we've all watched out for each other. Checked in with each other on a regular basis, even when someone's on vacation. For that matter, we often vacation together. Not one of us has ever had a holiday alone, unless we wanted it that way. And I can't, off the top of my head, ever remember any of us wanting it that way. And now, our family is growing. Hudson found out he had a thirteen-year-old daughter and married her mother, and we all have grown to love both of them. And Mariah, she's married and adopted an orphaned three-year-old."

Her abrupt stop caught his attention. Until she looked over at him and said, "Do I want to get married someday? Yeah, of course. But not until it's the right thing to do. Until it's something that's going to work."

He nodded then. And, knowing exactly what she was talking about, let the conversation die. He'd married for the sake of marrying, not because the woman was the right one for him, and had regretted having done so ever since.

Sometimes being alone really was the best choice.

Chapter Twenty-One

Levi wanted to bring a police dog out to accompany Kelly on her early-morning walk. She vetoed the suggestion immediately. In between phone calls with Sierra's Web and the sheriff's department, they'd only found a handful of protocols upon which they'd agreed.

She was going to have her phone in the pocket of her hoodie, with his number on speed dial on the lock screen. She could slide her hand in her pocket without causing alarm and push to call him every fifteen minutes. If he didn't get a call, he was heading after her.

She'd let him know, before she left, the direction she was traveling.

And she'd agreed not to go more than a twenty-minute walk from the cabin. Her victim clearly knew where she was.

They both believed that much—though she knew Levi's take was that her stalker knew.

If the woman truly wanted to be found, she'd be watching for Kelly to be available. Kelly was going to be out there.

And she'd do everything she could to keep herself safe in the event that Levi proved correct.

They'd moved to the living section of the L-shaped room. Were sitting at opposite ends of the couch. He'd had word that the last of his people were out of the hills and back in Idlewood.

And there they sat. With notes and jars, footprints, a missing quilt, a path and a tree climber, a missing fishing net and a couch moved away from a secret hole in the floor.

And a dead body.

All of which mattered.

And might not even be connected. Some of it. All of it.

The jars were definitely tied to the Yardle case.

"We've known the notes were a copycat of some kind from Maura," Levi said to her as she sat there trying not to ponder their earlier conversation about family—or lack thereof. Trying not to think about the insidious jealousy that had snaked through her at the sight of Levi and Deputy Williams talking in an intimate-looking fashion.

"Yeah," she said, welcoming the diversion from the things she wasn't thinking about.

"But the pencils, the charcoal that Glen called about. It all got overshadowed by the body ID and then the footprints," he said, "but it's key."

Glen had thought so. "It just verifies that whoever is sending the notes is using the same provisions," she said, stating what she'd assumed all along. "She's up there, Levi. She knew Maura. She knew about the notes. She probably knew Robin, too. Maybe was the one who'd found her and cut her down. Buried her…"

"The rope appears as though it had been chewed through," Levi said. "A raccoon probably."

"But then why wasn't her body eaten by the wildlife?"

"If there was a storm, you know how the wind gets up there—she could have been buried within hours."

Could have. Yes. But…

He looked at her. Hard.

And she knew what he wasn't saying. Animals could have been responsible for some of what she'd assumed was decomposition. She'd seen the shallow grave. The skeleton. She'd believed what she'd been comfortable with in the moment.

Not a mistake she'd usually make. But then, since she'd boarded the plane in Phoenix, nothing about her life had been anything close to usual.

"The pencils, Kelly," he said then. "If your victim is the one using them, why didn't we find a single one of them in the cabin?"

"She's clearly not staying there. There's no sign of habitation…"

"So you think she's running around the woods, living off the land, carrying around jars and pencils?"

She knew what he was doing. Trying to get her to see that there was no victim.

Because he didn't want her getting up at dawn and heading out.

"Obviously she has a place where she's camping," she said. "Just because your teams haven't found it, doesn't mean it doesn't exist. It took you fifteen years to find Yardle's place."

He cocked his head at that one. Stared toward the window.

"How does your stalker fit in with the pencils?"

"He found them during his search of Yardle's place. That's why he started writing the notes to begin with. He'd gone up looking for a way to get to you, to get us to reopen the case. It was such news in these parts, Kel, I'm telling you, the following of the articles, the social media posts, it was almost like a cult around here. He knew all you had to do was bring us one tiny piece of evidence of something ongoing and we'd bite like lions on meat. He lucked into the jars and pencils."

The relocated couch. The empty hole in the floor.

She was the one who'd thought the jars had been stored there. That her victim had taken them.

She and Levi were going in circles. They had hard evidence. Someone had used jars and pencils from a crime.

And had nothing, too, when it came to finding a suspect.

But they were getting closer. She really believed that. And knew he did, too.

Just as she believed that she had to stop thinking about Levi and Annie Williams. If they were on the verge of something…she was happy for him.

And he shouldn't be sleeping with Kelly.

Just as he shouldn't be living alone.

If anyone had thrived on being on the inside looking out, it had been Levi. He'd never even considered a life outside Idlewood. Had known when he was ten what he wanted to do with his life. Follow his uncle into law enforcement. And sit at family holiday dinners at a table big enough to hold all of the adults, cousins included, with a second table for the kids.

Just like he'd grown up.

Jen Montgomery, the woman he'd married, would have fit perfectly. A year older than Levi and Kelly, Jen came from a nice Idlewood family. She taught preschool.

"Why didn't you fight for her?"

Shaking his head, he glanced at her. "Fight for who?"

"Jen."

"There was no point."

"Because she'd slept with someone else? I get that it would be hard to get over that, Levi, but if you knew you'd neglected her, could understand, why not try to make it work? Why didn't you fight for the life you wanted?" A wife and kids had always been his number-one goal.

And if he was married, happy, Kelly could get over him once and for all.

"You want to know the truth?"

Not really. But she needed to, so she nodded.

"Because she wasn't you, Kel."

THERE WAS MOST definitely no one like Kelly Chase. Levi loved her the only way he could that night—with his body—pouring himself into her heart and soul. No words were spoken. No deep looks exchanged. Just two desperate bodies communicating in the only way they could.

And when sleep was done, Levi did as he'd done every day that he'd awoken in her bed. He quietly slid away.

He didn't shower. Wasn't going to risk Kelly heading out without him on immediate watch. He made coffee. Opened all but the porch bedroom shutters.

Thought about his marriage to Jen. The way he'd pictured the babies they'd make when he'd vowed to love her until death did them part.

He hadn't pictured her by his side forever.

Or felt her in his heart.

And Annie…she'd made it clear on more than one group outing, that if Levi wanted more from her, she'd gladly give it to him.

Bitch of it was, he really liked Annie. Admired her. Enjoyed her company.

Maybe he could even picture her in his mind, feel a swell of good emotion for her, if she ever walked down the aisle toward him.

He wasn't sure she wanted kids.

And he wasn't asking. For any of it.

Maybe he was more like Kelly than he'd known. Was that the point where he'd gone wrong in life? Thinking he needed to be like his aunts and uncles, his parents and grandparents? Married with children?

He'd made a good life for himself. Him and Betsy. He missed the girl. Had had daily reports from his mother regarding the dog's vacation with Grandma.

He thrived at work. Knew he was where he needed to be. Doing what he needed to do.

Thanks to Kelly.

Hard to believe that just a few long days before he'd been contemplating quitting. Making his temporary leave of absence permanent.

At the sink, staring out, he studied every dot on the horizon, and all sights closer in, too. Kelly was about to head out into that mass of land.

A crime had been committed there. A woman had been kidnapped, held hostage and abused to the point of being unable to walk out on her own. Or another man, a Yardle copycat, was up there holding a woman hostage, a Yardle copycat who was stringing along the River County Sheriff's Department, creating the use of massive police resources and thinking he could get away with it. Or…a stalker was running one hell of a campaign to discredit Kelly Chase. Or someone out for revenge was trying to torment her before killing her outright.

The last thought struck him cold as he heard Kelly stir around the corner.

The possibility of someone wanting Kelly gone had always been there. Even with the stalker theory, he'd known it could turn deadly.

And he had to stand back and watch her go. Everyone agreed there was someone out there. A person good enough at hiding to avoid capture from teams of trained professionals.

And Kelly was their only shot at luring the person out.

"There's an app. It tracks one phone's position using another phone signed into the account." He swung around as she came out talking.

"I'm familiar with it," he told her. Though, truthfully, he'd been so wrapped up in bigger picture things, he hadn't thought of it. If he needed something tracked, he had the means to do so. His uncle already had tracing set up on Kelly's and Levi's phones.

"I'd just feel better if we had it, and you watched me from the minute I leave here." She held her phone out to him. "Here's the app I'm using and my sign-in…can you get it set up on your phone while I go brush my teeth?"

He noted the app, her sign-in, and nodded as she took her phone and left the room.

She was scared. Maybe more so than she'd been since she'd seen the first note. Every instinct he had pushed him to stop the morning from progressing as planned.

Every personal instinct, that was. His professional ones… they forced him to stand in the kitchen downloading an app to his phone. Logging in. And seeing coordinates that let him know Kelly's phone was just yards away from him. In the direction of the bathroom.

The app was a good one. As he'd expect from someone who was partners with one of the nation's top IT experts. He'd be able to track Kelly for miles. Every step of the way.

And she was right. No waiting for a call from headquarters to alert him if she went off course. He'd know the second it happened and be out the door.

The woman was good.

The best.

But then, he'd known that since he was twelve.

IN BLUE DENIM, a sleeveless blouse and blue hoodie, Kelly left the cabin via the back door just as the sun was rising. Her hands were in her pockets. With one push of her finger, she made the first call. No vibration or any other indication that she'd dialed was forthcoming. Good.

Levi's ringtone, one set up just for her calls, sounded briefly and then quit.

Test complete.

She didn't turn around, look for him in the window. Didn't access any source of support from him. Other than the phone that was set to keep her safe.

And the pocketknife he'd insisted at the last minute, that she slide into the side of her bra.

It was uncomfortable. Would probably leave a bruise.

And was definitely overkill. Still, a part of her was glad it was there.

Crossing the yard, she could feel Levi's gaze on her back. She needed him there, at her back.

Needing him made her weak.

Took focus from her task.

Which was why she'd left without looking at him. Or saying a word.

She'd wanted to hug him.

Stupid. She knew better than to let feelings for Levi Griggs interfere with her life. Not only for herself, but for him.

The extent of her emotions, if he knew of them, would only hold him back from his best life.

And maybe, her knowing the extent of his, was holding her back, too.

Keeping her wits about her, she walked the bank, passed the bend where Levi was certain his stalker had been waiting to take her out the day before. She'd dialed him once, after what seemed like fifteen minutes. A plan was good, when being talked about in a room.

In reality? How did she keep looking at her watch, to be

aware of every fifteen-minute interval, without alerting who-ever might be watching her, assessing her for safety, that she wasn't actually alone?

When she'd gone what she thought was the predetermined distance upon which she and Levi had agreed, without a hint of another living being close by, she sat. Leaned against the bark of a tree as though she had all day to sit and pray. Or take in the serenity of her surroundings.

She did have all day.

In other circumstances, would have enjoyed the cool early-morning air.

Remaining vigilant, maintaining a constant watch around her, made appearing peaceful difficult.

The inactivity made keeping thoughts at bay even harder.

Damn Levi for bringing up the past. Talking about how she'd always felt like she was on the outside looking in.

He was completely right, of course. Had talked to him about it often enough.

It was just…she'd left all of that behind when she'd left Idlewood.

Except, talking to him the previous evening—maybe it hadn't all disappeared as completely as she'd thought.

Hud with his biological daughter, marrying the high school love of his life. Mariah—her newly adopted preschooler was one of Kelly's favorite dates every time the child life special-ist was in town.

And yet, with all of the newly forming families—she was a special aunt. With no real attachment other than bone-deep friendship.

If something happened to any of them, she wouldn't be part of a family notification.

More than a decade after leaving her past behind, she was

living right smack in the middle of it. On the outside looking in at the family she'd helped create.

Irritated with herself, growing impatient with the passage of time, Kelly stood, deciding to cross the stream and walk back on the opposite bank. A fallen tree gave her the idea. There was a particular swimming hole across her meadow where she used to go as a kid—the hole had a log across it and when Jolene was at the cabin with her, they'd spend the afternoon playing balance beam on the log—not swimming.

Funny how she had so many memories from just the few years she and Jolene had been friends. Odd how you could care so deeply for someone and then just move on.

Which is what should have happened with Levi.

What on earth was it going to take for her to get the man out of her system?

Another week of sleeping with him? Until the experience wasn't so new and exciting? If that was all it would take, she was willing to give it a try.

Hell, for all she knew, they were still going to be holed up at the cabin. At the rate they were going, who knew when they'd identify the note writer and bring justice where it would be served.

Hand in her pocket, she pressed her finger against the lock screen on her phone, sending yet another *I'm okay* signal to the detective partnering with her on the case.

And thought of Levi alone at the cabin—watching out the window, or walking the perimeter of the clearing, awaiting her return—as she expertly crossed the log, and reached the opposite bank. Once both tennis shoes were on solid ground, she took a few minutes to assess. To take in every view in a circle around her. Paying close attention to the opposite bank— the ground she'd just traversed—in case she'd see something she'd missed.

View was different. Result was the same.

By the time she made it back to her own property, she was gearing up mentally for her next time out. Planning the route. Maybe bringing a picnic.

A sign that she was in no hurry, that she was out for enjoyment, and…food. A desperate victim trapped in a life in the woods would most certainly be captivated by fresh, tasty food.

Thinking about the cookies she'd bake later that morning, with the idea that she'd head out again midafternoon, she pushed a finger to the upper right corner of her lock screen for the last time, and crossed into the woods that led her to the bank across from her cabin. Breaking free of the woods, she set out through the ferns.

It was just before she crested the small hill that would bring her cabin into view that she heard it.

A whisper.

And stopped in her tracks.

Chapter Twenty-Two

Phone in hand, Levi was watching the crest of the hill across the river, waiting to see Kelly's head and face appear. To sustain the purity of the mission, he'd remained inside the cabin the entire time she'd been gone.

Him seemingly on patrol, even in the yard, would likely spook anyone who might be watching to check that Kelly was truly alone.

Being able to track every step she made on the app she'd provided him had helped him stay on task.

Her head wasn't appearing.

Gaze shooting to his phone, he watched the red dot remain steady on the screen. She'd stopped. Just over the hill.

Over the next fifteen minutes, Levi's adrenaline level rose to explosive levels as he watched that red dot move forward, then back, then sideways, then back. Always returning to the original stopping point. She hadn't dialed him.

But if someone was harming her, she wouldn't be moving in circles, would she?

Unless a bear had her...

There were reports of bears being spotted in the hills occasionally. He'd never heard of one down at river level.

No. Clamping off that train of thought, Levi focused on

the movement. Always returning to the same spot...no wild animal would do that.

Nor would a kidnapper.

Had Kelly been right? Was she right then having her meeting? A touch-and-go attempt to get whoever had shown themselves to her to come fully out of hiding?

He could picture it.

Knew that if anyone could convince a panicked, untrusting individual to trust enough to make contact with another human being, it would be Kelly Chase.

He paced in front of the kitchen window. Cheering her on.

Wishing he was there. That he could help.

And his phone rang.

Kelly?

He hung up, as predetermined.

It rang again.

Seeing her name pop up a second time, he answered immediately.

"Levi?" Her tone was agitated, but didn't sound frightened. His gut dropped anyway.

"Are you okay?" The words flew out as bites.

"Yes, but can you come out?" She'd stopped moving fifty yards from the center of her circle. Toward the bank of the river.

He caught the coordinates as he ran across the yard and was already taking leaps across the water when he said, "On my way."

MAYBE SHE WAS in over her head. Thinking she could work a case with Levi Griggs, of all people. What had possessed her to mix her own personal angst with a case?

She wasn't the only expert psychiatrist employed by Sierra's Web. She had an entire team of them who worked for her. Should have called one of them to take over for her the second she'd seen Levi pull up in front of her cabin.

If a life was lost because of her...

Standing at the base of a tree, she watched her phone, tracking Levi's advance. The man was running, not walking, in her direction.

Watching the swift movement of that red dot brought tears to her eyes.

Another sure sign she was in the wrong place at the wrong time.

To hell with Levi's stalker trying to ruin her credibility. Levi was going to think she was paranoid.

She was beginning to doubt herself.

When ferns started to move like a tornado was shooting through them, she pocketed her phone. Tried not to notice when her entire body welcomed the sight of his.

Forced herself to maintain complete professionalism, as she said, "I heard a whisper. I couldn't make out what was being said, but I heard it, Levi. I'd bet my bank account, my job, my life on it."

His nod gave nothing to her. Could have been a pat on the head. Or total belief. She needed more than blankness.

"I heard it." In that moment, she didn't know if she was trying to convince him, or herself.

"Okay." His breath slowed a bit. "How many times?"

"Twice."

"Could you tell if it was words? Or just a blowing sound?"

"It wasn't a deer snort."

"I'm not saying it was. I'm trying to determine if someone was attempting to call out to you, or lure you into a trap."

She pointed to the tree branches directly above her. Waited to see if he noticed what she had. If not, it was time to speak with her partners about her suitability for the case.

What if she'd been leading Levi and his teams, her own team, wrong all along?

The notes were real. But the rest. She'd been so certain.

Levi's continued silence felt like nails on her coffin. Until she saw him start to climb the tree. And watched as he climbed branches, moving from one tree to the next, along the bank, continuing for a much greater distance than he had the day before.

On the ground, she followed right along with him. Watching for footprints, for anything dropping from the tree, or evidence that a human being had recently been there.

Had she really heard a whisper?

Closing her eyes briefly, she tried to quiet her mind. Left Levi in charge, up in the tree, fully trusting that if there was evidence to be found, he'd find it. She was in the ferns. Planning her next outing…the picnic…and—

She'd heard a whisper. More than air on the wind. Not a snort. A soft calling out—but no words. How could that be?

Searching in every direction from the initial spot where she'd heard the sound, she saw no trampled ferns. Found no one hiding.

But she'd heard the sound again. Standing in the initial spot. "Almost the word *hey*," she said aloud, softly.

With no long sound.

Like a huff or a puff? An old nursery rhyme came to mind. Something about a house being blown down.

Was that what was happening? Was she really going over the edge?

At the machinations of some sick dude out to get her as Levi thought?

He'd been trying to tell her for days.

And now she was sure she'd heard a whispered cry for help with no words?

Oh God. How could she expect anyone to believe her?

She was almost underneath a big oak tree when Levi started to descend from it. Kept her distance.

If she was being adversely affected by the current circumstances, she had to keep her focus on getting one of her psychiatry experts in immediately who could assist Levi while she took her own butt straight back to Phoenix.

"Kel, get over here."

The urgency in his tone wiped all other thought from her mind as she hurried the several yards to where he stood by the bank of the river.

His eyes were totally focused on a point on the ground. As though holding something in place simply by looking at it.

She looked to see what had his attention.

And almost fell to her knees.

"A CHILD!" KELLY'S PAIN-FILLED, guttural, soft-spoken cry hit Levi so hard he had to take a breath before he could respond.

He stared at the prints he'd seen from above, when the trail of broken twigs he'd followed had suddenly stopped. Until he'd looked at the branch directly below him and noticed some freshly torn leaves, with more on the branch below that.

Glancing up again, at the evidence that had first caught his attention, he cleared his throat and said, "It appears that the little one slipped…"

"And might be hurt?" Kelly's near whisper continued to tear at him.

While he'd been busy preparing to take on her stalker, she'd been right all along. He should have listened.

Done things differently.

Even as his cop's brain told him that there was nothing more he could have done, that he was hell-bent enough on finding the stalker to turn over every single hope of clue he'd had, Levi still ached for the little one who was out there. Hoped to God the child had a mother up there—even if that meant a third Yardle victim.

"Judging by the size of the print, I'm guessing the child is either three or four," Kelly said, her tone sounding more like the expert professional she'd more than proved herself to be.

Her gaze, as she looked up at him, tore at him anew. "As much as I hated to think that we had another female victim, we better hope that the footprint mold that was taken was from this baby's mother. It breaks my heart to think of a child out here all alone."

He didn't see how it could be possible. And told her so. But... "It's pretty clear that the child was alone this morning. There's no indication of anyone else having been in the tree. No other footprints down here. But, again, I don't see how it's possible for a little one to survive out here for any length of time."

"Children are resilient," Kelly said then. "You have to consider that this child was likely born out here, has been raised in the woods, much like a mother bear would raise her cubs. With a focus on teaching the child to survive alone. I'm guessing the child knows which berries to pick and eat. While most kids are learning to walk, this baby probably learned how to climb up to stay safe in the wild." Kneeling in some grass a good foot away from the two prints he'd found, Kelly leaned over the evidence as though she could shield the child from the atrocities, just as she was shielding the young one's prints.

And that's when Levi got on the phone and put in another call to his uncle.

THEY HAD A VICTIM—hopefully two—not a stalker. Kelly didn't feel any victory in vindication. Nor relief in knowing that she'd done her job just as she'd always done. Her heart was too busy breaking for the young child alone in the woods, apparently frightened of even her now.

She'd been visible.

Alone.

The child had called out to her and yet, in the end, had run away.

It wasn't a fail.

More like a critical first step.

They knew who was out there. At least in part.

She knew.

And from there, could create an entirely different profile, and build a plan specific to the needs of her little victim. If the mother was there, too, helping the child reach out, she'd see, by Kelly helping the child, that it was safe for her to come out.

Kelly's former idea to just present herself alone in the wilderness as many times as it took had been geared toward an adult, albeit one who'd likely have some slightly childlike tendencies. That changed immediately.

"We need only female personnel on the ground," she told Levi as they headed back to the cabin for supplies she might need throughout the day.

"I'm coming with you." His immediate response didn't surprise her. His reasoning did. "This little one climbs trees like a professional," Levi said. "You're going to need someone in the air, so to speak, following broken twig trails and, if we're lucky, spotting a young body moving on the ground."

He was completely right. And agreed that he should be a background member of the search party when it came time for her to head out. There was much to do first.

With a nod, she continued, "Please tell everyone to lose their uniforms. Have them in jeans or pants, light-colored shirts and tennis shoes. No guns or other weapons in sight."

"They can wear them in their waistbands, under their shirts," Levi agreed.

"Once they all get here, I'd like a quick meeting with them before we disperse."

"You've got it."

"And, Levi?"

"Yeah?"

"Could we have some cookies, cupcakes, peanut butter sandwiches and suckers brought out? Make sure the lollipops are big and colorful."

A child raised under Yardle's thumb in the woods wasn't likely to know what a sucker was. Or a cookie or cupcake, either, for that matter. But a toddler watching someone else eating any of the fun-looking confectionaries, and enjoying them, would be at least mildly curious.

And if a mother who'd been victimized as a young woman was behind the child, watching, encouraging them to seek Kelly out, the confections would speak of better times.

It could also be that the child and mother had been separated. That the mother had been sick, and thus seeking help. Or had had an accident, been bitten by a rabid animal, fallen. The mother could be prone somewhere, unable to get up anymore.

Kelly didn't want to bother waiting for Levi to bring waders over for her to get back across the stream to the cabin. Didn't care that she'd be getting her only pair of tennis shoes wet. As soon as he'd stepped into the stream, she sat down to slide in behind him, and felt hands at her waist, was in the air and then against his chest before she knew what was happening.

"You are not going to spend all afternoon traipsing in the woods in wet shoes," he told her.

She could have asked one of the deputies on her way out to pick up a pair of shoes for her. But didn't say so.

She was too busy allowing her body to take comfort against the warmth, the strength, of his.

Closing her eyes, she rode across the water in a pool of emotion, trying to absorb, to memorize every moment, thankful her life had given her the opportunity to know Levi Griggs.

Chapter Twenty-Three

Never in a million years would Levi have believed he'd be witnessing a ground crew of deputies and police officers from neighboring departments spreading out to canvass thousands of acres of wilderness with suckers in their mouths. The all-women brigade would be traveling in teams of two spread out around their given territories.

Kelly had insisted they all have sweets in their backpacks, explaining that if they believed the child was close, or in sight, the first thing they were to do was sit down and eat a sweet. While they hiked, they were to have the sucker in hand at all times, and occasionally at least look as though they were licking it.

They weren't searching for a wanted man, but, rather, a child victim who'd likely only ever seen two or three people ever—and could have witnessed the death of at least one of them.

And possibly the child's mother.

Hopefully there was another woman up in the hills, a third hostage. Standing side by side with Kelly, he felt her shiver, as she delivered that hope to a group of law enforcement officers. She also stressed that based on the child traveling alone that morning, and so close to Kelly's place, she was concerned that the mother might have become incapacitated.

Silently, he prayed that there was another victim, just as she'd been thinking all along. That Robin McKinney was not the child's mother.

"Why would a woman hang herself when she had a young child to provide for?" He asked Kelly what he imagined at least some of his deputies would be wondering. Because he was wondering as well.

"I can only guess," she said, her tone completely professional, confident, commanding. She took on leadership abilities as though born to them. "But unfortunately, immediate scenarios come to mind," she said, speaking to the group. "It was possible that Yardle had separated her from the child and she'd believed her baby dead."

And that made sense to him. He saw others nod, their faces grave. And fully attentive.

Every bit of it was supposition.

But based on investigative logic.

They had jars and pencils tied to the Yardle case.

A mother less than two months dead on Yardle's property.

A child traveling alone.

And a larger footprint found in a different place at a different time. But still recent. Hopefully meant the child's mother was still alive.

They had to go with what the evidence was telling them.

While Kelly's cabin was the search headquarters, law enforcement would be driving as far into the hills as they could to reach their areas in the most expedient fashion. They also wanted to have transportation as close as humanly possible in the event they found the child in a state of emergency.

After Kelly finished talking, Levi told everyone he was certain the little one had made it up a tree after whispering to Kelly. He also feared that, based on the broken leaves heading straight down—above the footprints—the child might have fallen out. Kelly had agreed with his theory that the steps they'd seen had been left when the little one jumped into the water, perhaps as a means of escape.

"That little one would have to be an amazing swimmer to make it upstream," he said quietly to Kelly as they finished their meetings with everyone and watched the teams disperse. They were going to hang back at the cabin, let everyone get into place and wait for first-impression reports.

"I'm guessing that baby has reached much higher than average proficiency on all skills needed to stay alive out here," she said.

She hadn't been herself since they'd arisen that morning. He'd first put the change in her down to fear—heading out alone to meet up with what could be her stalker.

And maybe the new Kelly, this woman who seemed almost to treat him as though they were strangers, was the professional most people encountered when they worked with her.

He had no doubt she was eating herself up with worry over the preschool-aged little one, possibly still all alone in the wilderness.

"We're going to find this baby, Kel. I swear to you."

"I know." Her glance didn't quite make it up to meet his gaze. "We just have to be prepared. If I'm wrong and there's no other woman… I can't explain the earlier footprint, but…a child alone for two months…clearly we can put that down to some resilience. And training. Kids at that age are less prone to depression and giving up. Toddlers, preschoolers are generally pretty adaptable. But two months, Levi? We have no idea what we're going to find. Malnutrition. A little body covered with insect bites. Possibly even animal bites. Rabies?"

She started to move away as her voice faded on the question and Levi meant to let her go. He needed the separation she was creating between them.

He reached an arm out to her, touched her shoulder and then pulled her body up against his. There was nothing the least bit sexual about his embrace.

And when she put her arms around him, he knew she wasn't a lover holding him. Their lower bodies didn't even connect.

They were two human beings facing an overwhelming task, knowing that if things didn't work out well, a child, and perhaps a vulnerable woman, could die.

And they'd be deeply marked for the rest of their lives.

He kissed the top of her head. Stood there as she pressed her face into his chest.

And then he let her go.

WHILE KELLY ACHED to be out in the woods, she knew the futility of her and Levi hiking around aimlessly. She needed to be on hand in the event that any of the women in the field were able to draw the child out. To help them, through the use of the earpieces they all wore, which were connected to police radios attached to their ankles under their jeans, and maintaining contact through signals bouncing off of power boosters attached to their vehicle antennas. The idea was to allow Kelly means to establish trust with what would most likely be an emotionally regressed child. If a woman was with the child, Kelly would have to be that much more astute. Making split decisions based on situations described to her.

It was critical that she and Levi remain centrally located, with access to a vehicle, in the event any of the officers on the ground found evidence, additional footprints even. Levi and Kelly were to be immediately notified so that they could be physically present on scene as soon as possible.

And if someone found the child... The plan, if anyone got lucky enough to lay eyes on the little one, was to radio Kelly, stay with her online, so the officer could help keep the child engaged—and at the very least in sight—while Levi and Kelly traveled to the site.

The poor baby had been in the woods alone for a couple of months—another hour or two to see that the youngster had the least emotionally traumatic trip out, and a start to the healthiest possible transition, was a blip.

And if there was a woman—Kelly was leaning toward injured at that point—that would require further transport. It was unlikely the child would be amenable to leaving the woods without her. And there was no way, unless it was a life-or-death situation, that Kelly would allow such a thing.

Still, doing virtually nothing other than monitoring maps and the tracking apps the deputies had willingly downloaded for Levi, Kelly was about to split out of her skin.

While the mold of the earlier, larger footprint they'd found had been sent to Michigan Forensics, Kelly sent a photo to Glen as well, just covering every single base she had.

And...determining that she had to do more to stay connected to her team. Her family. They grounded her. She told herself that if she turned to her own experts, relied on them, she wouldn't be needing Levi so much.

No matter how emotional the situation became.

She was monitoring half of the two dozen deputies' progress from the app on her phone, comparing movement to a large coordinate map of the hundreds of miles of wooded wilderness, while Levi handled the other dozen.

He'd chosen to monitor Annie's twosome. Kelly noticed, but couldn't care. She just needed the child found.

An hour after everyone set out, Kelly had the beginnings of a headache. Pure tension. Starting from her shoulders and neck and moving up the sides of her head. The pain was like a fly, pestering her, and she willed her muscles to relax. Was just thinking about going for some analgesic skin cream in the bathroom when her phone rang.

Levi's gaze was as sharp as hers, moving as instantly as hers, to the screen of the phone.

"It's Glen." She picked up the cell. Heard what Glen had to tell her. When her partner asked how she was doing, she told him she was holding up. And rang off.

"The earlier footprint… Glen says they've taken the exact measurements of all ridges in the marking, experimented with it in mud, and found that it matches the print you and I found this morning."

"That's impossible." Levi's immediate response mirrored what her own had been just seconds before.

She swallowed. "He said that the first print appears to be much larger because the child slid in the mud. He also said that he'd guess we're looking for a boy, but that it's only a guess. His lab has been following footprint evidence for determination of age and sex of individuals and while the science is still new, there are determining factors. Of course, this is all belied by the fact that this child has likely been barefoot in the wilderness since birth, so foot growth and structure won't compare the same…" She was rambling.

She heard it. Hated it. Couldn't help it.

Just as she couldn't stop the moisture in her eyes as she looked over at him. "He's been out there all alone, Levi. This baby…for two months?"

His lips thinning, chin jutting, he watched her for long seconds. Blinking a couple of times. Just stood there with the pain flowing out of her—and, she was pretty sure, out of him, too.

"He's not an average preschooler," he finally spoke. "You said so yourself. And look…he knew about the notes Maura sent, Kel. He's savvy enough, courageous and bold enough, to send some himself."

"I was wrong about the 'you,'" she said then. "No way a young kid like that, no matter how much schooling his mom or Maura must have given him, would be letting me know that only I could help. He's just writing the words he's been taught. Or had seen Maura write."

Which made sense and took her one step further. "I'm guessing he witnessed Maura writing them. Kids at that age are curious. Everything is always a 'why.' She must have told him, honestly, why."

"They needed him prepared in the event the notes finally worked," Levi said, straightening, his eyes filling with new purpose. "They probably taught him that if they ever got out of the cage, he was to run as fast as he could until he found someone who could help them…"

It all fell into horrifying place then. The way Levi's words broke off, she was pretty sure he'd seen the truth, too.

"That's why he wasn't around when me and my team… he'd run away. And by the time he made it back, his mother had given up hope of finding him, probably hoping that some-one had found him, taken him in, was loving him…and she hanged herself…"

Yeah, she'd seen it pretty much the same way. Except she asked, "You think he eventually made it back up to the shack?" She didn't even want to think about it. "It makes sense, with the missing quilt. That would be something a kid would take for security. Most particularly if his mother or Maura held him in it."

"He could have been the one who buried Robin."

Tears flooded her eyes as that piece fell so cleanly into place. A young child, covering the body of his dead mother… She couldn't just sit there and monitor maps like it was all in a day's work.

"We don't know for sure that the baby's mother isn't up

there, too, Kel." Levi's words reached her. She clung to them. "And if she is, maybe you were right, and she was watching you, asking for your help."

He was offering a version that she could live with more easily. And because she had work to do, because a child's life depended on her getting it right, she blinked away her tears, nodded and went back to monitoring progress.

LEVI HAD NEVER struggled so acutely to stay in work mode. The case captivated every bit of his mind—and was impinging on his heart as well.

For the child. For the women Yardle had hurt so atrociously. Turning their young lives into a never-ending nightmare.

And for Kelly, too. As they stood there at the table, watching phones and marking the map, it was almost as though he could feel her pain mingling with his own.

He could feel the day passing, too. While it was still not quite lunchtime, the hours were dwindling too quickly for the lack of progress. He had to find the kid before nightfall. No other option.

Logically, he knew that the child had likely survived many, many nights alone in the wilderness. But none while Levi was on watch. He couldn't know that little one was out there, and sleep.

Period.

He and Kelly both jumped when the phone rang again. His. Annie. Holding up his screen so Kelly could identify the caller, he put the call on speaker.

"Yeah," he said, as he always answered when working with his people on a case.

"We found another shack, Levi. It's straight uphill a couple of miles from Yard—"

"I see where you are," he cut her off.

"You'd expect, looking at the map, for access to the river to be impossible because of the drop-off from the hill, but it's a sand dune—"

"Is he *there*?" Kelly cut off the deputy that time, a testimony to how tense they both were.

"No, I'm sorry, ma'am, I should have led with that. There's no sign of the boy. We've checked the entire clearing. Found an open spot in the fencing where he obviously comes and goes, but the quilt you were missing, Levi, it's here."

Kelly was already heading for the door. Keys to his truck in hand, Levi wasn't even a full step behind her. "Is there any sign of recent habitation?" he asked, climbing into the driver's side of his truck as Kelly slid into the seat next to him. He leaned over and put the keys in the ignition.

"Yes. But, maybe just the child. There's a chair pushed up to what was being used as a cupboard, as though for him to reach. Another by some jars that hold macaroni. And one more by what looks like a firepit, some kind of really old heater maybe, raised off the ground being used as a stove. It has a rudimentary, aboveground gas line to it. The tank holds fifty gallons and is almost empty."

"Stay put," Kelly said then. "But casually. Sit outside, so he can easily see you, and let him choose whether or not to approach. And so that he doesn't feel as though his home is being invaded. You're a visitor. And keep that sucker handy. If you can't stomach licking it, at least pretend as though you are. It's big enough, he won't know the difference. If he starts to run, call out to him, try to engage. To assure him he's safe. That you want to help. That you won't hurt him. Talk about a tree near him or a bird he'd be able to see, anything that can distract his attention. Don't chase him unless you have to."

Levi heard the string of instructions coming from Kelly's lips, and throughout the harrowing forty-five-minute drive, and then the hour-long run in the hills, he listened to Annie's continued reports that were no signs of the boy at all.

And grew sicker by the moment as he flooded with dread.

There'd been another shack.

And he'd missed it.

If he'd worked harder, studied the scene more, done something besides sit at home and think about quitting, could he have found the child sooner?

Chapter Twenty-Four

The shack, much farther up in the hills, and higher above water level, than Levi and his team had ever searched, was a lot like the place where Levi had found Yardle and Maura two months before. A little bigger, a little nicer. With fencing that encompassed more than a couple of acres, all the way down the sand dune and across the water.

It looked more like a playground than a prison, but Kelly saw it immediately for what it was. Annie and her partner, Deputy Sandra Larson, were sitting on opposite sides of the compound when Levi and Kelly arrived, both licking big colorful suckers and looking like they were out on a pleasurable afternoon hike.

She wanted to hug them both.

While Levi checked out the perimeter of the grounds, Kelly stepped through the open spot in the fencing and headed inside.

Her eyes hadn't even adjusted to the darkness before she heard Levi call from outside. "Get Kelly."

She didn't wait to be summoned. Out the door, she was halfway to Levi before Sandra had a chance to round the shack.

"Look," he said, pointing upward.

Broken twigs.

"We specifically looked for branch trails," Sandra said.

"Those twigs are barely noticeable," Annie added, with Levi already half up the tree.

"You two stay here." He called down the command. "Same MO as before, Kel. Follow the trail on the ground."

As she'd done twice before, she walked the earth beneath Levi, keeping an eye out for footprints while watching him climb from tree to tree in one of the largest tight clusters they'd come across. It stretched about a quarter of a mile along the top of the hill. Parallel, at least in part, to the sand dune.

And explained why no aerial surveillance had ever seen the shack.

The cluster ended with no sign of human habitation, but Levi didn't seem deterred. He climbed down, intent, surveyed the area, checked another cluster of trees off to the left. Shook his head, then headed on along the edge of the hill, following the water line that was so far down below.

A few yards along, he was scaling another tree. She'd seen the cluster. Had looked for broken twigs, but hadn't noticed any.

Then, out of nowhere, she heard a rustle. Leaves in the trees. Farther ahead than Levi's current position. With a quick intake of stagnant, breezeless air, she moved quickly, outpacing Levi. Heart pounding, she didn't dare call out to him. Hoped he'd have the sense to stay back. He'd heard her mandates to the deputies, knew her professional opinion where approaching the child was concerned...

As though feeling every second on her skin, under her skin, Kelly forced her feet to slow, to stroll, while her blood seemed to pump out of her body and ahead of her. She could feel it pulling her. And held back.

Noticing at some point that Levi was behind her still.

Whether he'd heard the leaves, noticed movement or was just taking a cue from her, he was holding back.

Chest tight, Kelly stepped slowly, softly, consciously taking breaths deep into her belly. Exhaling slowly. She needed calm.

If she was tracking a child, and not a raccoon or buzzard or other tree creature, she needed him to feel her calm.

Not frenzy.

Not fear.

Keeping her sight pinned to the spot where she'd seen the movement after hearing the leaves, she approached slowly, wishing Levi wasn't so far back.

Knowing he needed to be.

And…nothing.

Standing beneath the tree, she stared upward, almost out of breath in spite of her lack of exertion. The leaves hung silently, still, mocking her.

A thorough glance around the woods, taking in all views, with her back to the dunes and the water below, she could barely contain her disappointment.

Levi had climbed down. She saw him quietly approaching. Hated for him to know she'd made something out of nothing. But faced him, waiting for him to determine what to do next.

They'd known the quest wasn't going to be easy.

Doubts assailed her anyway. They had footprints. Skeletal remains that had delivered a child in the past. And notes. No one had actually seen a child.

Chilled, she stared at Levi. "What if it's been the stalker all along?" she asked softly, so close she could feel his warmth against her arm. "What if he used a dummy to make the footprint? And here I am demanding an army of female deputies, making them eat suckers and sweets and…" Her panic was building.

Pushed largely by the awareness that the day was passing.

Levi was looking over her shoulder, as though he couldn't meet her gaze and not tell her *I told you so.*

The chairs in the cabin. Pushed up as though to allow...

Levi nudged her wrist. Glancing down as he touched her a second time, unable to figure out what he wanted, she looked at his face, and saw him nod behind her. Over the hill, toward the dunes and the water.

Slowly backing away, into the woods, he nodded at her a second time.

Feeling tension in every ounce of her being, Kelly slowly turned, mind fully engaged on what she'd find. Instructions to her senses filing in by one by one.

It took her a minute, stepping an inch or two at a time, peering out, and then...there it was. A shock of hair. It must have been what Levi saw, maybe only with a brief glimpse, but as she drew closer, she wished he was by her side with his gun.

Surely that wasn't human hair...it was so thick and... Another step and she saw a pair of big brown eyes. Peering right at her.

There was hair hanging down on both sides of his face, so that she could barely make out the corners of those eyes. And, badly cut bangs, a jagged swath of hair, partially covered the lids, too.

But not the eyes. Those frightened orbs, shining with tears, spoke to her.

And, heart crying out, she knew.

They'd found their baby.

IT TOOK EVERY bit of self-control Levi possessed to follow Kelly's earlier edict and stay back. He knew that she had eyes on the boy. The deep breath that had puffed her back out, the lowering of her shoulders, even the sudden tilt of her head, had told him.

He needed to get to the child, grab him up and run like hell out of those hills. Straight to a hospital.

"Hi." Unlike his own nearly explosive tension, Kelly's tone sounded...relaxed. Friendly. He listened for a response. The silence that followed was deafening.

Was the child okay? Should he move on getting him out of there?

"My name's Kelly."

She wouldn't be calmly introducing herself to a child in obvious physical distress.

With a view only of Kelly's back, he watched as she sat in the grass, reached behind her to her backpack and pulled out a couple of suckers and a package of two cupcakes. The swell of love that hit him at that sight almost knocked him on his ass.

"What's your name?" The psychiatry expert's voice brought him quickly back on point. Was the child male as they'd suspected?

Cellophane rattled. "You want a cupcake?"

No response from where Levi stood. He needed to know if the young one was creeping downward. If he slipped off the slight fern ledge he'd been on, he could slide down the sand all the way to the water. Backing to the nearest tree, he waited another couple of minutes. Thinking he'd climb up if Kelly didn't have hands on the child soon.

"Mmm, they're so good. Here, I have one for you." He saw her lean over. And when she straightened, she brought the arm she'd stretched out immediately behind her. He got her message. The child had taken the cupcake.

The woman was magic.

And Levi had never loved her more.

It took Kelly almost an hour to coax the small-boned, deeply tanned little body up the couple of feet that separated him from the grass upon which she'd perched. Based on his shirt-lessness, which, given the circumstances, meant nothing, she was pretty sure the child was a boy.

Had had proof of that fact when he'd suddenly stood and peed, right in front of her. With no sense of embarrassment or shame.

Acting as though kids relieved themselves in front of strangers all the time, she'd just continued to chat with him.

Anytime she'd tried to lower herself down, he'd started to scoot farther away and she'd stopped immediately. Afraid, every second, that he'd slip to the slide of sand down to the water. Keeping him where he was had to be her priority.

She talked about all kinds of things during the nearly sixty minutes that she sat there with him. Asked him if he liked blueberries or strawberries better. He'd just stared at her. She'd talked to him about her own memories of climbing around in those hills when she was a kid. About swimming in the river.

Through it all, those big brown eyes continued to stare up at her.

When she figured she'd gained enough equity to keep him listening, she brought the talk around to the bend where she and Levi had found the first set of footprints. She told him they'd seen where he'd gone into the river. And then, without pause, talked about how she used to catch frogs not far from there. Told him about the summer she and her friend had caught almost fifty frogs and had had races in the yard.

His eyes seemed to glisten with humor at that. She detected a slight upward tilt of his lips. And that's when she knew he could understand English.

She offered more cookies. A bottle of water.

Chatted about the time she'd come upon a deer bed that had a mama and baby deer in it. How the baby had been too young to run and so the mama had lain there with it. Watching her. The story was a true one. But the memory surfaced because she needed it. She talked about how the mama had trusted her not to hurt her baby.

"Do you think you can trust me?" she asked, wishing she knew his name. Young ones tended to trust easier when called by name.

The boy didn't nod. But he didn't shake his head, or make any movement toward sliding away, either.

"I'm just going to come a little closer and sit for a bit, if that's okay?"

Again, no sign of approval, but no movement toward descent, either. And so she went over the side of the hill. It took her another twenty minutes, and a bribe of more cookies, but she finally got the little guy to hold her hand, and together, they climbed back up to the top of the hill.

The child was small, but strong. Barefoot, and wearing only a pair of ragged-looking, too-long shorts made of cotton, not the more common silky basketball shorts that were currently so popular among young boys.

Leftover from Yardle purchases, she imagined. Or Yardle thefts. Maybe from garage sales. Or even a homeless shelter.

His dark hair, she could see once he stood, hung all the way to his waist. But he was clutching her hand as though he didn't want to let it go.

And she thought of the skeleton they'd found.

The boy's mother?

Hopefully she'd been permitted to raise him.

Probably in the shack Annie and Sandra had found.

All was going well with him. He walked beside her easily. Right up until Levi appeared several feet ahead of them. And said hello.

"Haaahhhh!" The sound the boy made was almost inhuman. He dug his feet into the ground. Clawing at Kelly's hand around his, trying to get her to let go of him.

"It's okay," Kelly said, crouching down, putting her knees on either side of the little body, holding him while she let go of his hand. And then patted his back. "That's Levi. He's not going to hurt you," she said.

Guttural sounds were coming from the child as he continued to fight her. Trying to get away. Glancing up, she saw Levi climb a tree. And move toward the shack branch by branch.

And she flooded with love.

HIS DEPARTURE ALLOWED Kelly to calm the child. He had no idea what she'd said initially, to restore calm, but Levi remained airborne until he saw her rise in the distance behind him, her hand once again held securely by the cute little guy. From there he hightailed it back to the shack. Filling in Annie and Sandra before continuing on his way to the truck.

He wanted that child fully in their custody, safely in a vehicle, and it was clear that a male presence was going to hinder the process.

Having met Yardle, it was a situation he fully understood. One with which he deeply sympathized.

Once out of earshot, he radioed the other deputies to head in. And asked someone to let the sheriff know that they had a victim in custody.

At his truck, he started the engine, and drove, but only far enough away from the Jeep Sandra and Annie had driven up to not be seen.

He wasn't going to leave Kelly and the others alone with their young victim, just in case.

As it turned out, his presence wasn't needed.

The three women were smiling, and all clearly doting on the child when the Jeep drove slowly past the curve where he'd hidden the truck. Whether any of them saw him or not, he didn't know. Until he saw Kelly turn around in the back seat and smile. Pulling out behind them, he followed them from a distance, down the dirt track in the woods, and finally to a dirt road that had been abandoned by the county decades before.

Kelly texted, as soon as they had phone service, and let him know the child was a boy, that he seemed overall healthy, though understandably underfed, and they were heading to the cabin. The child had started to exhibit severe anxiety as they'd sped up, and Kelly didn't want to remove him completely from the woods just yet.

Her cabin, while completely different from the one in which he'd grown up, was still a cabin. In woods he'd recognize.

While Levi didn't like the idea, afraid the boy would take off on them again, he didn't argue the point. Kelly would be well aware of the flight risk, and she'd still suggested the cabin.

He made a call to his uncle then, and by the time the women made it back to Kelly's cabin, a female pediatrician was there, waiting for them.

The grunts and noises he heard, some with clear levels of extreme distress, subsided fairly quickly and, at Kelly's request, the cabin slowly cleared out.

But as she tried, once again, to get the child loaded into a car, he flailed with all four limbs, shrieking and screaming, and she immediately called a halt. Levi, who'd been keeping tabs from outside the cabin, by text message and views through windows, had been poised to run, to chase the child before he got away, but stopped before reaching the clearing when Kelly glanced in his direction.

As though pleading with him.

Get me permission to keep him here, she quickly texted, once she had the child back inside the cabin.

And so he did.

Making it clear that he'd be staying, too, even if he had to sleep in the woods. Her credentials had won her the request to keep the child in her custody. His mandate was personal.

Kelly's text back, telling him to trust her, that she'd have him inside before dark, seemed far-fetched to him, but he did as she'd asked.

He trusted her.

His rusted-out heart—knowing her and bleeding for the child—gave him no other choice.

Chapter Twenty-Five

In full work mode, Kelly had handled the people in and out of the cabin as though they'd all been coming in and out of her office while she had a patient in residence. Her job had taken her to many out-of-the-way places, handling all kinds of psychological issues, and her success rate had given her enough confidence to trust her instincts.

By dinnertime, just she and the boy were in the cabin, but she wasn't done working. Not by a long shot. Her work had only begun.

"Am I Kelly?" she asked the boy, sitting with him on the bed in the porch room. He'd found the mattress to be of utmost interest and had varied between standing, jumping, lying and just sitting in the middle of it, which was where they were when he noticed the mirror over the dresser. It was only in view from parts of the bed, and when he finally slowed down his exploration of the mattress and noticed the reflecting glass, he quickly stiffened and scrambled behind her. Holding both of her arms, hiding his body behind her back.

"It's okay," Kelly told him. "It's a magic game, come look. It's not hurting me so it can't hurt you." After several minutes of coaxing, she finally got him to look long enough to point herself out. "See? It's magic glass. It's me."

The boy stared, open-mouthed, still just peeking from behind her. And then stuck his head out a little more, looking up at her with those big brown eyes. Her heart split wide open at that look and she had to blink away tears. "Yep," she said, smiling as she nodded. "That's you." She pointed at him. Waiting patiently while he took several minutes to stare, and slowly experiment with images in the mirror.

She picked up a hanger, slowly untwisted it so that it was a long poker and touched her image in the mirror, watching as those eyes followed the hanger all the way to the point touching her image, and then looked back at her to see that she wasn't being touched. When he looked back to the mirror again, she tapped her image and said, "Kelly."

And then she tapped him. "Who's this?"

He grunted. Looked at her. And then himself.

The little guy was nonverbal. That much had been obvious to her from the first. But how much was an emotional response to the past months obviously alone in the woods, and how much was a more serious condition, she didn't yet know.

"How about we give you a magic name to go with the glass?" she asked him then. Needing him to have a title that he associated with himself, but nowhere near ready to rename him, if it came to that. "Is that okay?"

His eyes lit up as she was already associating with his affirmative response, and she said, "How about Fluppbudgety?" She giggled as she said the word. He just watched her. In person, and in the mirror.

"How about Andrew?" she asked him. Then said, "Annndrrrew," very slowly. Showing him with exaggerated movement how her mouth and tongue were moving. "It means 'strong warrior,' and that's what you are, you know that? You're the strongest little warrior I've ever known."

His eyes glistened, his mouth tilted slightly upward.

And Kelly's heart was sunk.

IN A CLEARED space behind the shed, Levi chopped a lot of wood. The cabin had a wood-burning fireplace and there was a firepit down by the river, too, though both looked as though they hadn't been used in years. Still, the woodpile could be a selling point for Kelly. Fresh wood laid in the fireplace, in the pit and stacked by the edge of the clearing gave the place a "welcome home, move right in" kind of look. Or so he told himself. Every few logs he took a break, followed a now-beaten-down trail through the woods at the edge of the clearing, getting good looks inside the cabin from the various windows.

Enough to know that Kelly and the little guy were getting along.

The doctor had brought a fresh set of clothes for him. Navy shorts and a matching navy-and-red-striped shirt. She'd brought a few sizes of shoes, compliments of the River County Sheriff's Department, but he had no way of knowing if Kelly had managed to get anything on the child's feet.

Thinking about having someone drive out some dinner for him, he hadn't gotten as far as figuring out what he'd want, or who he'd ask, when his phone buzzed a text.

You're here to keep us safe so no one can hurt us. I've assured him that you don't have chains and don't yell. It would help if you can tone down the testosterone as much as possible. And sit on the floor when you first try to engage with him. Putting you lower than he is. I'm calling him Andrew. He seems to like it. Use it as often as you can when you address him. He's completely nonverbal. And you can come in now.

So Kelly, to write a letter with full punctuation and spelled-out words in text.

Completely nonverbal. Because she'd mentioned the condition last, and didn't seem concerned by it, Levi took that one in stride.

Smiling, feeling better than he had in far too long, more alive, he entered the cabin by the front door, careful not to let the screen door slam behind him. He wore a big smile, and immediately took a seat on the inch-high stone hearth in front of the fireplace.

"Hi, Andrew, I'm Levi."

He'd grabbed an old softball out of the shed on his way in, from the collection of outdoor games he'd remembered being there, and started to roll it around between his hands on the floor.

Kelly was at the stove, cooking what looked to be macaroni, and though Andrew didn't leave her side, was clutching her shorts so tightly his fingers were white, the little boy was watching Levi.

Those brown eyes, shining out through what seemed like a shield of hair around his arms and down to his waist, changed Levi. He wasn't sure how. Or why.

Or even if it mattered.

SHORTLY BEFORE EIGHT that evening, Kelly rolled softly off her bed. Still in the jeans and shirt she'd worn to the woods, and on top of the comforter, she'd lain with Andrew until he was asleep. And would be returning to spend the night with him.

His frightened expression when she'd pulled back the covers and told him to climb inside had prompted the promise. But she and Levi, by text message, had already determined that the boy was to sleep on the wall side of the bed, and she'd be between him and the door.

In case he woke up frightened.

Or tried to sneak out.

Levi, as added security, would be on the couch right around the corner outside the door. The little guy had started to droop sitting on the floor with his bowl of macaroni, eating it with his fingers. But when she'd taken him to the bathroom—he'd already had a lesson on how to relieve himself—and had him change into the brand-new pajamas that had arrived with the rest of the provisions the doctor had delivered, she'd figured she might be in for a struggle, getting him to sleep. As darkness fell, he'd grown more and more anxious.

As it turned out, it took him all of five minutes to fall asleep.

Half expecting Levi to be snoozing, too, she was way too happy to see him sitting up, waiting for her. At least that's the way she took his position on the couch, watching her as she walked out.

She needed a shower.

Needed time to close up her heart some and prepare for time with Levi. Andrew had required a completely open heart in order to be reached.

Giving as much to Levi would not only half kill her again, but in the end it would hurt him, too.

He moved to a kitchen chair, within full view and reach of the porch door. Told her quietly to take as long as she needed. And pulled out his phone.

Turned out, she didn't want long. The case was done. She could be leaving as early as morning, depending on child services and Andrew—or whoever he'd turn out to be.

The doctor had taken a DNA sample with her. The first step would be to find out if it was a match for Robin McKinney. And Yardle.

And she'd be leaving Idlewood.

Leaving Levi.

She was back in the kitchen, hair only towel dried, in

a clean pair of cotton pants and a T-shirt—an outfit she'd deemed suitable for sleeping attire while still allowing her to be dressed and ready for whatever Andrew's first night in civilization might eventually bring.

She'd planned to sit with Levi at the table. But a glance at the sleeping boy just a few yards away had her moving to the couch.

Her place was with Andrew. But she wasn't ready for sleep. And didn't want her restlessness to awaken the boy.

And she couldn't bear the idea of her and Levi parting ways the next day with others around. She needed one more chance to meet him eye to eye.

To bond.

And remember that they'd always be connected.

As traumatic moment soulmates.

When he grabbed a bottle of beer and poured her a glass of wine—all with hardly making a sound—she had the surprising thought that he was so ready for fatherhood.

Felt tears prickling at the back of her lids as she silently acknowledged that that part of his life was off-limits to her. Not part of their contract.

"What a day." She spoke just above a whisper as they softly touched their drinks together. "We saved a little boy today, Levi." They'd had help, most definitely.

But if not for her and Levi, out there every day, refusing to give up, following broken twigs in trees...

"He's rather remarkable, isn't he?" The compassion in Levi's tone tugged at the heart walls she was trying so hard to hold up.

And she thought about the little long-haired guy asleep in her bed. Maybe four. Could be five. Chances were they'd never know his birth date. "He thought the shower was fun," she said, smiling. And then sobered. "Chances are, if DNA comes back a match for Robin, he's going to end up in foster care."

They both knew that was how the system worked. Levi's silence was its own confirmation.

"You were right, Kel." He was shaking his head. Looking toward the shutters he'd lowered right after dinner.

For Andrew's sake. He'd texted that he didn't want the boy to think he could get through a window to the outdoors.

"I had such a strong feeling that there was a man after you..." he continued.

She nodded. "Truth be told, I was kind of afraid of that, too." Though maybe more from his constant reminders of his theory, his admonishments to her to be vigilant with her safety measures, than any real sense she'd had that someone was after her.

"The notes almost seemed like taunts to me."

Looking back, she could see that.

His sigh, so deep, followed by a longer-than-normal swig of beer, had her turning toward him, reaching out to run a hand across the frown marring his forehead.

"What's wrong?"

He shook his head, glanced at her and then back toward the shutters. Holding his bottle with one hand, he ran the other through his hair. Leaving it with a look reminiscent of lovemaking.

Something they'd done for the last time.

Without knowing it was the last time.

She knew it was for the best. Still felt consumed with sadness.

"I just keep thinking about that second shack," he said then, making her feel like a louse—a besotted, unprofessional and horny woman—with the direction her thoughts had taken.

"What about it?" Fully focused now, she sipped her wine, resting her glass against her thigh.

"I should have found it. If I'd even had my mind open to the possibility of more people living up there, which made sense. A sick dude like Yardle wasn't going to be content with just one conquest. If I had an open mind, which is something I've always prided myself on, by the way, I'd likely have found clues in that cabin pointing to other occupants."

She didn't see how.

"We didn't even dust for prints."

"Why would you? You'd already IDed the suspect. And since he was dead, there'd be no court case, no need for the evidence…"

"But if I had…what if I'd found Robin's prints?"

She got it. So acutely.

"It's like when we found Sierra dead," she told him softly. "All of us knew, once we started talking, that something horrible had happened to her. And we knew who the suspect was. Once we talked. Problem was, none of us talked to each other about her, put it all together, until it was too late."

The memory was as clear as it had been the day they'd gone to the crime scene together. To cry. To mourn. To leave doves and butterflies in honor of the woman who'd loved both.

"That right there, that feeling, it's what bonds us all," she told him. "And more importantly, it's what keeps us sharp, focused and able to help others resolve their traumas before it's too late…"

Which was why, no matter how much it shattered her heart to leave Levi, she couldn't stay.

With a sigh he set his beer on the table. Slouched down farther on the couch, and slung an arm around her.

"You're good for me, Kel."

"You're good for me, too, Levi Griggs."

She put her head on his shoulder. "We'll stay in touch this time, right?"

"If not, I'm coming looking for you."

He didn't mean it. She knew that.

If she chose not to respond to him in the future, he'd stay away just like he had in the past. Not because he was giving up.

But because he respected her that much.

"I'm holding you to that," she told him, anyway.

And fell asleep that night imagining how it would be, her missing a text from him, not responding, and having him fly to Phoenix and show up on her doorstep.

The dream was a good one.

Chapter Twenty-Six

The little one slept through the night, and the following day was as low-key a day as Levi could ever remember having outside his own home. With Kelly's blessing his mom and dad had come out, briefly, just to say hello—to let Betsy visit. His dad had been a little distant with Kel, but his mother had hugged her right up before turning her caring eyes on Andrew.

The boy shied away from both of the elder Griggses, but was fascinated with Betsy, and so, with Kelly's full blessing, the old girl stayed with them. Until the DNA came back, possibly ascertaining Andrew's identity, county family services had agreed to leave the boy in Kelly and Levi's care. She had credentials and a reputation that made the choice clearly better than any readily available foster care. He had the backing of state and local law enforcement.

As it turned out, Betsy was a godsend in that her obvious attachment to, and affection for, Levi—her propensity for sitting in his lap and laying her head on his shoulder—made Andrew less suspicious of him and the child slowly started to show interest, not fear, in the tall male cop who'd helped save him. Moving closer and closer, until he'd stand right next to Levi and pet Betsy. Glancing at Levi for approval as he did so.

Levi didn't need Kelly's coaching to smile and nod at the boy. To talk to him about Betsy's antics when she was younger, about the way she loved to dive in the water to fish. And to tell him that Betsy loved it best if you rubbed her chest, right between her front legs.

By midafternoon, the boy was sitting on the floor with the old softball Levi had brought in the night before, rolling it across the room, and laughing when Betsy went to get it and bring it back to him. The small room and the small boy were just the right size for the old dog to be able to play a game she used to love on a much grander scale.

"You got her." Kelly's soft words, as they sat together at the far end of the kitchen table, watching Andrew play with Betsy in the front of the fireplace, made no sense to him at first. Until he followed the direction of her gaze. She was watching Betsy.

And he nodded. There was no point in not.

That last summer they'd been together, a friend of theirs had purchased a female Jack Russell terrier as the beginning of a breeding business. He and Kelly had agreed that as soon as they graduated from college, and were both back in Idlewood full-time, they'd get one of the pups. As a start to the family they'd eventually have.

"The day that I got your letter," he told her.

And let the feelings lie there, right out in the open.

There was no more to be said. He was sorry. She was sorry. They both knew she'd done the right thing, if perhaps not in the best way.

"If I'd come back to tell you, if I saw you, or even heard your voice, I'd never have had the strength to follow through," she said then.

"I know." Just as he knew he wouldn't have made it easy on her. He'd have pulled her to him. Looked her in the eye. And they'd probably have been married within the year. And divorced…sometime later.

Betsy ran over to Levi, nudging his hand. Since he'd been shot the dog seemed more in tune than ever to Levi's moods. With the reminder to lighten up, he patted her head. And then stopped as Andrew slowly approached.

Leaving the dog's head for Andrew's smaller hand.

Just watching the kid made him want to smile. The little guy showed obvious signs of lagging development in some ways. And was so far ahead of kids his own age in others.

The boy drew closer. Raised his hand.

And Levi froze. Andrew hadn't reached for Betsy. He was gripping Levi's fingers. That small hand had an amazingly strong grip. The boy was pulling at him, grunting.

Levi glanced at Kelly, who nodded, and so he stood—tall guy that he was—and Andrew just kept pulling. Once they'd reached the fireplace, he stopped. And pointed at the floor. Then at Levi again, and at the floor.

Thinking he might just make a fool of himself by getting moist eyes, Levi sat. And wasn't at all surprised to see Kelly blinking back tears. She stood. And a minute or so later, after he'd just followed instructions to roll the ball to Andrew, he heard the boy laugh as Betsy intercepted, and felt his phone buzz a text, too.

Kelly was going outside for a few minutes. Wanting to leave Andrew alone with Levi. The boy had to acclimate without Kelly around or he'd become too dependent on her, which would make transition that much more difficult for him. Starting the separation, there at the cabin, was critical to the boy's success in the immediate future.

He glanced up. Nodded. And melted inside at the smile they exchanged over the little guy's head.

KELLY CRIED A little as she walked out into the pine trees in the front of the cabin, steering clear of the river for once. She'd spent too much time with that water over the past few days, frightened, worried, hurting...

She needed peace.

And enough space to distance herself from the moment and find the woman who yearned to get home to Phoenix, back to her everyday life. Because she did yearn.

She missed her partners. Her home. She missed the office. And worried about the jobs passing her by.

Just as she was going to miss Levi—and little Andrew— when she left.

A deer leaped up ahead of her. She'd been so engrossed in her own thoughts, she'd failed to see how close she'd come to the feeding trough her grandfather had put out decades ago. For old times' sake, she'd filled it from the corn feed bag she'd found in the shed when she'd first arrived. And had forgotten about it since.

She didn't get to see the deer—the purpose for filling the crib, as her grandfather had called it—but she saw the movement of brush and branches as it hopped away.

And then...no...the movement wasn't receding. It was there, still. Someone was there. In the woods. "Hey." She heard the whisper. Heard the word this time.

Andrew's mother! There *had* been another woman. One who'd kept Andrew fed. And in good health.

She slowly moved closer, approaching with a natural caution after spending twenty-four hours with the boy. A couple of feet away, she saw a brief movement backward.

"It's okay," she said softly, her tone filled with the compassion overflowing out of her. "I've got your son. He's safe and fine. You will be, too. I promise you."

Reaching out a hand, pushing it into the bramble of ferns within which the woman crouched, she almost cried when she felt the first touch of human flesh against her own.

She'd done—

"What!?" she screamed as, instead of smaller female fingers closing around hers, she felt the crush of a much larger grip around her wrist, yanking her forward.

Before she could get another sound out, a second large hand clamped over her mouth.

And darkness descended.

LEVI THOUGHT HE heard something. Betsy's bark and Andrew's laughter drowned it out. He told himself the job was done, that he was overreacting to Kelly out alone in woods that, for the past few days, had represented nothing but danger.

She was an adult. Had been traveling in dangerous situations her entire adult life without once needing him to come rescue her.

He had to somehow rein in his internal need to watch out for and protect her. And any other person in his sphere. But more acutely, Kelly.

Because she was the love of his life. He'd known that as a kid, though not understanding at the time that that's what he was feeling. He'd known it when she broke up with him.

And as ashamed as he was by the fact, he'd known it when he'd welcomed another woman walking down the aisle to him.

He'd been untrue to Jen from the beginning.

Just as his need to keep Kelly close, to keep her life small and safe, had been untrue to her. He wasn't a dumb guy. He got it.

And so he rolled the ball. He caught it. He teased Betsy and made Andrew laugh more. He laughed, too, out loud, at the small boy's innocent joy.

But when the game waned, twenty minutes later, he couldn't prevent himself from pulling out his phone. Dialing Kelly.

And getting a very sick feeling in his gut when she didn't pick up.

KELLY'S HEAD HURT. Not badly. Not like she'd been hit…

Memory hit her, though. A deer. Her wrist.

She'd been grabbed? Heart pounding, blood pouring, nerves so tight she feared they'd break, she told herself to concentrate on even breathing.

She knew how to maintain calm. It was a hallmark of her job.

Bring calm to help others find calm.

Calm. Calm. Calm.

Was there another word for calm?

She couldn't think of it.

Gentle movement distracted her.

Where was she? Movement again. Slight. Side to side?

Not a vehicle.

Not being carried, either. No stride bumps.

Air on her face.

Bird chirps.

She was outside. Coming fully conscious, she concentrated. Where outside? If she could figure out where she was…

The woman. The boy's mother.

Had she scared her? Had the woman brought her to a hiding place?

Taking stock of her body, still feigning sleep, Kelly didn't feel any pain. Other than her wrists. Was she tied up?

Big hand. Grabbing her wrist. She remembered clearly. Big, rough hand over her mouth. Stink of fish.

She'd been abducted!

Not a woman!

He'd given her something—maybe made her smell something?—that had knocked her out. Without moving anything but the muscles required to flex her wrist, she filled with horror, despair, as she realized she was tied up, hands above her head.

But they weren't hanging there. She was lying down. Her hands were on fabric.

A bed.

Movement again.

Her bed was moving.

Wind in the trees. Leaves rustling. She'd spent the past days with Levi, listening to them. Trying to gain clues through them.

And it hit her. Andrew up in trees. Poor Robin, up in a tree.

As the breeze picked up, she moved more. Swinging.

She was in some kind of hammock. Some distance above ground. Was there a sound that could tell her how high up? Did it matter?

Was *he* there? Watching her?

Not a stalker.

Another Yardle.

Oh God. Levi.

Please, Levi.

Find me.

Chapter Twenty-Seven

Within seconds of Kelly not answering her phone, Levi had a cavalry on the way. But he hadn't waited for everyone to drive out from Idlewood. He couldn't.

No way Kelly would have left the premises, or not answered her phone, unless she was in some kind of trouble. Especially not with Andrew there.

"Hey, Andrew, you want to go on an adventure in the woods? Maybe show me some of your favorite places?" he'd asked the young boy, waiting only to ensure no negative reaction before he'd picked the boy up, put him on his shoulders, told him they were going for a fun adventure and headed out the door.

He could be doing wrong. Very wrong. But he'd die protecting the boy, if it came to it. Very clearly, Andrew knew the hills. He'd survived in them alone. And he couldn't leave the boy alone.

Kelly might not have a chance to survive if he didn't get to her. He could be overreacting. Didn't give a whit.

He'd had their tracking app up on his phone from the second he'd hung up her unanswered call. Kept the window open as he'd called his uncle, who'd be running the show on this one.

Kelly wasn't moving. Or at least her phone wasn't. His call could have alerted her abductor to the device.

His damned attempt to check up on her could have stripped away the best chance he'd had to find her. And he couldn't worry about that.

It was possible she'd fallen, hit her head. Didn't matter what the emergency turned out to be—he wasn't stopping until he found her.

The boy was holding Levi's forehead as Levi ran, phone in hand, through brush and ferns and woods, getting to the stationary red dot on his screen. He jumped logs in his path, and Andrew laughed. Levi told himself to focus on that laugh.

To remember what mattered most—he and Kelly had saved a young life—and trust himself to get to her in time.

Rather than panicking that he might not.

He was going to save her. Period.

Mindset firmly in place then, he focused his thoughts on the sights, the sounds around him, as he ran. Any sign of human presence, either current or recent.

In jeans and a T-shirt, he was lacking Mace and Taser, but he had his gun tucked into his waistband. And a knife strapped to his ankle.

"Da."

Worried that Andrew was uncomfortable, not wanting the boy to panic, he slowed enough to glance upward. The boy didn't seem stressed. He was pointing.

"Da," he said again.

Since the direction the little guy was pointing matched the general vicinity he was heading, Levi said, "Yes! Da," and set out again, careful as he'd been since they'd set out, to make certain that Andrew remained clear of all leaves and branches in their path. He lowered the two of them, veered right and left, as obstacles presented, but he didn't slow down.

Until his location matched the red dot on his screen. In the middle of a grouping of trees, deep in the woods. Looking up first, and then around and down, he saw no sign of Kelly.

But he did find her phone.

Crushed and broken on a tree root.

As though someone had been very angry to find it.

"YOU AREN'T GOING to get away with this." Panicked to the point of nausea, Kelly managed to instill confidence in her voice simply by thinking of Levi.

Trusting him.

She'd rather die believing in Levi, with his love on her mind, filling her heart, than die focused on the fiend who had her tied to a hammock, so far above ground that if she moved too much, she'd swing upside down and hang there, facing the ground. A good ten feet up.

Been there done that. Twice in the time he'd held her captive.

He'd laughed the first time. And the second, had just let her hang there for a while—her hands and feet bound, but the rest of her weight pulling her down—before righting her.

"Uh-huh. I know how." Her captor sat in the vee of a tree trunk just far enough away that she couldn't reach him. Not that she wanted to.

How he'd gotten her into the roughly hewn hammock, she hadn't yet figured out.

His somewhat childlike quality of speech might have intrigued her more if she wasn't fully aware that the man was not planning to be kind to her. Whether he was going to hurt her first, before she died, she didn't know.

Didn't need to know.

Levi would save her.

"You know how what?" she asked, changing tactics as,

with thoughts of Levi, it occurred to her that she had to help save herself to give Levi time to find her. He needed her just like she needed him. And while it felt as though she was completely helpless, she wasn't.

She was an expert at drawing people out. Reading their nuances. Getting them to talk.

In her current case, buying time.

"I know how to take you away and how to show you that you have to stay and how to make you want to stay and how to be a family."

As much as the words horrified her, she was more than just a victim. She tuned in to the skills that had helped save lives.

And it hit her. The man's oddities. Not just speech, but the way he looked—his hair long, cut unevenly, the almost childlike expression he often wore, his vocabulary, his proficiency in the woods, the way he'd pulled a fish right out of the water down below, the second time she'd been hanging upside down—she'd thought the move a fit of cruelty at the time, his showing her what he was going to do to her. But it had almost been as though he was showing off.

"You grew up here, then," she said, playing off his family comment. Scared to death. And it hit with a force that stripped what breath she'd had. She was facing Yardle's *son*?

It was possible. Maura had been missing more than twenty years. Oh God.

Levi!

Stay alive so he can find you.

"Yes. I live here." His grin, black-toothed and slightly hungry, seemed to leer at her. "And our baby will, too," he told her then.

If Kelly hadn't been keeping Levi on her mind, she'd have puked right then. Lying flat on her back. Maybe choked herself with it.

For a second, she didn't care.

"Your father..."

"Da," the man said, nodding. "He loved Ma and I know how, he showed me. You use the chains so she needs you and then you give it to her." He spoke with no remorse.

As though there was no sense of right and wrong.

A condition that occurred sometimes when a baby was denied any kind of human cuddling or even contact during early life.

She didn't want to know what "it" was.

"You show her that she has to stay and then you make the baby and then you take the baby away from her to make her stay," he continued, by rote. At first she hadn't been sure if the man was simpleminded, or just taunting her. As he talked, she grew more terrified.

"But the baby is the most important and you have to care for it and teach it and then it will grow up and be you."

His sudden smile shocked Kelly. For a second or two, the man looked like he was besotted in love. Before he seemed to remember something, and started looking around.

"You have to let him run free," he said then. "He has to find his way back."

She felt the man's worry. And froze.

Andrew.

"You have a child," she said, as though getting to know someone she'd just met.

"Uh-huh," he said, still glancing around him. "And he is free and I have to wait, and he will find his way back. That makes it his home because he brings himself home."

He didn't know she and Levi had the child.

Her first ray of hope. She'd found his weak spot. Just had to figure out a way to use it.

"Weren't you afraid, sending him off alone? It's a big world out here." She played into the fear he'd shown her. If she could convince him that he needed to trust her, to find his son again...

"I wasn't going to," he told her, seeming ashamed of the admission. "When I got big enough to see Ma, she taught me stuff. That there was a land with water that runs through pipes like the river and you push a button and the fire is hot for cooking. She wrote notes so that we could go there. And it was our secret. But then the devil came. And then other stuff, and I didn't want it to happen to Eli like it did to me and I wrote notes, too. And then you came. And you are perfect and I needed you. And I knew that Da was right. This is the best place, not another land. So I sent Eli off to come back and know his home..."

He wasn't an evil man. But he'd kill her without conscience. The two facts presented clearly.

"Eli is mine and he will like you and you can see him, but first you have to have a baby and then I will take it and that will make you stay."

In a sick, twisted way, his thinking made perfect sense.

"I had Robin, but Da had to kill Ma because the devil came to get us and the devil killed Da, and then I had to kill Robin. She tried to take away Eli and that is wrong. That's the devil and she knew it was."

Robin. No need for DNA results.

Kelly had their answers.

She just had no means to do anything with it.

Sounds of shuffling against bark reached her. Turning her head, she saw the man shifting in his seat. Getting ready to make his move?

Reaching up, he grabbed for a branch above him. She saw the old pistol shoved into the waistband of his jeans. Remembered Levi saying that they'd rounded up all weapons and ammunition when they'd taken Yardle down two months before.

But they hadn't known about the second shack, then.

Her captor settled. Glanced over at her.

And she knew, by the way he was looking at her, that her time was running out.

He was a man.

And he'd chosen his wife.

AS LEVI CLIMBED, he switched to the radio he'd grabbed on his way out, to communicate with his teams. Cell service would get sketchier the higher he climbed. The ability to connect to another device via radio signals would have given him hope, if Kelly still had her phone.

Connecting to the shattered device in his front pocket wasn't going to help.

Martin was at the cabin. All other units had been dispersed. The prior days had served as trial runs as everyone set out to find the missing psychiatrist in time.

If the stalker had her, they might already be too late. He could have killed her and buried her anywhere within the thousands of acres.

And he could have removed her from the woods as well, but that was doubtful. Chances of that were less, due to how quickly Levi had alerted law enforcement to her disappearance. Roadblocks had already been set up. Anyone objecting to a vehicle search would need to wait until the roads opened up in order to pass through.

But more, he'd found Kelly's cell phone across the river and farther up in the hills. She was out there.

"Da!" Andrew said again. Levi had lost count of the number of times. But he always looked up at the child. One time Andrew had been reaching for some berries. He'd let him pick them. As he glanced up then, he noticed the boy pointing toward the trees.

And it hit him. Andrew had moved through the trees. He thought about the places they'd seen signs of the boy.

And the spot where he'd thought an adult had been. Turned out it was Andrew's footprint, but that didn't mean there wasn't another adult with the boy.

Kelly's woman? The victim she'd been so certain was there? Had she approached Kelly at her place?

Was Kelly with her? Trying to help?

The theory didn't fit her violently smashed cell phone.

But another, earlier one might.

Pulling the boy down from his shoulders, he calmed himself. Thought only of the child as he asked, "Does someone live out here with you?"

And tried to fight the futility that hit him as the boy said, "Da."

What would Kelly do?

The question wasn't new in his mind. But it was more than a decade rusty.

He held out his hand to the boy. "Can you show me some of the places you like to go?" he asked. "With your hand, show me."

Andrew pointed. Having no other viable plan, Levi loaded him up, and set off.

SHE WAS GETTING HOT. Sun shining through the leaves beat down on her head, so bright that she had to keep her eyes closed.

Her captor had disappeared. At first, she'd thought he'd just gone quiet. But when the silence went on for a while and she started to imagine what he was getting ready to do, she'd turned her head to find him gone.

Mixtures of relief and dread consumed her at his absence. He could be below her, in the river. On the bank. Getting ready to cut the rope holding up the hammock as she now figured he'd cut Robin's rope after hanging her?

If she was alone, Levi would be able to save her more easily.

A breeze blew. She wanted the coolness.

The rocking made her nauseous.

So Kelly kept her eyes closed, thought about Levi and waited.

Chapter Twenty-Eight

"Da! Da! Da!" Andrew's feet, clad in brand-new tennis shoes, kicked against Levi's chest as the boy jumped up and down on his shoulders.

Figuring he wanted down, that there was something he wanted to show him, Levi reached up and grabbed Andrew under his arms, intending to lift him down, when he heard the click of a gun.

The boy was under one arm, shielded against Levi's back against the tree he darted behind, as he reached for his own gun.

The woods were filled with sounds. And the silence was acute, too.

The sound of a revolver preparing to fire echoed through the trees. He couldn't see anyone, but he knew what he'd heard.

"Da!"

Levi realized in that second, far too late, why he shouldn't have brought the boy with him into the woods. The child was going to get them killed.

"Quiet," he said softly. "It's a game."

"Da," Andrew replied, but in a whisper.

Levi waited. Watching the area he could see. He didn't dare duck out from the tree. Not with the boy's life at stake.

And then it occurred to him to look up.

KELLY LURCHED WHEN she heard the gunshot. And again when the second loud crack sounded through the trees. Pulling with her arms and legs, she tried to loosen the knots that bound her, to knock herself loose from the tree, to do anything to help, and ended up swinging upside down. Her weight pulled her arms and legs behind her and she pulled back as best she could, feeling the strain.

And she cried out. What was it going to hurt?

If her captor was shooting something, he might as well shoot her and get it over with.

As loud as she could, between sobs, she screamed.

The one name that, in the end, meant the most to her.

"Levi! Levi! Levi!" Over and over long after her throat hurt. Even after she was hoarse.

She just kept calling.

HE'D ONLY HAD one shot. Levi hadn't thought about the young boy he shielded witnessing a murder; he'd only had thoughts of keeping the child alive when he'd seen the glint of metal pointing at him through a cluster of leaves one tree over.

He hadn't been able to prevent the shot the other man got off. But he'd deflected it so that it hit the tree behind which he'd been hiding.

He'd aimed, ready to fire again, but the body had fallen out of the tree, bleeding from the side.

Keeping the boy under his arm, locked behind him, he'd grabbed the gun, thrown it aside long enough to feel the body and make certain there were no more weapons before he'd collected the gun, tucked it into his waistband with his own and, pulling Andrew in front of him as he turned from the body, he held the boy with both arms and ran.

"Da! Da!" The boy kicked against him.

Da. He'd figured it out too late.

The boy hadn't been making a random sound. He'd been asking for his father.

Da.

Andrew's father? Not Yardle?

"Da! Da!" Andrew's small flailing body was strong for his age, but he was no match for Levi, who moved through the woods without stopping until he'd put hundreds of yards between him and the bleeding man.

Andrew's father?

He'd missed so much.

But they'd saved the boy. And he was going to save Kelly.

Keeping his mind on what he could control, Levi came to a stop, catching his breath as he put the boy on his feet, keeping enough of a hold of his arms to grab him up if Andrew tried to run. He wasn't going to lose the little tree climber again.

Kelly would never forgive him.

"We'll help Da, I promise," he told the boy. "We need to get someone who can fix his hurt, and I need you to help me, okay? Kelly will help, but we have to find her." He pulled out the only stop he had with the boy.

Whether Andrew fully comprehended his words, he didn't know. Didn't have time to find out, either, because once the boy quieted to listen to him, Levi heard another sound.

Faintly. From far in the distance. Echoing through the trees.

"Levi!"

Boy once again in his arms, Levi ran.

KELLY STRETCHED—WINCING AS the muscles in her arms and legs ached with the bruising they'd taken—and slowly opened her eyes. Eli, asleep on the mattress beside her, breathed easily. And just beyond him—Levi Griggs's beautiful blue eyes were open, gazing at her.

He was it for her. The love of her life. Her brief time in

captivity had shown that to her with a clarity that couldn't be denied. Just as she couldn't deny that her life would wither and she wouldn't be the woman he loved if she didn't continue on with her life.

The temptation to quit Sierra's Web, stop putting her life on the line to help others, was strong. So strong. But as she gazed silently into Levi's eyes, she knew that she'd lose his respect if she did so. Because she'd be doing it solely for him. Not because she wanted to live a quieter life.

For the two nights since he'd rescued her from the woods, they'd slept together in the porch bed, the child between them, while officials sorted out details over which she and Levi had no control.

While there'd been no birth certificate for Eli or his father, no official accounting that either existed, the courts were quickly making records. A plethora of them.

The man who'd captured her—Silas, he'd said he was called—was in the hospital, recovering from bullet-damaged organs, but was expected to live.

He'd already been charged with kidnapping and attempting to kill a police officer. Murder charges in the death of Robin McKinney were going to follow. He'd also already been seen by a state-appointed psychiatrist and a lawyer. Chances were, the man would spend time in a psychiatric facility. Maybe a lifetime. Either way, as soon as the DNA had come back confirming that Robin McKinney was Eli's mother, the boy had been made a ward of the state.

Eli had seen his father in the tree. But due to Levi's quick thinking, throwing the boy on his back, the child hadn't witnessed his father's fall. He'd only seen him, had a brief glimpse of him, on the ground hurt.

Kelly had spent a good amount of time over the past two days explaining to the boy that Daddy was gone, but that he'd have a new mommy and daddy who would love him forever, too.

From what she could tell, Eli hadn't known his mother well enough to bond with her.

The child still didn't speak, but based on the way he'd been raised, and the other markers she'd observed in him, she fully believed that in a matter of time, Eli would be sharing all of his opinions with anyone who'd listen.

The state, with Kelly's consultation and full support, had decided to leave Eli with her at the cabin while more final arrangements could be made for him. The boy was going to need a specialized foster family.

She had a few more days left of vacation and hadn't been able to think of anyplace she'd rather be to recover from her own near tragedy than in her cabin, safe with Levi and Eli.

It had been a strange, sweet time out of time.

That was coming to an end.

She slid out of bed, not surprised when Levi followed. His body bare except for the shorts and T-shirt he wore to bed. She'd continued to wear her cotton pants and T-shirt to bed every night. Eli recognized them as her sleep apparel. She wanted anything that could remain the same for him to do so.

Betsy jumped off the end of the bed as she awoke and realized that Levi was up, and followed them out to the kitchen, where Levi would let her out. The sweet old girl had been a godsend with Eli.

"He needs a dog in his new home," she said softly as she watched the boy continue to breathe deeply and steadily. So peaceful in sleep.

With such a tough road ahead of him.

They all had some adjusting to do. She planned to seek counseling for herself as soon as she returned home. Being held captive, even for a few hours, was not something she was going to let destroy any part of her.

While Levi watched Betsy outdoors and started the coffee brewing, Kelly made her quick trip to the bathroom. She poured the coffee when Levi headed back for his turn in the restroom.

They didn't assign tasks, or turns. Or even talk about them. They'd just become routine.

One of the many things she was going to miss.

But the ache that had been steadily growing in her, as her muscle pains lessened over the past couple of days, had receded some. Lying awake in the middle of the night, listening to the three other bodies breathing on the bed with her, she'd made a mammoth decision.

As soon as Levi sat at the table with her, coffee cup in hand, she shared it with him. "I'm going to petition to adopt him," she announced. "Under the circumstances, I should be able to get temporary custody. I want to bring him back to Arizona with me. Let him acclimate in a completely different world…"

There was more. She stopped anyway, assessing his reaction.

Levi sipped coffee. Nodded.

And nothing.

"I'm also planning to keep the cabin," she said, an assertion to herself of the truths she'd needed to let herself express long ago. "While I wasn't all that close with them, I loved my grandparents. This place is all I have of them. All my memories…right here. I know, with what happened, it seems odd, but I still find peace here." She'd found Levi again. Had accepted that she'd always love him. The man who'd promised they'd be friends for the rest of their lives.

"But that aside, Eli has left pieces of himself here. Someday he'll know something about the crimes that took place around him, but I want him to be able to grow up running in these hills. And maybe remembering bits and pieces of the real love his father felt for him."

He still sat silently. But he'd set his cup down. Was watching her. She'd said what she had to say. Sipped her coffee. Holding back tears at his lack of response.

"I had a talk with my cousin Tilly yesterday." He broke what, to her, had been stretching into an interminable silence. He'd had talks with pretty much everyone in Idlewood, every family member and friend since the news of the Yardle case addendum had hit. He'd put his foot firmly down against any press, though.

And after what seemed to her to be a mammoth announcement, those phone calls were all he could talk about?

She waited, though. Because she loved him for who he was. And if he wanted to talk about his cousin, she'd listen.

"Turns out, once she made it to the academy, she realized that she didn't really want to be a cop. Her quitting had nothing to do with me letting her down."

Eyes wide, Kelly hid behind her own coffee cup. She hadn't realized he'd thought so to begin with. "She's applying to law school," he said, staring toward the table.

"That's good." She'd opened the door to the first talk of the future they'd had since he'd charged through the woods, and with Eli's help, found the rudimentary tied log ladder the boy and his father used to access the hammock. He'd rescued her. And if he chose not to take up the future, she had to respect that.

"Thing is, you were more right in the past than you knew, Kel. You saw that I was trying to fit us into a mold of what I thought life was supposed to be."

Eyes filling with tears, she blinked them back. Sucked in her bottom lip. At least they had that. Agreeing that they hadn't belonged together. That she'd made the right choice when she'd broken both of their hearts.

His gaze bored into her. "You didn't get caught in my cage, but I did."

What?

She stared at him.

"I love my family."

She nodded.

"I love Idlewood."

She knew that. Had never questioned where he needed to be. Wasn't going to, either.

"And the cage I built around myself is so small…the only way I could fit in it, was to obsess over cases."

She shook her head. "No, Levi. You have real talent. An incredible ability to see the little everyday things that most people miss—"

"I know," he cut her off, but gently, with a nod. "Which is why I need more, Kel. More than one small town, one low-crime-rate county's work, to keep me in line."

She couldn't breathe. Was cold and hot and…

"I want to come to Phoenix with you, Kel, if you'll have me. I can get a place, apply to the police department. Betsy and I can help out with Eli—you're going to get him, you know. The county already asked me to find out if I thought you had any interest…"

Her eyes filled with the tears she could no longer hold back. She needed to run in the hills with her freedom and shout the energy from her lungs. To swim down the river with the glints going on to someplace else. Not to leave where she was, but to open her life to more.

"You don't need my permission to come to Phoenix," she told him, finding enough professionalism left in her to give him the semblance of a calm voice. "But can I ask you something?" Maybe it wasn't the time. But she had to know.

"Of course."

"Why aren't you asking me to marry you? And moving you and Betsy in with me? Or finding a new home there that we all choose together?"

The man's chin tightened. His lips pursed. He nodded.

And tears filled his eyes.

A sight she'd never seen.

Lovesick as she was, Kelly did the only thing she could. She left her chair, climbed onto his lap, wrapped an arm around his neck, wiped gently at his eyes and said, "I've been running ever since I left here, Levi. Running from my deepest truth. I've listened to my heart regarding my service to others, but not for myself. But I'm listening now. Loud and clear. So, in case you *are* going to ask, my answer's yes, Levi Griggs. And, if you do want to marry me, I'm not leaving without you this time."

"That's good to hear," he told her, his arms so tightly around her she could feel his heart beating against hers. "Because I still want what I want, Kel," he grumbled in her ear. "I want my wife and my kids. I want you. I've just finally found my missing piece to the puzzle."

Curious, she pulled back, held his chin, staring into those so-expressive blue eyes. "Oh? What's that?"

"Family isn't just about staying in one place with the people you're born to. It's about making a family with the people you love."

He kissed her then. Long and deep and hungry.

And minutes later, when they heard Eli stir, and separated to start the day as the parents they'd just agreed to become, Levi's words played in her mind again. *Family isn't just about staying in one place with the people you're born to. It's about making a family with the people you love.*

He was right. Again.

Though she hadn't been born to any of them, she'd made a real, loving family with her Sierra's Web partners. A family that would welcome Levi and Eli with open arms.

An extended family. And she wanted so much more.

She and Levi and Eli and any future babies they made or adopted were starting out differently, to be sure, but they were exactly what she'd always wanted, forever family, in the home they built together.

And she ought to know.

After all, she was the expert.

* * * * *

COMING SOON!

We really hope you enjoyed reading this book. If you're looking for more romance be sure to head to the shops when new books are available on

Thursday 9th November

To see which titles are coming soon, please visit
millsandboon.co.uk/nextmonth

MILLS & BOON

LET'S TALK
Romance

For exclusive extracts, competitions and special offers, find us online:

Get in touch on 01413 063 232